新历史主义视角下的唐·德里罗小说研究

范小玫 著

外国文学研究丛书

序

杨仁敬

近几年来，国内学术界对美国后现代派小说的研究日益深入，视野不断扩大，方法呈多样化趋势。比如20世纪90年代末以来，小说家唐·德里罗越来越受重视，其作品逐渐成了许多高校硕士生和博士生学位论文的研究课题，涉及其中的媒体文化、消费主义、生态意识、空间叙事以及恐怖主义等。如今，范小玫又从新历史主义视角，研究了德里罗的9部主要作品。这无疑将进一步推动国内德里罗小说研究，也为美国后现代派小说的研究增添光彩。

范小玫的专著《新历史主义视角下的唐·德里罗小说研究》是她在其博士学位论文的基础上修订而成的。这篇论文于2014年5月10日通过答辩，校内外专家评审结果为优秀。范小玫以不懈的努力换来了这可喜的成果。

范小玫对唐·德里罗的兴趣由来已久。1988年，她从本校外文系英文专业毕业后留校任教，2001年考取本系英美文学专业硕士生，曾以德里罗的长篇小说《白噪音》作为硕士论文的研究对象。2005年3月，她考取了博士生，跟随我研习美国小说。她一面教书，一面读书，刻苦努力，成绩优秀，还挤时间出版了《美国短篇小说选读》，并以此为教材，给全校同学开设了选修课——"美国短篇小说"。没料到，选修的同学很多，教学效果意外的好，接连开了几轮，深受同学们欢迎。该书第1版3000册很快售罄。

动笔写博士论文时，范小玫多次与我交流意见。她提出想继续研究德里罗。我觉得她在这方面有些基础，就欣然同意了。2010年9月，范小玫有幸赴美国北卡罗来纳大学教堂山分校进修一年。其间她一面选修相关课程，充实自己的理论知识；一面广泛汇集最新资料。回国后，她继续埋头修订论文提纲，开始撰写初稿。没想到另一位导师的一位博士生也在写评论德里罗的学位论文。我们及时进行了沟通，发现两人虽然都评论德里罗的小说，但视角不同，论文结构也很不同，不存在"撞车"问题。一个作家可以有多种不同的解读和评析方式，即使视角迥异，不同的评论者同样能写出优秀的论文。思想认识统一以后，范小玫终于定下心来，并接受我的建议：用新历史主义的视角来评论德里罗的主要小说。我很高兴并提出了一些参考意见。接着，她信心十足地抓紧研读有关新历史主义的论著，细读德里罗的小说文本，重新修订了论文提纲，使论文重点突出，并能发挥自己的优势。不久，论文的初稿完成了。

唐·德里罗是美国后现代派小说家的优秀代表。他和海勒、品钦、纳博科夫、加迪斯、梅勒、加斯、苏克尼克、莫里森、汤亭亭和多克托罗等人一道被载入史册。他在小说里构建了一个充满反讽、戏仿和去中心的后现代语境，同时杂糅了许多现实主义细节，深刻地揭示了当代美国后工业社会千奇百怪的生存状态，从不同的层面描绘了美国后现代社会的道德困境和精神危机，字里行间包含着可贵的人文关怀。因此，他的作品拥有大量读者，在美国国内外深受欢迎。

由此可见，本书将德里罗放入新历史主义的视野中加以重新认识，选题属于学科前沿。它将作品研究与西方文论相结合，展示了德里罗是个勇于批评美国后现代文化的美国当代编年史家。因此，它具有重要的理论价值和现实意义。

总体来说，本书的创新之处表现在以下四个方面：

第一，围绕中心，突出重点，兼顾一般。本书紧紧抓住新历史主义代表人物格林布拉特和蒙特洛斯的主要论点，尤其是蒙特洛斯的"文本的历史性和历史的文本性"，以此为中心，深入评析德里罗文本的历史性。作者将德里罗的小说置于美国社会、政治和文化的复杂关系中进行考察，探讨它们怎样表现美国后现代社会状况。《天秤星座》以独特的视角描述了前总统肯尼迪被刺事件及其对美国人的心理冲击；而《坠落的人》则揭示了美国人对"9·11"恐怖袭击的反应。德里罗通过他的小说文本揭示和批评了美国后现代文化。

同时，本书还进一步评析了德里罗的《白噪音》、《毛二》和《地下世界》如何展示历史的文本性。这些小说记录了德里罗所处的社会生活及其文化特征，重现了美国当代的秘密历史。德里罗以小说的形式书写历史，将历史表现为多种迷人的故事，从而挖掘出被历史表象和官方档案所掩盖的历史，成为一位出色的当代美国编年史家。

第二，重视文本分析，注重评析的广度与深度的结合。本书选取了德里罗已出版的9部小说进行评论。它们是：《美国志》、《玩家》、《白噪音》、《天秤星座》、《毛二》、《地下世界》、《大都会》、《坠落的人》和《欧米茄点》。这些涵盖了德里罗在不同时期的主要作品。评论的范围大大地超过了国内学界所关注的《白噪音》和《天秤星座》两部。不仅如此，本书还将这9部长篇小说与德里罗的一些短篇小说、重要文章和访谈录联系起来考察，使评论具有多角度和全方位的特点，立论也更客观公正。

本书一方面以新历史主义为中心，另一方面注意结合相关的西方文论，以加深对西方后现代社会的理论阐释，如本书第一部分梳理了4位后现代社会理论家的观点：丹尼尔·贝尔论后工业社会、利奥塔论后现代社会状况、鲍德里亚论消费社会和詹姆逊论晚期资本主义。这些理论与德里罗用小说记录的社会变态和历史真实具有异曲同工之妙。这不仅帮助读者加深了对德里罗小说文本的历史性的理解，而且体现了作者扎实的理论功底、丰富的专业知识和较强的科研能力及潜力。

第三，紧扣历史语境，注重虚构的世界与现实社会的对照。本书应用辩证唯物主义观点，注意文本、语境和理论相结合，处处将德里罗虚构的艺术世界与美国现实社会相对照，比出了二者的差异，也比出了德里罗小说文本的特色和意义。

在评论《天秤星座》时，作者首先探讨了美国前总统肯尼迪在达拉斯被刺杀的历史背景和民众的反应，然后再与《天秤星座》产生的时代背景及政府出台的《沃伦委员会报告》相对照，指出德里罗小说文本的反叙述特点，凸显他对美国媒体的戏仿和反讽。德里罗将对元小说的反思与对官方历史的质疑结合起来，使他虚构的人物与历史人物同台表演，让文本化的过去融入他构建的文本。

《坠落的人》也是个很好的例子。小说借鉴了许多媒体的报道和《"9·11"委员会报告》的调查结果，反映了德里罗自己独特的见解。本书认真考察了"9·11"恐怖袭击发生的历史背景和该事件前后美国人的种种反应以及当时充斥于美国媒体的各类宏大话语，展示了德里罗对美国后现代文化的尖锐抨击，显得生动有力，令人信服。

此外，本书对《地下世界》的评析也具有同样的特色。书中指出德里罗精心挖掘历史，选择美国中情局局长胡佛作为小说中的重要人物，以揭示美苏两国冷战时期的地下历史。小说从一场棒球比赛开始，描述苏联核爆炸成功后美国的核忧虑。有人宣称1951年10月4日苏联原子弹爆炸成功便是冷战开始的第一天。紧接着，美国加快了纳瓦达的一系列原子弹新试验。苏联的第二次原子弹爆炸，经过美国媒体的渲染，进一步加剧了民众的核恐惧，使20世纪50年代的美国人生活在核战争的阴影下。尽管棒球比赛空前活跃，核恐惧仍成为美国人日常生活的一部分。60年代美苏又爆发了古巴导弹危机，双方严重对峙。后来，肯尼迪与赫鲁晓夫互相妥协，和平解决危机。1991年苏联解体，冷战结束了，美国留下一大堆核废料。《地下世界》描写了核废料的历史：苏联哈萨克斯坦试验场和美国纳瓦达试验场。1945—1992年间，美国进行了1054次核试验，比苏联多了 300 次。核废料堆积如山，四周污染严重，平民死伤不少。德里罗认为 20 世纪后期的美国文化由两种废料组成：核废料和资本主义大众媒体产生的废料。许多地方成了艾略特所说的文化"荒原"。所以，美国虽然赢得了冷战，但付出了高昂的代价。核军备竞赛留下了无数埋藏新武器和核废料的地下世界，留下了一大片荒原，也许艺术是个忏悔的希望……

这些虚实结合的评论拓展了读者的视野，加深了对德里罗小说文本的理解，深刻地揭示了其小说创作的社会意义。

第四，关注小说文本的叙事策略，力求主题思想与艺术手法评论的统一。本书由绪论、结语和三个章节组成，结构严谨而合理，逻辑性强，概念清晰，层次分明，格式规范，资料翔实，文笔流畅，表述准确。本书不仅汲取了海内外本学科相关领域的最新成果，梳理了许多重要文献，提出了富有创意的见解，而且关注德里罗小说文本的叙事策略，做到主题思想与艺术手法评论的统一，展示了小说家德里罗的完整形象。

本书指出：多视角、非连续性叙述、黑色幽默和互文性构成了德里罗小说文本的四大叙事策略，它们有力地帮助德里罗再现了美国后现代社会的混乱、碎片化、随意性、荒谬性和不确定性。德里罗继承了乔伊斯、福克纳、梅勒、达戈尔和兰尼·布鲁斯等人的优秀传统，并加以大胆的创新，杂糅了许多现实主义的特质，集后现代派艺术手法之大成，形成了自己独特的艺术风格，对美国当代文学做出了巨大贡献。有人开玩笑地说，德里罗很像他小说《地下世界》里所描述的艺术家，他悄悄地从历史垃圾的填埋场寻找文学创作的视角和表现手法，揭示美国社会的阴暗面：现代科技和消费主义对自然环境的破坏、媒体操纵和消费文化造成社会的扭曲和变态、冷战带来的恐惧和困惑、"9·11"恐怖袭击给人们造成的心理创伤以及贫富悬殊、城市里许多无家可归的人……德里罗成了一位勇于揭露现实、有正义感和社会责任感的优秀小说家。

本书不回避矛盾，而是面对现实，大胆地表明自己的看法。评论界有人认为德里罗遵循狄更斯、马克·吐温和德莱赛的传统。他既不是个现代派作家，也不是个后现代派作家，而是一个批判现实主义作家。作者不同意这种看法，认为德里罗是个出色的后现代派作家。尽管他的小说里具有许多现实主义因素，但他巧妙地采用了独特的后现代派叙事策略，精心描绘了美国后工业社会的状况——媒体的垄断一切和消费主义的横行、人们的焦虑和社会的扭曲，反映了德里罗的后现代主义文化历史观。这些细致而客观的评析体现了我国青年学者的学术勇气。

古人云："成功在久不在速。"拿到了博士学位，又出版了博士学位论文，可算是双喜临门,可喜可贺!诚然,成功来之不易,这是范小玫长期努力的结果。学术的道路是漫长而曲折的,需要与时俱进,不断努力,一步一个脚印地往前走,不求快速,但求持续向前不停步。我希望范小玫以此作为自己事业的新起点,继续发挥正能量,向更高的目标奋进,稳步实现新梦想,争取获得美国文学教学和科研的新丰收。是为序。

2015 年 1 月 6 日
于西村书屋

前　言

唐·德里罗（1936—），美国著名作家，著有长篇小说、短篇小说、剧本和评论文章。至今他已出版了16部长篇小说，获奖无数，其中包括：1985年《白噪音》获得美国国家图书奖，1992年《毛二》获得笔会/福克纳奖，1999年获得耶路撒冷奖，2010年获得笔会/索尔·贝娄美国小说成就奖，2013年获得首届国会图书馆美国小说奖。德里罗在美国文学评论界备受赞誉。哈罗德·布鲁姆曾这样评论过：美国当代有四大小说家，德里罗是其中之一，另外三个是托马斯·品钦、菲利普·罗思和科马克·麦卡锡。目前大约出版了25部研究德里罗的专著。

自从20世纪90年代末以来，德里罗在中国得到越来越多的学者和读者的关注。他的一些小说有了中译本，一些评论其小说的文章陆续发表。2001年，本人完成了研究《白噪音》的硕士论文，这是中国第一篇研究德里罗小说的硕士论文。如今，已有近50篇研究德里罗小说的硕士论文。近年来有一些博士生研究德里罗，可以查到的有关德里罗作品研究的博士论文有5篇。这些论文主要集中研究其单部小说《白噪音》或者《天秤星座》，探讨媒体文化、消费主义和恐怖主义等主题。本书试图另辟蹊径，从新历史主义视角对德里罗的作品进行综合性评论，以研究其小说与美国当代文化、历史和社会的关系。作品分析涵盖其9部小说，它们是《美国志》、《参与者》、《白噪音》、《天秤星座》、《毛二》、《地下世界》、《大都会》、《坠落的人》及《欧米茄点》，此外还涉及他的短篇小说、重要文章和访谈。

蒙特洛斯的"文本的历史性和历史的文本性"最恰当地概括了新历史主义的特点。蒙特洛斯对这两个关键词的阐释表明："首先，文本总是产生于特定的历史背景中，因而不是'永恒'的艺术品。……我们所谓的历史本身是我们对历史文献，即文本，阅读的产物。"（Hiscock and Longstaffe 96）历史性是文本性的产物。海登·怀特认为，历史写作是个诗性的过程，历史叙述是"语言造物"。怀特关于历史叙述的理论填平了历史事实与虚构的鸿沟。历史与小说是可以互相转换的。"历史本质上是虚构的，或者是文本的，小说家和历史学家发挥相同的作用。"（Gu 14）在新历史主义的理论框架内，本书试图论证：德里罗用

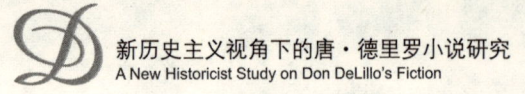

小说的方式书写了美国后现代历史,他也因此成为小说家中的历史学家。

首先,本书探讨了德里罗文本的历史性。德里罗的写作生涯始于20世纪60年代,与此同时,后现代主义在美国产生,在70年代逐渐发展,在80和90年代达到鼎盛。德里罗的小说探究了美国的后现代性,力图再现美国当代文化的整体风貌,记录了美国后现代化的过程。本书将德里罗的作品置于社会、文化与政治的关系中,在后现代的背景中进行研究,探究它们是如何反映后现代状况的。西方有不少理论家对后现代社会进行了理论阐释,本书梳理了其中4位后现代社会理论家的理论:丹尼尔·贝尔的后工业社会、利奥塔的后现代状况、布希亚德的消费社会和詹姆逊的晚期资本主义。这些理论家忙于建构后现代理论时,德里罗在忙于他的后现代小说的创作。他们所描述的后现代社会状况正是德里罗所经历的,本书视其为德里罗小说创作的理论和历史背景。后现代理论家们试图用理论描述他们所感受到的后现代思潮,而德里罗则用小说记录其所见的社会变化和历史现实。

蒙特洛斯的"文本的历史性"可以理解为"历史塑造当下,当下重塑历史"(Montrose 24)。本书以《天秤星座》和《坠落的人》为例进一步论述德里罗文本的历史性。首先,本书研究了"肯尼迪遇刺"的历史背景及其对美国人心理的冲击,研究了德里罗创作《天秤星座》的文化和时代背景,分析为什么德里罗要呈现一个不同于《沃伦委员会报告》的"肯尼迪遇刺"事件。本书还考察了美国人对"9·11"恐怖袭击的反应,分析了为什么《坠落的人》虽然严重依赖媒体的报道和《"9·11"委员会报告》的调查发现,但呈现的是一种反叙述,而当时美国媒体上则充斥着恐怖主义叙述和民族主义的宏大话语。对事件发生的历史背景和小说创作的历史背景进行分析研究,从而能洞悉德里罗如何通过其文本对美国后现代文化进行批评和解剖。

其次,本书探讨历史的文本性。本书分析了德里罗如何通过其小说《白噪音》、《毛二》和《地下世界》记录他那个时代的文化、生活,再现美国当代的秘密历史。新历史主义认为人类只有通过残存的文本痕迹才能接近历史。历史只有通过叙述化和文本化的方式才能显现。新历史主义的研究方向重点不是大写的历史,不是一个巨大的整体,而是小写的各种历史,充满了异质性、零碎化、矛盾和差异。这种观点与利奥塔的观点不谋而合。利奥塔认为,在后现代社会,我们应该摒弃历史总体化、主导叙事或者宏大叙事的观念。我们应该允许多个互相对抗、互相矛盾的小历史或故事共存。小说把历史呈现为多个故事。因为我们只能以故事的形式理解有关人的事件和经历。小说家有时等同于历史学家:他们以小说的形式写历史,他们的作品告诉我们很多过去的事情。德里罗就是这样一位伟大的小说历史学家，他详细地描述了 20 世纪末 21 世纪初美国的生活。他是当代美国的编年史家，是"秘密历史"的专家，能够挖掘被历史现象和官方档案所掩埋的历史。

最后，本书分析讨论了德里罗小说文本的叙事策略：多视角、叙事的非连续性、黑色幽默和互文性。这四种叙事策略帮助德里罗再现了美国后现代社会的混乱、碎片化、随机性、荒谬性和不确定性。这些叙事策略在文学中早已存在，但 20 世纪 60 年代以后成为后现代文学的主要叙事技巧。德里罗通过"回收"乔伊斯、福克纳、梅勒、戈达尔和兰尼·布鲁斯等前人的叙事手法进行加工，形成了自己独特的叙事方式，对美国后现代文学做出了巨大的贡献。他就像《地下世界》中的艺术家，在历史的垃圾填埋场中寻找创作的视野和手法。

蒙特洛斯的"文本的历史性和历史的文本性"表明：文学或是任何特别的文本不仅是社会的产物，而且也对社会产生影响 (Montrose 23)。德里罗的作品不仅是当代社会的产物，而且还通过建构美国后现代独特历史叙事、解剖美国后现代社会，像诺曼·梅勒一样，影响了美国当代的思想意识，同时把自己塑造成一个对抗性作家。

德里罗还是个颠覆性作家。他的小说致力于描写美国的阴暗面：这是国家及其话语常常掩饰或忘记的那一面。德里罗描写了美国自然环境如何遭到技术和消费主义的破坏；视觉导向的消费社会所具有的破坏性影响；美国社会由于媒体操纵和消费文化占主导产生了专制主义；城市的下层阶级和无家可归者；冷战带来的焦虑和多疑；"9·11"恐怖袭击造成的创伤。德里罗认为自己的小说关注的是"危险时代的生活"。他极力主张作家要抵制权力，"抵制权力试图强加于我们的一切" (Bou and Thoret)。由于他的作品揭露现实，他被当成坏公民和左派偏执狂而受到谴责。

德里罗的小说再现了美国的后现代现实，探讨了美国的后现代性，因而他是个编年史家。同时他还是美国的乔纳森·斯威夫特，讽刺了被消费主义吞噬、受恐怖主义困扰的美国社会；他是美国的查尔斯·狄更斯，利用后现代生活中的有毒元素来"表现产生这些元素的社会所存在的道德缺陷" (Ryan 794)。德里罗是美国社会的批评者，在他看来，美国社会"是人类追求个性与自我实现这个事业所遇到的最坏敌人" (Lentricchia, *Introducing Don DeLillo* 5)。德里罗在小说中刻画了很多抵抗性艺术家，他们抵抗自己深陷其中的权力制度。德里罗的小说展现了后现代时代难得的道德力量。尽管在这个全球化的世界，影像文化泛滥，消费主义盛行，文学已被边缘化，但德里罗依然坚持做美国社会忠实的镜子和良心。一些批评家认为，德里罗既不是现代派作家，也不是后现代派作家，他是个现实主义作家，因为他遵循狄更斯、马克·吐温和德莱赛的创作手法。但笔者认为，德里罗是个后现代派作家，因为其小说不仅描写了后现代社会、后工业社会、媒体饱和社会中的美国人的生活，而且也体现了小说作者对于历史与文化的后现代观，还例示了后现代主义小说颇具创新的叙事策略。德里罗小说中的现实主义元素表明，德里罗是个具有社会责任感、道德感和强烈历史意识的作家。可以认为，他是个美国后现代编年史家。他的小说尖锐地批评了美国后现代文化。

Contents

前言 /I

Introduction / 1

  I. DeLillo's Life and Career / 2
  II. Research Reviews on DeLillo in the United States and China / 11
  III. Theoretical Framework and Structure of the Book / 19
    1. New Historicism and the Key Representatives / 19
    2. The Structure and Contents of the Book / 24

Chapter One   The Historicity of DeLillo's Texts / 31

  I. **Context: The Postmodern Condition / 31**
    1. Daniel Bell's Theory of the Post-Industrial Society / 32
    2. Jean-François Lyotard's Analysis of the Postmodern Condition / 34
    3. Jean Baudrillard's Idea of Consumer Society / 36
    4. Fredric Jameson's Viewpoint on Late Capitalism / 41
  II. **The Chronicler of America: Historicizing the Present / 45**
    1. *Libra*: The Origin of American Postmodern Condition / 46
    2. *Falling Man*: A "Brave New Chronicler of the Age of Terror" / 60

Chapter Two   The Textuality of History: DeLillo's Chronicle of Postmodern America / 87

  I. *White Noise* / 89
    1. "Death Is in the Air" / 89
    2. "As Long as the Supermarket Did Not Slip" / 104
  II. *Mao* II / 114
    1. "When the Old God Leaves the World" / 115
    2. "Nothing Happens Until It's Consumed" / 121

    3. "Novelists and Terrorists Are Playing a Zero-Sum Game" / 133
  III. *Underworld* / 143
    1. "The Shot Heard Round the World" / 143
    2. "We're All Gonna Die" / 152
    3. "Waste Is the Secret History" / 158
    4 "Everything Is Connected in the End" / 172

Chapter Three Narrative Strategies in DeLillo's Fictional Texts / 175
  I. Multiple Points of View / 176
  II. Discontinuity in Narration / 182
  III. Black Humor / 186
  IV. Intertextuality / 191
    1. Allusion / 193
    2. Adaptation / 195
    3. Pastiche / 196
    4. Historiographic Metafiction / 198

Conclusion / 202

Works Cited / 215

Acknowledgments / 228

Introduction

Don DeLillo is a distinguished contemporary American novelist, playwright, and essayist. He has published 16 novels, more than 20 short stories, 5 major plays, and a few essays over the last 50 years. He has received the National Book Award, the PEN/Faulkner, the PEN/Saul Bellow Award, the Common Wealth Award of Distinguished Service for Achievements in Literature and various other distinctions internationally. According to a survey made by the *New York Times Book Review* in 2006, three of DeLillo's novels—*Underworld*, *White Noise*, and *Libra* were voted by 125 prominent writers, critics, and editors to be "the Best American Novel[s] of the Past 25 Years." DeLillo now stands "in the first rank with Thomas Pynchon, Toni Morrison, Philip Roth, and John Updike" (Duvall, Introduction 1).

DeLillo has been widely regarded as an important postmodern writer (LeClair 9; Keesey 198; Cowart 2; Schneck 204). He explores many postmodern themes: consumerism, paranoia, terrorism, conspiracy, simulacra, saturation of mass media, psychology of the crowd, and politics in American society. He depicts many historical events in his works: The assassination of President Kennedy (*Libra*), the 1951 National League playoffs of baseball, the Soviet Union's nuclear test (*Underworld*), environmental disasters (*White Noise*), Salman Rushdie's exile for *The Satanic Verses* (*Mao II*), and the 9·11 terrorist attacks (*Falling Man*, 2007). And he's also been writing terrorist novels for the past 30 years. "Terrorists have been making regular appearances in his books since *Players* (1977)" (Binelli).

DeLillo writes about contemporary American history and represents a panorama of American life from the 1950s to the early 21st century. His works show the complexity of history and the postmodernity of American society. They provide us an insight into American society and its culture which is saturated with mass media images so much that the very remarkable distinction between fact and fiction is almost erased. "What makes DeLillo one of the most important American novelists since 1970 is his fiction's repeated invitation to think historically" (Duvall, Introduction 2). He challenges the official history and gives the readers a different historical perspective. He is a cultural critic. He belongs to the kind of "writers who conceive their vocation as an act of cultural criticism; who invent in order to intervene; whose work is a kind of anatomy, an effort to represent their culture in its totality; and who desire to move readers to the view that the shape and fate of their culture dictates the shape and fate of the self" (Lentricchia, "The American Writer as Bad Citizen" 1).

For decades Don DeLillo has been engaged in an oppositional writing which challenges the consumer society in which, according to Jameson, "all aesthetic production now is nothing more than a form of commodity production" (Duvall, "The Power of History and the Persistence of Mystery" 2). DeLillo has been regarded as a social critic and cultural anatomist. He was criticized by "the media political right" as "a bad citizen" (Lentricchia, "The American Writer as Bad Citizen" 3), and was once "denounced as a member of the paranoid left" (DeCurtis 73). To the criticism, DeLillo replied in an interview: "Being called a 'bad citizen' is a compliment to a novelist, at least to my mind. That's exactly what we ought to do" (qtd. in Remnick 142). DeLillo admits that politics plays a part in some of his books (DeCurtis 73) and claims "fiction must contest in power" (Moss 165). Indeed, politics has been regarded as an indispensable theme in postmodern American literature. According to Linda Hutcheon, the cultural activity of postmodernism is "fundamentally contradictory, resolutely historical, and inescapably political" (*A Poetics of Postmodernism* 4). In my view, DeLillo is political in that his works launch a serious critique of postmodern America.

I. DeLillo's Life and Career

Don DeLillo was born into an Italian immigrant family in New York City on November 20, 1936. He grew up in the Italian-American neighborhood of the Bronx. It was a childhood of sports and games. As a teenager, DeLillo did not read much until he was 18 years old when he started to read William Faulkner, James Joyce, and Ernest Hemingway. DeLillo was raised as a Catholic. He came from a Catholic family and attended Catholic schools. In 1954 he graduated from Cardinal Hayes High School in the Bronx. After he received a bachelor's degree in Communication Arts from Fordham University in the Bronx in 1958, DeLillo took a job in advertising and worked for five years as an advertising copywriter at the ad agency of Ogilvy & Mather in Manhattan. In his spare time he started to write fiction. In 1964 he quitted his job in the agency and devoted himself to fiction writing. In 1975 DeLillo was married to Barbara Bennett, then a banker and later a landscape designer. They do not have children and now live in Bronxville, a suburb of New York City, the city which serves as the setting for many of his novels. In an interview he stated, "I became a writer by living in New York and seeing and hearing and feeling all the great, amazing and dangerous things the city endlessly assembles. And I also became a writer by avoiding serious commitment to anything else" (Bing).

In 1960 DeLillo's first work of fiction, a short story, "The River Jordan," was published in *Epoch*, the literary magazine of Cornell University, which also brought to light the first published fiction of Thomas Pynchon, and Stanley Elkin, along with early stories by Philip Roth and Joyce Carol Oates. The following years saw more of DeLillo's short stories appear in *Epoch*, *Kenyon Review*, and *Carolina Quarterly*. In 1971 DeLillo published his first novel *Americana*, which manifests his career ambition, recurring themes, styles and techniques in his works. What does *Americana* mean? It refers to artifacts, or a collection of artifacts, related to the history, geography, folklore and cultural heritage of the United States. It can be used to describe the studies of American culture. Since his first novel, DeLillo intended to take the entire American culture as the subject matter of his creative writing. "That DeLillo was deeply concerned with serious subjects—the failure of language, the state of the modern world, the Cold War, technology—had been evident as early as *Americana*…" (Ruppersburg and Engles 2). David Bell, the protagonist and the narrator, works for a television network as an executive that produces images. His father works with television advertising and believes that image is everything. With a movie camera in hand, David travels across the United States in quest of his own identity or the national identity. His journey is called "post-Kerouac pilgrimage" (Champlin 7). David plans to make his own film of discovering America, and in the meantime exploring part of his consciousness to discover himself.

Americana is a semiautobiographical novel. In an interview with Thomas LeClair in 1982, DeLillo said that this novel was the one closest to his own experience "in the sense that I drew material more directly from people and situations I knew firsthand" (DePietro 4). There are some references and allusions to the movies, novels, skills that have influenced him. David Bell thinks himself as a "child of Godard and Coca-Cola" (DeLillo, *Americana* 269), "a witty rephrasing, one step removed, of Godard's famous reference to himself as a 'child of Marxism and Coca-Cola'" (Keesey 14). When asked about the influence on his writing, DeLillo said, "I think more than writers, the major influence on me have been European movies, and jazz, and Abstract Expressionism" (qtd. in Passaro 79). DeLillo was strongly influenced by Jean-Luc Godard's movies which, "with their jump cuts and arresting images, would have a major impact on *Americana*" (Keesey 3). He admitted to Thomas LeClair about his affinities with

Godard: "Probably the movies of Jean-Luc Godard had a more immediate effect on my early work than anything I'd ever read" (DePietro 9). Godard's films express his political ideologies and existential and Marxist philosophy. His radical approach in movie conventions, politics and philosophies made him the most influential filmmaker of the French New Wave. Godard's influence can be keenly felt through much of DeLillo's fiction—his interest in images, his depiction of the media-dominated society, the ideology of his characters, and his concern with the important historical events.

In 1972 DeLillo published *End Zone*, a novel about language and football. The next decade saw the following books appear: *Great Jones Street* (1973), *Ratner's Star* (1976), *Players* (1977), and *Running Dogs* (1978). In 1978, DeLillo was awarded the Guggenheim Fellowship, which he exploited to fund a trip around the Middle East before settling down in Greece, where he spent several years. While he was there, DeLillo spent three years writing *The Names* which was published in 1982. *The Names* is a complex thriller concerning James Axton and a mystifying cult of ritual murder. James is an American political risk analyst working for multinational corporations primarily in the Middle East, Turkey, and India, and living in Athens, Greece, and also an unwitting agent for the CIA. The cultists live in caves along the Messinian Coast (though they also have cells in northern Iran and India) and call their organization "The Names." The cultists choose as their victims the people who are severely handicapped or dying anyway. But the key to their ritual is that their murders are committed in places whose initials correspond to those of their victims. In this novel DeLillo "verbally examines every state of consciousness from eroticism to tourism, from the idea of America as conceived by the rest of the world to the idea of the rest of the world as conceived by America, from mysticism to fanaticism" (*New York Times*). Also in 1982, DeLillo finally broke his self-imposed ban on media coverage by giving his first major interview to Tom LeClair. In 1984 he was given an award by the American Academy and Institute of Arts and Letters that "honored his work to date," but until the publication of *White Noise* in 1985 he was "a pretty obscure object of acclaim, both in and out of the academy" (Lentricchia, Introduction 1-3). *White Noise* helped its author win the National Book Award and has been regarded as a postmodernist classic which is often selected to represent the American postmodern novel to be read and taught in colleges both in and out of the United States. It depicts a society saturated with mass media and explores the effects of consumerism on the American society.

In 1988 DeLillo published his ninth novel *Libra*. It is a fictional portrayal of Lee

Harvey Oswald and the events surrounding the Kennedy Assassination, a historical event that shaped DeLillo's writing career. According to DeLillo, it was the Kennedy Assassination that "invented him" because when it happened he was not a fully formed writer. In an interview when he talked about the assassination's effect on him, DeLillo said:

> I don't think my books could have been written in the world that existed before the Kennedy Assassination. And I think that some of the darkness in my work is a direct result of the confusion and psychic chaos and the sense of randomness that ensued from that moment in Dallas. It's conceivable that this made me the writer I am—for better or for worse. (qtd. in Passaro 77-78)

It took DeLillo more than three years to write *Libra*. He did a lot of research in order to write this novel. He "went to New Orleans, Dallas, Fort Worth, and Miami and looked at houses and streets and hospitals, schools and libraries" (Begley 97), places which were related to Oswald's life and the conspiracy of the assassination. He had to dig into numerous materials concerning the Kennedy Assassination: the twenty-six-volume *Warren Commission Report*, a lot of biographies, reports, old magazines, old photographs, scientific reports, films, and audiotapes. When faced with these mazelike research materials, DeLillo had to "become part scientist, novelist, biographer, historian and existential detective" (Begley 98). The result is his subversion of the lone gunman theory. He sees a conspiracy at work in Kennedy's assassination. After it was published, *Libra* made an instant success. It was made a main selection of the Book-of-the-Month Club in the spring of 1988, and hit the best-seller list for several weeks in the summer of that year. DeLillo was invited to do interviews on National Public Radio and NBC's Today Show. In the meantime, for his conspiracy theory of the Kennedy Assassination he was criticized by George Will and Jonathan Yardley, who charged him with bad citizenship, bad influence and "something of a traitor to his country" (Lentricchia, Introduction 4).

In 1991, when the Soviet Union disintegrated, DeLillo published *Mao II*, which was inspired partly by the fatwa calling for Salman Rushdie's execution in 1989. Rushdie was condemned to death by the Ayatollah Khomeini for blaspheming Islam in his novel *The Satanic Verses* and was forced to go into hiding. DeLillo was upset by this event, not just because he shared a publisher with Rushdie, but also because the writer's rights to express freely and to speak against totalitarianism was now threatened. In order to show his support for Rushdie's rights to freedom of speech, DeLillo and other writers gave a public reading. In 1994 Don DeLillo and Paul Auster co-wrote *Salman Rushdie Defense* pamphlet in an effort to raise awareness about the plight of Rushdie. In the pamphlet they say:

> On February 14, 1989, the religious leader of one country issued a death edict against a citizen of another country. Five years later Salman Rushdie is still a man with no fixed address. [...] *The Satanic Verses* continues to be available in bookstores and libraries throughout the United States and many other countries. But Rushdie is in hiding, still writing nearly every day, making public appearances on occasion—but effectively under threat [...] He is alive, yes, but the principle of free expression, the democratic shout, is far less audible than it was five years ago—before the death edict tightened the binds between language and religious dogma. (DeLillo and Paul Auster)

Underworld was published in 1997. It is a novel about the history of Cold War, the postwar American underhistory. It manifests the power of history. It is a massive, 833-page masterpiece, DeLillo's "longest, most ambitious, and most complicated novel—and his best" (Remnick 132). Its title comes from *Unterwelt*, a rediscovered film by Sergei Eisenstein, a famous film director of the Soviet Union. *Unterwelt* is a silent film. But where was it made? How was it made? Where did the title come from? Nobody knows the answers for sure. "Unterwelt" is a German word, meaning "underworld." "Eisenstein knew German and may have had a reason for choosing a title in that language. But it's more likely the film acquired the title during its long repose in an underground vault in East Berlin" (DeLillo, *Underworld* 426). The title probably also refers to another film. "There is another movie called *Underworld*, a 1927 gangster film and box office smash" (ibid. 431). Then what is DeLillo's novel about? The key to understand it is the prefix "under-." In the novel there are many words that include "under-": the undervoice of America, the underdream of history, and the underbelly of the Bronx. In an interview DeLillo talked about the word "under," where the center of the novel lies:

> In this book "under" can apply to suppress or repress memories or even consciousness. [...] Aside from that, I think that all the unders spring originally from my sense of the physical meaning of the word as applied to the burial of nuclear waste. This is when I first hit upon the idea of calling the book *Underworld*. [...] and I thought of the word "plutonium." I thought of its source which is Pluto, god of the dead and ruler of the underworld. [...] I kept finding myself [...] treating subterranean realities of one kind or another [...] The other kind of underworld too, the underhistory of the Cold War, a curious history of waste which forms an underground stream in

> this book, waste and weapons, and then they merge toward the end. [...] There's a curious kind of cultural history, mostly informal, of drugs, garbage, condoms. The baseball forms a kind of underhistory as it bounces from character to character. (qtd. in Echlin 146)

Underworld is DeLillo's multilayered portrayal of American life during the Cold War, from the early 1950s to the early 1990s. The prologue, entitled "The Triumph of Death," relates to the famous baseball game between the New York Giants and the Brooklyn Dodgers at the Polo Grounds in the Bronx on October 3, 1951. Midway through the game, J. Edgar Hoover, director of the CIA, learns from Special Agent Rafferty that the Soviet Union has conducted their second atomic test. When George Thomson hits the homerun that wins the game for the Giants, the ball flies into the stands and Cotter Martin, a 14-year-old Harlem boy, wins the fight for it and takes it home. After the prologue the story is narrated in six parts and in reverse chronological order, beginning with the narration of Nick Shay, one of the novel's protagonists, in 1992's spring and summer and ending up in Nick's juvenile life between the fall of 1951 and the summer of 1952. The novel's "Epilogue: Das Kapital" brings the action up to the last decade of the 20th century when capitalism prevails in Russia and globalism gathers momentum.

After the formidably thick book *Underworld*, DeLillo published *The Body Artist* in 2001, a 128-page novella. It is a book about personal trauma, language and time. Like Bill Gray in *Mao II*, Klara Sax in *Underworld*, Lauren Hartke, the protagonist of the novel, is an artist of the book title. Bill worries about the artist's role in the contemporary society and fears that "writers are being consumed by the emergence of news as an apocalyptic force" (DeLillo, *Mao II* 72). He has hidden himself for 23 years from the media in an attempt to escape their increasingly pervasive influence and retain his individual voice. He believes that terrorists are taking over the role of the artist to shape the way people think and see. In *Underworld* Klara paints a fleet of military planes that once carried nuclear bombs during the Cold War and now become kind of waste in an unused military base in the Arizona desert, recycling the obsolete aircrafts into works of art. "As a result, her project is also an attempt to restore a kind of balance" (Bloom, *Don DeLillo* 144). In *The Body Artist* DeLillo again explores the role of the artist. Lauren is in great distress after her husband Rey Robles, a film director, commits suicide. But she overcomes her grief by transmuting mourning, a kind of waste, into an unsettling work of performance art.

DeLillo's 13th novel, *Cosmopolis*, appeared in 2003. It is a book about capitalism, violence, sex, and death. The novel is often compared with James Joyce's

Ulysses. The action is confined to a single day in April, 2000, when the "dotcom bubble" collapsed in the United States. Eric Packer, the narrator and protagonist, is a 28-year-old billionaire currency trader and fund manager. Eric is trying to cross traffic-clogged mid-town Manhattan in his luxurious and technologically sophisticated stretch limo to get a haircut in the barbershop where he had his first haircut in the neighborhood where his father grew up. On his way he encounters a presidential motorcade, the funeral procession of a rap star and a violent anti-globalist demonstration. In 24 hours the New Economy icon loses all of his money by betting against the rise of the yen, hence his empire tumbles. He kills his bodyguard and gets killed by his antagonist Benno Levin. *Cosmopolis* is the first of DeLillo's novels that is adapted into a movie. It was directed by Canadian director David Cronenberg and was released in 2012.

When the 9·11 terrorist attacks happened in 2001, DeLillo had nearly finished drafting *Cosmopolis*. The traumatic event affected almost every American, of course including DeLillo, a native New Yorker. After the terrorist attacks he claimed: "I took a long pause. I just didn't want to work for a while" (qtd. in Barron 1). He did take a long pause before he decided to write a book on this disaster. In May, 2007, more than five years after the catastrophe, *Falling Man* was published. It "examines the psychological trauma experienced by New Yorkers in the aftermath of the terrorist attacks of 9·11, once again underscores DeLillo's longstanding concern with the role of the artist" (Duvall, Introduction 9). The "Falling Man" of the title refers to a performance artist named David Janiak, who suspended from various structures in New York, dangling upside down from a harness, and dressed in a suit and tie, to remind New Yorkers of the catastrophe of 9·11. The opening of the novel describes the hellish morning of September 11, 2001. Keith, bloodied and dazed, carrying a suitcase, walks out of the North Tower before it collapses. Outside, it is all dust and ash. "It was not a street any more but a world, a time and space of falling ash and near night" (DeLillo, *Falling Man* 1). Keith returns home to his estranged wife Lianne and young son Justin. He has an affair with a black woman, Florence, a fellow survivor from the towers. He quits his job and becomes a professional gambler. From time to time the horrible scenes of that morning come to his mind: his seriously injured and dying friends trapped in the tower, men jumping from the burning towers. It seems hard for him to get out of the shadow. Gambling becomes a kind of medicine for the trauma.

DeLillo's latest novel, *Point Omega*, was published in 2010. Like *The Body Artist*, it is brief, spare and concentrated, merely 117 pages. There are only three main characters: Richard Elster, a 73-year-old scholar and advisor of the Iraq War, Jim Finley, a young film maker who wants to make a movie about Elster and has followed him to the Arizona desert, and Jessie, Richard's daughter, who comes to visit and then suddenly disappears. For most of the book, they sit on Elster's porch, drinking and talking. DeLillo's inspiration for the novel came from his visit to the Museum of Modern Art in New York in the summer of 2006 when he happened upon Douglas Gordon's *24 Hour Psycho*, a video installation that consists of Alfred Hitchcock's movie *Psycho* which has been slowed down to two frames a second so that it lasts for 24 hours instead of the original hour and a half or so. DeLillo was attracted by the slowness of the film, and the way it caused him to notice things he might otherwise have missed, so he decided to write a book about the mysteries of time and space. The novel is philosophical and experimental. The title "Point Omega" refers to the term "Omega Point" coined by the French philosopher and theologian Father Teilhard de Chardin who believed that there is a point of perfection that the universe will eventually achieve. The narrator of the novel is Jim Finley. The first part of the novel is entitled "Anonymity 1" in which Elster and Finley are in the Museum of Modern Art, watching *24 Hour Psycho* on September 3. The last part of the novel is entitled "Anonymity 2" in which the story of watching *24 Hour Psycho* continues in the gallery on September 4, but this time only Finley remains. The middle part consists of four chapters which tell the desert story. Elster said to Finley before his daughter disappears that the Omega Point is a concept of paroxysm, "[e]ither a sublime transformation of mind and soul or some worldly convulsion" (DeLillo, *Point Omega* 72). With Jesse's mysterious disappearance, Elster drops into the state of grief. "The Omega Point has narrowed, here and now, to the point of a knife as it enters a body" (ibid. 98).

There is one novel that is believed to be one of DeLillo's works. But DeLillo has never officially acknowledged it. The novel is entitled *Amazons*, co-written by Don DeLillo, and published under the pseudonym Cleo Birdwell in 1980. The subtitle is *An Intimate Memoir by the First Woman to Play in the National Hockey League*. The novel is a fictitious autobiography narrated by Birdwell centering on her experiences as the first woman to play professional hockey in the National Hockey League. The book represents a commercial, light-hearted effort between *Running Dog* and *The Names*.

In 2011 DeLillo published his first collection of short stories, *The Angel Esmeralda: Nine Stories*. Those stories were written between 1979 and 2011, chronicling—and foretelling—three decades of American life. This book consists of three parts. In Part One there are two short stories: "Creation" (1979) and "Human Moments in World War III" (1983). In Part Two there are three short stories: "The Runner" (1988), "The Ivory Acrobat" (1988), and "The Angel Esmeralda" (1994); and in Part Three four short stories: "Baader-Meinhof" (2002), "Midnight in Dostoevsky" (2009), "Hammer and Sickle" (2010) and "The Starveling" (2011). *The Angel Esmeralda* is a highly acclaimed book well received by both literary critics and ordinary readers. It is a finalist for the annual Story Prize for best story collection, awarded on March 21, 2012.

In addition, DeLillo is a playwright. He has written five major plays: *The Engineer of Moonlight* (1979), which has never been produced; *The Day Room* (first production 1986); *Valparaiso* (first production 1999); *Love-Lies-Bleeding* (first production 2005); and *The Word for Snow* (first production 2007). DeLillo also wrote a screenplay, *Game 6*, which was first produced in 2005. When he was asked "what got you interested in theater in the first place?", he answered, "Being a New Yorker, I always, even as a kid, was aware of theater…" Also he is attracted by the theater represented by Beckett and Pinter. For him, "each form, play and novel, is an antidote to the other" (qtd. in McAuliffe 173-74).

DeLillo occasionally wrote essays on movies, artists, art, and history. On December 8, 1983, in *Rolling Stone* he published his first major essay, "American Blood: A Journey Through the Labyrinth of Dallas and JFK," which is regarded as a precursor to *Libra*. In 1989 he published "Silhouette City: Hitler, Manson and the Millenium" in *Dimensions—A Journal of Holocaust Studies*, Vol. 4, No. 3. This essay was reprinted in full in the critical edition of *White Noise*. In 1994 DeLillo and Paul Auster wrote the pamphlet "Salman Rushdie Defense" in defense of Rushdie who was still in hiding five years after Khomeini's announcement of a fatwa upon him due to the publication of *The Satanic Verses*. In the September 7, 1997 issue of the *New York Times* appeared the essay "The Power of History" in which DeLillo explains how his interest in writing *Underworld* was ignited and how he used facts in his fiction. In 1999 DeLillo was awarded Jerusalem Prize for *Underworld*. He was the first American author to receive it. On the occasion of accepting the award, he delivered a speech entitled "A History of the Writer Alone in a Room" which was later printed in book form with two other addresses. In December 2001 DeLillo published an important essay, "In the Ruins of the Future: Reflections on Terror and Loss in the Shadow of September," in *Harper's*. It is an essay written by a native New Yorker as a response to the terrorist attacks, which provides easy access to his *Falling Man* and a deep insight into the Age of Terror. It "not only offers a penetrating reading of the relationship of globalization and terrorism but also provides a personal reflection on the tragedy" (Conte 191).

DeLillo is the recipient of numerous literary awards. In 1979 he was awarded a Guggenheim Fellowship. In the 1980s he received seven awards, including National Book Award for *White Noise* in 1985 and *Irish Times*, and Aer Lingus International Fiction Prize for *Libra* in 1989. In the 1990s DeLillo won eight different awards and award nominations: PEN/Faulkner Award for *Mao* Ⅱ in 1991, the Pulitzer Prize for Fiction nomination for *Mao* Ⅱ in 1992, the Lila Wallace-Reader's Digest Award in 1995, the National Book Award finalist (Fiction) for *Underworld* in 1997, *New York Times* Best Books of the Year nominee for *Underworld* in 1997, a Pulitzer Prize for Fiction nomination for *Underworld* in 1998, the American Book Award for *Underworld* in 1998, and the Jerusalem Prize awarded for *Underworld* in 1999. From 2000 to 2012, DeLillo received ten awards. They are the 2000's William Dean Howells Medal awarded for *Underworld*, the 2000's Riccardo Bacchelli International Award for *Underworld*, the 2001's James Tait Black Memorial Prize shortlist for *The Body Artist*, 2006's *New York Times*: The Best Work of American Fiction of the Last 25 Years (Runner-Up) for *Underworld*, 2007's *New York Times* Notable Book of the Year for *Falling Man*, 2007's Booklist Top of the List: A Best of Editors' Choice for *Falling Man*, 2009's Common Wealth Award of Distinguished Service for achievements in literature, the 2010's St. Louis Literary Award, the 2010's PEN/Saul Bellow Award for Achievement in American Fiction, the 2012's The Story Prize finalist (Runner-Up) for *The Angel Esmeralda*, and the 2013's inaugural Library of Congress Prize for American Fiction.

Ⅱ. Research Reviews on DeLillo in the United States and China

DeLillo is highly acclaimed by the literary critics both in the United States and abroad. So far, there are about 30 critical books on DeLillo and his works. The first is Tom LeClair's *In the Loop: Don DeLillo and the Systems Novel* which was published by University of Illinois Press in 1987 and is still highly regarded in the literary criticism of DeLillo. In this landmark work LeClair applies the systems theory to his detailed analysis of DeLillo's eight novels published before 1986. He regards DeLillo as a systems novelist and compares him with William Gaddis, Thomas Pynchon and Robert Coover who are also viewed by LeClair as system novelists. LeClair argues that with his unique literary achievement DeLillo deserves the kind of attention that Gaddis, Pynchon and Coover have received. "DeLillo's novels are deceptively artful, mysteriously profound, and wide ranging in their treatment of those qualities of American life that distinguish it as a postindustrial culture, America in the age of information and communication" (LeClair ix), expressing "his passionate concern with human survival, his rage at and pity for what humankind does to itself …" (ibid. 212). Apart from this book, LeClair published four book reviews of DeLillo's novels, the best of which is his review of *Underworld* entitled "An Underhistory of Mid-Century America" which appeared in the October, 1997 issue of *Atlantic*. It was Tom LeClair who did the first major interview with DeLillo in 1982. The interview was published in *Contemporary Literature*, 23, No. 1, 1982 and was republished in 2005 with 16 other interviews in the book entitled *Conversations with Don DeLillo* in which DeLillo talks about his life and his works, the only book that provides access to his biography and the process of his writing.

In 1991, two books about DeLillo were published. Both books were edited by Frank Lentricchia, a professor of English at Duke University. One book is entitled *Introducing Don DeLillo* which consists of 12 articles, two of which are contributed by Lentricchia himself. In "The American Writer as Bad Citizen," Lentricchia defends DeLillo who was criticized by George Will and Jonathan Yardley for *Libra*. Chapter 10 of *Ratner's Star* and an interview with DeLillo—"An Outside in This Society" are included in this book along with an essay on how to read DeLillo. The rest of the articles are critical essays on DeLillo's first eight novels. As is manifested by the title, the book provides some introductory knowledge to those who are not familiar with DeLillo. The other book is *New Essays on White Noise*. This is a short book of five critical essays on *White Noise*. The first essay is the editor's general introduction to DeLillo and *White Noise*. The other four essays focus on the postmodern conditions of American society: consumerism, mass culture, technology, and mass media. It is kind of groundwork for the studies of *White Noise*. With those two pioneering books, "Lentricchia has become DeLillo's canonical critic" (Bloom, *Don DeLillo* 1).

Three other books devoted entirely to *White Noise* are as follows: *Don DeLillo's White Noise* (edited by Harold Bloom and published in 2003); *Don DeLillo's White Noise: A Reader's Guide* (edited by Leonard Orr and published in 2003 as part of the Continuum Contemporaries series); and *Approaches to Teaching DeLillo's White Noise* (co-edited by Tim Engles and John N. Duvall, and published in 2006). Orr's book is very short, containing 88 pages. It is not a book for academics but for "members of book clubs and reading groups, as well as for students of contemporary literature at school, college and university," as the back cover of the book states. By comparison, Bloom's book is more academically profound. It is a collection of 11 classic critical essays written by influential critics of DeLillo like Harold Bloom, Tom LeClair, Frank Lentricchia, John N. Duvall. Some of the essays had already been published in literary journals like *Comparative Literature*, *Modern Fiction Studies*, and at least five essays had been collected in other books. With his sharp eyes, Bloom recollected these insightful essays to present the best literary criticism of *White Noise*. Engles and Duvall's *Approaches to Teaching DeLillo's White Noise* is so far the most comprehensive and pragmatic book on how to teach *White Noise*. It consists of two parts. The first part, "Materials," suggests readings and resources for both instructor and students of *White Noise*, in which the reader can even find detailed information on the novel's editions. The second part, "Approaches," contains 18 essays that establish cultural, theoretical, and technological contexts; place the novel in different survey courses; compare it with other novels by DeLillo; and give examples of classroom techniques and strategies in teaching it. The 19 contributors are professors of English, literature, or literary theories in colleges and universities. Their perspectives are varied and inspiring. It is not just a good know-how book of teaching *White Noise* which has become a popular text for American contemporary literature courses. It is also a good reference book for scholars on DeLillo's other novels.

White Noise is DeLillo's most discussed novel. The critical attention that it has received is not confined to the above books. In 1993 Douglas Keesey's *Don DeLillo* was published by Macmillan as a part of the Twayne's United States Authors Series. This book covers all of DeLillo's novels through *Mao II* with one chapter on each novel. It even includes a coda to introduce DeLillo's plays, stories, essays and the novel *Amazons*. "The focus of this book is on DeLillo's treatment of the media and mediating structures—words and music, names and numbers, film and television" (Keesey vii). It is the second monograph on DeLillo.

There are seven other monographs on DeLillo. Mark Osteen's *American Magic and Dread* (2000) is a work of cultural studies that covers all of DeLillo's novels through *Underworld* with particular emphasis on the issues of media, waste, consumerism and commodification. In *Don DeLillo: The Physics of Language* (2002), David Cowart examines all of DeLillo's novels through *The Body Artist* with an emphasis on language; on how DeLillo uses language in the novels, and how his characters are characterized by different types of language. Cowart applies language theory to his analysis, so his book is particularly illuminating and valuable for readers with some background in critical theory. In 2004 Jesse Kavadlo published *Don DeLillo: Balance at the Edge of Belief*, which is different from those previously published books about DeLillo. His standpoint is morality and his focus is on *White Noise*, *Libra*, *Mao* II, *Underworld* and *The Body Artist* which he believes are more concerned with spiritual crisis. Kavadlo says that his aim to write this book "is to show not just how DeLillo's work can be associated with or understood through systems, language, culture, or the postmodernism, but how it transcends all of these by revealing what it means to be human, not just at the end of the twentieth century, but for all of modernity" (Kavadlo 5).

In 2006 two monographs about DeLillo's works appeared. Routledge published *Don DeLillo: The Possibility of Fiction* by Peter Boxall who teaches English literature at the University of Sussex. This is the first book that reads all of DeLillo's works through *Cosmopolis* in the light of 9·11. As the back cover introduces, "In reading DeLillo's ambivalent engagement with globalization, and with global terrorism, Peter Boxall suggests ways in which his writing might help us to think about the possibilities of fiction in the post-9·11 global context." In his discussion, Boxall often refers to some theorists like Francis Fukuyama, Alexandre Kojève, Gilles Deleuze, Edward Said, Derrida, Wittgenstein, Kristeva, Lacan, Freud and Marx, which makes his book difficult to read in spite of his clarity in expression. In the same year, Joseph Dewey published his monograph: *Beyond Grief and Nothing: A Reading of Don DeLillo*. The book title comes from the famous line from Faulkner's *Wild Palms* that forms a motif in Godard's 1960 film *Breathless*. The book traces a thematic trajectory in DeLillo from his first short story "The River Jordan" to one of his major plays *Love-Lies-Bleeding* (2005). It examines DeLillo as a profoundly spiritual writer, perhaps the most important religious writer in American literature since Flannery O'Connor (Dewey, *Beyond Grief and Nothing* 13). The book is divided into three parts: the street, the word, and the soul, developing from narratives of retreat, narratives of failed engagement, to narratives of recovery, and narratives of redemption, ending up with parables of resurrection. The use of close reading techniques and simple diction make Dewey's book more accessible.

The Environmental Unconscious in the Fiction of Don DeLillo (2007) is about the environmental issues portrayed in DeLillo's four books: *Americana*, *The Names*, *White Noise* and *Underworld*. The book was published by Routledge as a part of Studies in Major Literature Authors. Elise A. Martucci, the author, applies the theories of Dana Philips, William Cronon, and Lawrence Buell in her discussion. She points out: "[H]is novels bring to light the environmental implications of consumerism and technology, and that they raise questions about how we can adapt to and survive in this environment" (Martucci 6). This is the only critical book that exclusively deals with the environmental concern in DeLillo's novels.

Many critics read DeLillo through Jean Baudrillard. They examine DeLillo's novels within Baudrillard's theoretical framework and analyze how DeLillo presents the postmodern condition which is dominated by consumerism. Marc Schuster's monograph, *Don DeLillo, Jean Baudrillard, and the Consumer Conundrum* (2008), belongs to this type of literary criticism. It is the first book-length "detailed and sustained comparison between DeLillo's novels and Baudrillard's works" (Schuster ix). DeLillo shares Baudrillard's interest in consumer culture. This book examines the ways in which both DeLillo and Baudrillard criticize the dehumanizing effects of consumer culture and, more specifically, the ways in which DeLillo's novels interrogate and refine Baudrillard's notion of ambivalence, "the term Baudrillard uses to denote the incessant potential for the destruction of the illusion of value that is at the heart of consumer ideology" (Schuster 187). The book is divided into ten parts with each part focusing on one novel, exploring the relationship between DeLillo and Baudrillard. Interestingly, of all DeLillo's novels published before 2008, four are excluded from the book's discussion: *End Zone*, *Great Jones Street*, *Ratner's Star*, and *Running Dogs*.

Though *Underworld* is a highly acclaimed novel, and has generated countless book reviews and critical essays, there are few monographs or collections of essays about the novel. In 2002 Joseph Dewey co-edited *Underwords: Perspective on Don DeLillo's Underworld*. From the title we know that this is a book entirely devoted to DeLillo's *Underworld*. This collection of 13 essays assesses the novel not only within the postmodern tradition but also within the larger patterns of American literature and culture. It is an illuminating and interesting book. In the same year, John Duvall's *Don DeLillo's Underworld: A Reader's Guide* was published as part of the Continuum Contemporaries series. The book's format is the same as that of Leonard Orr's *Don DeLillo's White Noise: A Reader's Guide*. The book consists of five chapters: "The Novelist," giving background on DeLillo; "The Novel," the main section of the book with an analysis of the main themes; "The Novel's Reception," on the initial reviews of *Underworld*; "The Novel's Performance," on the subsequent academic treatment; and "Further Reading and Discussion." The readership of the book consists of readers in reading clubs and students of contemporary literature in colleges and universities.

Apart from the books mentioned above, some collections of essays on DeLillo have appeared. *Critical Essays on Don DeLillo*, edited by Hugh Ruppersburg and Tim Engles in 2000, contains a section of book reviews and a section of essays, covering each novel through *Underworld*. *Don DeLillo*, edited and with an introduction by Harold Bloom, was published in 2003. The book consists of previously published critical essays on DeLillo's novels published before 2000. *The Cambridge Companion to Don DeLillo*, edited by John Duvall in 2008, features articles covering much of DeLillo's work by many familiar names of DeLillo criticism. It includes Duvall's introduction "The Power of History and the Persistence of Mystery," an excellent essay that covers all of DeLillo's novels through *Falling Man* from the perspective of history. The book is divided into four parts—aesthetic and cultural influences, early fiction, major novels, themes and issues, exploring DeLillo's relation to aesthetics of the 20th century and his major themes. It is a good guide to DeLillo scholarship.

In 2010 two books about DeLillo appeared. One book is Randy Laist's monograph *Technology and Postmodern Subjectivity in Don DeLillo's Novels*. Technology in postmodern society is one of the themes explored in DeLillo's novels. Through a close reading of four novels—*Americana*, *White Noise*, *Underworld*, and *Cosmopolis*, the book examines the variety of modes in which DeLillo's novels illustrate the technologically mediated confluence of his human subjects and the field of cultural objects in which they discover themselves. For those who are interested in contemporary cultural studies, this book will be very helpful and enlightening. The other book about DeLillo is published by Continuum: *Terrorism, Media, and the Ethics of Fiction: Transatlantic Perspectives on Don DeLillo*, a collection of essays from the DeLillo Conference held in Osnabrück, Germany in 2008, "to initiate a dialogue between DeLillo scholarship in Europe and the United States," as the conference organizers hoped. This collection of 14 essays "approaches DeLillo's reflections on the place of literary fiction in the age of mass media and global terrorism from a decidedly transatlantic perspective" (Schneck and Schweighauser 2). This book showcases DeLillo scholarship on both side of the Atlantic: his works' reception, and the similarities and the differences in reading DeLillo.

The newest books about Don DeLillo were published in 2011. They are Paul Giaimo's *Appreciating Don DeLillo: The Moral Force of a Writer's Work* (Prager in Santa Barbara) and Stacy Olster's *Don DeLillo: Mao II, Underworld, Falling Man* (Continuum in New York). In his book, Giaimo claims that DeLillo's body of work does not fit neatly into either the modern or postmodern categories so often assigned to it. He examines the themes and traces the style through DeLillo's award-winning novels, showing how they evolve from a more postmodern into a more modern, or neorealist sensibility. Giaimo is particularly interested in the moral force of DeLillo's works, as well as the Catholic Italian-American cultural background from which they spring. While Giaimo's book is a monograph, Olster's is a collection of ten essays by ten critics. The book consists of ten chapters in three parts. Chapter One is the editor's introduction "Don DeLillo and Dream Release", introducing DeLillo's entire works and the historical context. Part Ⅰ, dedicated to *Mao* Ⅱ, includes three chapters which discuss the themes in the novel "from a post-millennial perspective" (Olster 16). Part Ⅱ consists of three essays on *Underworld*, addressing "the union of high and low" (ibid. 67). The essays included in Part Ⅲ investigate DeLillo's *Falling Man* with respect to its very specific historical context of 9·11, yet in such a way that also extends the discussion to a broader historical continuum. *Don DeLillo: Mao* Ⅱ, *Underworld, Falling Man* reflects on the broad picture of American culture in the multidisciplinary light of modernist and postmodernist theories, artistic concerns and notions of identity. It provides "a critical approach that may develop existing perceptions or challenge them, but always expand the ways in which the author's work may be read by offering a fresh approach" (Tseti 4).

Five journals have devoted special issues to DeLillo's fiction. In 1990 *South Atlantic Quarterly* published such an issue edited by Lentricchia. One year later this collection was reprinted as *Introducing Don DeLillo*. The January 1994 issue of *Postmodern Culture* features the DeLillo cluster, four essays all dealing with DeLillo. In May 1999, an all-DeLillo issue of the online journal *Undercurrent* appeared. It contains six essays on *White Noise* and *Underworld*. Also in 1999, *Modern Fiction Studies* offered a special issue *Don DeLillo* (edited by John Duvall) containing ten essays on DeLillo's novels. In 2001, *Critique* devoted an issue to DeLillo's works with six essays.

The above works witness the development of DeLillo scholarship in America and Europe. But literary criticism of DeLillo is not confined to those works. There are reviews and essays published in journals and newspapers. At least a dozen books include a chapter or more for discussion of DeLillo. Arnold Weinstein devotes a chapter to DeLillo in his *Nobody's Home: Speech, Self, and Place in American Fiction from Hawthorne to DeLillo* (1993). Paul Civello sets aside three chapters to deal with *End Zone* and *Libra* in his book *American Literary Naturalism and its Twentieth-Century Transformations: Frank Norris, Ernest Hemingway, Don DeLillo* (1994). This kind of books on DeLillo—Steffen Hantke's *Conspiracy and Paranoia in Contemporary American Fiction: The Works of Don DeLillo and Joseph McElroy* (1994), Stephanie Halldorson's *The Hero in Contemporary American Fiction: The Works of Saul Bellow and Don DeLillo* (2007), Catherine Morley's *The Quest for*

Epic in Contemporary American Literature (2008) are too many for me to list them all in this book. The topics in DeLillo scholarship are as diverse as postmodernity, historiography, systems theory, technology, film, language, ecology, and terrorism, to name but a few. The body of critical literature and topics for discussion will continue to expand.

In China, Don DeLillo has gained more and more attention from the academic circles and ordinary readers. *The Names*, *White Noise*, *Libra*, *Cosmopolis*, and *Falling Man* have been translated into Chinese, each with an introduction by the translator. Even some of his short stories have been translated into Chinese and published in *Foreign Literature*, a Chinese journal devoted to the introduction of and research on foreign literature. "Human Moments in World War III" (1983) and "The Ivory Acrobat" (1988) are included in *Selected Readings of American Postmodern Short Stories* (2004), a collection translated into Chinese by Professor Yang Renjing and his doctoral students. Reviews and essays of DeLillo's works can be found in the journals of foreign literature, like *Foreign Literature*, *Contemporary Foreign Literature*, and *Foreign Literature Research*. There are a number of MA theses on DeLillo's novels. Whether in essays or MA theses, *White Noise* remains the most discussed novel, probably because it is the most accessible and successful DeLillo's novel. The topics concentrate on postmodernism, consumerism, and ecology. Though DeLillo's status and influence in American literature has been widely recognized in China, books on DeLillo are few, except Li Gongzhao's *Introduction to 20th Century American Literature* (2000), Chen Shidan's *A Study on the Art of American Postmodernist Fiction* (2002), and Yang Renjing's *The History of 20th Century American Literature* (2000) and *A Concise History of American Literature* (2008). No monographs or collections of essays on DeLillo have been published by Chinese scholars yet. There is only one interview, done by Chen Junsong, titled "Keeping Fiction Alive: An Interview with Don DeLillo," which was published in the first issue of *Foreign Literature Research* in 2010. Dr. Chen Junsong finished his dissertation "Political Engagement in Contemporary American Historiographic Metafiction" in 2010. He discusses political engagement in DeLillo's *Libra* as well as in E. L. Doctorow's *The Book of Daniel* and Robert Coover's *The Public Burning*. Additionally, four other PhD students have finished their dissertations on DeLillo's fiction, focusing on the themes of consumerism, media culture, paranoia, and terrorism. More PhD projects on DeLillo are under way, and hopefully, books fully dedicated to DeLillo will appear soon in China.

III. Theoretical Framework and Structure of the Book

1. New Historicism and the Key Representatives

New Historicism is a school of theory that arose "in the late 1970s and early 1980s, most prominently in writings by scholars of the English Renaissance" (Abrams 186), and gained wide acceptance in the 1990s. According to *New World Encyclopedia*:

> New Historicism is an approach to literary criticism and literary theory based on the premise that a literary work should be considered a product of the time, place, and historical circumstances of its composition rather than as an isolated work of art or text. It has its roots in a reaction to the "New Criticism" of formal analysis of works of literature, which was seen by a new generation of professional critics as ignoring the greater social and political consequences of the production of literary texts.

New Historicism was influenced by structuralist and post-structuralist theories, especially the work of Michel Foucault. Many New Historicists have acknowledged a profound indebtedness to Foucault for his theories of power. Foucault claims: "Power is everywhere; not because it embraces everything, but because it comes from everywhere" (Foucault 93), and "power exists in various relations" (Liu 13). Hence, power relations are viewed as the most important context for interpreting literary texts. New historicists believe that power is not simply repressive but it can be productive, while in the eyes of Marxists, power is repressive. "New Historicism is as much as a reaction against Marxism as a continuation of it" (Veeser xi).

Stephen Greenblatt (1943—) is one of the major figures in the school of New Historicism and co-founder of the literary-cultural journal *Representations*, which often publishes articles by New Historicists. He became famous for his brilliant studies of the English Renaissance. Greenblatt coined the term "New Historicism" in his introduction to a special issue of *Genre* in 1982. Due to his influence, New Historicism first gained popularity among Renaissance scholars, and then its popularity was spread to those engaged in culturally- and historically-minded studies which are often referred to as Cultural Studies. He remarked that the presence of Michel Foucault on the Berkeley campus, the influence in America of French anthropological and social theorists, and the Marxist courses he taught all had helped to shape his literary critical practice. He said that New Historicism is "a practice rather than a doctrine" (Greenblatt 1-2). He labeled his literary critical practice as "Poetics of Culture." In a number of articles and books he puts his "Poetics of Culture" into practice, in which he seeks to explore relationships between literature and history, between texts and their social-historical contexts and assumes "texts not only document the social forces that inform and constitute history and society but also feature prominently in the social processes themselves which fashion both individual identity and the socio-historical situation" (Veenstra 174).

"Toward a Poetics of Culture" is one of Greenblatt's important essays. In this essay, when addressing the question of "how art and society are interrelated," as posed by Jean-François Lyotard and Fredric Jameson, Greenblatt refers to "a brilliant paper" by American political scientist and historian Michael Rogin, in which he observed "the number of times President Reagan ha[d], at critical moments in his career, quoted lines from his own or other popular films" (Greenblatt 6). It is interesting to note that both Greenblatt and Rogin point out the social forces that fashion the self-identity in the age of mass media and "the collapse of the working distinction between the aesthetic and the real." The following are some insightful remarks:

> To a remarkable extent, Ronald Reagan, who made his final Hollywood film, The *Killers* in 1964, continues to live within the movies; he has been shaped by them, draws much of his cold war rhetoric from them, and cannot or will not distinguish between them and an external reality. Indeed his political career has depended upon an ability to project himself and his mass audience into a realm in which there is no distinction between simulation and reality.
>
> The response from Anthony Dolan, a White House speech-writer who was asked to comment on Rogin's paper, was highly revealing. "What he's really saying," Dolan suggested, "is that all of us are deeply affected by a uniquely American art form: the movies." (Greenblatt 6)

Like the characters in DeLillo's novels, especially *White Noise* and *Libra* which were both written and published in the 1980s, President Reagan, on the one hand, was deeply affected by the mass media. On the other hand, as an actor who starred in the movies and the President who often spoke on TV, Reagan influenced the large audience and American people who consumed his movies, his televised speeches, the news about him, and even his assassination attempt by John Hinckley, Jr., who was Lee Oswald's successor. The power of mass media to shape identity and the effects of rampant consumerism during Reagan's presidential terms (1981—1989) have been DeLillo's main concerns in his novels and essays.

In his important book *Renaissance Self-Fashioning: From More to Shakespeare*, Greenblatt observes that in the sixteenth-century England "there appears to be an increased self-consciousness about the fashioning of human identity as a manipulable, artful process" (2). The six English Renaissance writers that Greenblatt examines seemed to possess remarkable autonomy to shape themselves and the characters in their works. But as his work progressed, he "found not an epiphany of identity freely chosen but cultural artifact" (256). Greenblatt quoted Clifford Geerfz, an influential American anthropologist, as saying "that humans are cultural artifacts and that human nature cannot be independent of culture" (6). Greenblatt shares his conviction that identity is not a given; rather, it is a cultural or political artifact, "the ideological product of the relations of power in a particular society" (256). Living in the postmodern society, Greenblatt was aware of the fragmentation or loss of self. He engaged himself in the study of English Renaissance which emphasized the importance of the individual and explored "the role of human autonomy in the construction of identity" (256). Greenblatt finds that, in spite of the realization that there is "the most sustained and relentless assault upon the will" to fashion oneself, these Renaissance artists cling to "the human subject and to self-fashioning," for they understand that in their culture "to abandon self-fashioning is to abandon the craving for freedom, and […] is to die" (257). In the "Epilogue" of the book Greenblatt relates an anecdote to assert his overwhelming necessity of sustaining the illusion "that I am the principal maker of my own identity" (257). DeLillo portrays the effort and futility of self-fashioning in postmodern society. Lee Oswald, the fictional character in DeLillo's *Libra*, is trying to fashion his self and ends up being fashioned and cancelled by power.

Greenblatt and some other New Historicists approach the relationship between text and context, or literature and history, "with an urgent attention to the political ramifications of literary interpretation" (Brannigan 3). In their opinion, "literary texts are vehicles of power which act as useful objects of study in that they contain the same potential for power and subversion as exist in society generally." Thus it becomes clear that "the discipline of literary studies is not removed from the sphere of politics" (Brannigan 6). In his famous essay "Invisible Bullets", Greenblatt introduces the theory of subversion and containment which is a means of control. Greenblatt argues that "subversiveness is the very product of that power and furthers its ends" (48) and that the "production of subversion" is "the very condition of power" (57).

There is no effective space of resistance because "power is everywhere; not because it embraces everything, but because it comes from everywhere" (Foucault 93). DeLillo's texts contain subversive forces. DeLillo has been "writing against what power represents, and often what government represents, and what the corporation dictates, and what consumer consciousness has come to mean" (Remnick 142). DeLillo was criticized for writing "ideological fiction" and his satirical portrayal of American postmodern culture. He was called a "bad citizen" by George Will and some other critics in America. The power that the American government represents needs to have subversion because "subversion is always produced in the interests of power." But the power is so erosive and so pervasive that DeLillo's containment is inevitable and inescapable.

Another important New Historicist is Hayden White (1928—). He is a professor of comparative literature at Stanford University, University Professor Emeritus of the University of California, and a member of the American Academy of Arts and Sciences. White published his famous book *Metahistory: The Historical Imagination in Nineteenth-Century Europe* (1973) which marked what came to be known as the "linguistic turn" in historical theory. Since its publication, his theories have revolutionized thinking about historical representation and the intersection of history and literary studies. White regards history as narrative and says all historical explanations are rhetorical and poetic by nature. He argues that history is not a science, or a story told only in facts, but rather a form of discourse that relies on conventional narrative forms and the imagination. The techniques or strategies that historians and writers of fiction use "in the composition of their discourses can be shown to be substantially the same, however different they may appear on a purely surface, or dictional, level of their texts" (White, *Tropics of Discourse* 121). Both historians and writers of historical novels are concerned with the historical events and truth which can only be presented to the reader by means of fictional techniques of representation. White identifies four rhetorical styles through which the authors presented their interpretations: metaphor, metonymy, synecdoche, and irony, and four different literary genres by which the historians figured historical processes in their work as stories of a particular kind: Romance, Tragedy, Comedy, and Satire (ibid. 93). "On this basis alone, one is justified in speaking of history as a text" (White, "New Historicism: A Comment" 297). The similarities between histories and novels are so striking that

> [t]here are many histories that could pass for novels, and many novels that could pass for

> histories [...] Viewed simply as verbal artifacts, histories and novels are indistinguishable from one another. [...] In this respect, history is no less a form of fiction than the novel is a form of historical representation. (White, *Tropics of Discourse* 122)

White's view of history as text and historical texts as literary artifacts erases the distinction between history and fiction. White concludes that history is fiction with ethical consequences.

White's concept of history as narrative corresponds with Lyotard's view of postmodern knowledge. White and other New Historicists reject the Western tendency to write history in grand narrative strokes. They are instead more concerned with what Lyotard terms petits récits, particularly how such "little narratives" participate in the consolidation and maintenance of the status quo. Lyotard argues that in postmodern society people no longer believe the grand narrative and that postmodernity is characterized by an abundance of micro-narratives. A unified History is a myth "propagated by the ruling classes in their own interests. There are only "discontinuous and contradictory histories" (Zhu Gang 259). The grand narrative of official History has been challenged, rewritten, and even replaced by little narrative of histories. These little or personal narratives take part in the historical formations and contribute to the making of history. DeLillo has been writing about American contemporary history. His works belong to the type of little narrative. They interrogate and rethink about the official historical record. They form a counterhistory or an underhistory in tackling the historical events like the Kennedy Assassination, the Cold War, and the September 11 Terrorist Attacks. As little narratives, DeLillo's texts truly represent the historical process of America becoming postmodern. They provide a culture's sense of reality and interesting access to American contemporary society.

Since history is a text, a story, a narrative, it is subjective and fictive. As a reaction to old historicism, New Historicism calls this postmodern situation of history "textuality." It asserts that historical facts exist only as textual traces, and we can only know history in textual forms and "by way of prior textualization" (Jameson, *Political Unconscious* 82). Meanwhile, New Historicists regard both historical and literary texts as products of their social and cultural conditions. They also consider the historian or literary critic to be a product of specific historical conditions. In addition, they tend to read literary texts as functional components of historical formations. They think that literature is "an active part of a particular historical moment" and "see literature as a constitutive and inseparable part of history in the making" (Brannigan 3-4). This post-structuralist understanding of the relationships between literature and history, text and context, "may be characterized chiastically," by another key New Historicist, Louis A. Montrose, "as a reciprocal concern with the historicity of texts and the textuality of history" (20). The following is Montrose's definition of these two terms:

> By the historicity of texts, I mean to suggest the cultural specificity, the social embedment, of all modes of writing—not only the texts that critics study but also the texts in which we study them. By the textuality of history, I mean to suggest, firstly, that we can have no access to a full and authentic past, a lived material existence, unmediated by the surviving textual traces of the society in question—traces whose survival we cannot assume to be merely contingent but must rather presume to be at least partially consequent upon complex and subtle social processes of preservation and effacement; and secondly, that those textual traces are themselves subject to subsequent textual mediations when they are construed as the "documents" upon which historians ground their own texts, called "histories." As Hayden White has forcefully reminded us, such textual histories necessarily but always incompletely constitute in their narrative and rhetorical forms of the "History" to which they offer access. (Montrose 20)

This famous chiastic formulation coined by Montrose sums up the critical premise of New Historicism. In Montrose's view, history is a textual reconstruction of the past. He claims that the "writing and reading of texts ... are being reconstructed as historically determined and determining modes of cultural work" (Montrose 15). The literary text and the critical text reflect the historical, social, and political condition, and the understanding and interpretation of the text cannot be done independently of the historical context. Once the text is produced, it participates in the formation of history.

2. The Structure and Contents of the Book

This book will try to conduct a comprehensive exploration of DeLillo's works from the perspective of New Historicism. When Stephen Greenblatt announced the arrival of New Historicism in 1982, he defined it not as doctrine but as a practice which was "set apart from both the dominant historical scholarship of the past and the formalist criticism that partially displaced this scholarship in the decades after World War Two" (Greenblatt 5). "New historicism represented [...] a significant shift away from the kind of literary studies wherein the literary text was conceived to be an ahistorical linguistic structure, or the literary text was measured against a crude historical background" (Brannigan 204). New Historicism has come to be known as the turn to history in literary studies with its focus on the relationship between history and literature. Later Greenblatt substituted "Poetics of Culture" for New Historicism. DeLillo's writing career started from the 1960s, which parallels the high development of postmodernism in the United States. His works probe American postmodernity, document how America became postmodern, and are an effort to represent contemporary American culture in its totality. In this book I will place DeLillo's works in relation to society, culture and politics, study them in the context of the postmodern condition, and examine how they reflect this condition. According to the New Historicists, history is a verbal construct, and the past can only be "known from its texts, its traces, be they literary or historical" (Hutcheon, *The Politics of Postmodernism* 4). Hayden White claims that the writing of history is a poetic process, and that historical narratives are verbal artifacts. White's influential theory of historical narratives has resulted in the erasure of the distinction between fact and fiction. History and fiction are interchangeable. "History is in essence fictive, or textual, and a novelist performs the same role as a historian" (Gu 14). Within the theoretical framework of New Historicism I will argue that DeLillo's fiction can pass for a history of postmodern America in which popular culture dominated, mass media acted as social forces, and consumerism prevailed. In writing his fictional history, DeLillo became a novelist historian.

Montrose's "historicity of texts, and textuality of history" best sums up the main characteristics of New Historicism. According to his definition of these two terms in his essay "Professing the Renaissance: The Poetics and Politics of Culture," Montrose suggests "first, texts are always produced in a specific historical context, and are thus not 'timeless' work of art", and "what we call history is itself the product of our readings of historical documents, in other words, texts" (Hiscock and Longstaffe 96). Historicity is the product of textuality.

Based on the theories of New Historicism, this book will first examine the historical and cultural context of DeLillo's works and how DeLillo's texts reflect the context in which they were produced. DeLillo's novels come from a particular point in history: the late 1960s to the early 21st century—the postmodern era. Understanding of this period, namely, its history and culture, is, in part, shaped by texts such as DeLillo's works. As a distinguished author and "a strong candidate for the Nobel Prize in literature" (Gioia), DeLillo has made "raids on the consciousness" (Allen) of his time by means of his texts, influencing the formation of American history.

Chapter One "Historicity of DeLillo's Texts" will examine the context in which DeLillo's texts were produced. As with the old historicism, New Historicists argue that we cannot know literary texts independently of their historical and cultural contexts. Knowing the implied context that permeates a text helps us understand it more fully. Since the publication of his first short story "The River Jordan" in 1964, DeLillo's writing career has lasted almost 50 years. His writing took place in the postmodern era which is also referred to as the post-World War II era. According to the New Historicists, literary works and writers are products of their social and cultural circumstances and "literary texts can be illuminated by the study of their relations to their historical contexts" (White, "New Historicism: A Comment" 294). DeLillo lives and writes in the postmodern society, the society which Jean-François Lyotard, Jean Baudrillard, Daniel Bell, and Fredric Jameson reflected upon and wrote about. Their works about postmodern society are helpful access to understanding American postmodern society and its culture. Lyotard has analyzed the condition of postmodern society. Baudrillard, Bell and James call postmodern society "consumer society", "post-industrial society" and "late capitalism" respectively. This book will examine the four aspects of the postmodern society defined separately by these theorists and explore how DeLillo's works represent them.

In his much discussed book *The Coming of Post-Industrial Society*, Bell wrote about the transformation of capitalism from an industrial-based system to one built on consumerism. It is due to this book that the concept "post-industrial society" is popularized. Bell contends that "the post-industrial society is an information society, as industrial society is a goods-producing society" (467). It is a society of affluence and abundance. Bell predicts the global spread of service-based economies as generators of capital and employment. The post-industrial society emphasizes not the production of goods, but of services, which depend on intelligent designers and users of technology. In Bell's view, capitalism has come to rely on "mass consumerism, acquisitiveness and widespread indebtedness," "undermining the old Protestant ethic of thrift and modesty" that have long been credited as the reasons for capitalism's success (Kaufman). The post-industrial society first emerged in the United States. In *White Noise* DeLillo anatomizes American culture in the post-industrial society in which consumerism is rampant, media saturates, and technology predominates. I will investigate the social condition in which *White Noise* was produced.

Lyotard analyzes the condition of knowledge in the post-industrial society in his famous book *The Postmodern Condition: A Report on Knowledge*, "a report on knowledge in the most highly developed societies" (Lyotard xxv). He uses the word "postmodern" to describe this condition and defines "postmodern as incredulity toward metanarratives" (xxiv). In this book Lyotard argues that the status of knowledge has been changed "as societies enter what is known as postindustrial age and cultures enter what is known as the postmodern age" (3). He rejects the big stories, the metanarratives, as he urges at the end of the book: "Let us wage a war against the totality" (82). He argues for the fragmentation of beliefs and values and against a society unified under a grand narrative. He believes that no one can grasp what is going on in the postmodern society as a whole. This sense of fragmentation and uncertainty is shared by DeLillo and is represented in his novels. In an interview with Don DeLillo, Anthony DeCurtis asked: "There's something of an apocalyptic feel about your books, an intimation that our world is moving toward greater randomness and dissolution, or maybe even cataclysm. Do you see this process as irreversible?" DeLillo answered: "This is the shape my books take because this is the reality I see. This reality has become part of all our lives over the past twenty-five years. I don't know how we can deny it" (DeCurtis 73). DeLillo regards 1963, the year of President Kennedy's assassination, as the date for the beginning of the age of randomness and dissolution. Americans have lost a "sense of manageable reality", and "seem much more aware of elements like randomness and ambiguity and chaos since then" (DeCurtis 56).

Baudrillard's works also express this growing awareness of randomness, ambiguity, and chaos. Baudrillard has been regarded as a postmodern guru. He has become best known for his writings about consumer society, for his famous concepts of simulacra, simulation, and hyperreality. In his early books, such as *The System of Objects*, *For a Critique of the Political Economy of the Sign* and *The Consumer Society*, Baudrillard's main focus is upon consumerism, and how different objects are consumed in different ways. For Baudrillard, it was consumption, rather than production, which was the main drive in capitalist society. He claims, the Western societies have entered a new era of simulation in which "social reproduction (information processing, communication, knowledge industries, and so on) replaces production as the organizing principle of society" (Kellner 51). In his "Systems of Objects" and "The Consumer Society" Baudrillard clarifies in length how consumption creates and determines a person's identity within the consumer society and declares that we become what we consume. He argues that consumerism is a postmodern phenomenon. DeLillo examines the effects of this phenomenon on the American society. Like Baudrillard, DeLillo is fascinated with consumer ideology which "ensures that its subjects base their personal worth, their status, and their identity on the objects they own, buy, use, and consume, and the knowledge they possess" (Helyer x). Baudrillard was influenced by Saussurean semiotics. He claims that the consumption of commodities is primarily the consumption of signs in the capitalism of signs. With the massive increase in signs and images circulating in post-industrial media society, the distinction between objects and their representations has disappeared. There is no difference between the images and other orders of experience. Simulation is often taken to be reality.

In his essay "Postmodernism and Consumer Society" Jameson claims that after World War II the United States has entered a new era:

> At some point following World War II a new kind of society began to emerge (variously described as postindustrial society, multinational capitalism, consumer society, media society and so forth). New types of consumption; planned obsolescence; an ever more rapid rhythm of fashion and styling changes; the penetration of advertising, television and the media generally to a hitherto unparalleled degree throughout society. (Jameson 178)

Jameson himself prefers to call this new era "late capitalism" in which "reality has been transformed into images and time fragmented into a series of perpetual presents. In this way, then, postmodernism replicates or reproduces or reinforces the logic of consumer capitalism" (Jameson). The media (print, internet, television, film) constitutes one of the more influential new products of late capitalism and a new means for the capitalist take-over of consumers' lives. "Through the mediatization of culture, we become increasingly reliant on the media's version of our reality, a version of reality that is filled predominantly with capitalist values" (Felluga). DeLillo shares this view of the postmodern condition with Jameson. The interrelations between their thoughts on postmodern society have already been noted by John N. Duvall: "If there is a version of postmodernism with which *White Noise* deeply resonates, it is Jameson's view of the totalizing reach of multinational capitalism" (Duvall, "The (Super) Marketplace of Images" 118). But when it comes to the political commitment of writers in the postmodern age, DeLillo does not fall into Jameson's category of postmodernist writers whose texts are ahistorical and apolitical, playing pastiched images and aesthetic forms, lacking depth and affect. In my opinion, DeLillo often takes an oppositional stance in delineating the postmodern condition. His works attack "those aspects of postmodernity that would turn individuals into so many iterations of Madison Avenue's dream of America" (Duvall, "Introduction: The Power of History and the Persistence of Mystery" 3). In his major works DeLillo engages his cultural anatomization and social criticism from a form that Linda Hutcheon has termed "historiographic metafiction." For Hutcheon, postmodern fiction remains political, opening spaces for social and cultural critique through a parody that deconstructs official history.

Bell, Lyotard, Baudrillard, and Jameson have all agreed that a new age has emerged after World War II although they label it differently. They predict or describe the development of the postmodern era and each produces a certain theory of postmodernism. Their attitudes toward postmodernity may vary, but their views on "the most advanced societies", especially contemporary American society, provide a profound insight into the social and cultural contexts which are shared by those theorists, the New Historicists, DeLillo, and his fictional characters.

In the postmodern age DeLillo produces his works which in turn reflect the social life and history of postmodern America. In an interview, DeLillo attests to his affinity for contemporary cultural processes: "I try to record what I see and hear and sense around me—what I feel in the currents, the electric stuff of the culture. I think these are American forces and energies. And they belong to our time" (qtd. in Begley 332). DeLillo's works are a chronicle of postmodern America, documenting the ordinary Americans' life, deconstructing and reconstructing contemporary American history. He "emerges as the poet laureate of the media age" (Weinstein 301) and "is the laureate of terror, of modern or postmodern terror" (Amis). So DeLillo's fictional texts cannot only be read as material products of specific historical conditions, namely, American post-war society, but also functional components of historical formations, contributing to the making of American history.

The second part of Chapter One will focus on DeLillo's two historical novels, *Libra* and *Falling Man*, to exemplify the "Historicity of DeLillo's Texts." Both novels are about the traumatic events in recent American history: the assassination of President Kennedy and the 9·11 terrorist attacks. Those two texts will be analyzed in their historical contexts and compared with some other texts (three official reports: *The Warren Commission Report*, *The Report of the Select Committee on Assassinations of the US House of Representatives*, and *The 9·11 Commission Report*; DeLillo's two essays: "American Blood: A Journey through the Labyrinth of Dallas and JFK" and "In the Ruins of the Future: Reflections on Terror and Loss in the Shadow of September") in order to have a clearer picture of how DeLillo interprets and represents the historical events and to examine "the cultural specificity, the social embedment" of DeLillo's texts.

Chapter Two will deal with the textuality of DeLillo's American history. I will focus on DeLillo's three novels: *White Noise*, *Mao II*, and *Underworld* and employ the method of close reading. From reading literary works we can obtain historical knowledge of a society and its culture. But literature is more than "a medium of the expression of historical knowledge," it is "a constitutive and inseparable part of history in the making and therefore rife with the creative forces, disruptions and contradictions of history" (Brannigan 4). *White Noise*, *Mao* II, and *Underworld* chronicle American life from 1951 to the late 1990s, reconstruct the reality which is saturated by mass media and popular culture, and represent almost all major historical events in America during the Cold War. In my opinion, the boundary between history and fiction is blurred in DeLillo's texts. History does not work differently from fiction. I argue that DeLillo writes history as a form of fiction although he refuses the explicit role of historian. His postmodern American histories question the official version of historical events.

Chapter Three explores four major narrative strategies as shown in DeLillo's fiction: multiple points of view, discontinuity in narration, black humor, and intertextuality, and discusses how DeLillo's employment of those strategies helps to represent the chaos, fragmentation, randomness, absurdity, and indeterminacy in postmodern American society. The first two strategies are often associated with modernist literature. From the late 19th century and the early 20th century, modernist novelists like William Faulkner and James Joyce experimented with narrative points of view, narrative chronology and abandoned the linear order. DeLillo's exploitation of those narrative strategies manifests that he "has a greater formal and spiritual affinity with the early twentieth-century avant-garde in particular and modernism in general than with other contemporary postmodernist writers" (Knight 27). However, DeLillo's use of multiple points of view matches the postmodern spirit manifested by Lyotard's "petit narrative." Discontinuity in narration is used to render contemporary disorder and lost coherence. Black humor and intertextuality have existed for a long time. Jonathan Swift was identified as the originator of black humor. Since the 1960s black humor has been associated with postmodernism. DeLillo employs black humor to criticize American society. His black humor contains both realism and postmodernism. The term "intertextuality" was coined by poststructuralist Julia Kristeva in 1966. But it is not a new device. Now intertextuality has become the very trademark of postmodernist fiction, though modernist writers James Joyce and William Faulkner heavily relied on this technique. As intertextuality is an important narrative strategy employed by DeLillo, this book gives a detailed analysis of the relationships between DeLillo's texts and other texts. The discussion and analysis are based on the close reading of DeLillo's texts to examine how these narrative strategies contribute to the portrayal of postmodern reality and critique American postmodern culture.

Chapter One

The Historicity of DeLillo's Texts

Montrose says, "By the historicity of texts, I mean to suggest the cultural specificity, the social embedment, of all modes of writing—not only the texts that critics study but also the texts in which we study them" (20). What Montrose means is the context: the historical, social and cultural contexts of the textual production. New Historicism argues for the contextuality of all human thoughts and activities. When reading a literary text, the New Historicists put emphasis on placing the text in its historical context, and its place in a broader literary movement as well as the author's own context.

DeLillo published his first short story "The Jordan River" in 1960, which announced the beginning of his writing career, which parallels the progress of postmodernity in the United States. His works document how this country became postmodern. So first and foremost, let us examine the cultural, social, and historical contexts of his writing. A writer can never escape his/her time and history, and his/her works are products of the social and cultural circumstances, as Jean E. Howard states:

> A new historical literary criticism assumes two things: (1) the notion that man is a construct, not an essence; (2) that the historical investigator is likewise a product of his history and never able to recognize otherness in its pure form, but always in part through the framework of the present. (qtd. in Hoover, 361)

In order to better understand DeLillo's works, it is necessary to put them in the context of their production—the postmodern condition.

I. Context: The Postmodern Condition

The postmodern condition refers to the way that the world has changed in the period which started in the 1950s and continued until now, "due to developments in the political, social, economic, and media spheres" (Nicol 2). A number of theorists theorize the postmodern condition, such as Daniel Bell and the so-called "Holy Trinity" (qtd. in Nicol 184) of postmodern theorists: Lyotard, Baudrillard, and Jameson for their theories particularly offer insights into the conditions of the postmodern society in which DeLillo and his characters live.

1. Daniel Bell's Theory of the Post-Industrial Society

The American cultural historian Daniel Bell coined the term "post-industrial society" and popularized it through his 1973 book *The Coming of Post-Industrial Society*. In this book he foresaw "the global spread of service-based economies as generators of capital and employment," replacing those dominated by manufacturing and the capitalism in the United States has transformed "from an industrial-based system to one built on consumerism" (Kaufman). Bell sometimes uses knowledge society interchangeably with the "post-industrial society," because he viewed knowledge as a "fundamental resource," and the scientific personnel as the chief resource, of post-industrial society (Bell 221). The post-industrial society is an information society in which electronic communications technology dominates and the exchange of communications has replaced the production of goods.

The success of capitalism in the United States has long been credited to the old Protestant ethic of thrift and modesty. But increasingly the development of the American society relies on mass consumerism, acquisitiveness and widespread indebtedness. According to Bell, the post-industrial society is built on this "privileging of self-gratification and hedonism to keep the economy expanding," and due to the lack of Puritanism's balancing constraints, "eventually undermining traditional authority and promoting an 'anything goes' ethic of individual fulfillment at the expense of the social fabric" (Faigley 10).

White Noise is set in a technologically-oriented post-industrial society. It depicts the way the Americans live in this society in the 1980s. Jack Gladney, the narrator of the novel, is a history professor in College-on-the-Hill which is located in a small town named Blacksmith. The Gladneys "live at the end of a quiet street in what was once a wooded area with deep ravines," but there is "an expressway beyond the backyard now" (*White Noise* 4). In the era which technology dominates, Thoreau's "Walden" becomes a dream forever to contemporary Americans. In Jack's house, television is always on. The voice of TV accompanies their daily activities, giving its "incessant bombardment of information" (66). It is a vital constituent of life. Blacksmith is home to a university, a center of ideas, a place of knowledge production and dissemination. On the other hand, Iron City, its neighboring town, stands for the industrial age, witnessing "the decline in the preeminence of the occupations of the manufacturing sector of society" (Bryson and Daniel 65). Iron City, with deserted streets and abandoned factories, now is "a large town sunk in confusion, a center of abandonment and broken glass rather than a place of fully realized urban decay" (85). *White Noise* portrays an American society which shifts from the industrial society to the post-industrial society.

According to Bell, the post-industrial society or postmodern society values consumerism and the "anything goes" ethic. In this society, to be is to buy, to consume, use, and then throw away. The pursuit of gratification, pleasure, and private fulfillment is the supreme ideal. There is no more need for the truth. There is only relativism of morality. The mass media determines the standards of consumer spending and behavior, replacing religious interpretation and ethics with punctual, instant, direct, and "objective" information. In *White Noise*, the Boy Scout camp, where the Gladney family and other residents of Blacksmith stay during the "Airborne Toxic Event," is such a mini post-industrial society. "Here were the sources of information and rumor" (129). There is no authority whatever. Jack's 14-year-old son Heinrich is the center of information about the airborne toxic event. The unorthodox Christians Jehovah's Witnesses are preaching to non-believers. And ironically, a new state program uses this real disastrous event as an occasion to practice simulated evacuation. The technicians use the connected computers with "a massive data-base tally to check the degree of victims' exposure to the deadly emissions and chances for survival." The computers know everything about a person. Punch in the name and the information "comes back pulsing stars … and you are the sum total of your data" (141). Some blind and old people are listening with interest to Babette, Jack's wife, to read from "a small and brightly colored stack of supermarket tabloids" (142). There is a carload of prostitutes in the camp, too. They are from Iron City. Jack's colleague, Murray, in spite of "all these outbreaks of life-style diseases," picks up a prostitute who would like to accept his "Heimlich maneuver" for 25 dollars. During all these activities can be heard the intermittent voice of radio from somewhere.

Bell's views of the social changes that have taken place in contemporary American society are mostly negative. Bell "mourned the absence of any 'transcendent ethic' or 'meaningful purpose' to postmodern life" (Buhle). In this respect, he is different from the following three postmodern theorists.

2. Jean-François Lyotard's Analysis of the Postmodern Condition

Lyotard shares with Bell the view that since at least the end of the 1950s the Western societies have entered "what is known as the post-industrial age and cultures enter what is known as the postmodern age" (Lyotard 3). In his famous book *The Postmodern Condition* (published in French in 1979, in English in 1984) Lyotard argues that in this era "the status of knowledge is altered" (ibid.) and the legitimizing metanarratives are in crisis and in decline. This is how Lyotard understands postmodern: "Simplify to the extreme, I define postmodern as incredibility towards metanarratives" (Lyotard xxiv).

To replace "the grand narratives", Lyotard calls for a series of little narratives that are provisional, contingent, temporary, and relative. The history of everyday life, the history of marginalized groups, and the history of ordinary people belong to Lyotard's "little narratives." Postmodern fictions tend to re-write or to re-present the past in fiction and in history, the multiple and even contradictory histories which are, in Lyotard's words, petits récits. According to Hutcheon, since the 1960s American fiction has been "particularly obsessed with its own past literary, social, and historical" (*A Poetics of Postmodernism* 130).

DeLillo's novels document contemporary American reality and rewrite the past of America after World War II. They call official history into question and interpret historical events in new contexts. DeLillo writes about the JFK Assassination, the Cold War, the 9·11 terrorist attacks, and the Iraqi War. But he usually uses these events as the background for his stories and focuses more on the small, mundane details of daily living in a changed world and their shaping effects on Americans' consciousness at large. What DeLillo writes is the histories, not the History, of America, but his little narratives are necessary constituents of the History, offering a different historical perspective and an accurate insight into the American culture and society of the late 20th century.

The incredibilities against the metanarratives, skepticism toward certainty, moral relativism, and being on guard against control are characteristics of the postmodern age. Jack's son Heinrich is a postmodern child. Two dialogues between Jack and his son capture the spirit of the postmodern age. In Chapter 6, *White Noise*, Jack drives Heinrich to school. It is raining, but Heinrich doubts the existence of the rain since the radio said it wouldn't rain until evening. Jack presses Heinrich to tell him the truth whether it is raining or not. Heinrich plays a language game with him and demonstrates that there is only relativism and no absolute truth. Jack admits his failure in the debate: "A victory for uncertainty, randomness and chaos" (24). This dialogue dramatizes the uncertain and chaotic postmodern condition. Another dialogue between Jack and Heinrich takes place in Chapter 21, in the Boy Scout Camp during the airborne toxic event. Heinrich is skeptical of the triumph of science and progressiveness of history:

> "It's like we've been flung back in time," he said. "Here we are in the Stone Age, knowing all these great things after centuries of progress but what can we do to make life easier for the Stone Agers? Can we make a refrigerator? Can we explain how it works? What is electricity? What is light? We experience these things every day of our lives but what good does it do if we find ourselves hurled back in time and we can't even tell people the basic principles much less actually make something that would improve conditions. […] We think we're so great and modern. Moon landings, artificial hearts. But what if you were hurled into a time warp and came face to face with the ancient Greeks. The Greeks invented trigonometry. They did autopsies and dissections. […] Could you tell him about the atom? The Greeks knew that the major events in the universe can't be seen by the eye of man. It's waves, it's rays, it's particles."
>
> "[…] If you came awake tomorrow in the Middle Ages and there was epidemic raging, what could you do to stop it, knowing what you know about the progress of medicines and diseases? Here it is practically the twentieth-century and you've read hundreds of books and magazines and seen a hundred TV shows about science and medicine. Could you tell those people one little crucial thing that might save a million and a half lives?" (146-47)

In spite of the advanced development in science and technology, we are not better equipped than the ancient people when confronted with the ecological disaster. With all the knowledge of science we, in the late 20th century, are as vulnerable and gullible as people in the Stone Age or Middle Ages.

  The above examples show that DeLillo's fictional America is postmodern, as defined by Lyotard. In it the metanarratives like the objectivity of the truth, and the triumph of science have lost their credibility. However, DeLillo differs from Lyotard in the view of postmodernity. Lyotard depicts the "postmodern condition as potentially more positive, even liberating" (Nicol 11) while DeLillo "sees more of the loss, more of the cultural vacuity" in the postmodern age, "when there is no objective truth, no metaphysical court of appeals for humanity" (Rettberg).

Compared to Lyotard, Jean Baudrillard, another French philosopher, has a more radical and pessimistic take on the postmodern condition, although he also rejects the metanarratives like Lyotard. For Baudrillard, the postmodern world is a world of simulacra, where people can no longer differentiate between reality and simulation and lead meaningless lives.

3. Jean Baudrillard's Idea of Consumer Society

Jean Baudrillard has become well-known for his writings on consumer society: *The System of Objects* (1968), *The Consumer Society* (1970), *For a Critique of the Political Economy of the Sign* (1972), *The Mirror of Production* (1975), *Symbolic Exchange and Death* (1976) and *Simulacra and Simulation* (1981). These books are "attempts to provide ultraradical perspectives that overcome the limitations of an economistic Marxist tradition" (Kellner 51).

Postmodern consumer society is socially constructed by signs. In this society, symbols, signs, and simulations proliferate so much that it is no longer possible to distinguish the real and the symbol. Baudrillard thus argues that we have entered a new era that is beyond the modern, namely the postmodern era. In this society people live in "the hyperreality of simulations in which images, spectacles, and the play of signs replace the logic of production and class conflict as key constituents of contemporary societies" (Kellner 52). For Baudrillard, simulation rules in postmodern society in which "identities are constructed by the appropriation of images, and codes and models determine how individuals perceive themselves and relate to other people" (ibid.).

Many critics have identified the affinities between Baudrillard and DeLillo (Schuster ix). In the discussions of these affinities, these concepts developed by Baudrillard stand out: simulacra, simulation, and hyperreality.

For Baudrillard, postmodern culture is a culture of simulacrum. According to Baudrillard, a simulacrum is "an identical copy without an original" (Storey 187). "Simulacra" is the plural form of simulacrum. Baudrillard argues that there are three "orders of simulacra":

> (1) In the first order of simulacra, which he associates with the pre-modern period, the image is a clear counterfeit of the real; the image is recognized as just an illusion, a place marker for the real; (2) In the second order of simulacra, which Baudrillard associates with the industrial revolution of the nineteenth century, the distinctions between the image and the representation

> begin to break down because of mass production and the proliferation of copies. Such production misrepresents and masks an underlying reality by imitating it so well, thus threatening to replace it (e.g. in photography or ideology); however, there is still a belief that, through critique or effective political action, one can still access the hidden fact of the real; (3) In the third order of simulacra, which is associated with the postmodern age, we are confronted with a precession of simulacra; that is, the representation precedes and determines the real. There is no longer any distinction between reality and its representation; there is only the simulacrum. (Felluga, "Modules on Jean Baudrillard")

In a postmodern society the very distinction between original and copy has itself now been destroyed. Baudrillard calls this process "simulation" and defines "simulation" as "the generation by models of a real without origins or reality: a hyperreal" (qtd. in Storey 187). For Baudrillard, "Disneyland is a perfect model of all the entangled orders of simulation" (Baudrillard 153). He claims that the reason for Disneyland's success is not that it can allow the Americans a fantasy escape from reality, but that it allows them an unacknowledged concentrated experience of "real" America. He declares:

> Disneyland is there to conceal the fact that it is the "real" country, all of "real" America, which is Disneyland (just as prisons are there to conceal the fact that it is the society in its entirety, in its banal omnipresence, which is carceral). Disneyland is presented as imaginary in order to make us believe that the rest is real, when in fact all of Los Angeles and the America surrounding it are no longer real, but of the order of the hyperreal and of simulation. It is no longer a question of a false representation of reality (ideology), but of concealing the fact that the real is no longer real. (Baudrillard 154)

The imaginary world of Disneyland is neither true nor false. Baudrillard argues that "it is meant to be an infantile world, in order to make us believe that the adults are everywhere, in the 'real' world, and to conceal the fact that real childishness is everywhere, particularly among those adults who go there to act the child in order to foster illusion of their real childishness" (ibid.). Baudrillard refers to Disneyland as an exemplar of hyperreality, in which the distinction between simulation and the real implodes; the "real" and the imaginary continually collapse into each other. The result is that reality and simulation are experienced as without difference. Simulations can often be experienced as more real than the real itself. Baudrillard furthers his argument by referring to Watergate Scandal reporting. Watergate had to be reported as a scandal in order to conceal the fact that it was a commonplace of American political life. This is what Baudrillard calls "a simulation of a scandal to regenerative ends" (qtd. in Storey 190).

In the American society DeLillo depicts in his novels, images proliferate, the distinction between what is real and what is imagined is destroyed and meaning is systematically eroded—the postmodern world consists of simulations of reality, or hyperreality. According to David Cowart, "[m]-ore than any other contemporary writer, DeLillo understands the extent to which images—from television, from film, from magazine journalism and photography, from advertising, sometimes even from books—determine what passes for reality in the American mind" (132). Take for example, *Americana*, in which the protagonist David Bell exemplifies how hyperreality has been gradually replacing reality, when he behaves according to media codes, copying from Burt Lancaster and Kirk Douglas (two popular American film stars) a personal style that is considered the personification of the American dream, confusing the scenes he has seen in the films with his own reality.

> When I was a teenager I saw Burt In *From Here to Eternality*. He stood above Deborah Kerr on that Hawaiian beach and for the first time in my life I felt the true power of the image. Burt was like a city in which we are all living. He was that big. Within the conflux of shadow and time, there was room for all of us and I knew I must extend myself until the molecules parted and I was spliced into the image. Burt in the moonlight was a crescendo of male perfection but no less human because of it. Burt lives! I carry that image to this day [...] It was a concept; it was the icon of a new religion. That night, after the movie, driving my father's car along the country roads, I began to wonder how real the landscape truly was, and how much of a dream is a dream. (13)

The film images shape Bell's consciousness of self and perception of the reality and make him question his material reality. The distinction between the imagined and the real blurs in Bell's mind.

Bell's life is dominated by various images which form his consciousness. These images do not just come from films. They also come from advertisements, TV news and plays, and books. As he is a TV network executive in New York City, his work is about producing and selling images. His daily life is saturated with images. The Vietnam War "was on television every night but we all went to the movies" (5). Even when he is a child, Bell is exposed to the business of advertising. His father Clinton Bell works as a successful advertising executive and embraces the power of the image technology. He passes on the notion of image to his son David and projects the commercials which his agency has produced onto a basement screen for his children's entertainment. Watching TV commercials is thus a primal childhood diversion for David. "All the impulses of the media," he says, "were fed into the circuitry of my dreams. One thinks of echoes. One thinks of an image made in the image and likeness of images" (130). Now David is fed up with the ruthless power plays of the network and wants to escape from the mass media-saturated life. He starts a journey to the American West for exploration and self-discovery. On the journey David discovers that American innocence and uniqueness are being eroded by consumerism. He shoots a film of his family history, part of which serves as a critique of advertising business on which consumerism is built. In David's film the character Clinton is engaging in a dialogue about advertising's role:

> "How does a successful television commercial affect the viewer?"
>
> "It makes him want to change the way he lives."
>
> "In what way?" I said.
>
> "It moves him from first person consciousness to third person. In this country there is a universal third person, the man we all want to be. Advertising has discovered this man. It uses him to express the possibilities open to the consumer. To consume in America is not to buy; it is to dream. Advertising is the suggestion that the dream of entering the third person singular might possibly be fulfilled."
>
> [...]
>
> "[...] The third person was invented by the consumer, the great armchair dreamer. Advertising discovered the value of the third person but the consumer invented him. The country itself invented him. He came over on the Mayflower[...] He identifies only with the image. The Marlboro Man." (270-72)

"The Marlboro Man" stands for masculinity, strength, independence, and heroism. He is the universal third man that all men want to become. David Bell has been bombarded by media images and living the dream of entering the third person singular. With 28 years in the movies, he is making "a life so easily made that a hat on the head could become the man. The hat wore me" (287). The result is he has become a hollow man, a fragmented postmodern man.

The perfect images in movies and on television dispense with reality and replace it with media simulacra of reality. The images of the American West in the classics and mass media are romantic and pastoral, representing "American purity and innocence"

(Martucci 31). On his journey west, David finds out that the pure and innocent landscape is non-existent. "Industrialization and commercialization have consumed most of it" (ibid.). David drives along the road, exploring and wondering: "what could we see of the countryside through the smoke and the billboards?" (DeLillo, *Americana* 111) He notices jet trainers flying over the mountains and deserts. He also encounters acts of violence and sexual abuse of Mexican prostitutes. In the end. "wilderness will soon be nothing but a memory" (358). "The Marlboro Man", the image of a cowboy, reminds consumers of the American West in the imaginary—a nostalgia for a life close to nature. But it is only a media simulacrum, a copy without an original. David's spiritual journey ends up in failure, but it reveals the dramatic changes that consumerism has brought about in the 1960s' America.

In the process of exploring the heartland and rediscovering the past of both the family and the nation, David, the image-maker, records the rise of postmodernity in the United States. *Americana* demonstrates DeLillo's ambition to take the whole picture, the whole culture of America as the subject of his writing. DeLilo paints detailed portraits of American life in the late 20th and early 21st centuries and provides a provoking insight into contemporary America, "a thoroughly postmodern, dehistoricized America" (Duvall, Introduction 7). In DeLillo's later novels, such as *White Noise*, *Libra*, *Mao* II, *Underworld*, the world where the characters live is increasingly "divorced from the real as a result of the persuasive power of technology and systems of representation" (Nicol 184) which dominate American culture: film, camera, television, Internet, advertising, and marketing. For example, *White Noise* depicts a society in which TV is dissolved into life and life is dissolved into TV. As a character remarks in the novel, for most people in the postmodern society "there are only two places in the world. Where they live and their TV set" (66). In this society of simulacra, images and electronic representations replace direct experience. Here the line between the real and the unreal, the line between high culture and popular culture, are blurred.

Though Baudrillard was a post-Marxist, and Jameson is a Marxist, they share the same extreme pessimistic view of the postmodern world. Of course, they are also different in that Baudrillard stresses the logic of simulation in contemporary Western societies while Jameson emphasizes the lessening of the inter-relationship between signifers.

4. Fredric Jameson's Viewpoint on Late Capitalism

In 1984 Fredric Jameson published his influential essay "Postmodernism, or the Cultural Logic of Late Capitalism," which was expanded to a full-sized book with the same title in 1991. In this book Jameson claims that late capitalism dominates contemporary American culture.

In *Postmodernism, or the Cultural Logic of Late Capitalism*, Jameson claims that postmodernism reflects a new "cultural dominant" where cultural production has become integrated into commodity production. Jameson adapts the argument of Ernest Mandel in *Late Capitalism* that there have been three stages in capitalism: market capitalism, the monopoly stage of imperialism, and late or multinational capitalism. Jameson connects the trajectory of capitalism with the artistic movements of realism, modernism, and postmodernism through a mediation that would explain postmodernism as a new cultural logic. Jameson claims that postmodernism can be found in all the arts and there are a variety of forms. Most of the postmodernisms "emerge as specific reactions against the established forms of high modernism … This means there will be as many different forms of postmodernisms as there were high modernisms in place" (Jameson 164). Another feature of postmodernism is the "effacement in it of the key boundaries or separations, most notably the erosion of the older distinction between high culture and so-called mass or popular culture" (165). Postmodernism is not just another word for the description of a particular style. From Jameson's perspective, postmodernism is "a periodizing concept whose function is to correlate the emergence of new formal features in culture with the emergence of a new type of social life and economic order" (ibid.). According to Jameson, late capitalism

> can be dated from the postwar boom in the United States in the late 1940s and early '50s or, in France, from the establishment of the Fifth Republic in 1958. The 1960s is in many ways the key transitional period, a period in which the new international order (neocolonialism, the Green Revolution, computerization and electronic information) is at one and the same time set in place and is swept and shaken by its own internal contradictions and by external resistance. (Jameson 166)

In Jameson's opinion, late capitalism includes the following elements: (1) "new forms of business organization (multinationals, transnationals) beyond the monopoly stage" (qtd. in Felluga); (2) an internationalization of business beyond the older imperial model; in the new order of capital, multinational corporations are not tied to any one country but represent a form of power and influence greater than any one nation; (3) "a vertiginous new dynamic in international banking and the stock exchanges (including the enormous Second and Third World debt)" (qtd. in Felluga). Through such a banking structure, the First World's multinational corporations maintain their control over the world market; (4) "new forms of media interrelationship" (qtd. in Felluga). The media constitutes one of the more influential new products of late capitalism (print, Internet, television, film) and a new means for the capitalist take-over of Americans' lives. Through the mediatization of culture, Americans become increasingly reliant on the media's version of our reality, a version of reality that is filled predominantly with capitalist values; (5) American military domination. As Jameson writes in *Postmodernism*, "this whole global, yet American, postmodern culture is the internal and superstructural expression of a whole new wave of American military and economic domination throughout the world: in this sense, as throughout class history, the underside of culture is blood, torture, death, and terror" (qtd. in Felluga). Hence late capitalism has synonyms like "multinational capitalism", "spectacle or image society", "media capitalism", "the world system", even "postmodernism itself."

These elements that Jameson lists in his book are American reality that is represented in DeLillo's fictional world. This is a world of ubiquitous media, advertising and rampant consumerism. In *White Noise* DeLillo depicts a media-saturated American society where people are surrounded by all kinds of "white noise." In order to ward off the fear of death, Babette trades her body for Dylar with Mink who is in charge of the Dylar project which is financed by a multinational giant. Babette knows of Dylar by reading the tabloid the *National Examiner* to a group of old blind people who are obsessed with the tabloid stories. An American takes the commodity Dylar which is produced and advertised by a multinational corporation whose project manager is non-white, probably a new immigrant, who says he "learned English by watching American TV" (308). This condition DeLillo depicts in *White Noise* is typical of late capitalism defined by Jameson.

In *Mao* II, DeLillo portrays a contemporary world dominated by images. Even in war-torn Beirut, capitalism penetrates. In the street the photographer Brita hears a driver blow the horn "at a guy who carries a bayonet in an alligator scabbard and the horn plays the opening bars of 'California Here I Come'" (228-29). "The streets run with images. They cover walls and clothing … Brita thinks this place is a millennial image mill. There are movie posters everywhere but no signs of anything resembling a theater" (229). There are adverting placards for a new soft drink, Coke II. *Mao* II was published in 1991, the year when one of the two superpowers, the Soviet Union, collapsed and the Cold War ended. That the Russian communism lost in the contest means the multinational capitalism won. In the epilogue of *Underworld*, the capitalist and postmodern Russia is portrayed as follows:

> Capital burns off the nuance in a culture. Foreign investment, global markets, corporate acquisitions, the flow of information through transnational media, that attenuating influence of money that's electronic and sex that's cyberspaced, untouched money and computer-safe sex, the convergence of consumer desire—not that people want the same things, necessarily, but that they want the same range of choices. (785)

The United States is the only superpower left on the earth then. As DeLillo writes in *Underworld*: "Everything is connected." The East and the West, the Russians, and the Americans, are connected by the capital and the Internet. Capital rules the world. As postmodern globalization spreads quickly, America's influence is deeply felt in almost every corner of the world. As pointed out by Fredric Jameson, globalization is synonymous with Americanization and "the standardization of world culture, with local popular or traditional forms driven out or dumped down to make way for American television, American music, food, clothes and films" is "the very heart of globalization" (Jameson, "Globalization" 51). American cultural commodities are invading every corner of the world.

Accompanying the economic domination globally is the American military domination throughout the world. With the end of the Cold War did not come the age of the "end of history" claimed by Francis Fukuyama in 1989. There have been local conflicts and clashes all over the world and the American military interventions in different places around the world. For example, in the name of "war on terror," the United States sent its troops to Afghanistan and Iraq. DeLillo's novels represent the history of American military domination since the 1950s. To keep military domination throughout the world lea to the development of nuclear weapons and consumption of large quantities of other hi-tech weapons, hence the problem of the deadly waste which is difficult to dispose of. Waste is one of the themes tackled in DeLillo's *Underworld*.

Postmodernism, for Jameson, "equates purely and simply to the effects of late capitalism on contemporary culture" (Nicol 10). Like many theorists of postmodernism and postmodernity, Jameson tends to regard their effects as harmful. His "diagnosis of postmodernism trumps all other theorists of the postmodern in its references to pathological conditions, associating the phenomenon with schizophrenia, hysteria, nostalgia, paranoia, and a 'waning of affect'" (Nicol 9). Jameson claims that postmodernism is characterized by pastiche and a crisis in historicity. In postmodernism, parody is replaced by pastiche and the postmodern era suffers from a crisis in historicity. According to Jameson, "late capitalism has created a 'perpetual present' where time is dominated by the free-floating rhythms of the new electronic media" (Nicol 10), resulting in the disorientation in time and space.

As a Marxist, Jameson's attitude toward late capitalism is critical, and as a result he can be located within the tradition of the Frankfurt School pessimists. According to Jameson, unlike modernism, which taunted the commercial culture of capitalism, postmodernism, rather than resisting, "replicates and reproduces—reinforces—the logic of consumer capitalism" (qtd. in Storey 194). The postmodern collapse of the distinction between high and popular has been gained at the cost of modernism's critical space. Postmodernism "offers no position of 'critical distance'; it is a culture in which claims of 'incorporation' or 'co-optation' make no sense, as there is no longer a critical space from which to be incorporated or co-opted" (Storey 195). As Grossberg remarks:

> For Jameson ... we need new "maps" to enable us to understand the organization of space in late capitalism. The masses, on the other hand, remain mute and passive, cultural dupes who are deceived by the dominant ideologies, and who respond to the leadership of the critic as the only one capable of understanding ideology and constituting the proper site of resistance. At best, the masses succeed in representing their inability to respond. But without the critic, they are unable even to hear their own cries of hopelessness. Hopeless they are and shall remain, presumably until someone else provides them with the necessary maps of intelligibility and critical models of resistance. (qtd. in Storey 195)

For Jameson, the only way out of the postmodernist logic is through what he calls "cognitive mapping," the identification and analysis of all its effects.

Like Jameson, DeLillo is a critic of postmodern culture. As Frank Lentricchia puts it, DeLillo "takes for his critical object of aesthetic concern the postmodern situation" (Introduction 14). DeLillo sees the writer's role as a resistant one: "There are so many temptations for American writers to become part of the system and part of the structure that now, more than ever, we have to resist. American writers ought to stand and live in the margins, and be more dangerous" (qtd. in Arensberg 46). As we know, it is hard to take an oppositional stance toward postmodernism since it "has swallowed everything" (Nicol 10). Those in the margins will be incorporated into the dominant, as the New Historicists claim that "subversion is always already co-opted by power" (Brannigan 76). DeLillo, in his dialogue with contemporary American culture and history, attempts to enforce a critique as a public intellectual, but his subversion is contained by the dominant power. In other words, his critique of postmodernism turns out to be a kind of "complicitous critique" (Hutcheon, *The Politics of Postmodernism* 2).

Daniel Bell, Jean-François Lyotard, Jean Baudrillard, and Fredric Jameson all wrote books to formulate their theories about postmodern society or postmodernity though they might employ different terms to label it and focus on different aspects of the postmodern condition. My survey of their related postmodern theories is used to examine the cultural context in which DeLillo wrote his works and to present an insight into the social condition which influences DeLillo, shapes his fictional characters and their consciousness. DeLillo has publicly remarked that he does not read much of "the theoretical work being done in philosophy and literary criticism these days" (qtd. in Morley 124). "Yet to read DeLillo is to encounter in his fiction many of the observations articulated by contemporary theorists of the postmodern. His work lends itself to definition by way of example rather than formulation" (Morley 124). The social and cultural changes that were taking place were felt by both the theorists and writers. DeLillo observed the changes in his surroundings, his life, and society and recorded them in his works. Thus DeLillo's fiction can be read as a fictional history of the process of American postmodernity.

II. The Chronicler of America: Historicizing the Present

The age of multinational capitalism or late capitalism, for Jameson, suffers a crisis of historicity. He calls postmodern culture schizophrenic, which means that it has lost its sense of history. "It is a culture suffering from 'historical amnesia,' locked into the discontinuous flow of perpetual presents" (Storey 193). Thus Jameson calls for "always historicize!" in his 1981 book *The Political Unconscious: Narrative as a Socially Symbolic Act*. DeLillo and Jameson have the same view in this respect. According to Duvall, DeLillo "has a rare gift for historicizing our present, a gift that empowers engaged readers to think historically themselves" (Introduction 2). This is what makes DeLillo stand out among contemporary American writers as "one of the most important American novelists" (ibid.).

DeLillo's writing career almost parallels the process of American postmodernity. For 50 years, DeLillo has been writing about America and offered an unofficial version of American contemporary history, thus he is called "the chronicler of America" (Adams). DeLillo said in an interview: "It was no coincidence that my first novel is called *Americana*. That became my subject, the subject that shaped my work." (qtd. in McCrum) DeLillo's works tackle American historical events as well as ordinary American life. Therefore, they can be treated as a history of contemporary America and DeLillo a writer of fictionalized history. Hayden White has argued that since history is a narrative art, it must be understood as a form of narrative representation analogous to fiction. In fact, as he sees it, history works no differently than fiction. The best novelists compel their readers to accept their narratives as true in the same way that historians expect their readers to accept their narratives as true. These novelists write history as a form of fiction. According to Timothy Parrish, in the twentieth century, "the most powerful works of American history were written by William Faulkner, Toni Morrison, Thomas Pynchon, Don DeLillo, Joan Didion, and Cormac McCarthy," who are regarded as the great modernists or postmodernist historians (back cover).

According to New Historicism, a literary or non-literary work should be considered a product of the time, place, and historical circumstances of its composition rather than an isolated work of art or text as the "New Criticism" advocated. This is what Louis A. Montrose means by the "historicity of texts": "the cultural specificity, the social embedment, of all modes of writing—not only the texts that critics study but also the texts in which we study them" (20). Since a literary work is the social and political product, it is necessary to study the historical context in which the work is produced in order to understand the work and the culture.

1. *Libra:* The Origin of American Postmodern Condition

Libra was published in 1988. DeLillo's composition of this novel started in the early 1980s when he returned to the United States after he had lived abroad for there years and was surprised to find television had become the primal force in the American home. "I began to notice something on television which I hadn't noticed before. This was the daily toxic spill—there was the news, the weather and the toxic spill" (qtd. in Rothstein 23). This phenomenon probably caused him to reflect upon the media-saturated culture and its influence on the psychology of the individuals and led to his publications of the essay "American Blood: A Journey through the Labyrinth of Dallas and JFK" in 1983 and the book *White Noise* in 1985. These two works are related to *Libra* thematically, focusing on American postmodernity.

As a writer whose main concern is the postmodernity in the Uuited States, DeLillo keeps referring to the JFK Assassination in his works. He views the assassination of the President as the origin of the American postmodern condition. The deaths of President Kennedy and Lee Oswald ushered in the society of spectacle in the United States. For the week following the murder, television kept replaying Jack Ruby's murder of Oswald and then the President's funeral, which were turned into media products and sold to the audience addicted to consuming images of disasters and violence. The media coverage on the Kennedy Assassination has never been equaled. Because of the national sense of loss and mourning, all three networks (ABC, CBS, and NBC) suspended all regular programming for nearly four days and devoted all of their programming time to the coverage of the investigation, arrest of Oswald, background of Kennedy's administration, the Kennedy family, Oswald's background, and retelling of the motorcade and shooting. The power of image-obsessed media was felt for the first time. All the Americans seemed to be watching the footage of the shooting, "which deepened and prolonged the horror. It was horror on horror… After some hours the horror became mechanical" (*Libra* 446-47). Even Oswald seemed to be watching his own death when he was shot. "Through the pain, through the losing of sensation except where it hurt, Lee watched himself react to the augering heat of the bullet" (*Libra* 439). Oswald, who used to identify with the image of Kennedy in the media, now has become an image on TV and achieved the same status of celebrity as Kennedy with the acts of violence. He prefigures people like Arthur Bremer and John Hinckley, the would-be assassins of the Presidents, presidential candidates, and other celebrities. "After Oswald, men in America are no longer to lead lives of quiet desperation" (*Libra* 181). Lee Harvey Oswald "exemplifies this new regime, where acts of consumerism and violence overlap, where anomie and lethal intent feed off media attention" (Green 97).

For DeLillo, the postmodern condition originated from the assassination of Kennedy because this traumatic event has changed the ways the Americans view knowledge, reality and government, which matches Lyotard's postmodern condition characterized by the incredulity towards meta-narratives. DeLillo mentioned this change in an interview:

> As the years have flowed away from that point, I think we've all come to feel that what's been missing over these past twenty-five years is a sense of a manageable reality. Much of that

feeling can be traced to that one moment in Dallas. We seem much more aware of elements like randomness and ambiguity and chaos since then. (qtd. in DeCurtis 56)

In the following section I shall discuss how this change has been brought about and elaborate it in more details.

1.1 The JFK Assassination: "The Seven Seconds that Broke the Back of the American Century"

On November 22, 1963 President John F. Kennedy was assassinated in Dealey Plaza of Dallas, Texas. The assassination was regarded by the Americans as the most traumatic moment in the 20th century since the Pearl Harbor. As DeLillo wrote in *Libra*, this was "the seven seconds that broke the back of the American century" (181).

A. Various Reactions to the Assassination

In America and around the world, there was a stunned reaction to the assassination of President Kennedy. In the days following the assassination, people wept, lost their appetites, had difficulty in sleeping, and suffered nausea, nervousness, and sometimes anger. On November 28, 2003, the 40th anniversary of the assassination, BBC held an online debate about the impact of the assassination. I read the comments and found all of the participants of the debate remembered where they were and recalled the crying and emotional breakdown of themselves and people around them when they heard the tragic news.

Americans' grieved reaction to the assassination was depicted in *Libra*. "There were wreaths and flower clusters arrayed on the lawns of Dealey Plaza, marks of sadness and farewell." (428) Normal life seemed to stop for most Americans. Most businesses were closed on the weekend due to the national pain. In the eyes of Jack Ruby, the murderer of Oswald, the assassination of President Kennedy was "an event that had the possibility of being bigger in history than Jesus, he thought. So much impact and reaction. It was almost as though they were reenacting the crucifixion of Jesus" (ibid.). Like many others, Ruby cooked a meal "but didn't have the heart to eat it" (429). He wept and was angry. He was overwhelmed by the constant replays of Kennedy's assassination on TV and tortured by the repetition of the assassin's name, Lee Harvey Oswald, on the radio news. In the end, Ruby, owner of a nightclub, who was connected to the Mafia, shot Oswald when authorities were preparing to transfer Oswald from the police basement to the nearby county jail—Ruby stepped out from a crowd of reporters and fired his revolver into Oswald's abdomen, fatally wounding him. The shooting was broadcast live nationally and replayed over and over again during the weekend, and millions of television viewers witnessed it. "In his televised death," Oswald "becomes part of American consciousness in a way unique to its history" (qtd. in Cowart 101).

B. The Camelot Presidency of Kennedy

American people were stunned and saddened by the assassination of the President. In their hearts, Kennedy was a charismatic leader, hero and martyr for civil rights and equal justice. His assassination was compared to the fall of King Arthur as his term was said to have potential and promise for the future, and many were inspired by Kennedy's speeches, vision, and policies. In an interview shortly after the funeral of her husband, Jacqueline Kennedy likened John F. Kennedy's 1000-day presidency to King Arthur's Camelot (Streich). Camelot is a castle and court associated with the legendary King Arthur. In the Broadway musical *Camelot*, King Arthur sings these lines as he is dying: "Don't let it be forgotten, that once there was a spot, for one brief shining moment that was known as Camelot." She quoted these lines and added: "There'll be great Presidents again, but there'll never be another Camelot again … it will never be that way again" (Streich).

Kennedy's reputation as a great president is due mainly to this Camelot image of his time as president. This is an image constructed by the media, especially television. John F. Kennedy once worked as a journalist. This experience made him realize how much a politician could manipulate the news media and how much that could help his career. The televised debates between him and Nixon had a profound influence on the 1960 election, and helped him win the presidential election. "A master of the spotlight" (Scheiber), he was the first American President to understand and exploit the power of television to showcase himself, his family and the White House, the first president to effectively use the new medium of television to speak directly to the American people. His media image communicated intelligence, confidence, articulation, youth, good looks, and humor. Both men and women were attracted to him by his charisma. For women, Kennedy was the object of sexual fantasies, the lady killer. For men, he was their hero, the symbol of the American Dream. The media constructed John F. Kennedy as "a universal third person, the man we all want to be" (*Americana* 270). In *Libra*, Kennedy dominated in the sexual fantasies of Marina, wife of Oswald:

> In pictures taken near the sea, with the wind ruffling his hair, the President looked like her old boyfriend Anatoly, who had unruly hair and kissed her in a way that made her dizzy.

[…]

She wondered how many women had visions and dreams of the President. What must it be like to know you are the object of a thousand longings? It's as though he floats over the landscape at night, entering dreams and fantasies, entering the act of love between husbands and wives. He floats through television screens into bedrooms at night. He floats from the radio into Marina's bed. […] (323-24)

Perhaps Marina identified with the image of the first lady, young, charming, and eloquent. The media's successful marketing certainly found "a buyer in Lee Oswald" (Keesey 167) and brought Oswald's strong identification with the President. Oswald finally became the double of Kennedy in the world of celebrity.

Among John F. Kennedy's most notable and long-standing accomplishments was the establishment of the Peace Corps, an organization responsible for sending thousands of American volunteers around the world to help the needy. It was Kennedy's support of space exploration that enabled the accomplishment of landing a man on the moon. Kennedy was also dedicated to reducing poverty and high rates of unemployment and ending segregation in the southern states although these issues remained serious at the end of his presidency. Kennedy helped promote the arts by holding concerts, plays and musicals at the White House. For Kennedy, the Round Table Knights were the heroes—the Peace Corps volunteers, the scientists and technicians at NASA, and the Civil Rights advocates. Kennedy's Camelot represented "a magic moment in American history, when gallant men danced with beautiful women, when great deeds were done, when artists, writers, and poets met at the White House, and the barbarians beyond the walls held back" (qtd. in Streich). The media promoted the magic of JFK's Camelot. Both Oswald and DeLillo were "a little dazzled" (*Libra* 353) by this magic. DeLillo said that the United States "was riding a benevolent whirlwind" while Kennedy was the President. The assassination slowed down the growth of the United States "as the dominant world power. And it had an effect on Americans that we'll probably never recover from" (qtd. in Arensberg 42). As DeLillo put it in *Libra*, the assassination was "the seven seconds [that] broke the back of the American century" (181).

According to David Cowart, "all historical fictions reflect and comment on the present of their writing and presentation to the public" (94). The historical novelists explore the past in order to comment on the society in which they compose and publish their novels and to find out how the present acquires its character. When he was a university student, DeLillo majored in Communication Arts and after graduation worked as a copywriter in a New York advertising agency for five years. He knows how the media affect people's consciousness and behavior, which is one of the themes explored in his works. *Libra* was written in the mid-1980s when television had its explosive growth. The cultural environment in that decade is his main focus and concern when he deals with Kennedy's assassination. On June 1, 1980, CNN (Cable News Network) was introduced to American viewers, providing 24-hour news, reporting comprehensively on violence, disaster, and crisis, such as the Iran hostage crisis. President Reagan served two terms for a total of eight years, from 1981 to 1989. He was a former movie actor. Even after he became the President, to a remarkable extent, Ronald Reagan

> continues to live within the movies; he has been shaped by them, draws much of his cold war rhetoric from them, and cannot or will not distinguish between them and an eternal reality. Indeed his political career has depended upon an ability to project himself and his mass audience into a realm in which there is no distinction between simulation and reality. (Greenblatt 6)

As a serious writer with a strong sense of social responsibility, DeLillo was very much concerned with the dangers of living in this society where the line between the simulation and reality blurs. People are bombarded by the images of the media and live their daily lives according to them. When they identify with the images dramatizing the fulfillment of the American Dream, but find themselves battered in life again and again, they will resort to violence and get their dreams fulfilled. DeLillo's Lee Oswald prefigures the killer who testifies

> to the power of publicity and the random streams of disaffection running through the land. The killer prepares by wandering in empty spaces, watching television, reading books about previous killers. He gets himself photographed […]goes back to his hotel, as Arthur Bremer did, to put on a better set of clothes in which to commit the act, for the sake of his self-image. (DeLillo, "American Blood" 27)

In DeLillo's view, the JFK Assassination started the age of conspiracy in the United States. It changed this country, "put an end to its innocent conviction of invincibility, gave birth to the culture of paranoia, the perception of history as 'the sum total of what they're not telling us'" (qtd. in Cowart 95).

1.2 The Age of Conspiracy: "History Is the Sum Total of All the Things They Are Not Telling Us"

After the JFK Assassination, these questions haunted America and the world: "What was the President's killer really like? How did he grow up to commit this terrible act?" (Keener 70) Did he act alone? "In the United States and abroad, these events evoked universal demands for an explanation" (*Warren Commission Report* ix). For this purpose the new President Johnson created the Warren Commission to "evaluate all the facts and circumstances surrounding the assassination and the subsequent killing of the alleged assassin and to report its findings and conclusions to him" (ibid.). The result of the investigation is the 888-page *Warren Commission Report* in 26 volumes. *The Warren Report* concludes that Lee Harvey Oswald was a lone gunman and there was no conspiracy involved.

Since its publication, the official account of the Kennedy Assassination has been regarded with suspicion and has been questioned by more and more people with the passage of time. The Kennedy Assassination remains the greatest mystery in American history although it was witnessed by crowds of people at the site, recorded in the Zapruder film and investigated by the government twice in the past 50 years. Interpretations of this historical event proliferate. Some confirm the conclusion of the Warren Commission, but more challenge it. According to Peter Knight, the assassination of JFK "has inspired more conspiracy thinking in America than any other event in the twentieth century" (*Conspiracy Culture* 76). It is often referred to as "the mother of all conspiracies" (Knight, *Conspiracy Theories in American History* 383). "There is a vast literature on the Kennedy Assassination, with over 2000 books, countless newspaper and magazine articles, along with novels and films, not to mention the dozens of journals and websites devoted to the topic," the overwhelming majority of which challenge the *Warren Commission Report* and develop a "conspiracy theory of one stripe or another" (Knight, *The Kennedy Assassination* 75).

Nicholas Branch, the CIA analyst-turned historian in *Libra*, is faced with this postmodern condition which originated in the death of President Kennedy, the condition in which incredulity against metanarratives is promoted and little narratives prevail. Branch is trying to find out the secret to the mystery of the assassination and to provide a grand historical narrative. When the novel unfolds, he has already spent 15 years collecting, reading and analyzing historical material and data in order to write a secret history of the Kennedy Assassination for the CIA. He is hopelessly stuck in an endless stream of material concerning the JFK Assassination: "files, testimony, ballistics reports, surveillance logs, Zapruder's home movie of the assassination, biographies, and even works of fiction" (Green 98). He sometimes feels helpless and even frustrated buried in the piles of documents, without much progress in his work. At the end of the novel, Branch still struggles in his room of documents for writing a true and accurate history of the assassination which is an impossible task in the postmodern era when metanarratives are supposed to have ceased being credible and also due to the overwhelming number of documents which are sometimes contradictory and forged.

Branch's labor to write an accurate history of the Kennedy Assassination dramatizes DeLillo's process of preparing for *Libra*. In order to write *Libra*, DeLillo undertook a vast research project. He read the *Warren Commission Report*, studied its 26 volumes of testimony and exhibits, and travelled to the places in the southern states where Oswald once lived or stayed. He also read a lot of biographies and reports in newspapers and magazines like *Journal of Forensic Sciences*. Like Branch, DeLillo was overwhelmed by the amount of the data generated by the assassination, which seemed endless. Walking into them was like walking into a maze or labyrinth. "Anyone who enters this maze" has to become "part scientist, novelist, biographer, historian, and existential detective. The landscape was crawling with secrets" (qtd. in Begley 98). Branch's documents for study are forwarded to him by the CIA curator. Branch feels that the CIA and the government are holding back some secret documents. This feeling that history is manipulated is shared by DeLillo, who said in an interview:

> Even after all these years we still can't agree on the number of gunmen, the number of shots, the time span between the shots, the number of wounds on the President's body, the size and shape of those wounds. And even beyond this confusion of data there's a sense of the secret manipulation of history. This has certainly entered our mass consciousness. Documents are lost or concealed. Official records are sealed for fifty or seventy-five years. A curious number of suspicious murders and suicides. And I think this current runs from November of 1963 right through Viet Nam and Watergate, and into Iran-Contra. (qtd. in Connolly 28)

Here what DeLillo means is that the JFK Assassination was the origin of the Americans' distrust of their government or the authorities. This is DeLillo's hindsight. In fact, this kind of distrust was incited by American media's revelations about the covert and illegal operations of the intelligence community in connection with the Vietnam War and the Watergate scandal. Especially after the Watergate Scandal, conspiracy theories about the Kennedy Assassination proliferated.

The following exposures of the CIA scandals eroded Americans' trust in the intelligence community and their government. The Vietnam War was one of the events that led to the pervasive distrust of the American government. Ngo Dinh Diem was the first president of South Vietnam, who was a staunch anti-communist. He and his powerful brother were assassinated on November 2, 1963, during a coup d'état that deposed his government which was originally supported by the United States government. The CIA was involved in the coup against and the murder of the Vietnamese President, but they told the White House and the American public that Diem and his brother committed suicide. Later, American media uncovered the secrets and reported CIA's conspiracy in Vietnam and the subsequent cover-up to the American people, who were very much shocked. During the early years of the Vietnam War the American public showed high support on the grounds of the "fight against communism." It was until President Nixon ordered the invasion of Cambodia that many protests occurred. The protests on campus led to the United States government censoring American media which exposed the Nixon Administration's manipulation of the war news reports. Towards the end of the American involvement with Vietnam, the trust in the government was truly damaged by the censorship of the media and the Watergate Scandal.

The Watergate Scandal brought about a pervasive cynical attitude toward the American government and "echoes in American culture four decades later" (Finney). On June 17, 1972, five burglars broke into the Democratic Party's National Committee offices located in the Watergate Hotel in Washington D.C. The arrest of these burglars led to the investigations into the Watergate. Initial investigations were heavily influenced by the media, particularly the work of two reporters from the *Washington Post*, Bob Woodward and Carl Bernstein. By early 1974, the United States was consumed by the Watergate Scandal which was sensationalized by the media. On August 8, 1974, Nixon delivered a nationally televised resignation speech and was forced to resign. At one time, "everybody believed what the government said. People disagreed over policy, but not over honesty. The myth of the president as always a great, trustful, moral leader ended" (Finney).

The Iran-Contra Scandal, also referred to as Irangate, was exposed by the media in November 1986. During the Reagan Administration, senior officials secretly facilitated the sales of arms to Iran, the subject of an arms embargo, in the hope that the arms sales would secure the release of seven American hostages being held by a group with Iranian ties connected to the Army of the Guardians of the Islamic Revolution and allow the United States intelligence agencies to continue to fund the Nicaraguan Contras. According to the American law, funding of the Contras after

1984 by the government had been prohibited by Congress. The investigation into Iran-Contra was stopped because large volumes of documents relating to the scandal were destroyed or withheld from the investigators by the Reagan Administration officials for the purpose of covering up. News reports about the hearings and investigation of the scandal were watched by millions daily. Television and radio talk shows debated over it. But unlike the Watergate Scandal, the Iran-Contra affair did not bring down Reagan because he made friends with many powerful media executives and celebrities, and enjoyed a warmer relationship with the media than many former presidents.

When the Irangate was revealed and covered daily by newspapers and TV, DeLillo was composing *Libra*. As mentioned in the previous section, the 1980s of the United States was a media-saturated era. In those months when the Irangate was revealed and debated, the Americans were daily bombarded by the media reports of the scandal, investigation and Senate hearings so much so that they became tired of it all. They became used to the culture of conspiracy. DeLillo was of course influenced by this kind of culture, since humans, as New Historicism declares, are "cultural artifacts" (Greenblatt, *Renaissance Self-Fashioning* 3). DeLillo perceives the history of the JFK Assassination through the lens of post-Watergate-Iran-Contra America. Reading his *Libra*, one gets the impression that the Watergate and Iran-Contra events seemed to precede November 22, 1963, "as if the novel's narration of the events of twenty-five years past made that day in November contemporaneous with its retelling" (Lentricchia, *Introducing Don DeLillo* 200). He sees his own effort to reconstruct American history as uncovering the secrets hidden underneath the official documents and behind the news reports of the media manipulated by the government. He believes, as he writes in *Libra*: "There's something they aren't telling us. Something we don't know about. ... This is what history consists of. It's the sum total of all the things they aren't telling us." (321) Even before *Libra*, DeLillo's novels are engaged with the paranoia that "has, since Dallas, infected American culture, a sense that history has been manipulated" (Green 95). A character in his *Running Dogs* (1978) says: "This is the age of conspiracy, the age of connections, links, secret relationships" (111). Many American people have the same feeling that the postwar era is an age of conspiracy. "The rhythm of conspiracy, once background noise, is now a dominant theme of everyday life" (Melley 7). DeLillo recreates the inception of the age of conspiracy in *Libra*.

Libra consists of three narratives: Oswald's biography, the CIA's conspiracy against President Kennedy and Nicholas Branch's effort to write a secret history of the Kennedy Assassination. The novel's strength lies in that it skillfully interlaces those narratives. The narrative of Oswald and the narrative of the conspirators unfold simultaneously, in alternating chapters. Oswald's chapters are titled by the places where Oswald stays, from the Bronx of New York to Dallas. The conspiracy chapters are titled by the dates when the conspirators plot against the President, from April 17, the second anniversary of the Bay of Pigs Invasion, to November 22, 1963. Oswald's story and the conspirators' story converge when Oswald joins the conspirators preparing for the attempt on the President's life. Branch's narrative is cleverly inserted into the story of the conspirators. The conspiracy chapters start with the narrative of the retired CIA analyst, Nicholas Branch, who is hired by the CIA to write a secret history of the Kennedy Assassination. He sits in his room packed with documents provided by the Curator. He guides the reader to "follow the bullet trajectories backwards to the lives that occupy the shadows, actual men who moan in their dreams. … There is much here that is holy, an aberration in the heartland of the real" (*Libra* 15). He appeals to the reader, probably more to himself: "Let's regain our grip on things" (15). Branch "enters a date on the home computer the Agency has provided for the sake of convenient tracking. April 17, 1963. The names appear at once, with backgrounds, connections, locations" (15-16). The conspirators "come back to life" with the click of the mouse.

Win Everett, the instigator of the plot against the President, was a CIA agent involved in the Bay of Pigs Invasion in 1961. He was angry with Kennedy for he thought the President did not give the landing anti-Castro Cuban exiles the help he had promised and that this failure to keep his promise led to the deaths of the ground troops. He was also angered by his demotion by the Kennedy Administration from active status as a CIA agent to semiretirement as an instructor at a college for women. On April 17, 1963, Everett and two other CIA agents, T. J. Mackey, Laurence Parmenter, were plotting a mock assassination of President Kennedy in order to prevent him from negotiating with Castro:

> "The movement needs to be brought back to life. … We need an electrifying event. JFK is moving toward a settling of differences with Castro."… "… I am convinced this is what we have to do to get Cuba back. This plan has levels and variations I've only begun to explore but it is already, essentially right. I feel its rightness. I know what scientists mean when they talk about elegant solutions." […] There was a silence. Then Parmenter said dryly: "We couldn't hit Castro. So let's hit Kennedy. I wonder if that's the hidden motive here." "But we don't hit Kennedy. We miss him," Win said. (*Libra* 27-28)

After they agreed on the mockery, they decided to look for a patsy:

> They wanted a name, a face, a bodily frame they might use to extend their fiction into the world… someone who would be trailed and possibly apprehended … Spanish-speaking men, Mexican, Panamanian, trained specifically for this mission in Cuba … to be trailed, found, possibly killed by the Secret Service, FBI or local police. Whatever protocol demands …. Mackey would find this man for Everett. They needed fingerprints, a handwriting sample, a photograph. Mackey would find the other shooters as well. We don't hit the President. We miss him. We want a spectacular miss. (*Libra* 50-51)

Through David Ferrie, another conspirator, Mackey found Lee Oswald whom they thought perfectly fit for the role of a patsy. Ferrie was a fatherly figure to Oswald who was fatherless. By means of threat, persuasion, and temptation, Ferrie and Mackey made Oswald agree to be the lone gunman. But Oswald did not know there would be other shooters and that he would be forever silenced by the conspirators after the assassination. In Mackey's eyes, Oswald's "role was to provide artifacts of historical interest, a traceable weapon, all the cuttings and hoardings of his Cuban career" (*Libra* 386). In Mackey's hands the mock assassination designed by Everett was turned into the real one. Mackey secretly changed the original plan. To him, "the main thing is Kennedy dead. The next thing is Oswald dead" (388). He recruited Ramon Benitez and Frank Vasquez from the growing community of Cuban exiles in Miami, and Wayne Elko, but failed to inform them that the shooting had to be a miss and not a hit. Ramon and Frank went to the Dealey Plaza and assassinated Kennedy. Wayne went to the cinema where Oswald hid after the shootings. Oswald was caught by the police before Wayne could kill him. By employing the conspiracy plot, DeLillo subverts the conclusion of the *Warren Commission Report* that Oswald was the lone gunman and that there was no conspiracy involved in the Kennedy Assassination.

In both *Libra* and his interviews, DeLillo compares the *Warren Commission Report* to fiction. In *Libra* he writes: "There is also the *Warren Report*, of course, with its twenty-six accompanying volumes of testimony and exhibits, its millions of words. Branch thinks it is the megaton novel James Joyce would have written if he'd moved to Iowa City and lived to be a hundred" (181). In an interview with DeCurtis, DeLillo said, "I asked myself what Joyce could possibly do after *Finnegans Wake*, and this is the answer" (62). In another interview he referred to *The Warren Report* as "the Joycean novel" (qtd. in Begley 98). In writing *Libra*, DeLillo relied heavily on this "Joycean novel," for this document "captures the full richness and madness and meaning of the event" (ibid.). By making these remarks DeLillo blurs the distinction between fiction and history. DeLillo regards James Joyce's novel as a history and *The Warren Commission Report* as a fiction. In this respect, DeLillo shares the postmodern view of history with Hayden White, who declares "history is no less a form of fiction than the novel is a form of historical representation" (122). According to New Historicism, both history and fiction are linguistic constructs. Language has its ideological connotations, so history can be distorted and manipulated for certain political purposes. *The Warren Commission Report* has been questioned and criticized since its release. Critics have argued that the Commission, and even the government, covered up crucial information pointing to a conspiracy. DeLillo once mentioned that the *Warren Commission Report* "omits about a ton and a half of material" (qtd. in Begley 98). "There are worrisome omissions, occasional gaps in the record" (*Libra* 442). Nicholas Branch depends on the mysterious Curator to supply him with the research material, which confirms the New Historicists' view that historical facts can exist only as textual traces, and we can only know history in textual forms and by way of prior textualization. It also suggests that the Curator is in control of the access to all the secret information about the Kennedy Assassination and holds back crucial information even to Branch, "one of their own, someone pledged to confidentiality" (*Libra* 442), let alone to the public.

Behind the conspiracy are "the interlocked representatives, as in Iran-Contra, of American power" (Lentricchia, *Introducing Don DeLillo* 200). Cuba adopted Communism under the leadership of Fidel Castro in 1959 and came to become pro-Russian. The anti-Castro Cubans went to exile in Miami, waiting for chances to overthrow Castro. The United States was afraid of the spread of Communism across the border and attempted hundreds of ways to murder Castro to curb Cuban Communism and regain their interests there. The CIA supported and trained the Cubans to engage in the activities of subverting Castro's government. The core conspirators were the CIA agents who regarded themselves as "free fighters." As is depicted in *The Names* and *White Noise*, in the Cold War the CIA agents operated in the Mideast, Asia and South America to subvert the Communist regimes in these regions. But not all CIA agents' activities were the Cold War ideology-oriented. Larry Parmenters, one of the conspirators, realized that "there was a natural kinship between business and intelligence work" (*Libra* 126). There were "legally incorporated businesses actually financed and controlled by CIA," and the businesses set up as cover for the Agency operations "held potential for legitimate profits." Larry took advantage of his position and power as a CIA agent "for enormous personal gain." After the Cuban revolution, Larry's fortune "was still in the ground of the unexpected oil properties of Cuba" (ibid.). Carmine Latta, the Mafia boss, who was involved in the Kennedy Assassination, had a happy memory of Cuba. He "had a third of the Cuban dope before Castro" (170). Havana was then a "fucking paradise," and Cuba was a whole country "to pluck like a fruit" (172). Carmine was investigated by FBI and his Mafia business was curbed by Robert Kennedy, the Attorney General. If they could get Cuba back, they "would have leeway, with Cuba back in the firm" to help to "relieve pressure on the mainland" (171).

According to Branch in *Libra*, conspiracy means plot. "Plots carry their own logic. There is a tendency of plots to move toward death" (221). The plot against the President ended with death, the deaths of John Kennedy and Lee Harvey Oswald. It also led to the unnatural deaths of those involved in the assassination. Jack Ruby died of cancer "while waiting retrial for the murder of Oswald" (443). He confided to Chief Justice Earl Warren that he had been used for a purpose. It was believed that he was poisoned to death. The mysterious nature of the assassination leads to many versions of conspiracy in which motives are speculated and some political figures like President Johnson were involved. Before he died, Ruby wanted to talk to President Johnson, who had the resources and power to manipulate the investigation and the cover-up. In the past, Americans tended to believe the honesty and uprightness of their presidents who would not resort to means of craft and deceit like the European emperors. But after the JFK Assassination, "a culture of conspiracy has become an implicit mode of operation in American politics" (Knight, *Conspiracy Culture* 3). The pursuit of power and policy objectives through clandestine means has "come to be taken for granted by the political establishment" (ibid.). In this sense, DeLillo chronicles the origin and the development of American rogue government conspiracies.

Libra tackles the traumatic event of the Kennedy Assassination and explores how this event inaugurated postmodernity in America. DeLillo, as a postmodern theorist by proxy, comments on the psychological effects of the assassination on Americans and their changed perception of American history. On September 11, 2001, the Islamic terrorists attacked the World Trade Center in New York, causing the collapses of the twin towers and the deaths of more than 3, 000 people. As he is a writer whose fiction "has been closely attuned to moments of cultural transformation in American history" (Conte 190), it is not surprising that DeLillo has come to deal with the traumatic event of 9·11 in *Falling Man*, offering a counter-narrative to the prevailing nationalistic rhetoric after 9·11 and the narrative of terrorism.

2. *Falling Man:* A "Brave New Chronicler of the Age of Terror"

Since the mid-1980s, the Cold War entered its final years and the capitalist globalization gained its momentum. With the fall of the Berlin Wall in 1989 and the dissolution of the Soviet Union in 1991, the United States has turned out to be the only superpower in the world. As DeLillo writes in his 2001 essay "In the Ruins of the Future": "In the past decade the surge of capital markets has dominated discourse and shaped global consciousness. Multinational corporations have come to seem more vital and influential than governments."

According to Jameson, globalization means Americanization, which the Islamist terrorists wanted to hold back and destroy. Bin Ladin and his followers hated America and what it stands for. DeLillo writes in "In the Ruins of the Future": "It was America that drew their fury. It was the high gloss of our modernity. It was the thrust of our technology. It was our perceived godlessness. It was the blunt force of our foreign policy. It was the power of American culture to penetrate every wall, home, life and mind." Americans are "rich, privileged and strong", but the terrorists are ready to embrace martyrdom. Ladin called for the murder of any American, anywhere on earth, as the "individual duty for every Muslim who can do it in any country in which it is possible to do it" (qtd. in the *9·11 Commission Report* 47). The Arabic terrorists assaulted the American embassies. On September 11, 2001, 19 terrorists, led by Mohamed Atta, hijacked four commercial planes and staged the most devastating terrorist attacks in American history, which, in the eyes of many Americans, ushered in the age of terror.

2.1 The Age of Terror in the 21st Century

On September 11, 2001, the whole world was stunned to learn that the World Trade Center in New York City was attacked by terrorists and the twin towers collapsed. The horrible scenes were played and replayed on TV all over the world. "The events of September 11 were covered unstintingly. ... The event dominated the medium" ("In the Ruins of the Future"). The terrorist attacks were made all the more horrible through the coverage of mass media, especially the live television broadcast of the collapse of the towers, deeply impacting America and its people. On watching the disaster on TV again and again, the Americans were saddened to find that their nation was vulnerable to attacks, even with the most advanced technology possessed and with the two oceans safeguarding it against attacks from other continents. They were awakened to the fact that they were living in an age of terror. The land of

America has become a place of danger and rage.

The terrorist attacks of 9·11 were described as follows:

> At 8:46:40, American 11 crashed into the North Tower of the World Trade Center in New York City. All on board, along with an unknown number of People in the tower, were killed instantly. [...] At 9:03:11, United Airlines Flight 175 struck the South Tower of the World Trade Center. All on board, along with an unknown number of people in the tower, were killed instantly. [...] At 9:37:46, American Airlines Flight 77 crashed into the Pentagon, traveling at approximately 530 miles per hour. All on board, as well as many civilian and military personnel in the building, were killed. (*The 9·11 Commission Report* 7-10)

The fourth plane, United Airlines Flight 93, took off from Newark Liberty International Airport bound for San Francisco at 8:42. The objective of the terrorists on board was to crash the plane into "the symbols of the American Republic, the Capitol or the White House" (ibid. 14). The passengers realized the plane was hijacked and all joined in the battle for the control of the plane. When the passengers had "only seconds from overcoming" the four terrorists, the plane crashed to "an empty field in Shanksville, Pennsylvania, at 580 miles per hour, about 20 minutes' flying time from Washington, D. C." (ibid. 14). According to the 9·11 *Commission Report*, America suffered the single largest loss of lives from an enemy attack on its soil.

The September 11 terrorist attacks not only caused a great loss of lives, but also impacted Americans' psyche. As DeLillo remarks, what had happened on that day affected "the air around us, psychologically. We are all breathing the fumes of lower Manhattan, where traces of the dead are everywhere, in the soft breeze off the river, on rooftops and windows, in our hair and on our clothes" ("In the Ruins of the Future"). One week after the attacks of 9·11 came the anthrax attacks. Letters containing anthrax spores were mailed to several news media offices and two Democratic United States Senators, killing five people and infecting seventeen others. These terrorist acts caused the Americans to fear that biological and chemical weapons would contaminate the air they breathe and the water they drink. Some became so scared that they carried gas masks with them when they took subways to work. Public places like shopping malls, restaurants, movies theaters saw decreases in attendance because they represent potential targets for terrorist attacks. Many New Yorkers fled New York City, as is described in the novel *Falling Man*. The Americans were haunted by the nightmares of terrorism and dread.

On the night of September 11, 2001, President Bush addressed the whole nation.

He condemned the terrorist attacks as "evil, despicable acts of terror" and these acts filled him "with disbelief, terrible sadness and a quiet, unyielding anger" ("Text of Bush's Address"). He pledged to bring to justice those who were responsible for the terrorist attacks. His remarks "We will make no distinction between the terrorists who committed these acts and those who harbor them" foreshadowed the upcoming war on terrorism in Afghanistan, the Taliban government of which was believed to have harbored Bin Ladin and the terrorist organization al-Qaeda. On September 16, the Bush Administration announced a "War on Terror" to defend freedom and "all that is good and just in our world" that the United States stands for. On October 7, 2001, the war in Afghanistan began. In less than two years, America-led coalition invaded Iraq, hence launched the Iraq War.

The September 11 terrorist attacks and the subsequent "War on Terror" were covered by mass media, thus became something consumed by viewers all over the world. "The pictures of airplanes flying into buildings, fires burning, huge structures collapsing" (Bush) kept being replayed on TV. President Bush's address was televised, reassuring Americans that their great country was strong and invincible. He said: "Today, our fellow citizens, our way of life, our very freedom came under attack in a series of deliberate and deadly terrorist acts. … Terrorist attacks can shake the foundations of our biggest buildings, but they cannot touch the foundation of America. These acts shatter steel, but they cannot dent the steel of American resolve." With his televised address, the President was trying to unite his people under the cause—justice and freedom. With the nation thrown into fear and chaos, the mass media attempted to promote a spiritual unity and restore faith and confidence in their nation, by providing untiring coverage of the apocalypse and celebrating heroic deeds of the firefighters. The dominant media narratives of 9·11 and the aftermath were full of super-patriotism and militarism, expressing a "puzzling unanimity and even monotony" (qtd. in Chermak et al. 5).

2.2 "America under Attack": The Media's Representation of September 11

On the morning of September 11, 2001, two passenger planes hijacked by the Islamic terrorists crashed into the twin towers of the World Trade Center complex in New York City. Within two hours both towers collapsed, killing nearly 3000 people. The mass media, especially TV, were quick to break the news to people in America and beyond and turned the tragedy into a media event 9·11, like the Holocaust, was the kind of event that defied representation. Yet it was through the media coverage that we could know what was happening to the World Trade Center and to the United States. The media represented the reality of the September 11 terrorist attacks for us. Only through the texts, whether in the form of the image or the discourse, could we get access to the traumatic reality.

On the tragic day of September 11, CNN and other mass media gave 24 hours' breaking live coverage of the terrorist attacks and repeatedly broadcast the images of the hijacked airplanes crashing into the World Trade Center towers in New York City. People around the world watched the towers collapse "live" on television and panic-stricken people fleeing massive debris clouds and running for their lives. Americans were shocked and terrified at the images presented on the TV screens. It was such a hellish world as described by DeLillo at the very beginning of *Falling Man*:

> It was not a street anymore but a world, a time and a space of falling ash and near night. [...] there were people running past holding towels to their faces or jackets over their heads. They had handkerchiefs pressed to their mouths. They had shoes in their hands, a woman with a shoe in each hand, running past him. They ran and fell, some of them, confused and ungainly, with debris coming down around them and there were people taking shelter under cars.
>
> The roar was still in the air, the buckling rumble of the fall. This was the world now. Smoke and ash came rolling down streets and turning corners, busting around corners, seismic tides of smoke, with office paper flashing past, standard sheets with cutting edge, skimming, whipping past, otherworldly things in the morning pall. (3)

Even the journalists could not keep their detached manners when they saw these apocalyptic scenes and were often plunged into nearly stunned silence: "Good Lord. There are no words. … This is just a horrific scene and a horrific moment" (qtd. in Reynolds and Barnett 85).

The terrorist attacks struck terror in the hearts and minds of most Americans, who equated the 9·11 event to something like the Pearl Harbor. The attacks shattered the sense of invulnerability that had existed among Americans. For the first time the American people realized that their country was vulnerable to the attacks of international terrorism and that every aspect of their ordinary life could be filled with dangers. The media coverage of the terrorist attacks was dominated by the nationalistic rhetoric which "sought to transform vulnerability into triumphant profiles in courage" (Versluys 23). First the media arouse the American viewers' anger and bloodlust by focusing on the horror and devastation which the terrorist attacks had caused and by indoctrinating them with the belief that America was under attack. The then New York Governor George Pataki was quoted as saying: "Clearly this is an attack upon America, it's an attack upon our freedom and our way of life and we must retaliate and go after those who perpetuated this heinous crime against the people of America" (qtd. in Reynolds and Barnett 93). This kind of comments could be often heard in the media's coverage. The impression that their country and ideals were in crisis was created by the media. The news headlines ran like "America on Alert," "War against Terror," "America Attacked," "America at War" (ibid. 107). The media also repeatedly gave Americans the perception that the entire country and the two dominant political parties were unified when confronted with their national enemies.

The post-9·11 media were not only infiltrated with the patriotic message of unity and solidarity, but also were informed with heroism. The survivors in the Twin Towers, the passengers of United Airlines Flight 93, police officers, emergency medical technicians, military officers and the firefighters were the heroes most used by the media in an attempt to provide hope to what was a hopeless situation. In the meantime, the picture of the man who jumped from one of the burning towers and committed suicide was withdrawn from all the media. This picture had originally been published by the September 12 *New York Times* and then was carried by hundreds of newspapers all over the country, even all over the world. Americans did not want to look at this picture which reminded them of the trauma and their vulnerability and they had it banished from the record of September 11 terrorist attacks. The picture made people realize that Americans responded to "the worst terrorist attack in the history of the world with acts of heroism, with acts of sacrifice, with acts of generosity, with acts of martyrdom, and, by terrible necessity, with one prolonged act of—if these words can be applied to mass murder—mass suicide" (Junod, "The Falling Man").

To these mainstream narratives of the media and the narrative of terrorism, there have been countless counter-narratives. Among them are the literary works interpreting 9·11 and its aftermath. They are called post-September 11 fiction. In his essay "In the Ruins of the Future" published three months after the attacks, DeLillo writes: "Many things are over now. The narrative ends in the rubble, and it is left to us to create the counter-narrative." Many writers take up DeLillo's call to construct a counter-narrative to grapple with 9·11 and its psychological fallout. Some famous 9·11 novels are Jonathan Safran Foer's *Extremely Loud and Incredibly Close*, Ian McEwan's *Saturday* and DeLillo's *Falling Man*. These novels focus on the daily lives of individuals. In *Extremely Loud and Incredibly Close*, a 9-year-old boy Oskar Schell experiences the trauma of 9·11 through the loss of his father who worked in the World Trade Center during the terrorist attacks. McEwan's *Saturday* narrates how Henry

Perowne and his family struggle with the vicarious traumatization that they experience living in an anxious post-9·11 culture. In both of these novels the protagonists are not immediate victims or survivors of the attacks while in *Falling Man,* Keith Neudecker is one of the survivors of the physical attacks upon the Twin Towers and struggles with the direct traumatic experience of the attacks.

It came as no surprise that DeLillo confronted 9·11 and offered his own interpretation of this traumatic event. DeLillo is "the writer who seemed best equipped to respond to our paranoid moment" (Kirsch). DeLillo has been writing towards an event like 9·11 in his whole career. Terrorists have been making regular appearances in his books since his 1977 novel *Players.* He almost predicted the September 11 event in *Mao II*, in which Bill argues that in modern writing, "the major work involves mid-air explosions and crumbled buildings. This is the new tragic narrative" (157). More than any other novelist, DeLillo "has always worked at the intersection of public terror and private fear" (Kirsch). His novels explore the way the disaster, mediated through mass media, becomes collective experience: the Kennedy Assassination in *Libra*, the airborne toxic event in *White Noise*, the atomic bomb and highway killer in *Underworld*. In *Falling Man* DeLillo narrates a petite histoire of the September 11 terrorist attacks and its aftermath. He creates a counter-narrative to the prevailing heroic and nationalistic rhetoric of the mass media by focusing on the emotional effects of the attacks on the victims and survivors rather than writing "a novel that had a great deal of political sweep" (qtd. in Binelli).

2.3 DeLillo's Counter-Narrative to the Discourses of Terrorism and Politics

Three months after the 9·11 terrorist attacks, DeLillo published his essay titled "In the Ruins of the Future": Reflections on Terror and Loss in the Shadow of September" in *Harper's*. In this essay he asserts "the world narrative belongs to terrorists" and the narrative of the future "ends in the rubble and it is left to us to create the counter-narrative." "There are 100,000 stories crisscrossing New York, Washington, and the world" in the mass media, as DeLillo observes in the essays. They were stories of heroism, patriotism and spirit unity. Finally, in 2007 DeLillo published *Falling Man*, a counter-narrative to challenge the media and official accounts of the tragedy, representing the unrepresentable.

2.3.1 "This Was the World Now": Witnessing the Trauma

Falling Man begins with the detailed realistic description of the street scenes after the fall of the South Tower of the World Trade Center. Keith Neudecker, survivor of the terrorist attacks,

> was walking north through rubble and mud and there were people running past holding towels to their faces or jacket over their heads. They had handkerchiefs pressed to their mouths. They had shoes in their hands, a woman with a shoe in each hand, running past him. They ran and fell, some of them, confused and ungainly, with debris coming down around them, and there were people taking shelter under cars. The roar was still in the air, the buckling rumble of the fall. This was the world now. (1)

Keith walks out of the rubble, carrying a briefcase, with blood on his face and clothes, and instead of going back to his apartment, goes to the home and the bed of his wife, Lianne, from whom he is separated for more than one year, and to his son, Justin.

As a native New Yorker, DeLillo witnessed the traumatic event and his pain at the devastation can be felt in the essay "In the Ruins of the Future" and the novel *Falling Man*. In the essay DeLillo narrates how his nephew's family survived the September 11. Marc and Karen and their family lived close to the World Trade Center and witnessed the collapses of the Twin Towers and the chaos following the attacks. "From the window she saw people running in the street, others locked shoulder to shoulder, immobilised, with debris coming down on them. People were trampled, struck by falling objects, and there was ash and paper everywhere, paper whipping through the air, no sign of light or sky" ("In the Ruins of the Future"). DeLillo was worried about his nephew's family. He writes in the essay: "When the second tower fell, my heart fell with it. I called Marc, who is my nephew, on his cordless. I couldn't stop thinking of the size of the towers and the meagre distance between those buildings and his." "They all moved into the stairwell, behind a fire door, but smoke kept coming in. It was gritty ash and they were eating it." (ibid.) They thought they would die. But luckily with the help of their friend and the policemen they successfully evacuated from the damaged building and

> came out into a world of ash and near night. There was no one else to be seen now on the street. Grey ash covering the cars and pavement, ash falling in large flakes, paper still drifting down, discarded shoes, strollers, briefcases. The members of the group were masked and towelled, children in adults' arms, moving east and then north on Nassau Street, trying not to look around, only what's immediate, one step and then another, all closely focused, a pregnant woman, a newborn, a dog. (ibid.)

DeLillo's nephew, his family, and other tenants of the building were led to safety, food and water. They had just walked out of the apocalyptic world.

In the essay Marc and Karen relate what they saw and did in the building which is two blocks away from the Twin Towers when the September 11 terrorist attacks took place. In *Falling Man* DeLillo not only portrays the terrific outside world, but also walks into the towers and enters the inner world of the victims, revealing the psychological trauma suffered by Americans. Keith and Florence Givens, whose briefcase Keith carried unknowingly when fleeing the burning, are victims of the terrorist attacks. They are haunted by the memory of the attack on the workplace and attracted to each other by their common traumatic experience. Florence needs someone to listen to her talk about her haunting experience inside the tower moving downward the stairway with a crowd. "There were people everywhere pushing into the stairwell" (58). She was scared and did not know how to get out of the burning building. It is "when she saw a blind man and a guide dog, not far ahead, and it was like something out of the Bible, she thought. They seemed so calm. They seemed to spread calm, she thought. … She believed in the guide dog. The dog would lead them all to safety" (57-58). She keeps talking, for talking about the traumatic event can help healing. Keith was in the same building and came down from the same stairs. They share the same memory, reliving every possible detail of the moving down the stairs. "This was their pitch of delirium, the dazed reality they'd shared in the stairwell, the deep shafts of spiraling men and women" (91). They have a short-lived love affair, for comfort and healing.

But the trauma of 9·11 is not easy to heal, for the victims like Keith who saw friends and workmates get seriously injured and die in the towers. The nightmarish scenes of that day keep coming back to him even after the lapse of three years. Keith, at the end of the novel, relives the attack of the terrorists on the North Tower where he worked on that day. After having been hit by the plane, the tower began to move. "It was the tower lurching. … He saw the ceiling begin to ripple" (240-41). His friend, Rumsey, who worked in the same hall, was badly injured. "His face was pressed into his shoulder … and bleeding badly" (241-42). Rumsey died in Keith's arms. Keith was also injured. His face "felt like a hundred pinpoint fires" (242). Embedded in his face were some small fragments of glass. He joined thousands of people walking down the stairwell. Finally Keith and the other survivors "came out onto the street, looking back, both towers burning, and soon they heard a high drumming rumble and saw smoke rolling down from the top of one tower, billowing out and down, methodically, floor to floor, and the tower falling, the south tower diving into the smoke" (246). With the fall of the tower, the illusion of America's invincibility was shattered.

Through the accounts of Keith and Florence, victims and direct witnesses to the trauma of the day, DeLillo reconstructs the horrible scenes of the terrorist attacks in a vivid way comparable to the medium of TV which covered the event unstintingly but "cheapened trauma into mere sensationalism" (Versluys 75). DeLillo admits that this event was "so vast and terrible that it was outside imagining even as it happened" and that the Americans "have to take the shock and horror as it is" ("In the Ruins of the Future"). But he realizes that it is a writer's responsibility to create a counter-narrative, "trying to imagine the moment, desperately" (ibid.). The place which used to be occupied by the Twin Towers is called Ground Zero, leaving something empty in the sky. "The writer tries to give memory, tenderness and meaning to all that howling space" (ibid.). The September 11 event also left a gaping hole in the hearts of the Americans. The trauma takes time to heal, and may never heal some victims. It has been three years since the attacks, yet the characters in *Falling Man* are still struggling for ways to cope with the trauma and to make their life return to normal.

2.3.2 Individuals' Reactions to the Trauma

As has been mentioned in the above section, Keith and Florence are two survivors of the September 11 attacks. Because they were in the same tower and connected by their common experience, they develop an intimacy, though it does not last long. Although her credit cards and driving license were lost, she "didn't do anything, basically, but sit[s] in the room" (54). She was in the post-traumatic inertness. When Keith comes to her apartment to return the briefcase, her memory of the trauma comes to her and tortures her. She keeps talking to Keith about her story in the tower. Talking about her traumatic experience is a positive way of healing. Florence is a black woman of Keith's age, in her late 30s. She had a short-lived marriage 10 years ago. Now she starts a love affair with Keith, by which means she begins to actively cope with the trauma. She is thankful to Keith for not only "saving" her briefcase, but also her life. She explains: "After what happened, so many gone, friends gone, people I worked with, I was nearly gone, nearly dead, in another way. I couldn't see people, talk to people, go from here to there without forcing myself up off the chair. Then you walked in the door … to keep me alive" (108-09).

The September 11 tragedy has changed the life and impacted the psyche of the Americans in *Falling Man*. Keith is an immediate victim and Lianne a vicarious victim. How do Keith and Lianne react to the trauma? In the novel DeLillo explores different reactions of individual Americans and their ways to cope with the trauma.

A. Drift "in the Ruins of the Future"

In his essay "In the Ruins of the Future," DeLillo writes: "The dramatic climb of the Dow and the speed of the Internet summoned us all to live permanently in the future, in the utopian glow of cyber-capital," and the technological development makes it possible for the Americans to claim the future. On September 11, terrorists, who "want to bring back the past," "hold off the white-hot future" and change everything. The World Trade Towers, a symbol of advanced technology and America's supremacy, were completely destroyed. The terrorist attacks exposed the vulnerability of the superpower. Has the country regained its power and vitality? The title of DeLillo's novel *Falling Man* implies the answer. The United States started a "War on Terror" after 9·11 and since then has been involved in the wars in Afghanistan and Iraq. While the "War on Terror" is going on, the victims of the terrorist attacks are struggling with a life impacted by the event.

Keith's life has been totally changed by the September 11 event. "These are the days after. Everything now is measured by after" (138). It is true that he survives the attack, but from then on, he drifts like an empty shirt out of the sky, which he saw when he was trapped in the tower. After he gets out of the leaning tower, Keith, who is too much traumatized by what he witnessed, walks on the street aimlessly. A truck driver, seeing Keith "scaled in ash, in pulverized matter" (6), gives him a lift. "It wasn't until he got in the truck and shut the door that he understood where he'd been going all along" (ibid.). Keith, driven by his instinct for love and warmth of the family, drifts back to the apartment he previously shared with his son Justin and estranged wife Lianne. But after he resumes the intimate relationship with Lianne, he drifts into the bed of another woman. Keith is a changed man now. He "used to want more of the world than there was time and means to acquire" (128), but he does not want this anymore. He used to look shiny, but now he does not care about his appearance anymore. He was a corporate lawyer, but after 9·11, he quits his job and becomes a professional poker player and stays in Las Vegas for most of his time or tours the world to play in professional poker tournaments. For him to sit at the table in the casino and play is to escape the recurring memory of hellish scenes he witnessed in the tower. "He was never more himself than in these rooms ... He was looking at pocket tens, waiting for the turn. These were the times when there was nothing outside, no flash of history or memory that he might unknowingly summon in the routine run of cards" (225). Keith drifts away from his job, wife and child and escapes into the meaningless rituals of shuffled cards and stacks of brightly colored chips.

Instead of pulling himself together, Keith chooses to fall. "He heard the sound of the second fall, or felt it in the trembling air, the north tower coming down … That was him coming down, the north tower" (5). He falls with the tower. There is no way to save. Is it possible for his self-recovery? Just like those people who jumped from the towers, once the fall starts, there is no way to stop it. Kristiaan Versluys remarks in his book *Out of the Blue: September 11 and the Novel* that *Falling Man* "is, without a doubt, the darkest and the starkest" of 9·11 narratives because it "allows for no accommodation or resolution" (20).

Contrary to the heroic and uniting rhetoric of the mass media, *Falling Man* portrays the vulnerability of America. Not only America is vulnerable to the terrorist attacks, but victims are also vulnerable psychologically. Life in Keith's eyes makes no sense now. He is so stunned by the atrocity of the terrorists and so overwhelmed by the tragedy that he becomes a man without compass or heart. Shocked and disoriented, he drifts "in the ruins of the future." He survived by chance and now he lives by chance, going wherever the fate takes him.

But not all victims react to the trauma like Keith who practices escapism first by indulging in a love affair and then gambling, which can help him temporarily forget what he underwent during the terrorist attacks. Florence and Lianne have come to confront the trauma in a more active and courageous way.

B. Confront the Horror of 9·11

As I have mentioned above, Florence Givens recovers from the trauma by confronting the horror of 9·11 and talking about it and by entering an intimate relationship, after the initial traumatic inertness. Like Keith, she is an immediate victim. But unlike Keith who keeps the trauma to himself and tries to forget it by playing poker, Florence is willing to confront it bravely, which finally heals her.

Lianne is not an immediate victim, but she is traumatized by living in the attacked New York, watching the TV coverage of the terrorist attacks, and having an ex-husband who worked inside one of the towers. Whenever she watches the videotape of the planes hitting the towers, she will bite her lip and think that they "would all be dead, passengers and crew, and thousands in the towers dead, and she felt it in her body, a deep pause, and the thought there he is, unbelievably, in one of those towers, and now his hand on hers, in pale light, as though to console her for his dying" (134-35). The videotaped attacks of the terrorists and the collapses of the towers produce an impact on Lianne's psychology and make her a vicarious victim.

Lianne demonstrates the symptoms of a trauma victim in her daily life. She is often worried, agitated, irritable and paranoid. Her perspectives on things are affected by 9·11. Everything she sees or hears reminds her of what happened that day. Two dark objects in the painting in her mother's home remind her of the twin towers. She becomes paranoid after 9·11. The Islamic music played by her neighbor Elena irritates her. She knocks open Elena's door, slaps her hand across her neighbor's face and mashes the hand into the eyes, which is a crazy thing to do. Also since 9·11, she starts to have insomnia. 9·11 also triggers the trauma Lianne experienced from the unexpected suicide of her father when she was 22. She is troubled by memory lapse and panicked by the possibility of developing dementia because this is the family history.

However, she confronts the trauma, struggles with it, and gradually recovers from it. She accepts Keith who has separated from her for more than a year and they—the husband, wife and kid—become a family again. She understands the importance of the family in time of crisis, as she says to Keith: "This is the point I want to make, that we need to stay together, keep the family going. Just us, three of us, long-term, under the same roof, not every day of the year or every month but with the idea that we're permanent. Times like these, the family is necessary. … This is how we live through the things that scare us half to death" (214). Keith's coming back and retaking the roles of being husband and father contribute to Lianne's recovery from the trauma. Lianne is thankful for Keith's help, as she remarks: "You were stronger than I was. You helped me get here. I don't know what would have happened" (215). What Lianne means is that she has moved beyond the toughest stage of traumatic recovery with Keith being always there.

In addition, Lianne's story sessions help her recover, too. Every week, in the afternoon, a group of elderly people in the early stages of Alzheimer's disease gather in East Harlem. In these gatherings, Lianne and the members of the group first talk about events in the world and in their lives and then she suggests a topic they might write about or ask them to choose one. "This group had been started by a clinical psychologist who had left Lianne alone to conduct these meetings, which were strictly for morale" (29). The story sessions started before the fall of the twin towers, but after the fall of the towers they take on a measure of intensity, for speaking and writing about themselves and the planes can produce healing effects after they have experienced the collective trauma. It is especially true of Lianne who is traumatized by her father's suicide, by seeing Keith, covered in blood and ash, walk in her apartment and by watching the TV news coverage of the planes hitting the towers. Lianne feels she needs the story sessions more than her group members. "It was possible that the group meant more to her than it did to the members. There was something precious here, something that seeps and bleeds. These people were the living breath of the thing that killed her father" (62). As Linda S. Kauffman comments, these Alzheimer's patients "are crucial to Lianne's spiritual transformation … and give her some sense of proportion and perspective about the magnitude of her loss, which hardly compares to theirs" (143-44). She has come to understand why her father committed suicide. She says to Keith: "My father shot himself so I would never have to face the day when he failed to know who I was" (130). She uses the story sessions to mourn for her father, work through the loss of him and help her recover from the trauma.

Unlike Keith, who has recovered from physical injuries but whose psychological trauma lingers, Lianne confronts the horror of 9·11 and positively copes with her trauma by resorting to language and art. By the end of the novel, she has attained a state of spiritual awareness that mimics the peace of her pre-9·11 existence: "She was ready to be alone, in reliable calm, she and the kid, the way they were before the planes appeared that day, silver crossing blue" (236). But "[n]o one can ever be the way as they were prior to September 11" (Linda S. Kauffman 151). She has learned to live with the changed reality, as many Americans do. Lianne starts to go to church which she thinks can bring people closer, although she still has her doubts about God. In the church she meets more people, attends the mass, watches the rituals, and says her prayers, which consoles her. With the regained peace, strength and courage, she decides to carry on alone, without Keith, who is a fallen man by the end of the novel, drifting into the sin city, Las Vegas, plunging into professional gambling.

The American people reacted to 9·11 differently. In the weeks and months after 9·11, the images of the falling towers and their piled rubble pervaded most TV programmes and documentaries. DeLillo does not depict the anger, the patriotism and the revenge that dominated the coverage, but focuses on the personal trauma of the victims. He explores the different ways that the victims of 9·11 cope with their traumatic experiences and suggests that the victims can overcome the trauma and be healed by bravely confronting the horrors of the event, sharing their stories of sufferings and being integrated into a community built on love and Christianity, which in my view had suffered a decline but saw a revival for a time after 9·11. When the American government was busy fighting the "War on Terror" in Afghanistan and Iraq, many Americans were quietly struggling with their pains at home to overcome the trauma and trying to bring back their life to normal. With sympathy, DeLillo looks into the life of the individual victims and their innermost world and accurately represents their daily struggles, which may be too trivial when compared with the ongoing "War" but constitutes part of the 9·11 history.

2.3.3 "To Die with Your Brothers": The Terrorists' Conspiracy

At the end of the novel *Falling Man*, a hijacked plane flies into the north tower where Keith works. At this point, the plot of the novel reaches its climax, when the fusion of the perpetrator and the victim occurs:

> A bottle fell off the counter in the galley, on the other side of the aisle, and he watched it roll and that, a water bottle, empty, making an arc one way and rolling back the other, and he watched it spin more quickly and then skitter across the floor an instant before the aircraft struck the tower, heat, then fuel, then fire, and a blast wave passed through the structure that sent Keith Neudecker out of his chair and into a wall. He found himself walking into a wall. He didn't drop the telephone until he hit the wall. The floor began to slide beneath him and he lost his balance and eased along the wall to the floor. (239)

DeLillo enters the minds of the terrorist Hammad and the victim Keith and heroically enters the tower as a witness, giving a more realistic representation of the 9·11 attacks and offering a more humanistic characterization of the terrorists.

A. Terrorists in *Falling Man*

DeLillo portrays two Islamist terrorists in his *Falling Man*. One is the ring leader, Amir, whose full name is Mohamed Mohamed el-Amir Awad el-Sayed Atta. The other is Hammad, a young terrorist. DeLillo traces how a secular individual develops into a terrorist who "becomes deeply committed to a grave act of terror" (qtd. in Binelli). The image of the young terrorist is different from the mass media-generated image of the terrorists. This fictionalized terrorist discovers his religion, "through the power of deep companionship with other men" (ibid.). Amir acts as a spiritual guide to Hammad, who joins other 18 terrorists, pledges to accept their duty "to kill Americans" and dies with these brothers by flying the plane into the tower.

The American media and the Bush Administration officials described "terrorists" as hateful, barbarous, mad, perverted, faithless, and, most commonly, evil. DeLillo presents us a different terrorist by focusing on his psychology. He humanizes the young terrorist Hammad, who is different from the mass-mediated images of the terrorists and also different from the young terrorist portrayed in John Updike's 2003 novel *The Terrorist*, who was born in America but grows up to be a fervent extremist Muslim. Hammad is capable of feeling sorry for those shouting Iranian boys killed in the war between Iran and Iraq. He is a man of flesh and blood. He has sex before marriage with a girl named Leyla, which is regarded as sinful in the Koran. Sometimes he wants to get married and have babies. But as the time for action is coming, Hammad puts an end to their relation. He misses his parents, to whom he writes a letter before he sets out for the devastating duty, lying to them that he will be traveling for a time and that he works for an engineering company and soon he will get promotion (173). But then he tears up the letter and lets "the pieces drift away in a rip-tide of memories" (ibid.). He feels sorry for the pretty girl he sees at the checkout of the American supermarket, the people jogging in the park, and the old men who sit in the beach chairs, when he thinks of the plot to kill them. He questions Amir why taking the lives of the others. Sometimes he has doubts about martyrdom: "But does a man have to kill himself in order to accomplish something in the world?" (174)

Hammad could be like any ordinary American young man, living a normal life: going to college, dating girls, drinking, smoking and partying. When in America, Hammad and the other terrorists live the way Americans do: shopping in the supermarkets, using credit cards, being clean-shaved, wearing T-shirts, cotton slacks and tennis sneakers, eating fast food, ordering takeout and watching American TV. Hammad likes to "imagine himself appearing on the screen, a videotaped figure walking through the gate-like detector on his way to the plane" (173) they intend to hijack. In this aspect, this young terrorist is no different from "the self-watcher, the soft white dangling boy who shoots someone to keep from disappearing into himself" ("In the Ruins of the Future")—Lee Oswald, Arthur Bremer and John Hinckley. The corrupting American culture begins to have an effect on Hammad. He feels attracted to the Western culture that the Islamic terrorists renounced and plotted to subvert. In his heart he probably does not hate Americans when he comes to live close to them. There is even a possibility of them becoming friends as one day Hammad observes in the street: There is a car with six or seven young Americans crammed in, laughing and smoking, "maybe college kids, boys and girls. How easy would it be for him to walk out of his car and into theirs? Open the door with the car in motion and walk across the roadway to the other car, walk on air, and open the door of the other car and get in" (172). Instinctively he feels attracted to the joyous group of young Americans and longs for being part of them.

But Hammad ends up being one of the 19 terrorists launching the attacks on the World Trade Center and the Pentagon, as a result of the brainwashing which he gets in Afghanistan and the influence which Amir has over him. Hammad receives training in Afghanistan where he is brainwashed to believe that Americans are doomed because they oppress and control the Islam world. In Afghanistan, he began to understand that "death is stronger than life" and that "he was a man now, ready to close the distance to God" (172). Amir, whose name is Mohamed Atta, serves as Hammad's spiritual guide. He is a frantic Islamic fundamentalist. DeLillo bases his fictional Atta on the historical Mohamed Atta, the hijacker and pilot in the American Airlines Flight 11. In the novel he is the head of the terrorist group, leading the discussion of the conspiracy and the reading of the Koran, giving discipline, offering theories and guidance to unify their thoughts so that they become one mind and "each other's running blood" (83). Amir watches Hammad and alerts him to his base self and sins so that Hammad has to "fight against the need to be normal. He ha[s] to struggle against himself, first, and then, against the injustice that haunted their lives" (83). When Hammad raises doubt about the plot to take the lives of others as well as themselves, Amir impresses him by saying:

> The end of our life is predetermined. We are carried toward that day from the minute we are born. There is no sacred law against what we are going to do. [...] there are no others. The others exist only to the degree that they fill the role we have designed for them. This is their function as others. Those who will die have no claim to their lives outside the useful fact of their dying. (175-76)

Thus Hammad is trained to be cold-hearted. He is indoctrinated with the anti-Western thoughts and the idea that Islam is under attack. With the training, discipline, and praying together with the other terrorists, Hammad is "becoming one of them now, learning to look like them and think like them" (83). They are becoming total brothers bent on suicidal terror.

In the eyes of Hammad, Amir is authoritative and charismatic as well as frantic. As their plot moves deathward, Hammad finds a life in Amir too intense to last another minute, "maybe because he never fucked a woman" (176). When the young terrorists are waiting for the time to destroy and die, Amir stimulates and unites them with the power of brotherhood. This is the force, "a kind of blood bond with other men", that drives Hammad deathward. (DeLillo, "In the Ruins of the Future") On September 11, 2001, a few seconds before the plane's crash into the tower, Hammad recalls what Amir says to him: "This is your long wish, to die with your brothers" (238). He and his brothers are performing their duty to kill Americans and bring destruction to this nation, soon to become martyrs together. He thinks of the Iranian boys: "mouths open in mortal cry … cut down in waves by machine guns" (ibid.) in the thousands. He is now able to join them in the paradise and enjoy the eternal life.

B. Al-Qaeda and Its Plot against the United States

In *Falling Man*, Amir serves as a tool for DeLillo to bring out the terrorists' motivations for the terrorism against America. Amir is the mouthpiece of Al Qaeda, though the latter is not mentioned in the novel. Only the training camp in Afghanistan is referred to: "In the camp on the windy plain they were shaped into men. They fired weapons and set off explosives. They received instruction in the highest jihad, which is to make blood flow, their blood and that of others" (173). In the novel Bin Ladin becomes Bill Lawton as is mistakenly pronounced by Justin and his friends, who keep searching the sky for more planes after 9·11.

Al Qaeda is a global terrorist organization founded by Osama Bin Ladin in the late 1980s, with its origins traceable to the Soviet War in Afghanistan from 1977 to 1989. "Young Muslims from around the world flocked to Afghanistan to join as volunteers in what was seen as a 'holy war'—jihad—against an invader." (*The 9·11 Commission Report* 55) As a result, Afghanistan became Islamist extremists' rallying point and training field. "Mosques, schools, and boardinghouses served as recruiting stations in many parts of the world, including the United States" (ibid.). Bin Ladin became a leader among the volunteers "because he had access to some of his family's huge fortune" (ibid.) and thus could provide funds for recruiting and training the "holy warriors." After the Soviet War in Afghanistan ended in 1988, Bin Ladin founded a base or foundation, known as al-Qaeda, as a general headquarters for future jihad, and unquestionably was its number one figure.

Bin Ladin believed that the United States is the biggest enemy of the Islamists, the thief to steal their land, wealth, and even their souls. He repeatedly called on his followers to embrace martyrdom since "the walls of oppression and humiliation cannot be demolished except in a rain of bullets" (qtd. in *The 9·11 Commission Report* 50-51). Bin Ladin and al-Qaeda hated and attacked America for its foreign policy. Ladin and his followers believed that America had attacked Islam and should be responsible for all conflicts involving Muslims. They were angry at the United States "because of issues ranging from Iraq to Palestine to America's support for their countries' repressive rulers" (ibid. 51). They wanted to destroy America and end "the immorality and godlessness of its society and culture" (ibid.) that pose a threat to their faith or traditions. After 9·11, many Americans have wondered why the terrorists hated them. DeLillo summarizes the reasons in his essay "In the Ruins of the Future": "It was America that drew their fury. It was the high gloss of our modernity. It was the thrust of our technology. It was our perceived godlessness. It was the blunt force of our foreign policy. It was the power of American culture to penetrate every wall, home, life and mind."

The extremists believed that Islam had been oppressed by the Westerners, the Americans in particular. They wanted to fight back and bring back their glorious past, hence the revolt of Islam. DeLillo writes: "We are rich, privileged and strong, but they are willing to die" ("In the Ruins of the Future"). They embraced terrorism, "a tactic used by individuals and organizations to kill and destroy" (*The 9·11 Commission Report* 363). They encouraged armed martyrdom and suicidal bombings. As DeLillo points out, the global theocratic state of Islam, "unboundaried and floating and so obsolete," "must depend on suicidal fervour to gain its aims" ("In the Ruins of the Future"). For their evil aims, Ladin and al-Qaeda built a global terrorist network to prepare for the assaults on the land of America.

Before plotting the 9·11 terrorist attacks, al-Qaeda had organized the terrorist attacks on the World Trade Center in 1993 and the American Embassies in 1998 by providing funds, training and weapons for actions carried out by members of allied groups and later by planning, directing and executing under the direct supervision of Bin Ladin and his chief aides. In 1999 the terrorists started to think about attacking the United States by using commercial planes as weapons, which could inflict massive casualties. Bin Ladin and his aides developed a list of targets—the World Trade Center, the Pentagon, and the United States Capitol—and began the recruitments of suicide operatives. This plot against America was referred to within al-Qaeda as the "planes operation" (*The 9·11 Commission Report* 154).

Mohamed Atta and other core members who would be involved in the "planes operation" were recruited by al-Qaeda's leadership and got trained in the training camps of Afghanistan. They were Arabic young men who had formed a close-knit group as students in Hamburg, Germany. They could speak fluent English, and were familiar with life in the West, due to the fact that each of them had spent many years living in Germany. When in Hamburg, they had already held extremist beliefs of violent jihad and were ready to abandon their student lives in Germany to put their beliefs into action. Atta rented an apartment on the street of Marienstrasse as a center for the group of radical Muslims in Hamburg. In the apartment they hosted sessions that involved extremely anti-American discussions. In late 1999 Atta and his group traveled to Afghanistan to be trained for jihad. Their Western-educated background and possession of technical skills and knowledge attracted the interest of al-Qaeda who recognized their potential for the "planes operation" and enlisted them in its anti-United States jihad. Atta and his Hamburg group became core members of the 9·11 conspiracy.

After the Hamburg group left Afghanistan, they returned to Hamburg and looked for flight schools and aviation training. They finally decided to go to the flight schools in Florida, for they were less expensive and required shorter training periods. Al-Qaeda provided these suicide operatives with nearly all the money they needed to travel to the United States, train and live. The Hamburg group arrived in Florida to get flight training in the early summer of 2000. They changed their appearance and behavior. They wore Western clothing, and shaved their beards, trying to avoid appearing radical. They lived the way as Americans do. They opened bank accounts, used credit cards, rented post-office boxes and did shopping in the supermarket. Atta was appointed to be the leader of the group by Bin Ladin. He stayed in a town in Florida, waiting for the arrivals of the muscle hijackers—"operatives who would storm the cockpits and control the passengers" (*The 9·11 Commission Report* 231). These muscle hijackers were 13 young men from Saudi Arabia, most of whom were unemployed, unmarried and had no more than a high school education. They were required to be clean shaven and well-dressed so that "others would think them wealthy Saudis and give them less notice" (ibid. 245). The majority of them settled in Florida. Atta and his team of hijackers began to make final preparations for the planes operation. They bought 19 air tickets for September 11 and left Florida for departure positions respectively.

On the morning of September 11, 2001, "weather conditions could not have been better for a safe and pleasant journey" (*The 9·11 Commission Report* 1). The 19 hijackers headed to the airports. They checked in and boarded 4 commercial planes: American Airlines Flight 11, United Airlines Flight 175, American Airlines Flight 77 and United Airlines Flight 93. At 8:46:40, the hijacked American 11 crashed into the North Tower of the World Trade Center; at 9:03:11, the hijacked United Airlines Flight 175 crashed into the South Tower of the World Trade Center; the hijacked American Airlines Flight 77 struck the Pentagon; finally the hijacked United 93 plowed into an empty field in Pennsylvania, "about 20 minutes' flying time from Washington D. C." (ibid. 14) These terrorist attacks brought down the fall of the Twin Towers and the fall of numerous lives inside them, causing massive causalities and a terrible impact on the psyche of Americans.

Al-Qaeda's 9·11 conspiracy is accurately represented by DeLillo in *Falling Man*. In the novel the terrorists' stories are told in three chapters under the headings "On Marienstrasse," "In Nokomis" and "In the Hudson Corridor." These headings serve as the geographical markers of the terrorists' plot. The fictional terrorists are the notorious Hamburg group in history. Al-Qaeda, whose name is not mentioned in the novel, has recruited some young Muslims to launch a terrorist attack on the American symbol buildings. Seven young men, disguised as university students, are trained in Germany. The group leader, Amir, rents a flat on Marienstrasse in Hamburg. The young Islamists come to Germany to pursue technical educations, but in the flat they speak about the struggle against "the enemy, near enemy and far, Jews first, for all things unjust and hateful, and then Americans" (80). They talk about their lost history, about "being crowded out by other culture, other future, the all-enfolding will of capital markets and foreign policies" (ibid.). They are sent to Afghanistan camps for training and brainwashing. They fly to America and arrive in Nokomis, Florida, to take the flight training, pledging to "accept their duty, which was for each of them, in blood trust, to kill Americans" (171). They disguise themselves so well that none of the Americans ever suspects that a group of Arabians are plotting in the land to kill them. On September 11, 2001, without warning, the terrorists hijack American planes which are forced to fly toward the Hudson corridor and crash into the World Trade Center, bringing the collapse of the Twin Towers, killing nearly 3000 people and causing trauma to numerous Americans.

With his humanistic characterization of the terrorists and his realistic representation of the conspiracy, DeLillo launches a sharper criticism of terrorism than otherwise. He describes the terrorist Hommad as some parents' son and treats him as a human being by showing us his desire, love, fear and dream. Hammad is nothing but cannon fodder employed for political and religious reasons like thousands of Shia boys on the battlefield in the Shatt al Arab during the Iran-Iraq war in the 1980s who were brainwashed and saw themselves as "the martyrs of the Ayatollah" (77). Many of those boys were even too small to carry their weapons and were "cut down in waves by machine guns" (238). At the end of the novel, when the plane crashes into the tower, Hammad, who is about to die, thinks of those Iranian boys "coming out of trenches and redoubts and running across the mudflats toward enemy positions, mouths open in mortal cry" (ibid.). He identifies with them and takes comfort from the belief that he will go to the paradise as a martyr and join them in the eternal life. The Islamist extremists often attack American capitalism. But they themselves are practicing capitalism, operating al-Qaeda in the way a businessman runs his company and indoctrinating young Muslims that they can purchase "tickets" to the paradise with the "heroic" death. With the intensive indoctrination of Islamic fundamentalism and Bin Ladin's inflammatory messages of hatred, which act like the daily bombardment of advertisements in the Western media, many young Muslims like Hammad, after having been recruited, turn into ruthless terrorists who embrace suicidal terrorism, taking the lives of the innocent people as well as their own.

What makes *Falling Man* stand out among the 9·11 novels is its juxtaposition of the perspectives of the attacker and the attacked, the victimizer and the victim. At the end of the novel these two perspectives merge when Hammad's plane crashes into Keith's tower, which makes the tragedy more provoking and the terror more graspable. The Islamic fundamentalists take the moral high ground to criticize American culture for its evil and corrupting influences while Americans often criticize Islam for its backwardness in culture, economy and politics. But in fact, the terrorists and the Americans are similar human beings, or more exactly, they are all "falling men" in the dangerous world.

2.3.4 The Falling Man in and out of the Novel

As the title of the novel and the central image, "falling man" has been differently interpreted by critics. John Carlos Rowe thinks that "falling" refers to the "fall" of America (131), while Kauffman remarks, "the novel portrays many falling men—and women" (135). Some critics compare the falling man to the dangling man of Saul Bellow: "This dangling man does not dangle between different alternatives of life, as the protagonist of Saul Bellow's debut novel does, but between postponed and immediate death" (Keskinen 73). The falling man's performances are viewed as "tantamount to the news coverage in the aftermath of 9·11; coverage whose repetition of images served to propagate a 'favorable' narrative among a world-wide audience" (Radar). But in the eyes of Versluys, DeLillo's use of this image "provides a counter-discourse to the prevailing nationalistic" rhetoric after 9·11, which seeks to transform vulnerability into triumphant profiles in courage (23). Of all these views, Versluys' is closest to mine. In this section I will discuss the imagery of the falling man.

Falling man is a character in the novel. He is DeLillo's vivid personalization of the tragic events of 9·11 and their aftermaths. Ten days after the planes hit the towers, Lianne finds a man dangling over the street. He is a performance artist known as falling man. His name is David Janiak. He reenacts the apocryphal spectacle of the World Trade Center jumpers:

> He'd appeared several times in the last week, unannounced, in various parts of the city, suspended from one or another structure, always upside down, wearing a suit, a tie and dress shoes. He brought it back, of course, those stark moments in the burning towers when people fell or were forced to jump. He'd been seen dangling from a balcony in a hotel atrium and police had escorted him out of a concert hall and two or three apartment buildings with terraces or

accessible rooftops. (33)

The performances of the Falling Man cause the consternation and outrage of many New Yorkers, just as the picture of Richard Drew, which appeared in the *New York Times* and in newspapers around the country of America on September 12, 2001, provoked public outrage. When the fictional Falling Man performs his jumping, there are "people shouting up at him, outraged at the spectacle, the puppetry of human desperation, a body's last fleet breath ..." (ibid.). In real life Mr. Drew's famous Associated Press photo of a man falling headfirst from the North Tower was pulled from circulation after that day, "out of respect for the families of those so publicly dying" (Junod) and also "on the grounds that this image was immoral, a voyeuristic invasion of the privacy of a man just moments before his death" (Duvall, "Witnessing the Trauma: *Falling Man* and Performance Art" 163). In fact, the underlying reasons for censoring Drew's photo are as follows: this image captures the vulnerability of the victims and the falling man in the photo "seems to be bespeaking the end of the American Dream of an unassailable global supremacy in the Post-Cold-War era ..." (ibid. 165). Drew's "Falling Man" is the intertext of DeLillo's *Falling Man*. The performance artist attaches himself by a harness to buildings and structures around New York and assumes the posture of the man in Drew's photograph, reminding the witnesses of the vulnerability of individuals and the nation of America as well as the horror of the terrorist attacks.

The title does not only refer to the performance artist who reenacts the falls of bodies from the burning World Trade Center, but also refers to Keith and his inability to cope with his traumatic experience. Keith falls, succumbing to the powers of chance that terror has so strengthened. Figuratively speaking, the Falling Man can also refer to the United States which has fallen since 9·11. The Falling Man's repeated enactment of falling "reminds New Yorkers of the pathos of the American 'fall'" (Rowe 131). 9·11 ended the era of innocence for the Americans. America is no longer unassailable as a superpower. "America is going to become irrelevant," as Martin, long-time lover of Lianne's mother, remarks. "Soon the day is when nobody has to think about America except for the danger it brings. It is losing the center. It becomes the center of its own shit. This is the only center it occupies" (191). Martin criticizes America for its hegemony and in the meantime foresees the decline of American international influence and the fall of its national power—an aftermath of 9·11. Martin is not alone in his views. It was true that after having learnt the news of the 9·11 terrorist attacks, people all over the world were shocked and stood shoulder-to-shoulder in mourning, solidarity, sympathy and friendship with the American people. But with the shock receding, people began to reflect on the tragedy and ask why the terrorists hated Americans so much that they launched such horrible suicidal attacks. Some famous intellectuals implicate America as the ultimate cause of the September 11 attacks although they condemned the terrorists' ferocity. They argued that the American government should reconsider its foreign policy which had triggered the hatred for America among some Muslims in the Middle East. Others criticized the globalization which meant Americanization and regarded America as the cause of the Muslims' poverty and oppression. The view that America was to blame is shared by some intellectuals both in America and beyond. But America's increasingly dominant power in the Arabian world should not have been used as an excuse to kill innocent people. Nothing can justify the terrorist violence against the civilians. In spite of America's seemingly unequalled power in military, economy and technology, a group of Islamic terrorists should not have caused the fall of the World Trade Center, a symbol of America's superpower and capitalism. The 9·11 terrorist event may signify America's fall in the eyes of people like Martin who comes from Germany, both an ally and rival of America. From my perspective, what concerns DeLillo most is not the fall of America's influence as a superpower, but the fall of the spirituality of the American people.

After the 9·11 terrorist attacks the American government has launched two wars against terrorism under President Bush's leadership, one in Afghanistan, the other in Iraq, which were daily covered by the media but are only remotely referred to in the novel. Keith and Lianne watch the news coverage of the "War on Terror" on TV: "[T]hey watched in silence as a correspondent in a desolate landscape, Afghanistan or Pakistan, pointed over his shoulder to mountains in the distance" (130-31). Many American servicemen and servicewomen were killed in the wars. According to Kauffman: "War brings an even more somber significance to the idea of falling bodies: the fallen soldiers join the ranks of all the men, women and children who have fallen at home and abroad." (151) The two wars are costly because thousands of young lives have been lost and a huge sum of money has been spent in the war efforts. Before the 9·11 terrorist attacks, globalization or Americanization had been spread to all over the world with America's booming economy. The United States was building the dream of an unassailable global supremacy in the Post-Cold-War era. The September 11 terrorist attacks triggered the fall of America in security, freedom, democracy and economy.

The Falling Man is also emblematic of what DeLillo is doing in the novel: try to make art out of horror and reenact the suppressed history of 9·11 as a chronicler and reminder. Many people develop amnesia when they come out from disasters, as the condition of the Alzheimer patients symbolizes. It is heroic of DeLillo to attempt to reconstruct that awful day, including a view inside one of the planes and a view inside the tower itself, and to characterize a performance artist who reproduces the hellish séance of men and women jumping from the towers. In a sense, the Falling Man is the double of DeLillo. The Falling Man suffers from "a heart ailment and high blood pressure" (220). Yet he jumps from high buildings, bridges, the bell tower of a church, and so on. His falls are said to be "painful and highly dangerous due to rudimentary equipment he use[s]" (222). No one can understand his motives for the dangerous performances. "He'd been arrested at various times for criminal trespass, reckless endangerment and disorderly conduct. He'd been beaten by a group of men outside a bar in Queens" (220). He dies at 39, according to the obituary, of "natural causes" (ibid.). In my view, he dies for the art which he employs to chronicle the history which is so unpleasant that the authorities try to cover up and which serves to remind people not to forget the history. Before his death he has made plans for a final fall which does not include a safety harness. His performances are not announced to the media in advance. He lives in the margins of the society and stays away from the media and the public life: "He turned down an invitation to fall from the upper reaches of the Guggenheim Museum at scheduled intervals over a three-week period. He turned down invitations to speak at the Japan Society, the New York Public Library and cultural organizations in Europe" (222). His falls are controversial. To witnesses like Lianne, the Falling Man is "a falling angel and his beauty [is] horrific" (222). To some critics he is a "Heartless Exhibitionist." To me, he is a "Brave New Chronicler of the Age of Terror" (220), like the author DeLillo.

DeLillo confronts the tragedy and the aftermath of the 9·11 terrorist attacks and draws the readers' attention to the impact of the 9·11 terrorist attacks on the Americans, especially on their psyche, recording their struggles for meaning, relief, safety and new identity, which started right after the catastrophe and moved on to 2004, the period which *Falling Man* covers. As a lifelong New Yorker, DeLillo witnessed the September 11 disaster and documented it as part of American contemporary history. Within days following the attacks, DeLillo went to the site, and recounts what he saw in the essay "In the Ruins of the Future":

> There stands the smoky remnant of filigree that marks the last tall thing, the last sign in the mire of wreckage that there were towers here that dominated the skyline for over a quarter of a

century.

Ten days later and a lot closer, I stand at another barrier with a group of people, looking directly into the strands of openwork facade. It is almost too close. It is almost Roman, I-beams for stonework, but not nearly so salvageable. Many here describe the scene to others on cellphones.

"Oh my God, I'm standing here," says the man next to me.

Like the immediate victims, DeLillo bears witness to the traumatic history and provides a different narrative, a counter-narrative to the terrorist narrative and the prevailing nationalistic rhetoric in American media. "In the Ruins of the Future" and *Falling Man* give truthful historical accounts of the 9·11 terrorist attacks, complementing the official record, even challenging it. "*Falling Man* is a memorial, an evocation, an unresolved argument with itself, an elegy, and the closest fiction has so far come to catching up with this huge piece of history" (Jones). Though it is a fiction, it can be argued that *Falling Man* offers testimony to at least some aspects of the disaster and its aftermath and becomes a significant part of the record of a moment of history.

DeLillo is an acute observer of American life which terror permeates. It is said that DeLillo used to keep two folders on his writing table, labeled "Art" and "Terror" respectively. Many of his novels and short stories are about violence and terrorism. In the postmodern consumer society violence and terrorist acts are often televised. In his works DeLillo has discussed how easily such televised acts of violence are transformed into images for visual consumption. "We consume these acts of violence," he told David Remnick in an interview. "It's like buying products that in fact are images and they are produced in a mass-market kind of fashion" ("Exile on Main Street: Don DeLillo's Undisclosed Underworld"). Even the 9·11 terrorist attacks, the most horrible disaster that happened to the American people, were turned into a media event and consumable products of patriotism and heroism. DeLillo's novel *Falling Man* centers on the 9·11 event and its aftermath, but tries to shy away from the news coverage which is "the narrative of our time" (qtd. in Remnick), the dominant media representations of the event, and creates a counter-narrative of his own. Certainly the terrorism in *Falling Man* relies heavily on the mass-mediated images of itself and the findings of *The 9·11 Commission Report*. DeLillo presents the hellish world after the World Trade Center was struck by the planes, the scenes which were caught by the media and played again and again. But in most of the novel, DeLillo refuses to reproduce the mass-media's representations of the 9·11 terrorist attacks which readers are used to. Instead, he focuses on the private lives shattered by the terrorism. He leads the readers to go inside the towers and the minds of the victims and terrorists, to witness what was going on there: the terror, blood, death, struggle and final fall.

DeLillo is regarded as "the laureate of terror" (Amis, "Laureate of Terror"). This is not just because DeLillo has been writing about terror of various kinds that exist in the postmodern world, to be more exact, the TV representations of these forms of terror, and also because he has the ambition of employing art to shape and alter people's consciousness in ways similar to the terrorists'. DeLillo said in an interview, in a postmodern society "that's filled with glut and repetition and endless consumption, the act of terror may be the only meaningful act" (qtd. in Passaro 84). As Bill Gray in *Mao II* puts it: "Years ago I used to think it was possible for a novelist to alter the inner life of the culture. Now bomb-makers and gunmen … make raids on human consciousness" (41), by their horrible terrorist acts and, more importantly, by mass-media's reproduction of terrorism. For DeLillo, the artists in the contemporary American society should take a stance of opposition and meanwhile stand in the margin of society, like the terrorists, to make raids on human consciousness. Indeed, DeLillo portrays an array of such artists in his works, for example, the performance artist in *Falling Man*, the body artist in *Body Artist* and the graffiti artist in *Underworld*. Like their creator, they produce art of terror in opposition to power structures and the dominant cultural logic of late capitalism while remaining in the social margin. Their works of art make impacts on their audience's consciousness, as DeLillo's works do. For decades, DeLillo has been writing with his ambition to "make raids on human consciousness." He has achieved a success in changing people's perception of the JFK Assassination, American culture, terrorism and the role of the artists in a postmodern society.

But compared to Norman Mailer, who voiced his aspiration of "making a revolution in the consciousness of our time" in his 1959 literary manifesto *Advertisements for Myself* (Gu 76), DeLillo has met greater challenges in his attempt to shape the public perception and keep the individualism and autonomy as an artist. DeLillo admitted Mailer's influence in an interview: "[I]n a number of ways, Mailer was a strong force, because he was at the center of the culture and I was at the opposite end, so to speak. And I admired his writing and his opinions and the fact that he was a writer who was highly visible" (qtd. in Binelli). DeLillo tries to distance himself from the contemporary culture dominated by manipulative mass media and rampant consumerism, to be dangerous to the dominant power structures and to avoid being incorporated into the system which threatens to absorb everything and assimilate every individual. But in the age of high postmodernism, with the publication of *White Noise*, it is impossible for DeLillo to stay in the margin of the society and to live the way as Thoreau did. He, as an individual and artist, has been shaped, too, by the times and the culture in which he lives and writes his novels. Thus on the one hand, he takes an oppositional stance of postmodern culture, criticizing its dangerous consequences, but on the other hand, he seems to be contained by the power structures he has opposed. So unsurprisingly, DeLillo has been read "both as a denouncer and as a defender of postmodern culture" (Osteen 3).

Chapter Two

The Textuality of History: DeLillo's Chronicle of Postmodern America

New Historicists regard literary works as products of their social and cultural circumstances. In the meantime they also consider history and culture as a product of literature and art and that history works no differently than fiction. Hayden White and Linda Hutcheon have argued that history is a narrative art, and must be understood as a form of narrative representation analogous to fiction. In White's view, "the techniques or strategies that they use in the composition of their discourses can be shown to be substantially the same, however different they may appear on a purely surface, or dictional, level of the texts" (*Tropics of Discourse* 121). Therefore, White continues:

> There are many histories that could pass for novels, and many novels that could pass for histories [...] Viewed simply as verbal artifacts, histories and novels are indistinguishable from one another. [...] In this respect, history is no less a form of fiction than the novel is a form of historical representation. (ibid. 121-22)

We often read novels as if they were histories and histories as if they were novels. It is the case even with postmodern American fiction, the ground of which, according to Timothy Parrish, is history. In his book *From the Civil War to the Apocalypse: Postmodern History and American Fiction*, Professor Parrish shows "how the best postmodern novelists compel their readers to accept their narratives as true in the same way that historians expect their readers to accept their narratives as true. These novelists write history as a form of fiction" (the book back cover). In the twentieth century, Parrish argues, the most powerful works of American history were written by William Faulkner, Toni Morrison, Thomas Pynchon, Don DeLillo, Joan Didion and Cormac McCarthy.

The New Historicists believe that one can never have access to the historical past except through surviving textual traces. History can reveal itself only through narrativization and textualization. As Montrose puts it:

> By the textuality of history, I mean to suggest, firstly, that we can have no access to a full and authentic past, a lived material existence, unmediated by the surviving textual traces of the society in question—traces whose survival we cannot assume to be merely contingent but must rather presume to be at least partially consequent upon complex and subtle social processes of preservation and effacement; and secondly, that those textual traces are themselves subject to subsequent textual mediations when they are construed as the "documents" upon which historians ground their own texts, called "histories." As Hayden White has forcefully reminded us, such textual histories necessarily but always incompletely constitute in their narrative and rhetorical forms the "History" to which they offer access. (20)

The implication of Montrose's view is that interpreting history as textual reconstruction inevitably leads to the erasure of the distinction between fiction and factuality. The past is always the historian's construction, and as such it possesses no authoritative materiality. As Lyotard urged, in postmodern society we should dispense with the notion of the totality of history, of one master narrative, or of one grand story. Rather, one should allow for the coexistence of multiple, competing and conflicting histories. This view differs fundamentally from the previous understanding of history. "The earlier historicism tends to be monological; that is, it is concerned with discovering a single political vision" (Greenblatt 5). The new historical orientation features not History, a single gigantic totality, but histories, full of the forces of heterogeneity, fragmentation, contradiction and difference.

What is history? According to White, history can be considered simply as the past, the documentary record of this past, or "the body of reliable information about the past established by professional historians … 'history' comprises everything that ever happened in 'the past'" ("New Historicism: A Comment" 295-96). This historical past is, as Fredric Jameson and Hayden White have argued, accessible to study "only by way of its prior textualizations …On this basis alone, one is justified in speaking of history as a text" (ibid. 297). The novels present history as plural stories. We can only make sense of any human event or experience in the form of a story, hence the inseparability of historical events from textuality. As mentioned above, novelists are identified with historians in some cases. They write history as a form of fiction. Their works tell us a lot about the past. DeLillo is such a great fictional historian who paints detailed portraits of American life in the late 20th and the early 21st centuries. He is a chronicler of contemporary American life and a specialist in the "secret history" of observable phenomena and recorded facts.

I. *White Noise*

"Who Will Die First?" Crisis of Survival in the Postmodern Age

In *White Noise* DeLillo portrays a society of spectacle and expresses his concerns about social, cultural and ecological conditions in the postmodern age. In an interview he told Mervyn Rrothstein:

> I lived abroad for three years, and when I came back to this country in 1982, I began to notice something on television which I hadn't noticed before. This was the daily toxic spill—there was the news, the weather, and the toxic spill. This was a phenomenon no one even mentioned. It was simply a television reality. It's only the people who were themselves involved who seemed to be affected by them. No one even talked about them. This was one of the motivating forces of *White Noise*. (23-24)

DeLillo was shocked by the reality he observed and this reality triggered his reflection upon postmodern American culture. Like the outstanding French novelist Balzac, he confronts and portrays postmodern social reality. The postmodern history he documents in the novel provides the readers, especially those in a different society and different times, an access to the life in postmodern America.

1. "Death Is in the Air"

In *White Noise,* which was published in 1985, DeLillo captures the atmosphere of dread in the early 1980s when cable television and FM commercial radio were just getting started in the United States and began to affect Americans' lives enormously. The individual increasingly felt threatened by the annihilation of self, both physically and metaphorically, and loss of freedom in this media-saturated, tech-crazed and mass consumer society.

DeLillo originally titled the novel "The American Book of the Dead," because death is the book's subject and theme. Murray and Jack discuss the Egyptian Book of the Dead, the Tibetan Book of the Dead, and the Mexican Book of the Dead. The industrial accident the "Airborne Toxic Event" threatens Blacksmith and its neighboring towns. Death stalks here and there, with the deadly poisonous substance leaking into the air and seeping into the soil. When evacuating, Jack is exposed to the toxic cloud. Death enters his body and blood. The threat of death is everywhere, as Murray puts it, "because death is in the air" (151) which they breathe. Death is white noise, "you hear it forever. Sound all round" (198). White noise comes from the TV, the radio, the tabloids, the shopping mall, the supermarket and all the other electrical household appliances. The menacing black toxic cloud is a more urgent and visible version of the white noise, heralding the danger of death. Like the white noise, death permeates every aspect of contemporary American society.

The question "Who will die first?" haunts Jack and his wife Babette. Why are they so obsessed with the fear of death? The answer lies in the social and cultural environments in postmodern America. All human beings are afraid of death and more so as we get old with years. On the one hand, we try every possible means to hold off old age and death. On the other hand, we search for ways to relieve our fear of death since we know that we are destined for death. In the Western societies which Christianity dominated, believers could always get comfort in their belief in the afterlife bliss in the paradise when faced with death. The Bible writes: by his death Jesus "might destroy him who holds the power of death—that is, the devil—and free those who all their lives were held in slavery by their fear of death" (Hebrews 2: 14-15). In the postmodern society where grand narratives are in crisis, Christianity as a master narrative has declined, resulting in a spiritual void which consumerism tries to fill. But consumerism cannot provide people with life's ultimate meaning and help them combat their fear of death. On the contrary, it aggravates the fear. *White Noise* depicts two types of fear of death. First is the fear of the physical death. Second is the fear of the death of self.

1.1 Fear of the Physical Death

Jack Gladney is a fifty-year-old family man and a college professor. He lives in an out-of-the-way suburb named Blacksmith with his wife Babette and their children from their previous marriages. The novel unfolds as the first-person narrative of Jack. Through his narrative, DeLillo demonstrates the effects of consumerism in contemporary American society.

1.1.1 The Fictional Environmental Accident

From early on in the novel, Jack discloses his fear of death. "Who will die first? This question comes up from time to time, like where are the car keys" (15).

Sometimes at midnight Jack will be awoken by his fear of death: "I woke in the grip of a death sweat. Defenseless against my own racking fears. ... Sweat tricked down my ribs" (47). Jack's fear of death originates from his concern with the increasingly deteriorating environment which is undermining his health and the health of his family. He observes the hairline of Heinrich, his son, is beginning to recede at the age of 14 and wonders: "Did his mother consume some kind of gene-piercing substance when she was pregnant? Am I at fault somehow? Have I raised him, unwittingly, in the vicinity of a chemical dump site, in the path of air currents that carry industrial waste capable of producing scalp degeneration, glorious sunset?" (22) Jack's interior monologue reveals his sense of insecurity of living in the environment "unintentionally produced by advanced technology, the effects of technology, the by-products, the fallout" (Lentricchia, *New Essays on White Noise* 99). Jack's awareness of the insidious dangers that accompany the technological advances is strengthened by other events that happen in his life. One day the children in the grade school of Blacksmith are getting headaches and eye irritation, tasting metal in their mouths. They are evacuated from the grade school because of an unidentified toxin in the atmosphere:

> No one knew what was wrong. Investigators said it could be the ventilating system, the paint or varnish, the foam insulation, the electrical insulation, the cafeteria food, the rays emitted by micro-computers, the asbestos fireproofing, the adhesive on shipping containers, the fumes from the chlorinated pool, or perhaps something deeper, finer-grained, more closely woven into the basic state of things. (35)

The men "in Mylex suits and respirator masks" are sent to give "systematic sweeps of the building with infrared detecting and measuring equipment" (ibid.). But the results tend to be "ambiguous" and no one knows for sure where the toxin comes from. "Because Mylex is itself a suspect material" (ibid.) and the toxins, in the form of white noise, are embedded in the environment, hence there is nowhere to escape and no one, not even pregnant women and school children, can escape.

Jack's fear of death is substantialized by an industrial accident the "Airborne Toxic Event." A tank car derails in a place not far from Blacksmith, causing a major chemical spill. There is a lot of smoke that forms a heavy black billowing cloud hanging in the air beyond the river, more or less shapeless. People call it the "Airborne Toxic Event." It is said that everything in the tank is dangerous. The inhabitants in Blacksmith and other nearby towns are urged to evacuate. On the way to their shelter the "abandoned Boy Scout Camp", Jack is exposed to the toxic atmosphere for about two and a half minutes when he stops and gets out of the car to fill their gas tank. According to the radio which Jack's family carry with them, the spillage contains toxic stuff called Nyodene D, a "whole new generation of toxic waste" (138). Jack thinks he is dying, for a medical checkup confirms that the toxic substance has entered his body.

The uncertainty about the outcome of being exposed to the toxic atmosphere increases Jack's fear of death. The information provided by the radio is very confusing and keeps changing. The exposure may result in skin irritation, sweaty palms, nausea, vomiting, short breath, heart palpitations, a sense of déjà vu, convulsion, coma, miscarriage or death. Since the computer in the checkup center shows Jack that Nyodene D has entered his body and blood, there is no way for him to escape death, but when will he die? No one has a definite answer, for even scientists do not have much knowledge of Nyodene D. It takes years, perhaps 15 years, to find out more about Nyodene D which has a life span of 40 years in the soil and 30 years in the human body. "So, to outlive this substance, I will have to make it into my eighties. Then I can relax," Jack says helplessly to the technician. Like waiting for Jesus Christ's Second Coming, Jack has to be always ready for his death. This absurd situation renders him helpless and terrified.

Heinrich's receding hairline, the evacuation of the grade school and finally the airborne toxic event work together to constitute the motives of Jack's fear. Jack and Babette's fear of death mirrors the mental state of Americans when they are surrounded by white noise, the reminder of the death that lurks beneath the technological society. It also reveals the American intellectuals' spiritual crisis and the middle class' confusion and anxiety in the postmodern age. The concerns over the threats to the humans and the environment posed by technology have become the collective unconsciousness of Americans since the Hiroshima Atomic Bombing and the Cuban Missile Crisis. During the Cold War the Americans had been living in the shadow of nuclear annihilation. *White Noise* was written in the early 1980s when the threat of the nuclear war had reached new heights not seen since the Cuban Missile Crisis. The Americans were seized with the terror of the seemingly upcoming nuclear war and its resulting mass destruction. As an American, DeLillo experienced the same fear and anxiety which can be felt in his works. In *White Noise* he represents the fear of death not by directly tackling the nuclear war threat, but by describing an industrial accident which is a fictional version of the Three Mile Island Accident. The media coverage of the accident both in the real life and in the fiction scares the Americans who are in the grip of the nuclear terror, exemplifying the manipulation of the mass media and criticizing the American government's cover-up of the adverse effects of the accident on the local people.

1.1.2 The Three Mile Island Accident

On the morning of March 28, 1979 a partial nuclear meltdown occurred at a nuclear power plant, located on Three Mile Island in the Susquehanna River, south of Harrisburg, Pennsylvania, and it released radioactive gas and iodine into the air. This was the infamous "Three Mile Island Accident," "the worst accident in the American commercial nuclear plant history" (Nuclear Regulatory Commission, "Backgrounder on the Three Mile Island Accident").

The news of the Three Mile Island Accident was as confusing as the coverage of the "Airborne Toxic Event" in *White Noise*. The public was told the releases were insignificant, there was no danger of an explosion, and there was no need to evacuate anyone from the area. But later all these assertions were proved to be false. There was a hydrogen explosion. Helicopters hovering above the plant reported radiation readings of up to 1, 200 millirems per hour, more than 1200 times the normal background level. It was ordered that everyone within five miles of the plant should evacuate. People did evacuate as if all hell broke loose. "There was an evacuation of 140,000 pregnant women and pre-school age children from the area" (ibid.). Residents soon began returning from their places of escape. There was no report of deaths or injuries to plant workers or members of the nearby community. But in the months, even years after the accident, questions were raised by the media about possible adverse effects from the released radiation on human, animal and plant life in the Three Mile Island area. The 24 hours' national news of the accident on cable TV led to the increased public fear and distrust. In order to dispel the public distrust, after some investigation, the government concluded that in spite of serious damage to the reactor, most of the radiation was contained and that the actual release had negligible effects on the physical health of individuals or the environment. For more than 30 years a growing body of witness stories and scientific evidence contradict the official United States government's conclusion that the Three Mile Island Accident posed no threat to the public. In 1984, for example, psychologist Marjorie Aamodt surveyed residents in three hilltop neighborhoods near the plant. Dozens of the surveyed people reported a metallic taste, nausea, vomiting and hair loss as well as illnesses including cancers, skin and reproductive problems and collapsed organs—all associated with radiation exposure. "Among the 450 people surveyed, there were 19 cancer deaths reported between 1980 and 1984—more than seven times what would be expected statistically"

(Sturgis).

The Three Mile Island Accident happened at the time when the environment movement had gained a quick development in the United States, which improved the environmental awareness of the American public and the media's interest in the environmental problems. Through his depiction of the Airborne Toxic Event, DeLillo dramatizes the American historical, social and political conditions in the early 1980s when *White Noise* was produced. In his first term, President Reagan launched the "Star War" to compete against the Soviet Union in military power, thus more nuclear bombs were produced. Domestically he encouraged consumption to develop economy. Yet too much emphasis on the consumption aided by technology, whether in military or civilian life, creates more problems, which contribute to and manifest in the fear of death. Technological capitalism has changed the picture of America, even the shape of the world. But it cannot provide a way to eliminate people's fear of death.

1.1.3 The Magic and Dread: Technology in the Consumer Society

One third of *White Noise* is about the environmental disaster the "Airborne Toxic Event," thus the novel can be labeled as a disaster novel. Or more exactly, *White Noise* is a screenplay of disaster. The evacuation is comic, detailed and realistic. Reading the novel is like watching a disaster movie, or watching the TV footage of the Three Mile Island (TMI) Accident. As is claimed in the government report of the TMI Accident, no one dies in the fictional disaster, either. The computer pronounces Jack's sentence of death, but no one knows for sure the date of execution. Because of his exposure to the toxic Nyodene D, Jack's life is forever changed.

The world depicted in *White Noise* is "a product of technology" (Moses 63). In this world, technology has become not only "a pervasive and mortal threat" (ibid.) to its residents, but also a godlike thing which people put their faith in. Technology brings forth the magic and dread to the postmodern American society.

The TMI Accident, the Airborne Toxic Event and the white noise in daily life point to the dangers of technology in American consumer society. Since the 1960s American environment has been changed by technological capitalism. This change is also documented by DeLillo's first novel *Americana*. David Bell, the main character in *Americana*, is a television network executive in New York City. He travels to the American West to escape from the corporate world to find his true identity and the identity of America. To his shock, David sees test jets flying overhead. Commercialism and industry pervade the mountains and the desert. The American West, which represents American purity and innocence, has been penetrated and transformed by technological capitalism. In *Underworld* DeLillo also depicts how the West is destroyed by the war industry, which dumps the nuclear waste on the sacred Indian land. "The way the Indians venerate this terrain now, we'll come to see it as sacred in the next century. Plutonium National Park. The last haunt of the white gods. Tourists wearing respirator masks and protective suits" (289). Through the use of black humor, DeLillo draws a dreadful picture of the American land contaminated by nuclear and other toxic materials. The Indian Reservations, possibly the least technological places in the United States, which depend on tourism to develop their economy, should become too toxic for Indians to live.

"All technology refers to the bomb" (*Underworld* 467). In the 1980s there was a horrible disaster which caused great damage to the environment and the humans. It was the Chernobyl disaster, the worst nuclear power plant accident in history. It occurred on April 26, 1986 at the Chernobyl Nuclear Power Plant in Ukraine, which was under the direct jurisdiction of the central authorities of the Soviet Union. An explosion and fire released large quantities of radioactive particles into the atmosphere, which spread over much of the Western USSR and Europe. An indirect consequence of the Chernobyl disaster was the collapse of the USSR. After the event, the Russians started to do business with Americans, trading nuclear waste and helping destroying it by explosion. Nuclear waste and nuclear explosion all become commodities which can be sold and bought. "They sell nuclear explosions for ready cash. They will pick up waste anywhere in the world, ship it to Kazakhstan, put it in the ground, and vaporize it" (*Underworld* 788). The inhabitants living close to "The Kazakh Test Site" have suffered terribly from the fallout: "The clinic has disfigurations, leukemia's, thyroid cancers, immune systems that do not function" (ibid. 800). Besides, some unknown diseases developed among the villagers who are the patients of the clinic.

Another disaster associated with the Airborne Toxic Event in *White Noise* is an industrial catastrophe that occurred in Bhopal, India, on December 2, 1984, just before the novel came out. There was a big American chemical plant in Bhopal called Union Carbide that manufactured chemical pesticides. Like what is described in *White Noise*, some chemical leaks from the plant entered the air over Bhopal. This accident killed more than 3, 000 people and injured 200,000. The catastrophe quickly became an international symbol of the hidden threat chemical factories can pose to their host communities. Greenpeace scientific survey reveals persistent contamination of land and water at the Union Carbide factory site 15 years after the disaster. Among women who were pregnant at the time of exposure, 43 percent suffered spontaneous abortions, four to seven times the usual rate in Bhopal. Many surviving infants had multiple birth defects.

But the ecological disasters were not the only dread which DeLillo was concerned about in life. Another dread caused his concern and inspired him to write *White Noise*. In 1981 when he came back to America from Greece where he had lived for a couple of years, he "began to notice something on television which [he] hadn't noticed before. This was the daily toxic spill—there was the news, the weather and the toxic spill" (qtd. in Rothstein 23). DeLillo observed that death, the highest form of disaster, permeates the mass media. "Death seems to be all around us —in the newspapers, in magazines, on television, on the radio" (ibid. 24). This cultural phenomenon appeared when CNN, the first all-news television channel in the United States, was founded in 1980, providing 24-hour television news coverage to millions of American households. In the age of information explosion, only sensational news can attract people's attention. Thus postmodern media always take great interest in covering disasters and breaking the news, which results in the phenomenon depicted in *White Noise*. Exposed to all kinds of dreadful news in the mass media, viewers very often become paranoid about disasters which might befall them. Therefore, viewers like Jack Gladney and Babette live in constant fear of death.

In addition to dread, technology produces magic. In the mass media there is always the news of new scientific developments which help people to live longer. In *White Noise* Dylar is such a highly technological product. This is a new medicine developed by Mink who secretly tests it on humans, which is prohibited by the government and the pharmacy company. This medicine is not a tablet in the old sense, but a highly efficient drug delivery. The medication in Dylar is encased in a polymer membrane. The water from the gastrointestinal tract seeps through the membrane at a carefully controlled rate. The controlled dosage is meant to eliminate the hit-or-miss effect of pills and capsule. After the medication is pumped out of it, the polymer tablet self-destructs. Once the plastic membrane is reduced to microscopic particles, it passes harmlessly out of the body in the time-honored way. According to Mink, the project manager, Dylar is designed to solve an ancient problem: fear of death. It encourages the brain to produce fear of death inhibitors. It would be a perfect magic medicine and a wonderful medical breakthrough if it were found to be working on humans. Tortured by the fear of death, Babette volunteers to try this tempting medicine. Even Jack wants to take this magic drug in order to relieve his fear of death. In the society where people develop a strong faith in technology, "everything is correctible" (191) and to every problem there seems to be a solution:

> It got you here, it can get you out. This is the whole point of technology. It can create an appetite for immortality on the one hand. It threatens universal extinction on the other. Technology is lust removed from nature. [...] It prolongs life, it provides new organs for those that wear out. New devices, new techniques every day. Lasers, masers, ultrasound. (285)

Technology, which combines the forces of capitalism and consumer culture, determines people's life and death and replaces nature. The development of technology provides the consumers with all kinds of products for consumption: the objects catalogued on the first page of *White Noise*, the electrical household appliances and the computers, as seen when the agent from SIMUVAC punches in a few numbers and gets Jack's history. With the popularity of cable television in the American households, anything can be transformed into a commodity for mass consumption. "CABLE HEALTH, CABLE WEATHER, CABLE NEWS, CABLE NATURE" (231). Health, weather, news, all are at the disposal of the consumers, who can watch the disasters and catastrophes that happen elsewhere without going to the scenes. Disasters are turned into addictive televised commodities. Even death is transformed into a consumable object by the technological media.

In the early 1980s DeLillo noticed that "a sense of death had begun to permeate not only television but the media in general ... in the newspapers, in magazines, on television, on the radio ... I can't imagine a culture more steeped in the idea of death" (qtd. in Rothstein 24). Death is "in the air." Immersed in this culture, people suffer from anxiety and insecurity, worrying not only about the physical annihilation, but also the death of self.

1.2 Fear of the Death of Self

As a fifty-year-old professor, Jack is of course concerned about the death of the body, but what he is most concerned with is the death of self. His views of the technological mass media and consumerism are similar to those of the theorists in the Frankfurt School. In this sense, Jack is more a modernist than a postmodernist.

Jack's fear of death partly originates from his worry about his loss of self. The loss of self in the postmodern society can be attributed to the influence of the mass media. The society depicted in *White Noise* is media-saturated. The characters are bombarded by news coverage, advertisements, weather forecasts, talk-shows and other programs. DeLillo regards this information bombardment as the "daily toxic spill" (Rothstein 23). This phenomenon caused DeLillo's concern. He admitted: "This was one of the motivating forces of *White Noise*" (ibid. 24). The "toxic spill" has started to influence the children. While sleeping in the evacuation center, Jack's seven-year-old daughter Steffie utters "Toyota Celica" (155) which is the name of an automobile advertised on TV. Steffie is repeating some TV voices in her sleep. The children are taking shape in their character and identity, and if often exposed to the toxic spill on TV, they would be poisoned to death spiritually and end up with a decentered and fragmented identity.

Due to his overexposure to the mass media, Mink becomes a man who has lost the self. According to New Historicism, self-identity is socially constructed. In the media-saturated society, mass media like radio, film and television are important social forces which impose images, role models and values that shape the identity of the individual. As an immigrant, he learns English and the American lifestyle by watching American TV and movies, takes the image for the real and identifies with the images. "I had American sex the first time in Port-O-Sex. Everything they said is true." (308) Mink becomes fascinated by American popular culture and believes in the technology of consumer fulfillment. He is lured by American sex and success. But when he tries to imitate the ways the Americans do things on TV, he meets his downfall. Kicked out by his company, Mink loses his mind. He stays in a motel in a deserted Germantown, consuming Dylar with his eyes focusing on the flickering screen. When Jack comes to the motel, he finds "Mink is a compacted image of consumerism in the electronic media, a figure of madness" (Fan 54), a completely hollow man who has lost his human agency. When Jack talks to him, he only replies with fragmentary and disconnected sentences from TV. Even when he is taken to the hospital, seriously wounded by Jack, Mink should comically babble: "No one knows why the sea birds come to San Miguel" (316), obviously a line taken from the narration of an animal TV program. Mink becomes merely a voice without center, a jumbled bunch of fragments from various contemporary jargons, mostly emanating from the TV "floating in the air, in a metal brace, pointing down at him" (305).

Mink is dead in terms of the self. In the philosophy of Hobbes and Locke, the individual is viewed "as a rational, motivated agent with a protected interior core of beliefs, desires, and memories" (Melley 14). Individualism makes the individual its focus. But with the arrival of the consumer society, this individualism and unique personal identity are becoming things of the past (Jameson, "Postmodernism and Consumer Society"). In the world of *White Noise*, the mind and behavior of the individual are controlled and manipulated by the mass media and corporate technologies, the result of which is the death of the self. Mink is such a case in point. He and the TV have become one, thus dehumanized. His behavior is governed by external suggestions and messages. Mink has lost his individuality and rationality, incapable of distinguishing the reality from its linguistic representation. Consumerism has reduced him to an alienated man, out of touch with himself as he is out of touch with the world outside.

Jack's fear of death of self originates from the cultural environment of the postmodern society which is media-saturated, highly commodified and morally degraded. Blacksmith is such a society in miniature which DeLillo paints from Jack's perspective. Television occupies an important position in the American home. For "most people there are only two places in the world. Where they live and their TV set" (66). In Jack's home, TV is always on. Even when they are not watching it, its voice accompanies their daily activities like eating, sleeping, cooking and washing. But too much TV is harmful. It may result in the viewer's alienation from the authentic existence, and from his genuine self. It may lead to a "one-dimensional" universe of thought and behavior in which the very aptitude and ability for critical thinking and oppositional behavior is withering away. In Douglas Keesey's view, television "dulls perception, flattens consciousness, manipulates desires, breeds decadence, fosters escapism, insulates the senses, rebarbarizes, infantilizes, is a narcosis or a plug-in drug, mediates experiences, colonizes, pollutes, encourages commodity fetishism, leads to psychic privatization, makes us narcissistic, passive and superficial" (133-35). Jack is aware of the harmful effects of television, but he knows that its pervasion is unstoppable.

American society is not only media-saturated, but also highly commodified. The university which used to be regarded as "an ivory tower" is invaded by the consumer culture. Jack, as a department chairman at the College-on-the-hill in Blacksmith, witnesses the commodification of an American university. In the opening paragraph of the novel Professor Gladney watches his students return to the campus from their summer holidays. DeLillo carefully catalogues the students' possessions:

> The roofs of the station wagons were loaded down with carefully secured suitcases full of light and heavy clothing; with boxes of blankets, boots and shoes, stationery and books, sheets, pillows, quilts; with rolled-up rugs and sleeping bags; with bicycles, skis, rucksacks, English and Western saddles, inflated rafts. As cars slowed to a crawl and stopped, students sprang out and raced to the rear doors to begin removing the objects inside; the stereo sets, radios, personal computers; small refrigerators and table ranges; the cartons of phonograph records and cassettes; the hairdryers and styling irons; the tennis rackets, soccer balls, hockey and lacrosse sticks, bows and arrows; the controlled substances, the birth control pills and devices; the junk

> food still in shopping bags—onion-and-garlic chips, nacho thins, peanut crème patties, Waffelos and Kabooms, fruits chews and toffee popcorn; the DumDum pops, the Mystic mints. (1)

Jack has witnessed this spectacle of September wealth demonstration for 21 years. If the narrator did not mention it is the college students' returning to the campus, the reader would think it is some young people's coming back after shopping in a supermarket. Those items of objects, the assembly of station wagons, the "well-made" faces, the "massive insurance coverage" and the high tuition they can afford all tell us these students come from wealthy families and are the so-called elite of the consumer society. They are not bound together by their noble pursuit of knowledge but by consumerism. They are "a collection of the like-minded and the spiritually akin, a people, a nation" (2), immersed in the world of commodities and popular culture which images dominate.

One outcome of consumer culture's invasion of the university is the academic commodification. In 1968 Jack invented Hitler Studies in North America and with the consent of the chancellor he built "a whole department around Hitler's life and work" (4). The project was "an immediate and electrifying success" (ibid.). It was so successful that "the chancellor went on to serve as adviser to Nixon, Ford and Carter" (ibid.). Jack has become a distinguished professor and chairs the Department of Hitler Studies in the college. As his colleague Murray comments: "Nobody on the faculty of any college or university in his part of the country can so much as utter the word Hitler without a nod in your direction, literally or metaphorically. … The college is internationally known as a result of Hitler studies" (12). Jack's Hitler Studies is more a commercial success than an academic one. In the postmodern society the image of Hitler is sold as a commodity. "He's always on. We couldn't have television without him" (63). The movies about Hitler are still popular around the world. Even on the Internet, objects with the image of Hitler, swastika armbands and the Nazism symbol can be sold at wholesale or retail in public. Hitler would seem to symbolize all the irrational and dangerous forces that have destabilized modern life, but for Jack he provides the solid foundation of a successful career. Like a good businessman, Jack comes up with the idea of Hitler Studies as a clever gimmick at a specific moment, when no one else sees the potential in the enterprise. Jack's appropriation of Hitler follows familiar patterns of capitalist enterprise, including product promotion and consolidation of a territory. When he started his enterprise of Hitler Studies in 1968, the chancellor advised him to do something about his name and appearance if he "wanted to be taken seriously as a Hitler innovator" (16). "Jack Gladney" is too common. Finally Jack and the chancellor agreed that Jack should be called "J. A. K. Gladney" after adding an extra initial. The chancellor also strongly suggested that Jack gain weight so that he would have "an air of unhealthy excess, of padding and exaggeration, hulking massiveness," which would help his career enormously (17). Additionally, Jack wears a pair of "glasses with thick black heavy frames and dark lenses" (ibid.) and a black academic robe whenever on campus. With his changed name and appearance Jack hopes to give his colleagues and students the impression of dignity, significance, power and prestige. In the consumer society education is commercialized in all of its aspects. In order to attract more customers, the university, the discipline and even the professors need to be packaged, promoted, and then put onto the market. The culmination of the marketing of Hitler Studies is the conference of Hitler Studies, the academic equivalent of a trade show. "Three days of lectures, workshops and panel. Hitler scholars from seventeen states and nine foreign countries. Actual Germans would be in attendance." (33) Even the academic language is infected by the hucksterism of the advertising world. Jack's Hitler Studies exemplifies the all-pervasiveness of the capitalist ethos in contemporary America.

Jack's success with Hitler Studies should be attributed to his marketing rather than his academic ability. In spite of his success, Jack does not feel secure in his professional reputation. In order to get more funding and promotion, Jack commits academic cheating. As a famous expert in the field of Hitler Studies, he does not know German. With the approaching of an international conference on Hitler to be held in his university, Jack secretly hires a tutor to teach him German, but there is not much progress. In the opening address at the conference he "spoke in German, from notes, for five minutes" (274). He talks about Hitler's mother, brother and dog. His dog's name was Wolf. This word is the same in English and German. "Most of the words I used in my address were the same or nearly the same in both languages. ... Of course there was Hitler himself. I spoke the name often, hoping it would overpower my insecure sentence structure" (ibid.). Not only is the address comic but the fact is also absurd that this address for the important conference should have been prepared with the help of Steffic, Jack's seven-year-old daughter. After the opening ceremony, Jack spends most of his time trying to avoid the German scholars. "Even in my black gown and dark glasses ... I feel feeble in their presence" (ibid.). Jack's postmodern Hitler Studies is commercialized and trivialized, lacking academic profundity and failing to confront the seriousness of Hitler in any way.

The academic commodification leads to a shallow and vulgar intellectual environment. Some professors are not only academically dishonest, but also morally degraded. *White Noise* is often regarded as a "campus novel" (Lentricchia, *New Essays on White Noise* 7). Besides Jack, it depicts some other professors. Murray is one of them. He is a villain. He is lascivious and covets Babette. In the evacuation camp he goes whoring. What is most impressive about him is his postmodern theories. He is something of a postmodern guru. He tutors Jack in violence and urges him to kill Mink, the man who seduces his wife Babette. He tells Jack that he can try to be a killer to cure himself of death:

> I believe, Jack, there are two kinds of people in the world. Killers and diers. [...] The more people you kill, the more credit you store up. [...] In theory, violence is a form of rebirth. The dier passively succumbs. The killer lives on. [...] Kill to live. [...] The more people you kill, the more power you gain over your own death. [...] But think how exciting, to come out a winner in a deathly struggle, to watch the bastard bleed. (290-91)

Jack takes Murray's advice to be a killer in order to survive. He goes to look for Mink and finds him in a motel. He fires at Mink. Ironically, the injured Mink shoots at Jack and wounds him, too. The novel does not tell whether Mink dies, but Jack is sure to survive although he is a killer. He gets away with killing, or more exactly, injuring another human being.

Jack has a fragmentary identity. He is "a sharp observer and commentator who at the same time participates … in an action which fatally shapes him" (Lentricchia, "Tales of the Electronic Tribe" 93). Jack is the first-person narrator. Everything that happens in the novel is filtered through him. His narration reveals his attitude toward what is narrated. His attitude toward the consumer culture is schizophrenic. In order to survive and get promotion in the academic market, Jack caters to the dominant capitalist ideology, inventing Hitler Studies, conducting it like a businessman, and making the maximum profit from it. He changes his name and appearance to package himself and the department of Hitler Studies which are commodities in the consumer society and which are truly sold well. But on the other hand, he feels he has lost his authentic self. He thinks: "I am the false character that follows the name around" (17). He fears that he will be turned into an image which has the void at the core and lacks substantial selfhood. With the bombardment of consumerism, Jack's sense of identity is dying. On an outing to a hardware store, for example, he bumps into his colleague Eric who acts slyly surprised to see Jack off campus without his academic dark robe and heavy-framed dark-lensed glasses. Eric describes him as "a big, harmless, aging, instinct sort of guy" (83). This obvious slight to Jack's sense of himself as a distinct being puts him "in the mood to shop" (ibid.).

According to the Frankfurt School, commodification may result in man's alienation and threatens to annihilate the self. Alienation refers to "an extraordinary variety of psycho-social disorders, including loss of self, anxiety states, anomie, despair, depersonalization, rootlessness, apathy, social disorganization, loneliness, atomization, powerless, meaningless, isolation, pessimism, and the loss of beliefs or values" (Josephson 15). Central to the definition of this term is the idea that man has lost his identity or selfhood. It is assumed, implicitly or explicitly, that in each of us "there is a 'genuine', 'real' or 'spontaneous' self which we are prevented from knowing or achieving" (ibid.). In American consumer society where the material side of existence is highlighted and the pursuit of material wealth and consumption is its priority, alienation is almost total. Obviously Jack suffers from alienation.

Unlike postmodernists who celebrate the fragmentation of self, modernists mourns for the loss of self. Jack fears that he will lose the self and tries his best to hold onto selfhood, "even selfhood conceived as a fiction" (Greenblatt, *Renaissance Self-Fashioning* 257). His confrontation with his physical death impels him to reflect on the reasons for his anxiety and fear. One day he goes home and throws away the objects he accumulates and threatens to annihilate his true self:

> I threw away picture-frame wire, metal book ends, cork coasters, plastic key tags, dusty bottles of Mercurochrome and Vaseline [...] I threw away candle stubs, laminated placemats, frayed pot holders [...] I was in a vengeful and near savage state. I bore a personal grudge against these things. Somehow they'd put me in this fix. They'd dragged me down, made escape impossible. [...] I threw away diplomas, certificates, awards and citations. (294)

Commodity fetish causes people to focus on the pursuit of happiness, safety and success brought about by possessing material things, which leads to the reification of man. Knowing that he is dying, Jack even throws away his "diplomas, certificates, awards and citations" which used to prove his qualifications and academic success which now he thinks are useless in protecting him, a desperate attempt to retain his autonomy.

Contemporary America has seen a great development of science and technology which has boosted social progress and improved people's health, but it has also brought about many problems like pollution and alienation. When Christianity has declined and people are confronting death in American postmodern society, who can protect them and where can they turn for comfort and peace?

2. "As Long as the Supermarket Did Not Slip"

In a traditional society where the belief in the afterlife is popular with people, when faced with death, one usually turns to religion for comfort and peace. In the consumer society where the traditional religion declines, "when the old god leaves the world" (*Mao* II 7), there seems nothing except consumption that can sustain people spiritually. In the society of *White Noise*, where consumer culture dominates and commercialization prevails, the characters plagued by fear of death can only turn to consumerism for comfort and peace, which is temporary and transient.

In the postmodern society, according to Lyotard, people have now lost the ability to believe in meta-narratives. Christianity, as one of the meta-narratives, used to play a dominant role in an individual spiritual life and serve as a social bond, but it has come to lose its credibility. Since people have rejected grand narratives, what they have fallen back on is little narratives. Instead of the traditional religion, the postmodern mass media creates its own set of myths, cults, gods and immortals to fill the psychological and spiritual need in the American people. When they are confronted with fear, especially fear of death, people in a traditional society will seek help from the Almighty God whom they believe can protect them, thus can remain calm and peaceful. They read the Bible, go to church on Sundays, and say prayers for themselves or others. In this way their fear, anxiety and sense of helplessness can be alleviated, even eliminated, for they believe God is omnipotent and omnipresent. After "the death of God" there is a great spiritual void left in people's life which needs to be refilled. Individuals in this fragmented society are susceptible to any power that gives them the sense of security, the sense of belonging, comfort and peace. *White Noise* depicts this postmodern social condition in great detail.

2.1 Hitler Studies

Hitler Studies is not just an academic commodity which Jack sells to make a living, but also a quasi-religion which Jack takes to shield him from death. Tormented by his fear of death, Jack is attracted to Hitler who "is larger than life" (287) and thinks that Hitler can protect him. As Murray says: "Helpless and fearful people are drawn to magical figures, mythic figures, epic men who intimidate and darkly loom" (ibid.), Jack wants to use Hitler to absorb his fear and conceal himself in Hitler and his works.

Jack does not condemn the Holocaust, the mass murder of about six million Jews committed by Hitler during the Second World War. Hitler is not a moral issue for Jack. His Hitler Studies focuses on the charisma of Hitler in order to "cultivate historical perspective, theoretical rigor and mature insight into the continuing mass appeal of fascist tyranny" (25). No matter whether in class or on TV, Hitler is an icon, juxtaposed with Elvis Presley, achieving a kind of celebrity status, which is a familiar postmodern phenomenon. But "even all the forces of the postmodern world cannot wholly drain him of his frightening aura" (Cantor 47). Beyond the overwhelming horror that Jack believes to be able to shelter him from fear of death, there is "a quasi-religious dimension to Hitler's power and mystique" (Cantor 50):

> Hitler [...] spoke to people [...] as if the language came from some vastness beyond the world and he was simply the medium of revelation. [...] Crowds came to hear him speak, crowds erotically charged, the masses he once called his only bride. [...] Crowds came to be hypnotized by the voice, the party anthems, the torchlight parades. (72-73)

Not only can Hitler himself be used as a mysterious yet powerful "protective device" (31), but the German language which Hitler speaks might be hopefully protective. For example, Jack named his first son Heinrich because the name has "a kind of authority" that might protect him. Another example is Hitler's book *Mein Kampf* (*My Struggle*). One night Jack finds someone sitting in his backyard and thinks it is Death at his door. He is so scared that he takes a copy of *Mein Kampf* as a holy shield and clutches it to his stomach for protection. When he opens the door, to his surprise, it is not Death that stands before him but only Vernon Dickey, his father-in-law.

Hitler, "the incarnation of absolute evil" (Cantor 39), becomes a depoliticized commodity, a media celebrity and a fascinating idol in the postmodern society. "He's always on. We couldn't have television without him" (63). Jack discovers the religious nature of Hitler and idolizes him. But Hitler's powerfulness is illusory. Even Jack himself admits that Hitler Studies fails to help him cope with his fear of death. Although he is "the most prominent figure in Hitler Studies in North America" (31), Jack does not know German, he cannot speak or read it, cannot "understand the spoken word or begin to put the simplest sentence on paper" (ibid.), and if exposed, it would be a big academic scandal. His speech at the International Conference of Hitler Studies is a laughing stock. The idolatry of Hitler cannot protect him against death, nor give him comfort and peace when he is faced with death. At last, desperate Jack becomes a killer in order to seize some Dylar from Mink.

With Jack's Hitler Studies, DeLillo dramatizes the spiritual crisis and belief crisis that the Americans underwent in the postmodern society and subtly delineates the anomie and the decline of religion in that society.

2.2 Dylar

One reason for Jack's fascination with Hitler is that he believes that Hitler is "larger than life" (287) and able to protect him against death. But as Hitler Studies brings him more success and fame, his fear of death increases. The marketing of Hitler Studies makes him feel more like a commodity rather than a human being with autonomy and free agency. In the meantime his inaccessibility to the German language makes him feel for many years he is "living on the edge of a landscape of vast shame" (ibid.). To make things worse, Jack is exposed to Nyodene D, which is likely to nourish within him a lethal "nebulous mass" (280), as if its "enormous dark mass" (127) has taken up residence inside his body to give physical form to his nebulous fear. Thinking he is technically dying and the doctors cannot do anything about it, Jack decides to go to find Mink from whom he hopes to get some Dylar.

Dylar is a high-tech product designed and founded by a multinational pharmaceutical company to cure human's fear of death. Babette comes across an ad about Dylar which the project manager Mink puts in a tabloid, advertising the recruitment of some volunteers to try the new medicine which can heal the fear of death. Tortured by her fear of death, she secretly meets Mink and has sex with him in a motel to exchange for some bottles of Dylar. After some months' trying, Babette finds Dylar does not work at all. Worse, she develops memory loss. The pharmaceutical company prohibits Dylar on humans before it is put on the market. Mink sees its business opportunities and tries it on the human subjects regardless of morality and professional ethics. After the company learns about Mink's secret deal with Babette, they fire him. With his American dream shattered and spirit ruined, Mink turns to Dylar for comfort and protection. But it turns out that Dylar does not work, either. Instead, taking Dylar has impaired his ability to distinguish signifier from signified. When Jack says "hail of bullets," Mink ducks in terror. After Jack whispers "fusillade," Mink is so terrified that he tries to hide behind the bowl, "both arms over his head" (311). However, Babette continues to take it, Mink increases its dosage and Jack seeks desperately for it. Their obsession with Dylar reveals their spiritual emptiness and their desperation for a spiritual sustenance.

With the "death of the God," there have appeared multiple gods to compete for filling the spiritual void left. Since the age of the Enlightenment, technology has been worshipped like a god. In the eyes of many people, technology is an almighty God who has infinite power and can help people to the happy realm. It seems to be omnipotent. For every problem, there is a solution. For every desire, there is a technique. Moreover, it gives the promise of immortality: the conquest of the final natural limit—death. Dylar, a technological pill, symbolizes the ambition of modern science and exemplifies human's faith in technology for solutions to all problems, including the ancient fear of death and mortality. The new God offers Babette, Jack and Mink consolation and the hope for a life free from fear of death. According to Mink, though "Dylar failed [...] there will eventually be an effective medication [...] A remedy for fear" (308).

With its human-oriented design, Dylar is regarded as the "technology with a human face" (211). It is efficient and user-friendly. The controlled dosage is meant to eliminate the hit-or-miss effect of pills and capsules. After the medication is pumped out of it, the polymer tablet self-destructs. Once the plastic membrane is reduced to microscopic parties, it passes harmlessly out of the body in the time-honored way. In spite of its advancement, Dylar fails to fulfil its purpose. In my view, there will never be such a technological product that can succeed in eliminating human's fear of death. Were it successful, it would be to return human beings to a subhuman state, free of either logos or the knowledge of personal finitude. It is true that technology, in all its forms, dominates every aspect of people's lives by making it possible for human beings to manipulate any physical or mental activity dealing with domestic, social, political, economic, medical and aesthetic concerns, facilitating means of transportation and communication, enhancing conditions of work and play, and helping in harnessing the forces of nature and in transforming raw materials. But it cannot satisfy man's longing for peace and salvation, and more importantly, it cannot answer the questions related to the ultimate meaning of life.

So neither Hitler Studies nor Dylar can help cure Jack's fear of death. They are just commodities. Consumerism cannot solve spiritual problems. Instead, it has caused moral decadence and religious decline. Jack used to be a believer of afterlife. He was "a Buddhist, a Jain, a Duck River Baptist" (310). Now he is a nonbeliever. He will not take an old belief to help him get rid of his fear of death. The postmodernist Murray says to Jack: "[T]he afterlife is [...] a sweet and terribly touching idea. You can take it or leave it" (ibid.). To Murray, the belief of afterlife is like a convenient fantasy. It is not an obligation or absolute truth. In fact, the number of believers in the postmodern society is declining. Even the nuns do not believe in "angels, in saints, all the traditional things" (317). They pretend to be believers by wearing the old uniform: the habit, the veil and the clunky shoes to "embody old things, old beliefs" (318). The nuns claim: "It is our task in the world to believe things no one else takes seriously.

To abandon such beliefs completely, the human race would die" (ibid.). They dedicate themselves for the sake of the nonbelievers, as the nun, who takes care of the injured Mink in the hospital, confides to Jack: "There must always be believers […] We are your lunatics. We surrender our lives to make your nonbelief possible" (ibid.). Without the religion which provides moral values, life meaning and spiritual sustenance, the society would not function properly and would suffer the anomie as described by DeLillo: fake professors in the universities, newspapers selling fake medicines, people tortured by anxiety and fear of death, unfaithful wives and fake nuns.

In postmodern America where the old God leaves, consumerism and technology are worshipped as a new religion, substituting for the traditional religion. Supermarket becomes the church of the new religion in the new era.

2.3 Supermarket

Supermarket is the center of Blacksmith and the symbol of postmodern America. It is the place where people shop, meet and chat. It is the place where families unite and individuals get comfort, peace of mind and security. It seems to be the postmodern church. "This place recharges us spiritually, it prepares us, it's a gateway or pathway. Look how bright. It's full of psychic data […] Here we don't die, we shop" (37-38).

In the past, the church was a gathering place for villagers and townspeople. It was the custom that on Sundays or some special holidays for Christians, parents and children, in their best formal clothes, went to church to worship and to socialize. They listened to the summons of the ministers, joined the choirs, sang songs to praise the Lord, said prayers and studied the Bible. Through these formal liturgies, they formed a community of "the like-minded and the spiritually akin" (4). They were peaceful when they were dying because they thought that after their bodies perish they would go to the paradise which they regarded as the home in the heaven where the Lord is waiting for them. With the decline of the traditional religion, American society is falling apart. In the pluralistic society people may have different values and beliefs. What unites people in this fragmented society is consumption, which is the social cement and an aesthetic. Consumerism becomes a new religion.

White Noise depicts the American family's crisis which dates back to the latter part of the 20th century, due to the Sexual Revolution, the Women's Liberation Movement, and the decline of the parental authority. Jack had been married four times before he married Babette less than two years ago. He and Babette have six or seven children from their previous marriages, but only four live with them. "Not a single child whom Babette has borne or whom Jack has fathered, whether in their custody or not, is living with both parents or even a full brother or sister" (Ferraro 17). It takes quite some time to sort out the complicated relationships in the Gladneys, a contemporary typical family. In this increasingly fragmented society which lacks the traditional family bond, consumerism offers a new binding force of the family, the community and the nation.

At the very beginning of the novel, Jack narrates his students' return to the campus from their summer vacation that "has been bloated with criminal pleasures, as always" (1). He catalogues their belongings in detail. Without the context, the passage would be read as a description of a supermarket in an affluent society instead of the luggage of the college students coming back to campus after the summer vacation. The rich parents "stand sun-dazed near their automobiles, seeing images of themselves in every direction" (1). This is a community that is immersed in the consumer culture. The consumer happiness shines about these people. "This massive assembly of station wagons, as much as anything they might do in the course of the year, more than formal liturgies or laws, tell the parents they are a collection of the like-minded and the spiritually akin, a people, a nation" (4). Here DeLillo suggests how attenuated America has become as a community, how little it holds together as a nation except for consumerism. The Americans in this society are no longer united by a common religion or even by political forces. They are in desperate need of new binding forces of the family, the community and the nation. Only consumerism provides a sense of connectedness and solidarity. Throughout the novel, the Gladneys give themselves over whole-heartedly to energizing rituals of familial consumerism: the lunch of "crumpled tinfoil" and "shiny bags," the Christmas-in-September shopping spree at the Mid-Village Mall, the night of watching natural disasters on TV. They consume fast food, catastrophes on television, postmodern sunsets, and Christmas gifts together, and go to the supermarkets shopping together. Consumerism produces what we might call an aura of connectedness among individuals: an illusion of kinships, transiently functional but without either sustaining or restraining power, a stimulant that at the same time renders one unable to feel either the sacredness or the tyranny of the family bond. Thus consumerism functions as a communalizing power under consumer capitalism.

The parents of the college students can afford station wagons which Babette admires. The "massive insurance coverage" (1) can protect them against diseases, disasters and death. Thus they live in happiness and satisfaction, seemingly free from anxiety and fear. Consumption is equated with personal well-being, economic progress and social fulfillment. Supermarket serves as a postmodern church, a clearing house for solace—an icon of consumerism. Just as cathedrals provided spiritual rebirth long ago, today supermarkets offer comfort to those who lack any other religious belief. In purchasing items at the supermarket Jack finds his inner happiness and security. Jack himself is aware of the role of supermarket in their emotional and spiritual life:

> It seemed to me that Babette and I, in the mass and variety of our purchases […] in the sense of replenishment we felt, the sense of well-being, the security and contentment these products brought […] it seemed we have achieved a fullness of being that is known to people who need less, expect less, who plan their lives around lonely walks in the evening. (20)

So when he suffers from insecurity, anxiety and fear, he will resort to conspicuous consumption to seek for security and comfort he is desperately in need of. Once in a supermarket, Jack encounters Eric Massingale, his colleague, who tells him that, without the academic gown and heavy-framed dark-lensed glasses that he wears on campus, he looks "so harmless"—just "a big, harmless, aging, indistinct sort of guy" (83). Jack feels hurt by Massingale's comment which in fact makes him realize his weaknesses and inability, hence feels his survival is under threat. This encounter puts him in the mood to shop. He gathers Babette and children together for a daylong shopping. By shopping "I began to grow in value and self-regard. I filled myself out, found new aspects of myself, located a person I'd forgotten existed" (ibid.). The goods the Gladneys purchase are viewed as a reflection of their owners' worth, thus provide them with the consumer fulfillment and a sense of security. Following the grief the airborne toxic event causes, Jack looks to the supermarket for comfort. "Everything was fine, would continue to be fine, would eventually get better as long as the supermarket did not slip" (170). As a spiritual seeker, Jack "finds moments of transcendence not in traditional religion but in shopping" (Eaton 151).

At the end of *White Noise*, Jack goes shopping and finds the "supermarket shelves have been rearranged" (325), which causes confusion, agitation and panic among the shoppers because the change comes without warning. "There is a sense of wandering now, an aimless and haunted mood" (326). The shoppers feel betrayed. But in the end it doesn't matter, because

> the terminals are equipped with holographic scanners, which decode the binary secret of every item, infallibly. This is the language of waves hand radiation, or how the dead speak to the living. And this is where we wait together, regardless of age, our carts stocked with brightly colored goods. A slowly moving line, satisfying, giving us time to glance at the tabloids in the

racks. Everything we need that is not food or love is here in the tabloid racks. The tales of the supernatural and the extraterrestrial. The miracle vitamins, the cures for cancer, the remedies for obesity. The cults of the famous and the dead. (ibid.)

This passage offers a realistic picture of the consumer society where the traditional religion is replaced by the new religion of capitalist consumerism. It is a paradoxical society: diverse yet totalitarian; highly technological yet extremely superstitious; materialistically affluent yet spiritually deprived. In this society, people resort to consumerism for consolation and peace of mind. They do not depend on their old religion for spiritual sustenance any more. Tweedy, one of Jack's ex-wives, puts all her energy into a kitchen with "a stove that belongs in a three-star restaurant in the provinces" (95) in order to forget her worries and unhappiness. Old Man Treadwell takes tabloids as something like the Bible to fill the spiritual vacuum and offer him comfort and spiritual satisfaction. In the above quoted passage, the consumers are waiting in line to check out. But metaphorically, they are also waiting to check in for a dwelling place in the consumer paradise where the consumers presumably find the happiness and contentment promised by consumerism. The terminals of the supermarket are "the commercial/technological gate of heaven where not people but products are judged by omniscient gods" (Osteen 190).

The supermarket, like a postmodern church, or more exactly a temple of multi-god worshipping, sells tabloids to the spiritually hungry people who need a regular dose of the tabloids in order to live. Babette belongs to a group of volunteers who read to the blind. Once a week she reads to an elderly man who is known as Old Man Treadwell from the tabloids like "the *National Enquirer*, the *National Examiner*, the *National Express*, the *Globe*, the *World*, the *Star*. The old fellow demands his weekly dose of cult mysteries" (5). In the evacuation camp, with the threat of the toxic cloud, Babette volunteers to read to Old Man Treadwell and "a number of other blind people… from a small and brightly colored stack of supermarket tabloids" (142). The tabloids are full of tales of celebrities, dead or alive; mysteries and wonder drugs:

She reported a front-page story. "Life After Death Guaranteed with Bonus Coupon." […]
"The no-risk bonus coupon below gives you guaranteed access to dozens of documented cases of life after death, everlasting life, previous-life experiences, posthumous life in outer space, transmigration of souls, and personalized resurrection through stream-of-consciousness computer techniques." (145-46)

Babette seems to be leading a Bible study group who are listening attentively, piously and hopefully. Just as the Christians believe in the predictions in the Bible, the small audience of the old and blind believe in the predictions in the tabloids. DeLillo once told an interviewer that the tabloids "ask profoundly important questions about death, the afterlife, God … in an almost Pop Art atmosphere" (qtd. in Osteen 179). "Everything we need that is not food or love is here in the tabloid racks" (326). Jack, who is dying but there seems to be no way out, in the end professes a sort of transparent faith in the tabloid promises of super-cures that can temporarily help him get through his life but cannot give him comfort and peace.

Up to the early 1980s when the novel was written, the American society had been conquered by consumerism. Commodity messages become the "natural language of the culture" (9) and humans are turned into commodities in this postmodern consumer society. Consumerism, like a dictatorship, has even colonized the unconscious of the children. "Toyota Celica" (155), the name of an automobile which is advertised in the commercial, finds its way into the dream of Steffie, a seven-year-old child. Consumerism has eroded the traditional values which used to bind a family, a community, a people and a nation. There is no spiritual life as we used to see in the family. What we see everywhere is the commodity fetishism, a postmodern religion which proffers consumers peace of mind and comfort.

White Noise ends with "three discrete scenes that are narrated without comment" (Osteen 188). Wilder, Babette's three-year-old son, rides his plastic tricycle across the interstate with passing cars and vans. He meticulously escapes the harm of the busy traffic. He is too young and ignorant to have fear of death. When he grows as old as his parents, he will naturally develop this anxiety. If Dylar were successful, would people be reduced to Wilder's state of ignorance which probably means greater danger than suffering fear of death? The characters in *White Noise*, who live in a highly technological consumer society, believe in the consumption of technological commodities. Besides Dylar, they consume the postmodern sunsets. The second scene to end the novel with is crowds of people watching the sunset, which becomes extremely beautiful after the Airborne Toxic Event. "We go to the overpass all the time. Babette, Wilder and I. We take a thermos of iced tea, park the car, watch the setting sun." (324) More and more people join them. Their attitude toward the sun is awe. "Certainly there is awe, it is all awe, it transcends previous categories of awe" (ibid.). Some people are scared while others are overjoyed. "No one plays a radio or speaks in a voice that is much above whisper" (325). "The highway overpass has become an outdoor cathedral where 'the middle-aged, the elderly'—those confronting their mortality—gather to watch the sky" (Osteen 189), the poisonous sunset. The third scene to conclude the novel is the supermarket. The shelves have been rearranged. Jack and some older "well-dressed" shoppers feel agitated, panic and confused because they do not know where to find what they need. But in the end it doesn't matter "what they see or they think they see. The terminals are equipped with holographic scanners, which decode the binary secret of every item, infallibly" (326). The machines know everything about each item of commodity, just as the computer at the Autumn Harvest Farms (275) knows everything about Jack's health. Technology-aided consumerism, like dictatorship, has colonized subjectivity, the very being of the characters. American society has become a big supermarket where people are sourrounded by all kinds of commodities and bombarded by mass media which speaks everywhere in *White Noise*, issuing from the mouths of marginal characters babbling about decongestants, appearing as "psychic data" (51) emanating from supermarket packages, holographic scanners, radios, TV, tabloids, and "punctuating the narrative in the form of triadic lists of brand names" (Osteen, "The Natural Language of the Culture" 192). "Faith in the power of unadulterated nature, individual humanity, and religious mystery has been replaced by belief in an unholy trinity of radio, TV, and tabloids" (Keesey 141).

By chronicling Jack's journey to find ways to cope with his fear of death, *White Noise* represents America in the early 1980s as a nation which is thoroughly postmodern and dehistoricized. Since the 1960s, America has embraced late capitalism, "a new type of social life and a new economic order—what is often euphemistically called modernization, postindustrial or consumer society, the society of the media or the spectacle, or multinational capitalism" (Jameson, "Postmodernism and Consumer Society" 165-66). According to Fredric Jameson, the consumer society has the following features:

> A new kind of depthlessness, a weakening of historicity, the commodification of objects and humans alike [...] a globalized economy in which power has shifted from nation-states to huge conglomerates, and the penetration of capital into those enclaves—notably nature and the unconscious—that formerly had resisted economic colonization. "[G]lobal, yet American," as Jameson states, postmodern culture originates as "the internal and superstructural expression of a whole new wave of American military and economic domination throughout the world" but eventuates as a universal "dominant" so that even aesthetic production—of any kind and any place—has now become a form of commodity production. (Olster 80)

The society inhabited by the Gladneys is the consumer society defined by Jameson. In this society, Adolf Hitler and Elvis Presley, "icons free of their historical context" (ibid.), can become "nearly interchangeable figures in a culture of celebrity" (Duvall, Introduction 7) and "are impressed into academic service in exchange for high tuition payment" (Olster 80). There are full professors in the popular culture department who "read nothing but cereal boxes" (10). The college students, joined by "the language of economic class" (41), are more indulged in pleasure and fun than their books. The "College-on-the Hill" parodies the theocratic "City on a Hill" aspired by the early Puritans in the colonies who wished that their new community on the new continent would be a "city upon a hill," watched by the world. Americans have always used this potent metaphor to define their national identity. Now they use consumerism to define their national identity, believing that "they are a collection of the like-minded and the spiritually akin, a people, a nation" (4) bound by the shallow and quasi-religious commodity culture. In this nation where consumerism becomes a new religion, the tabloids are the spiritual food and the supermarket is the postmodern church. The television is "a primal force in the American home" (51) and, as DeLillo noticed after he came back from abroad in 1981, Americans were fascinated by TV disasters just as the characters in *White Noise* are.

Leonard Orr regards *White Noise* as a "realistic" novel (20), for its plot and characters have the exact look and feel of contemporary American reality. As Stacey Olster states, *White Noise* depicts the "(postmodern) way we live now" (79). It paints a picture of postmodern America which is media-saturated, technology-oriented, consumption-obsessed, and spirituality-deprived and presents the postmodern condition by taking up "the signs of our contemporaneity, things which seem to distinguish our time as different from the past" (Douglas 106). To conclude, *White Noise* is a chronicle of postmodern America in the early 1980s and a satire of the television-saturated and consumption-based culture.

II. *Mao* II

"The Future Belongs to Crowds"

As in *White Noise*, in *Mao* II DeLillo offers his insightful reflection on the American society in the late 20th century, in which individual identity sustains itself with increasing difficulty. Fear of the loss of self is DeLillo's concern when he observes the rampant consumerism in the postmodern society. Consumerism takes its toll on the wholeness of the individual personality. With the falling apart of the traditional community, new communities appear. People in these new communities are bound by consumerism and postmodern culture more than "formal liturgies or laws" (*White Noise* 2). Crowds and masses who are controlled by mass-media and are guided by the flickering images on the screens throng the object-centered supermarkets. Individuality is lost to the crowd. In the crowd there is no individual identity except the group identity. In *White Noise* DeLillo delineates crowds of consumers: college students with their parents on campus; visitors of the most photographed barn in America; evacuees in the camp; the shoppers in the supermarket; and crowds of people watching the postmodern sunsets. All such crowds "derive from the same totalitarian template" (Cowart, *Physics of Language* 120) as the crowds in Hitler's Germany did. DeLillo continues his exploration of the nature of crowds and their relation to personal and collective identity in *Mao* II. In this novel he depicts many kinds of crowds and asserts "the future belongs to the crowds" (16). By drawing on the historical events in 1989, DeLillo anatomizes the postmodern culture that breeds the mass appeals of celebrities and reveals how detrimental cult and crowds can be.

1. "When the Old God Leaves the World"

Mao II presents the postmodern world in which metanarratives are replaced by local and small narratives, as is claimed by Lyotard in his famous work *The Postmodern Condition: A Report on Knowledge*. In the postmodern condition he describes, there is an increasing skepticism toward the totalizing nature of "metanarratives," for example, Christianity. When the old beliefs decline, the world falls in pieces. In *Mao* II DeLillo portrays this chaotic and de-centered world as it is.

DeLillo asks through a narrator in *Mao* II: "When the Old God leaves the world, what happens to all the unexpected faith?" (7) America is a nation that was so rooted in Protestantism. But the late 20th century saw the loss of Christianity's monopoly in American society, leaving a void in people's spiritual life. With the decline of Christianity, American society falls apart. People lose their traditional bearings in life and are susceptible to any power that will give them the sense of belonging to a meaningful group and provide peace of mind and comfort when confronted with fear and death. In the postmodern society where consumerism is celebrated, the spiritual void that people experience is great. They desperately need something to meet the psychological and spiritual needs and to restore meaning to their lives. "When the Old

God goes, they pray to flies and bottle tops." (ibid.) In *Mao* II, DeLillo explores "the continuing mass appeal of fascist tyranny" (*White Noise* 25). As Hitler's Germany crowds dominated, in the late 20th century crowds dominated the TV news. Crowds feature heavily in *Mao* II, from the opening crowds of thousands at the mass-wedding at Yankee Stadium to the thousands of mourners at the Ayatollah's funeral as observed on television by Karen. The masses embrace a charismatic figure, confident in the idea that faith—in a person or a religion—can provide some comfort in the increasingly unstable world.

1.1 The Mass Wedding at Yankee Stadium

Like in *White Noise*, DeLillo starts *Mao* II with a crowd scene. In the prologue a mass wedding is being held at Yankee Stadium. "Six thousand five hundred couples" (4) get married on this day. The parents and relatives attend this grand ceremony. Rodge and his wife Maureen come to attend their daughter Karen's wedding. They are searching for Karen in the crowd, but it is extremely difficult for Rodge to spot her in this undifferentiated mass, even with his binoculars, "[t]he bridegrooms in identical blue suits, the brides in lace-and-satin gowns" (ibid.). The future of the world is in the hands of these young people just as the future of American society is in the hands of the college students in the College-on-the Hill in *White Noise*. "Here they come, marching into American sunlight" (3), telling the spectators "they are a collection of the like-minded and the spiritually akin" (*White Noise* 4). Faceless and anonymous, these crowds "derive from the same totalitarian template" (Cowart, *The Physics of Language* 120). In *White Noise* the individual identity is in crisis of dying while in the age of *Mao* II, "the individual has been supplanted by the mass mind" (Osteen 260). We cannot imagine what kind of future there will be if individuality in a society is all lost to totalitarianism.

In *Mao* II DeLillo portrays a similarly grim reality. In the late 1980s capitalist consumerism was not only rampant in America, but also began to affect other parts of the world, like the Middle East and the communist countries. It was the age of globalization. As critic Jameson claims, globalization is Americanization. According to some critics, "globalization is nothing more than the imposition of American culture on the entire world" (Ssenyonga). The most visible sign of globalization seems to be the spread of Coca Cola to nearly every country on the earth. In the streets of the war-torn Beirut in *Mao* II, there is an ad of Cola, or Cola II. On the other hand, in the American society, the declined Christianity is being replaced by new religions. The disoriented Americans need to put their "unexpended faith" (7) in a strong and powerful person who can protect them and give them a national identity, meaningful life and salvation. "The terrible thing is they follow the man because he gives them what they need. He answers their yearning, unburdens them of free will and independent thought" (ibid.). *Mao II* reveals DeLillo's concern about this totalitarian tendency in the American society.

The man who marries the 6,500 couples at Yankee Stadium in *Mao II* is the Reverend Sun Myung Moon, the Korean minister of the Unification Church. In the eyes of these young couples, Mr. Moon is "their true father, Master Moon" (6). The members of the Church are called Moonies. They put their faith in Master Moon and believe he can "lead them to the end of human history" (6) and to the eternity in the Last Days. Mr. Moon "lives in them like chains of matter that determine who they are" (ibid.). These young people come from "fifty countries, immunized against the language of self. They're forgetting who they are under their clothes … They stand and chant, fortified by the blood of numbers" (8). Chanting together with the Master at Yankee Stadium, they look happy and feel "intact, rayed with well-being" (ibid.). The Master has a complete control over the Moonies who are required to give up their possessions, parents, personal histories, and bodies and souls to follow him. To enforce total obedience, Moon uses brainwashing, thought control, and coercion. Let's take Karen for example. She is a young Moonie. He can enter her dreams to control her unconsciousness: "She does not dream anymore except about Master. They all dream about him. They see him in visions" (9). He controls his Moonies through match-making: "Master chooses every mate, seeing in a vision how backgrounds and characters match" (10). Karen is married to a Korean whom she met just two days before the wedding. "Fifteen minutes in a bare room and they're chain-linked for life" (5). The mass wedding makes the Moonies realize they are "a world family now, each marriage a channel to salvation" (10). After they get married, Master requires husband and wife to live separately, in different countries, "doing missionary work, extending the breadth of the body common" (ibid.). The Master instills in his children the idea that people "must sacrifice together" (8). Karen and her sisters have a shared past of sleeping in a van or crowded room and getting up early to sell flowers for their Master. These girls live a very tough life without freedom.

Moon starts a flower selling contest to drive the girls to attain the "monetary goal." He employs their labor "to forge a new economy of subjectivity and a new measure of value that nevertheless owes much to American consumerism and its fetishization of images." He is a "capitalist of faith. His aura is the reflected glow of money" (Osteen 196). Moon's imported religion, after having been adapted to

American environment and incorporated into the commodity culture, has become a powerful threat to individualism which has been viewed as one of the founding pillars of the United States.

1.2 Sun Myung Moon and the Unification Church in the United States

Master Moon in *Mao* II refers to Sun Myung Moon (1920—2012), who was a Korean religious leader. He founded the Unification Church in Korea in 1954. In the early 1960s Moon started to hold mass weddings pairing up strangers from different parts of the world. After he moved to the United States in 1971, Moon held mass weddings in some American cities. "The mass weddings look set to prove the enduring image of his organization" (Coonan). One of the most famous ceremonies was in Madison Square Garden in New York—the first held outside Korea. As a New Yorker, DeLillo must have heard about or read about it. For in an interview with William Leith, DeLillo revealed that a photo of a Unification Church mass wedding triggered his interest in Mr. Moon and promoted him to explore the Moon phenomenon in his fiction. The mass wedding ceremony at Yankee Stadium which is portrayed in the prologue of *Mao* II exemplifies the cult of Moon and the popularity of the Unification Church in the United States in the 1970s and 1980s. Moon was a controversial figure in the eyes of many Americans. He died at the age of 92, leaving behind "a vast business empire and a reputation tainted by accusations of brainwashing" (ibid.). The Unification Church owned the UPI wire service, the *Washington Times*, the swish New Yorker Hotel in midtown Manhattan, and a vast seafood distribution firm. His church was criticized for its greediness: it "too readily emptied the pockets of its members" (ibid.). Moon was put in prison for tax evasion. He was accused of brainwashing, torturing and beating in order to recruit and control his members. "Despite his sponsorship of state terror" (Kauffman, "The Wake of Terror" 36), his followers regarded him as their "true father."

The Moon phenomenon was part of the postmodern culture DeLillo has devoted his whole career to anatomizing. Stephen Greenblatt writes in his book *Renaissance Self-Fashioning*: "… the questions I ask of my material and indeed the very nature of this material are shaped by the questions I ask of myself" (5). DeLillo's consistent concern about the postmodern condition in American society is a major reason for his interest in Moon's mass weddings. He focuses on the social, political and cultural environments which breed and sustain the Moon phenomenon and on the harm that the phenomenon may cause to the society.

Moon had a cult following in the world, in America in particular. In the

1970s he had already become the best known Korean in the world. In the 1980s and beyond, Moon consolidated and expanded his influence. The Church says it has three million members. It held mass weddings which manifested the Moonies' intensity of love for the Master Moon. "To its critics the Unification Church is a dangerous cult" (Coonan). In the eyes of many Americans the Moonies were crazy people because they equated Moon to God. For their Master, their "true father", they "are willing to live on the road, sleep on the floor, crowd into vans and drive all night, fund-raising, serving Master … weeping through hours of fist-pounding prayer" (*Mao II* 9).

Why could the Unification Church be accepted, developed fast in the United States and spread to other countries in the 1980s? First, with the impact of consumerism, American traditional religion has declined since the 1960s. "When the Old God leaves, what happens to all the unexpended faith?" (*Mao II* 7) People spend their unexpended faith on a religious leader who can give them what they need and answer their yearning. The void left by the Old God needs to be filled with a new God who can give the followers "a supportive community that lends meaningful order to their lives" (Osteen 195) in the world which is in pieces. Many young people are attracted to Moon and regard him as their Master, who replaces the Old God in their lives. They readily put everything, including their possessions, freedom, marriage and self, in the control of their Master. They believed in every word uttered by Master and memorized every word of his teaching. Second, after he arrived in America, he launched a massive recruitment drive. He promoted himself "as a Divine Salesman or Capitalist of Faith" (ibid. 196). He presided over the mass weddings as if he were presiding over a company's pep rally. "He leads the chant. … He leads them out of past religion and history, thousands weeping now, all arms high. They are gripped by the force of a longing" (*Mao II* 16). He sent out many Moonies to work as missionaries in 50 states. He used brainwashing to recruit members and control the newly recruited members so that they became his staunch adherents who in turn helped him get more Moonies. He instilled in young people that they were living in the fallen world owned by Satan and that he was the "Lord of the Second Advent, the unriddling of many ills" (*Mao II* 15). Moon often proclaimed that he and his wife "are the True Parents of all humanity" and that they "are the Savior, the Lord of the Second Advent, the Messiah" (*Unification Church and Rev. Sun Myung Moon*). According to the Bible, they were heretical because they wanted to replace Jesus.

Another reason for Moon's popularity lies in the political environment of America. Moon was not just a religious leader. He was also a businessman and media mogul. He invested in hotels, restaurants, real estates and some other businesses. He bought *The Washington Times* in 1982, which was called "a three billion dollar propaganda organ for the Republican Party" (Kauffman 36). He supported the Republican President Nixon and was highly appreciated by Nixon. Moon found common ground with strongly anti-communist leaders of the 1980s, including United States President Ronald Reagan. The political views of *The Washington Times* are often described as conservative. Due to his connection to American political figures and his support to the anti-communist drive reinforced by the Republican Party, Moon consolidated and expanded his influence in the United States. In the 1980s the Unification Church flourished in America and spread to other parts of the world, especially the communist countries.

DeLillo chronicles the late 1980s' American reality in *Mao* II, satirizing the commodification of religion and the manipulation of mass media which are among his main concerns in his fiction. Moon was a postmodern icon. His image circulates via the mass media and is consumed like the image of Elvis Presley. He was a religious leader who "exploits the American entrepreneurial spirit" (Osteen 195) to expand his church. He was the Messiah "in a business suit" (*Mao* II 186). "Whoever controls your eyeballs runs the world" (*Underworld* 530). Moon understood the power of mass media which he used as his propaganda organ and the instrument of brainwashing. His disciples memorize every word of his teaching and repeat it to their audience. After having been brainwashed, Karen "had Master's voice total voice ready in her head" (ibid. 194). She goes to Tompkins Square Park in New York to preach Master's teaching to the homeless people. It is Master's speaking through Karen: "We will all be a single family soon. Because the day is coming. Because the total vision is being seen. ... Prepare the day. Be ready in your mind and heart. There is plan for all mankind" (193). Karen's repeating of Moon's words reminds me of Mink sitting in the motel room repeating the words from TV. Both Karen and Mink are brainwashed, which results in the loss of their individuality and independent thinking. Mink lives in the society of rampant consumerism, gets poisoned by TV culture and finally engulfed by white noise. He is Mr. Gray, a man without identity. Karen is also addicted to TV and likes to watch the current world news. In her life, images proliferate. It is an image-bound society, a world dominated by images. In today's world nothing happens until it is turned into an image and consumed. Our concept of the world all depends on the media.

2. "Nothing Happens Until It's Consumed"

Mao II presents us a media-saturated society where people heavily rely on the media version of the reality. Like in *White Noise*, Jack goes to the airport in Iron City to pick up his daughter, Bee. He hears a passenger narrate his panic experience of their plane losing power and almost crashing. Bee asks her father where the media is. Jack informs her there is no media in Iron City. Bee is disappointed and says: "They went through all that for nothing?" (92) A disaster is not a disaster until it is put on the media as a commodity and consumed by the viewers. The media representation has become more real than the reality itself in the society of media simulacra. Bill remarks on this phenomenon: "There's the life and there's the consumer event. Everything around us tends to channel our lives toward some final reality in print or on film. ... Nothing happens until it's consumed" (*Mao* II 44).

Mao II portrays a society which is oversaturated by images and spectacles. In this society people's life is surrounded by an immense accumulation of spectacles. Things that were once directly lived are now lived by proxy. This is "the society of the spectacle" put forward by Guy Debord in his 1967 book, *The Society of the Spectacle*. In its limited sense, spectacle means the mass media. Debord declares: "All that once was directly lived has become mere representation" (12). He argues that reality has turned into an immediate spectacle, a spectacle in which we perceive and experience reality directly through the media which constitutes one of the more influential new products of this society. Some synonyms for "the society of the spectacle" include "late capitalism," "multinational capitalism," "image society," "media capitalism," "the world system," even "postmodernism" itself (Felluga, "Modules on Jameson: On Late Capitalism"). Whatever name the society is labelled, in this society the medium of communication is the image, literacy is increasingly image- rather than print-oriented and the economy is increasingly dependent on the re-production and circulation of images. As a result, the spectacle is an important force driving globalization, in no small part because it erases regional distinctions in favor of a homogenous monoculture. Through the mediatization of society and culture, people become more and more dependent on the media's version of reality that is filled predominantly with capitalist values and are unconsciously incorporated into the capitalist ideology, losing the power to subvert the system which turns people into assembly line commodities.

2.1 Andy Warhol and American Society

The cover of *Mao* II is crowded with the images of Chairman Mao. It is a reproduction of "New Series 1972—1974," the famous silkscreen series of Chairman Mao done by Andy Warhol, an American pop artist. The novel depicts the exhibition of Andy Warhol's works at the Metropolitan Museum of Art in New York City in 1989. Scott, Bill Gray's admirer and assistant, visits the exhibition and finds "a room filled with images of Chairman Mao. Photocopy Mao, silk-screen Mao, wall-paper Mao, synthetic-polymer Mao. A series of silk screens was installed over a broader surface of wallpaper serigraphs, the Chairman's face a pansy purple here, floating nearly free of its photographic source" (21). He is attracted to the works that are "unwitting of history" and finds them "liberating" (ibid.). DeLillo's choice of Warhol's work for the cover manifests the major themes of *Mao* II.

Andy Warhol and his works represent the postmodern society which DeLillo depicts and anatomizes in *Mao* II.

Warhol was a leading American pop artist. He started as a commercial illustrator and was quite successful with his exhibitions in the 1960s. It was during the 1960s that Warhol began to make paintings of iconic American objects such as dollar bills, Coca-Cola bottles and celebrities such as Marilyn Monroe, Elvis Presley, Muhammad Ali and Elizabeth Taylor. His art involved many forms of media, including hand drawing, painting, printmaking, photography, silk screening, sculpture, film and music. In the 1980s Warhol repeated his critical and financial success of the 1960s. Warhol's works were both popular and controversial. He was attacked for "capitulating" to consumerism (ibid.) and criticized for becoming merely a "business artist" (ibid.). Some critics comment that Warhol's works "are produced cheaply to be sold dearly by an artist in the capitalistic capital of the world" (qtd. in Keesey 181). In spite of its superficiality, Warhol embraced popular culture which he thought stands for democracy and equality. This is how he summed up his career as an artist: "After I did the thing called 'art' or whatever it's called, I went into business art. I wanted to be an Art Businessman or a Business artist. ... [M]aking money is art and working is art and good business is the best art" (qtd. in Keesey 181). His works include some of the most expensive paintings ever sold.

Warhol's superficiality and commerciality can be viewed as the most brilliant mirror of his era, for Warhol captured something irresistible about the zeitgeist of American postmodern culture. He was a critical observer of American society. He found American values were altered and saw a chance to highlight how easily people are influenced by the media and pop culture. He was concerned with painting icons of the mass consuming, over-advertised, popular culture, and celebrities, and Campbell Soup Cans, Marilyn Monroe and Elvis Presley are representative of these kinds of items. His paintings expose Americans' attraction to consumerism and their fascination for sensational journalism. He was interested in fame and fascinated by the celebrity culture in American society. He found celebrity was the opiate of the masses. He coined the term "15 minutes of fame," which was insightful and to the point as the era was shifting to the society of spectacle. He noticed celebrity worship in the society and was eager to participate in it. President John Kennedy was the first TV president, young, handsome and charismatic. In the entertainment industry, Presley and Monroe were the king and queen. Their images circulated in the mass media and were worshipped by people. Warhol took these images and repeated them in his paintings as mass-produced commodities. And they sold well in the art market.

Warhol became synonymous with pop art and American postmodern culture. Pop artists celebrate popular culture in all of its forms. They approve of using mass media and mass production as an influence in their art. Pop art reflected the rise in wealth and the importance of owning things that America experienced since the late 1950s. Through his works Warhol subverted the traditional understanding of art. He played upon the increasing bombardment of advertising and media images. He not only painted the portraits of famous people, but also food cans supermarkets, car crashes, death and disasters. He painted the famous *Campbell Soup*, the soup produced by one of America's most popular food companies, Campbell's. The paintings looked like the same as if they came out of the same factory that made the soup cans. Warhol also made paintings using images such as Coca-Cola bottles, dollar symbols and popular cleaning products. "Indiscriminately appropriating everything from the Old Masters to Brillo boxes, Warhol erases the distinction between high and popular culture, showing how art is anything packaged as such" (Osteen 199). He often repeated the same image many times in one artwork. He liked the idea of mass-produced art, the idea which retracts the individuality of the artist. He once said that he thought everyone should think alike and be like a machine. He set up his studio which he called "Factory" which turned out mass-produced visual commodities in artwork. Warhol conceived the idea, and an assistant—a "worker" in his factory—carried it out. His idea of art is opposed to that of Bill Gray, the arch-individualist in *Mao* II, and also opposed to DeLillo's view of art.

In 1989 Warhol's works were exhibited in the Metropolitan Museum of Art in New York City. The highlight of the exhibition was the portraits of famous personalities. Images of the political figures like John F. Kennedy, Jimmy Carter, Ronald Reagan, Queen Elizabeth II, Mao Zedong, Gorbachev, among others hung side-by-side with the icons of Marilyn Monroe, Elvis Presley. Warhol's images of these powerful personalities comment on the interrelationships between politics and celebrity culture in the late 20th century, blurring the boundaries between art and popular culture. Warhol pictured these celebrities in his graphic style which likened them to commercial products like Campbell's soup and Coca-Cola. In so doing, Warhol connected his images of these famous people to America's fascination and consumption of all aspects of contemporary culture. His depictions of John F. Kennedy, Mao Zedong, Queen Elizabeth II, and others were derived from widely circulated official or media photographs. Warhol's appropriation of these stock images signaled his interest in how political leaders ascended to celebrity status as a result of their constant representation in the media.

Warhol rose to fame in the 1960s and regained popularity in the 1980s, which was an image-driven and increasingly materialistic decade. Warhol's paintings of food cans and portraits of celebrities appealed to American mentality in this decade. Warhol himself had become a celebrity and iconic figure in American culture and embodied the spirit of the era which was dominated by postmodern pastiche, images and spectacle. The Americans saw many fundamental changes in their standard of living in the 1980s. One major change was the new, expanded role of television. Cable Television, available in the 1970s, became standard for most American households. This transformation ushered in a whole host of new programming. The Americans could catch up with the news at any time by watching CNN. President Reagan's two terms brought a growing economy and an upsurge in American consumerism. DeLillo's *White Noise*, *Libra* and *Mao II* all depict this culture dominated by rampant consumerism and mass media spectacles. So from this perspective these novels give realistic portrayals of the postmodern American society based on the production and consumption of images, commodities and staged events.

Both Warhol and DeLillo are exemplary postmodernists whose works mirror the zeitgeist of the postmodern society they lived in. They broke down the barriers between art and popular culture. Both had media working experience. They were familiar with media culture and drew on the materials in it. The media and advertising were favorite subjects for Warhol's celebrations of the consumer society. Warhol loved all forms of daily media and collected various newspapers, magazines and supermarket tabloids. He recognized the power of mass-circulated media images in American culture and appropriated these as source material for his artwork. Warhol not only painted the coke, Campbell's soup cans, and the supermarket which sells them, but also the celebrities. He not only painted the stars in the entertainment industry, but also political figures. He not only painted Queen Elizabeth, President

John Kennedy, and President Reagan, the political leaders in the capitalist countries, but also painted Mao Zedong, the Communist "dictator" in the eyes of the Westerners. The multiple images of Chairman Mao are juxtaposed with the images of President Reagan and the food cans on the wallpaper. Like the daily objects sold in the supermarket, people, regardless of beliefs and political leanings, are all turned into images—the major commodities in the media society. As commodities, the images are duplicated and repeated, thus lose their uniqueness and individuality, which mirrors the repetition evident in society through media and technology.

Warhol represented American culture which was becoming postmodern. His artistic practice reflects American culture and documents significant socio-cultural events of the 20th century. In the same way, DeLillo's novels like *White Noise* and *Mao II* "have a way of representing our lives that feels very immediate, very authentic, very sharp" and are "veritable textbooks of cultural commentary" (Bloom, "The Terrifying World of *Mao II*") of the late 20th century. DeLillo's fictional world is fragmented, "cluttered by the swarming of information and the numbing detritus of postmodernity" (ibid.). DeLillo chose Warhol's work of Mao Zedong's portrait for the cover of *Mao II*. The title of the book also refers to this series of Mao's image that perversely strips the photograph of all meaning. The book has a fixation with the image; fragmented streams of visual information engulf its characters with a crushing weight. They are spectators to disasters, but disasters as "channeled through satellite and contained behind monitor. DeLillo's prose lingers coldly over the incongruous distance between people and this hyperreality of terror" (ibid.). In my view, in *Mao II* DeLillo sounds like Jean Baudrillard, commenting on the increasing dominance of technologies of mass mediation; and the role of globalized consumerism in reshaping the world, a world that responds only to the acts of terrorists or to the daily image bombardment of popular culture.

2.2 "Whoever Controls Your Eyeballs Runs the World"

The mass media plays a tremendous role in the American society of the late 20th century. The characters in *Mao II* are bombarded by visual images every day. The opening scene is a mass marriage of 6500 couples performed by Reverend Moon at the Yankee Stadium. There is massive media coverage of this spectacular event. Thousands of people, standing everywhere in the stadium, take pictures. "There may be as many people taking pictures as there are brides and grooms. … They're here but also there, already in the albums and slide projectors, filling picture frames with their microcosmic bodies, the manikin selves they are trying to become" (10). Karen, one of the Moonie brides, knows that their pictures will be put in the family albums, appear in the newspapers, and be showed and watched on TV. This is the society of the spectacle. "There's the life and there's the consumer event. Everything around us tends to channel our lives toward some final reality in print or on film. … Nothing happens until it's consumed" (44).

As mentioned before, the cover of the Penguin *Mao* II is decorated with 32 Mao's portraits, a reproduction of Warhol's famous series of Mao Zedong's portrait. Warhol based his portrait on a photograph of Mao which appeared in a newspaper. Mao Zedong, "a man who is immersed in wars and revolutions becomes a sort of icon painted on a flat surface" (Nadotti 118). The image is repeated many times and there are no distinctions between the images. And "when the images are identical to each other, consumerism and the mass production of art in their most explicit form take over" (ibid.). The images of Chairman Mao are mass produced and consumed as commodities sold in art markets, exhibited in museums, and taken as an example of postmodern culture. Warhol's portrait of Chairman Mao was created in 1973. A year before President Nixon paid his ice-breaking visit to China which was mysterious and exotic in the eyes of the Westerners. Though liberated from history, "beyond parody, homage, comment and appropriation" (134), this series of Mao's portrait attracted the public attention and sold well in the market, for some political and historical reasons. In 1989 Warhol's works including Mao's portrait were exhibited in New York, in the summer when the whole world focused its attention on China, due to the students' parade in the Tian'anmen Square. Many people went to visit Warhol's exhibition. *Mao* II makes references to this exhibition. In the beginning of the first chapter, Bill's assistant Scott visits the exhibition. "The museum lobby was crowded" (20). In the museum Scott purchases some pencils with Mao's image on them and later gives them to Karen as souvenirs. Brita, photographer in the novel, also visits the exhibition where Warhol himself is turned into images on exhibition and consumed by the audience:

> Andy's image on canvas, Masonite, velvet, paper-and-acetate, Andy in metallic paint, silk-screen ink, pencil, polymer, gold leaf, Andy in wood, metal, vinyl, cotton-and-polyester, painted bronze, Andy on postcards and paper bags, in photomosaic, multiple exposures, dye transfers, Polaroid prints. Andy's shooting scar, Andy's factory, Andy's tourist-posing in Beijing before the giant portrait of Mao in the main square. […] He was all here now, reprocessed through painted chains of being, peering out over the crowd from a pair of burnished Russian eyes. (135)

Andy Warhol's life, works and career all become commodities. His own images and his creations of the celebrities' portraits are transformed into consumable spectacles.

In the society of the spectacle the images dominate, as DeLillo, in the voice of Bill, states, "In our world we sleep and eat the image and pray to it and wear it too" (36). It is a fact that every day people are bombarded by media images which help shape the personal identity and the cultural identity. In an interview DeLillo says that we are in the age of images and "I don't think any attempt to understand the way we live and the way we think and the way we feel about ourselves can proceed without a deep consideration of the power of image" (qtd. in Howard). In this regard DeLillo, Warhol and Jean Baudrillard share the same view: The image has replaced the reality in the postmodern age. According to Baudrillard, what has happened in postmodern culture is that the postmodern society has become so reliant on models and maps that people have lost all contact with the real world that precedes the map. Reality itself has begun merely to imitate the model, which now precedes and determines the real world. To explain this loss of distinctions between reality and simulacrum, Baudrillard points to a number of phenomena among which are media culture and ideology. Mass media (television, film, magazines, billboards, the Internet) are concerned not just with providing information or stories "but with interpreting our most private selves for us, making us approach each other and the world through the lens of these media images" (Felluga, "Modules on Baudrillard: On Simulation"). Baudrillard also points out that postmodernism understands ideology as the support for people's very perception of reality. "There is no outside of ideology ... Because we are so reliant on language to structure our perceptions, any representation of reality is always already ideological, always already constructed by simulacra" (ibid.).

In the media society, people depend upon the visual images to apprehend the world. They watch TV news to be informed of what has happened in the world. Karen is a TV-poisoned deprogrammed Moonie. At night she watches the news on TV, often with the volume turning off. "On any given day it was mainly the film footage she wanted to see and she didn't mind watching without sound" (32). The images matter most to her. The TV news is full of disasters and violence, as Bill insightfully remarks: "News of disaster is the only narrative people need" (42). Information overload has numbed the audience. Only the most shocking images can arouse their interest. One night Karen watches the news footage of a football disaster which took place on April 15, 1989 at the Hillsborough Stadium in Sheffield, England. The crush resulted in the deaths of 96 people and injuries to 766 others. The incident ranked as the worst stadium-related disaster in British history and one of the world's worst football disasters. The sufferings, torture, agony and pain were filmed in great detail and were presented to the audience:

> There are bodies packed solid, filling the screen, and people barely moving at the fence, pressed and forced into one twisted position. [...] they are writhing and twisted with open mouths and bloated tongues showing. [...] She sees people caught in strangleholds of no intent, arms upflung, faces popping out at her, hands trying to reach the fence but only floating in the air, a man's large hand, a long-haired boy in a denim shirt with his back to the fence [...] (33-34)

The news of the disaster seems to be presented in a neutral and objective way. The reporters behind the camera manifest their aloofness and their so-called professional ethics, standing just outside the fence shooting straight in through the heavy-gauge steel wire so that the media can provide the viewers, who are obsessed with disaster news and novelty, with the eye-catching "naked" truth.

But there is no so-called "naked truth." As Hayden White claims, any representation of reality is always already ideological. The news images in *Mao* II confirm White's view. Each section of *Mao* II is preceded by a photograph: a rally in Beijing, a mass Moonie wedding, the tortured crowd on the terraces at Hillsborough Stadium in England, Khomeini's funeral, the cracked streets in war-torn Beirut. "A photograph is a still, fixed representation of a fragment of reality, a slice of reality that shows objects frozen, instead of naturally moving" (Riepe 11). Visual images can be regarded as texts. According to New Historicism, "all texts are ideologically marked" (Montrose 22). The photographs included in *Mao* II are marked by the western ideology. Except the picture of Hillsborough football disaster, all the other pictures were taken in Asia and the Mid-East: The picture of the Moonie mass marriage was taken in Korea, the picture of the students' rally at the Tian'anmen Square taken in Beijing, China, the picture of the Ayatollah Khomeini funeral in Iran, and the picture of the cracked streets with kid soldiers in Beirut. Those pictures portray the Christian cult, Chinese Communism, Islamic fundamentalism and Maoist terrorism in Beirut. The Western media demonized Chairman Mao, Ayatollah Ruhollah Khomeini, and the Maoist leader in Beirut as authoritarians or tyrants for the mind control and tyranny. But they treated Reverend Moon differently for Moon was one of them ideologically, though physically he belonged to the Oriental, the "Other." Chairman Mao and Ayatollah Ruhollah Khomeini, who was an Islamic leader who issued a fatwa calling for the assassination of Salman Rushdie in early 1989, were obviously the "Other" in the eyes of the Westerners. In Part Two of *Mao* II, Karen is watching the world news at night which includes a news report on the death of Khomeini, who died on June 3, 1989. The news coverage of his frenzied funeral on TV reveals the media's perspective of Orientalism. The American media represents Khomeini's funeral as a black comedy, a farce, a consumable media event.

The final section of *Mao II* is titled "In Beirut." Beirut may be seen through the eyes of Brita, a photographer, who is in Beirut on assignment for a German magazine to photograph a local leader named Abu Rashdi. Beirut is a war-torn city, witnessing many years' military conflicts and political turmoil which lasted from 1975 to 1990. In history, the government of Lebanon had been dominated by Maronite Christians since the state was founded by France as its colony in the Mid-East. However, the country had a large Muslim population and many pan-Arabist and Left Wing groups which opposed the pro-Western government. The establishment of the state of Israel and the displacement of a hundred thousand Palestinian refugees to Lebanon changed the demographic balance in favor of the Muslim population. In the Cold War Maronites sided with the West while Left Wing and pan-Arab groups sided with Soviet-aligned Arab countries. Due to America's support of the pro-West groups in Lebanon, the Reagan Administration witnessed terrorist attacks against American and Western interests in the Mid-East. The Taif Agreement of 1989 marked the beginning of the end of the fighting. In *Mao II* Beirut is represented as a home of violence and terrorism, as is demonstrated by the three stories told by Brita's driver:

> First one, people are burning tires. In the midst of car bombs and street skirmishes and the smash of long-range field guns and buildings coming down and whole area lost in smoke, people are burning tires to drive away mosquitoes and flies.
> Second, a pair of local militias are firing at portraits of each other's leader. These are large photographs pasted to walls or hanging from awning poles in the vegetable souks [...] and they are shot up and quickly replaced and then ripped apart again. [...]
> Last, they are making bombs that contain flooring nails and roofing nails. The police are finding quantities of common nails, nails sprayed and dashed and driven into the bodies of victims of random blasts. (227)

Brita has become tired of this kind of stories because there are too many such stories in media. "They're all the same and all true" (228). Beirut has become a battlefield and a hellish place to live. There is bad hygiene, violence and poverty. The bombing and street fighting resulted in casualties every day. In the shot-up streets "weeds and wild hibiscus crowd out of alleyways and the women wear headscarves and stand on line, long lines everywhere for food, drinking water, bedding and clothing" (ibid.). The images become the language by which they describe the reality, the languae of Orientalism and global capitalism, identifying the East with religious cults, terrorism and other amorphous sources of evil.

All the events narrated by those pictures took place in 1989, the year when the Berlin Wall collapsed. Owing to these two characteristics: the historical references and the characters, who serve as the doubles of the author, making comments on them, *Mao* II can be regarded as a postmodern novel termed by Linda Hutcheon as "historigraphic metafiction," a form of novel which "intentionally and self-consciously blurs the boundary between history and fiction" (Duvall, "The Power of History and the Persistence of Mystery" 3). The novel's blend of recent history and fiction "creates an art with the potential to comment critically on the culture of which it is nevertheless inescapably a part" (ibid.). DeLillo, who is a prophet as well as a chronicler of American history, predicts the end of the Cold War and warns of two effects of globalization: authoritarianism and terrorism.

Globalization increased its speed of development in the 1980s which was called the age of Reagan. It was eight years of rampant consumerism and witnessed a restoration of prosperity in the United States. At the end of the Reagan Administration, American society was completely colonized by consumerism. With the renewed national strength and self-confidence, America made its influence felt more strongly in the world. With the weakening and collapse of the Soviet Union, the United States has become the only superpower. It dominates through the mass media and consumer culture as well as the economic and military hegemony. Globalization was predominantly driven by the outward flow of culture and economic activity from the United States and was better understood as Americanization or Westernization. For example, one of the most successful global beverages, Coca-Cola is often cited as an example of globalization and Americanization.

Mao II represents the quick development of globalization. In Beirut, Brita is surprised to find this war-torn city should be dominated by images so much so that Brita thinks it is "a millennial image mill" (229). The streets run with images. Brita finds "cigarette vendor's Marlboro cartons, movie posters, and posters of bare-chested men with oversized weapons," (ibid.) and "signs for a new soft drink, Coke II" (230). Like the images in Warhol's works, the Coke logo is mechanically reproduced in a series, hence Coke II in Beirut. Coke is a symbol of American culture. Coke II represents the invasion of American culture in Beirut and the penetration of consumerism in the society. Its juxtaposition with the images of Marlboro, Khomeini and the Lebanese soldiers recalls Warhol's work exhibition. The "image mill" is like Warhol's factory. Images proliferate in Beirut just as they do in American society. They mediate the reality and narrate the Lebanese history through the visual language. The tragedy that Beirut is going through is transformed into images and spectacles and becomes world news which the Western audience watch. The image proliferation affects people's conception of the world. When on a certain street, Americans find there are water-main breaks and steam-pipe explosions, asbestos flying everywhere, mud propelling from "caved-in pavement," they will keep saying: "It's just like Beirut, it looks like Beirut" (146, 173, 174), which almost becomes a refrain of the novel. The reality is beginning to imitate the media representations which have had impact on the viewers' consciousness and changed their perception of the world. Beirut has become a synonym of violence, chaos, poverty, and terrorism to the Westerners who were bombarded daily by the mass media's representations of Beirut as an "Other" for a decade.

Globalization met fierce resistance from Islamic fundamentalists in the Middle East, for they saw globalization as Americanization and Americanization as hegemony, as an invasion of the Islamic culture and countries. They attributed their problems to America and attacked it, as is analyzed by DeLillo in his essay "In the Ruins of the Future": "It was America that drew their fury. It was the high gloss of our modernity. It was the thrust of our technology. It was our perceived godlessness. It was the blunt force of our foreign policy. It was the power of American culture to penetrate every wall, home, life and mind." The Islamic extremists thought they had no equal footing for dialogues with the West. When they spoke, the Westerners would not listen. So they resorted to terrorism, like taking hostage of and bombing the innocent people, to achieve their goals. In *Mao II* the terrorists carried out explosions in London and took hostage of a Swiss poet and a UN worker to attain their political goals. I do not agree with John McClure who accuses DeLillo of Orientalism in his *Late Imperial Romance*. He argues that DeLillo is "a novelist who both questions and rejects the premises of Western imperialism in the twentieth century but who also declines to endorse or even to recognize the struggle of its victims" (Ruppersburg and Engles 15). In *Mao II*, the victims of Western imperialism not only include the people in Beirut who suffer from the domestic war but also the Western people like the unknown poet who had been helping the war victims when he was taken hostage. DeLillo does not endorse the victims' employment of violence for whatever reasons, which in my view is not Orientalism by any means. By portraying the Muslim wedding at the end of the novel, DeLillo expresses his hope for a peaceful Beirut in the future.

DeLillo has been committed to the critique of authoritarian thinking. *Mao* Ⅱ expresses his concern about the authoritarian tendency in postmodern American society. The crowds feature in the novel: the Moonies at the mass wedding, the students in the Tian'anmen Square, Shiites mourning the death of Khomeini, the soccer fans in the Hillsborough Stadium, Abu Rashdie's boys, the mass-market readers, exemplifying the global forces which threaten individuality. DeLillo juxtaposes the crowds with different religions, from different social systems and areas: Christianity, Islamism, Communism, Capitalism, the West and the East. But in his eyes, those crowds, in spite of their different backgrounds, are not different from each other: faceless and anonymous. In Cowart's words, "all such crowds derive from the same totalitarian template" (*The Physics of Language* 120). Through the use of the mind control, the Reverend Moon, Abu Rashdie, Khomeini and capitalism incorporate the individuals into religions. The individuals lose the self and passively follow their charismatic leaders. They lose individuality and independent thinking; hence the crowds like the Moonies and Abu Rashdie's murderous followers. A type of crowd—consumers in the postmodern American society—has caused DeLillo's great concern. The crowd consists of Americans like Karen and Scott. Karen worships Master Moon; Scott admires Bill Gray. Their desire to lose the self in the personality of the charismatic leaders does not collide with the desire to consume. They are all consumers of images. In consuming the commodities of images, the Americans are transformed into "xerox copies," mass-produced, without individuality, like the reproduced images of Chairman Mao on the cover of *Mao* Ⅱ.

Capitalist consumerism is so powerful that it incorporates everything. Not only material objects but humans are also turned into commodities. Even the "aesthetic production—of any kind and any place—has now become a form of commodity production" (Olster, "*White Noise*" 80). This is the postmodern culture DeLillo has been exploring and commenting on through his works. In *Mao* Ⅱ the protagonist Bill Gray meditates on this culture: "Everything around us tends to channel our lives toward some final reality in print or in film. ... Everything seeks its own heightened version. Nothing happens until it's consumed" (43-44). Life or death, love or disaster, the media can turn it into an image, a consumable commodity, and by repeating it, influence and even change the viewer's perception of the world. Thus Guy Debord asserts: "The society of the spectacle does not dominate ... solely through the exercise of economic hegemony. It also dominates ... in its capacity as the society of the spectacles." (qtd. in Olster, "*White Noise*" 80) As DeLillo writes in *Underworld*. "Whoever controls your eyeballs runs the world" (530).

In his works DeLillo depicts the increasing influence of mass media in shaping the individual identity and the cultural identity and shows his concern with its relation to terrorism. With the deepening of globalization, the Reagan eighties witnessed the powerful penetration of American culture into the communist countries and the Mid-East as well as the permeating hegemony of the global capital over the world culture. Baudrillard writes in his essay "The Spirit of Terrorism": "When the world has been so thoroughly monopolized, when power has been so formidably consolidated by the technocratic machine and the dogma of globalization, what means of turning the table remains besides terrorism?" (14) According to Gabriel Weimann and Conrad Winn, terrorism involves three major elements: "the use of violence or its threat toward some political end; the transgression of accepted rules or humanitarian conduct; and the use of publicity, along with surprise or unpredictability, to generate fear" (qtd. in Osteen, *American Magic and Dread* 206). For their political purposes, the terrorists take hostages, kill people and destroy buildings. Also they employ the mass media to publicize their political visions and acts of violence to make raids on human consciousness. Like Bill Gray in *Mao II*, DeLillo thinks that novelists are connected to terrorists in a certain way. The power of the novelists to "alter the inner life of a culture" (41) is usurped by the terrorists who understand the mechanism of the society of the spectacle and thus are able to influence the mass consciousness.

3. "Novelists and Terrorists Are Playing a Zero-Sum Game"

Mao II discusses an artist's role in the media-saturated society through the portrayals of the novelist Bill Gray, an unknown Swiss poet, and the photographer Brita Nilsson, and explores the global forces which have caused the novelist's weakened position in the world.

3.1 The Novelist's Position in the Postmodern World

Two events caused DeLillo's concern over the novelist's position in the contemporary world and inspired him to write the novel. One event concerned Salman Rushdie. On Feburary 14, 1989, the Iranian government decided to impose a fatwa upon Rushdie for his *The Satanic Verses*. Ayatollah Ruhollah Khomeini condemned Rushdie to death for blaspheming Islam in his novel and called on Muslims to hunt for and kill Rushdie anywhere and anytime. The controversy caused much violence and even death. Copies of *The Satanic Verses* were burnt in Britain, Iran and some other places. It was an enormous political and media event that threatened to swallow up

Rushdie. DeLillo was one of a group of writers who came out in support of Rushdie, reading from the book in New York City, in the tumultuous days just after the fatwa was issued. Five years later, in 1994, DeLillo and another writer Paul Auster wrote a pamphlet in an effort to raise awareness about the plight of Rushdie who was still under the death threat. Though *Mao* II contains no direct references to the Rushdie event, Gerald Howard suggests that *Mao* II can be read as an engagement with Rushdie's plight: "I think this is a book that's about Salman Rushdie in a way. Don was very upset about the Rushdie Business, and I think you can sense that feeling of threat all the way through *Mao* II" (qtd. in Passaro 84). In the interview with Passaro, DeLillo admits that *Mao* II bears some connection to Rushdie's situation: "It's the connection between the writer as the champion of the self, and those forces that are threatened by this. Such totalitarian movements can be seen in miniature in the very kind of situation Rushdie is in. He's a hostage" (ibid.). Rushdie was not the only hostage taken by totalitarian regimes and political religion. Writers are always seen as oppositional forces to the state, the government and the status quo, which explains why some writers are persecuted, and even put in prison. In *Mao* II a poet is taken hostage by the totalitarian Abu Rashdie. Bill Gray is also a hostage. He is held hostage by the celebrity culture which threatens individualism.

The other event which triggered DeLillo's concern over the writer's situation and provided him an inspiration for the novel is J. D. Salinger's photo event. In the summer of 1988, DeLillo came across a photograph of Salinger which appeared on the front page of *The New York Post*. The newspaper had sent two photographers to New Hampshire where Salinger lived, to stalk him. "It took them six days, but they found him. And they took his picture. … When they took his picture, he came at them. His face is an emblem of shock and rage. It's a frightening photograph" (qtd. in Passaro 80-81). *Mao* II makes a direct reference to this photo event through Bill's comment:

> The image world is corrupt, here is a man who hides his face. […] People may be intrigued by this figure but they also resent him and mock him and want to dirty him up and watch his face distort in shock and fear when the concealed photographer leaps out of the trees. In a mosque, no images. In our world we sleep and eat the image and pray to it and wear it too. The writer who won't show his face is encroaching on holy turf. He's playing God's own trick. (36-37)

In my opinion, Bill is modelled on Salinger as far as his reclusiveness is concerned. Both Bill and Salinger are famous reclusive novelists. It has been 30 years since Bill's picture appeared in the media. He has done all he can to keep others from invading his privacy, which is also true of Salinger. Both try their best to escape from the celebrity culture. Besides, there is another parallel between them. Bill has not published anything for 23 years. Salinger had not published fiction since 1966, that is, for 23 years to 1989 when DeLillo wrote *Mao II*. However, they are strangely at the height of their fame. Their books have become modern classics and sell well in bookstores. Their celebrity status is maintained by their mystery which arouses the curiosity of the public and is used as a marketing strategy to sell their books. It is ironic for Bill, or a Bill-like writer, who remains in reclusion in order to escape from the influence of the society which transforms everything into a spectacle, to end up as a commodity himself, subject to the manipulation of the publishers and "the machinations of Scott Martineau—his fan, factotum, and finally captor" (Osteen, "DeLillo's Dedalian Artists" 140).

Bill realizes his failure to resist the incorporation by capitalist consumerism and decides to go out of hiding into the world of media consumption and political violence. He accepts the invitation of Charlie Everson, his publisher and "chairman of high-minded committee on free expression" (98), to show up and participate in a reading in London which is to be organized for the release of a Swiss poet, a young man held hostage by the terrorist Abu Rashdie in Beirut. Why does Charlie choose Bill to do this job? Because Bill is an iconic figure in American society. There will be cameras and journalists in the meeting. Bill's presence will be a big spectacle and produce a profound influence on the Western society which will form pressure on the hostage-takers. As soon as the image of the famous writer addressing the suffering of the young unknown poet appears on live television, Charlie promises, the terrorists in Beirut, because of the pressure from the Western media, will set the hostages free. But the terrorists will not allow the reading to take place. A bomb explosion cancels the meeting. Bill is advised to go back to America. But he decides not to go home. He meets George Haddad, spokesman of a terrorist group in Beirut, who lures Bill to travel to Athens where the terrorists will have a press conference. George tells Bill if in the conference Bill makes a statement supporting their career, the young hostage will be freed. But the terrorists change their plan. They plan to take Bill hostage in place of the poet in Athens or Beirut, which will catch instantaneous worldwide attention. Bill asks George what if he gets aboard a plane right now and goes home instead of following their plan. George tells him that they will kill the young hostage. They will also photograph his corpse and the picture will appear in the media, which will terrorize the public, and make their presence felt by the Western society. So Bill decides to go to Beirut to save the hostage although it is fatally dangerous. He hopes "to return a meaning that had been lost to the world" (200) by his act. Bill believes that "when the terrorists inflict punishment on someone who is not guilty, when they fill rooms with innocent victims, they begin to empty the world of meaning" (ibid.). He will meet the terrorist leader Abu Rashdie face to face and declare himself a threat to terrorism. Just before he goes to Beirut, Bill is hit by a car in London. On the ferry to Beirut, he dies from the injury to his side. A cleaning man takes away his passport, "and other forms of identification, anything with a name and a number, which he could sell to some militia in Beirut" (217). When alive, he is a famous recluse, hiding from the media and his fans and living in reclusion to keep his individuality. Now dead, he joins the crowd of the dead and becomes an anonymous corpse. All his life Bill resists commodification and incorporation. His resistance fails. Before he goes to London, he agrees to let Brita photograph him after 30 years of disappearance from the public. His books and pictures are commodities like any others. After he dies, the passport with his image on it will become a commodity and be sold to the terrorists, which may become a spectacular news story in the Western media.

Through the fictional novelist Bill Gray, DeLillo deplores the loss of writers' power to have impact on the society and its people. In Bill's opinion, the writer "belongs at the far margin" of the society, "doing dangerous things" (97) to "alter the inner life of the culture" (41). Many years ago Beckett and Mailer were able to make raids on human consciousness. Now writers have been incorporated by the consumer society and become commodities, losing the power to shape and influence. "Now bomb-makers and gunmen have taken that territory" (ibid.). He says to George Haddad, a political scientist whom he meets in London: "For some time now I've had the feeling that novelists and terrorists are playing a zero-sum game" (156). He explains why he thinks so: "What terrorists gain, novelists lose. The degree to which they influence mass consciousness is the extent of our decline as shapers of sensibility and thought. The danger they represent equals our own failure to be dangerous" (157).

Mao II reveals DeLillo's concern of the writer's fate in the contemporary world and expresses "its author's mid-career doubts about the effectiveness of fiction in a world largely given over to the electronic media" (Keesey 177). According to DeLillo, the world, which Bill enters and which DeLillo lived in when he wrote *Mao* II, has become

> a book—more precisely a news story or television show or piece of film footage. And the world narrative is being written by men who orchestrate disastrous events, by military leaders,

> totalitarian leaders, terrorists, men dazed by power. World news is the novel people want to read. It carries the tragic narrative that used to belong to the novel. (qtd. in Begley 101)

It was "a world that responds only to the acts of terrorists or to the daily image bombardment of popular culture" (Cowart 116). Many people who used to read novels have become the consumers of the spectacular images and fall to the attraction of media news. The readership of long and serious novels keeps decreasing year by year. The situation which Rushdie and Salinger encountered shocked DeLillo into awakening to the plight of novelists in the world increasingly dominated by media images. In the novel, DeLillo's double, Bill, says to Brita: "In the West we become famous effigies as our books lose the power to shape and influence." (41) Another famous American novelist Philip Roth echoes DeLillo's concern over the status of the novel in the digital era in an interview: the novel has declined into an object of mere "cultic" interest (Raab). Novels are marginalized and lose the power to alter the consciousness of the people. They have been replaced by the news with the help of advanced communication technologies which enable the media to document terror and highlight the plight of the victims but in doing so, offer more opportunities to perpetuate terror. Novelists have been incorporated and silenced by the commodity culture. They lose their individuality and independent thinking. They become commodities, just as Bill tells Brita that he is nothing more than "someone's material" (43). The writer ceases to have importance for his society and its collective consciousness and can no longer pose a threat to the forces that turn him and the books he writes into commodities and reduce the individual into mass consciousness.

Terrorism is a ubiquitous presence in the world of *Mao II*: the terrorist-haunted London; the terrorist-haunted Athens; and the terrorist-thronged Middle East. Indeed in history, international terrorism abounded in the late 20th century and became "the new tragic narrative" (157) of the world. According to RAND, "[t]hroughout the 1980s, terrorism increased throughout the world and also became increasingly bloody" (Gardela and Hoffman). Especially in 1988, right before DeLillo began to compose *Mao II*, international terrorist activities increased. Terrorists killed more people in 1988 than in any year since 1985. A case in point is the notorious Luckerbie plane crash in 1988 which killed 270 people. A long-standing pattern evident in 1988 was "the preponderance of terrorist attacks on American targets" (ibid.). The terrorists "see symbolic value inherent in any blow struck against U. S. 'expansionism,' 'imperialism,' or 'economic exploitation'." They want to employ the American news media, the world's most extensive, to present "unparalleled" opportunities for exposure and publicity (ibid.). Due to the media's coverage of the terrorist acts, terrorism is able to cause fear as well as the immediate physical damage to the victims. "The motives of all terrorists are political." (ibid.) DeLillo points out in *Mao* II, the terrorist groups "are backed by repressive governments. They're perfect little totalitarian states. They carry the old wild-eyed vision, total destruction and total order" (158).

Bombing is the way most used by terrorists. There are many references to terrorist bombings in *Mao* II. Terrorists can enter a code in Brussels and "blow up a building in Madrid" (91). They can put a bomb in a passenger plane and explode it, killing hundreds of people. With the mass media in compliance, the terrorists have succeeded in causing fear and intimidating. People are worried about terrorist attacks when they travel by plane. Brita, who has to travel all over the world to take pictures, reveals her fear by this remark: "Yes, I travel. Which means there is no moment on certain days when I'm not thinking terror" (40-41). For her, the terrorists "have us in their power" (40). For Bill, what is more threatening and irritating is not that he can be physically harmed by the terrorist acts, but that the terrorists usurp the power of writers to shape the way people think and see. In his opinion, the major influential work which is able to make raids on human consciousness "involves midair explosions and crumbled buildings" (157). The terrorist spectacles of violence are able to capture people's imagination in a way his literary work can no longer. The only narrative which people need now is the addictive news of disasters.

3.2 "Make Raids on Human Consciousness"

Bill Gray's death symbolizes the loss of the writer's power to shape and influence in the postmodern society. Bill tells Brita: "Years ago I used to think it was possible for a novelist to alter the inner life of the culture. Now the bomb-makers and gunmen have taken that territory. They make raids on human consciousness, What writers used to do before we were incorporated." (41) Indeed, the writers' power to shape and influence is inconsequential in societies "reduced to blur and glut" where "terror is the only meaningful act" (157). According to George, only the terrorists, the "lethal believer[s]," can stand outside and resist being "absorbed, processed and incorporated" (ibid.) by the culture of the media and consumer capitalism.

Mao II depicts the writer's position in the media-saturated society: the writers have been either preempted by terrorism or incorporated by consumerism. What role can a writer play in such a society? DeLillo expressed his view in a 1988 interview: a writer ought to be dangerous, but at the same time "ought to live in the margins" (qtd. in Arensberg 46) to avoid being incorporated. By saying that a writer should take an oppositional role and be dangerous, DeLillo echoed the language with which Norman Mailer had announced his literary ambition in his literary manifesto, *Advertisements for Myself* (1959): "The ambition of a writer like myself is to become consecutively more disruptive, more dangerous, and more powerful." Mailer added that he was "imprisoned with a perception which will settle for nothing less than making a revolution in the consciousness of our time" (17). In the interview DeLillo implied the change in the writer's power to shape and influence in the past three decades:

> I wonder if modern writers have felt preempted by terrorism, have felt that they've lost a certain influence that violence, a particular kind of theatrical violence, has seized from them. Mailer once said he had hoped to alter the consciousness of our time. I wonder if any writer harbors such a thought now, in the light of what political terrorists have managed to do in that regard, and in so few years. (qtd. in Arensberg 45)

DeLillo recognized that the novel as an art form has been marginalized by terrorism and its media confederates in the late 20th century and that the majority of the writers, confronted with this reality, lose confidence in their power to make a difference to the mass consciousness and to the inner life of the culture. The forces of the media and capitalism are so powerful that everybody is absorbed. "The artist is absorbed. The madman in the street is absorbed and processed and incorporated. Give him a dollar, put him in a TV commercial" (157). Even resistant writers like Bill have been assimilated and become "famous effigies" (41). DeLillo notices this totalitarian tendency in American contemporary society and calls on writers to be resistant to the power: "There are so many temptations for American writers to become part of the system and part of the structure that now, more than ever, we have to resist" (qtd. in Arensberg 46).

DeLillo admitted to having a spiritual kinship with Mailer. Their works reveal that they were concerned about the negative effects of technological development and the totalitarian aspects in American life and shared the sense that "social control should be so ubiquitous, so effective, so total" (Melley 6). As Tony Tanner remarked: "The possible nightmare of being totally controlled by unseen agencies and powers is never far away in contemporary American fiction" (qtd. in Melley 8). Mailer and DeLillo belong to the group of American writers who believe that individualism is increasingly challenged by postwar economic and social structures. They have both produced narratives in which "large governmental, corporate, or social systems appear uncannily to control individual behavior and in which characters seem paranoid either to themselves or to other characters in the novel" (Melley 8). They both chose Lee Harvey Oswald as the subject of their novels, which resulted in DeLillo's *Libra* and Mailer's *Oswald's Tale* (1995). In a 2007 interview entitled "Intensity of a Plot," Mark Binelli asked DeLillo: "Who would you say were your biggest literary influences?" DeLillo made a list of writers: Joyce, Faulkner, Hemingway, Flannery O'Connor, and Norman Mailer. But he singled out only Mailer to elaborate. He said, "[P]eople don't seem to link my name with Norman Mailer, but in a number of ways, Mailer was a strong force." He admired Mailer's writing and opinions, which have disturbed and shaken the totalitarian way of thinking and acting in Mailer's time. DeLillo told Binelli: "I remember living in one room for years, and one of the books I kept picking up was Mailer's *Advertisements for Myself*." This book, an inventive collection of Mailer's stories, essays, polemics, meditations and interviews, contains and explores the core of Mailer's philosophy. It is regarded as Mailer's literary manifesto to call upon people in postwar America to wage a war against the totalitarian social milieu, to assert one's individuality, and consequently, to make a revolution in the consciousness of his time. *Mao* II is an exploration of the artist's role in postmodern society. Bill's discussion of novelists being preempted by terrorists is undoubtedly an allusion to Mailer's view of his role as a writer in postwar America. With the novel, DeLillo paid homage to Mailer.

  Different from Mailer who was at the center of American culture and made raids on the consciousness of his time by way of his works, Bill stays at the far edge of the society and practices escapism for 23 years during which he has not published anything. In the end, he decides to end his reclusion and to assume an artist's social responsibility. He dies on the way to save a captive poet and ends up as an anonymous moral hero. DeLillo is known for his social engagement as he advocated the cause of artistic freedom for Salman Rushdie and the release of some writers in prison. In *Mao* II, DeLillo depicts another artist, Brita Nilsson, an independent female photographer whose relation to society is what DeLillo advocates for an artist: "[A]lthough among the crowd, she remains somewhat detached from it, buffeted by its currents but not immersed in them" (Osteen, "DeLillo's Dedalian Artist" 142). She is doing a project of photographing writers from country to country. Her purpose is "commemoration and resurrection" (ibid. 145) through making a record of writers who have become a dying breed. She says to Scott: "I'm simply doing a record. A species count, one writer said. I eliminate technique and personal style to the degree that this is possible" (26). She sees her photographing as a chronicle, "a basic reference work" (ibid.), instead of commercial images for consumption. "She uses her craft to create a counter-narrative to the dominant one" (Osteen, "DeLillo's Dedalian Artist" 144). In the novel's final section when Brita comes to Rashid's retreat, she sees all the boys close to him wear hoods. They wear Rashid's picture on the shirts. They have no personal identity. "The image of Rashid is their identity." (233) On an impulse, she removes one boy's hood, exposes his face and snaps his picture. She is challenging Rashid's authority by recovering the boy's individuality. Before she leaves, she makes a point of shaking Rashid's hand, and "actually introduces herself, pronouncing her name slowly" (237), as if to say, "I am not merely a recorder. I am a challenger. I can contest your authority." Brita is a socially engaged artist, yet able to remain somewhat apart and detached from the culture. She exemplifies what role an artist can play in contemporary society. As a successor to Bill Gray who has lost his power to shape and influence, Brita has a more powerful weapon to document history and to make raids on the human consciousness from within the culture itself.

Photography is both an art and a form of media, thus more powerful and more capable than Bill's written medium of documenting and criticizing the reality and the postmodern culture. For DeLillo, Brita's subversive art remains the best hope for resisting media-saturated culture and changing social consciousness.

Photographers are everywhere in *Mao II*: at the mass marriage in Yankee Stadium; in Bill Gray's home; at Khomeini's funeral in Iran; in the students' rally in Tian'anmen Square; in the Hillsborough Stadium; at the site of explosion in London; and in war-torn Beirut. The photographers' pictures are shown as news images and consumed by the crowds watching TV news and reading newspapers. They present portraits of the global culture in the late 1980s, the culture increasingly dominated by media images and capitalism, which gives rise to conformism, terrorism, and totalitarianism which can be seen in America, China, Britain, Iran and Lebanon. This globalization threatens to incorporate everything, turn everything into commodities, and produce assembly-line human beings. Through *Mao II*, DeLillo expresses his concern over the loss of personal individuality in the consumer society of America. "All the news is bad. We can't survive by needing more, wanting more, standing out, grabbing all we can" (89), Bill, DeLillo's double, comments. At the end of the prologue of *Mao II*, DeLillo asserts: "The future belongs to crowds." (16) What kind of crowds does he refer to? He depicts many different kinds of crowds. In my view, the future belongs to the crowds who are more concerned about the souls of their own and other people instead of accumulating and consuming material things. They care for the poor people and the homeless. The future belongs to the crowds who protest against totalitarianism and sacrifice for democracy. Finally the future belongs to the crowds who participate in the wedding in the night street of Beirut, who remain optimistic and transcendent despite the reality that the wedding has to be protected by the militia and the tank because of the war—the crowds who suggest warmth, hope, genuine love and peace.

DeLillo incorporates many historical events into *Mao* II to address the position of the novelist in postmodern culture, to explore the themes of art, terrorism, crowd, and globalization, and to criticize the culture dominated by images and consumerism, the culture which is so powerful that it incorporates everything into it. With the commodification of art and photography as a dominant narrative in the society of the spectacle, photographers have replaced novelists to have the power to make raids on public consciousness. They produce photographic or televised images which are circulated widely and played again and again on TV. Thus it is the media, not the terrorists as argued by Bill Gray, that supplant novelists as the shapers of culture. In *Mao* II, DeLillo seems to propose that a novelist must be terroristic in order to be influential "in a society that's filled with glut and repetition and endless consumption" (qtd. in Passaro 84). In my opinion, DeLillo seems to be more like a photographer "who simultaneously documents and criticizes the culture in which he resides" (Osteen, "DeLillo's Dedalian Artist" 145).

Photos can document history. The five interpolated photos in *Mao* II give us access to what happened in history in 1989. They share a common feature: the crowd, which reminds me of the famous saying: "It is the crowd/mass who creates history." The photos also serve as inspiration of his novels. Before he wrote *Mao* II, DeLillo came across two photos:

> I saw a photograph of a wedding conducted by Reverend Moon of the Unification Church [...] a wedding in Seoul in a soft-drink warehouse, about 13,000 people. And when I looked at it again, I realized I wanted to understand this event, and the only thing to understand it was to write about it. [...] And I had another photograph—it was a picture that appeared on the front page of *The New York Post* [...] it was a photograph of J. D. Salinger. [...] His face is an emblem of shock and rage. It's a frightening photograph. I didn't know it at the time, but these two pictures would represent the polar extremes of *Mao II*, the arch individualist and the mass mind, from the mind of the terrorist to the mind of the mass organization. (qtd. in Passaro, 80-81)

These photos published in the newspapers provided inspiration for *Mao* II. They stimulated DeLillo to examine and reflect on the postmodern culture in which they were taken, circulated and consumed. DeLillo is a photographer-novelist. In an interview he told Begley: "I try to record what I see and hear and sense around me—what I feel in the currents, the electric stuff of the culture. I think these are American forces and energies. And they belong to our time." (107) His writing is both a chronicle of America and an act of cultural criticism. Media images and newspapers record what is happening locally and globally, thus constitute an important part of historical documents. They provide not only inspiration, but also materials for DeLillo's books, for "the historical past is, as Fredric Jameson has argued, accessible to study 'only by way of its prior textualizations,' whether these be in the form of the documentary record or in the form of accounts of what happened in the past written up by historians themselves on the basis of their research into the record" (White, "New Historicism: A Comment" 297).

III. *Underworld*

"Everything Is Connected"

Like in *Mao* II, DeLillo begins the story of *Underworld* with a huge crowd. In the former, 6500 couples are being married by a Korean priest while in the latter the finale of the 1951 Baseball National League play-offs is being held. Many Americans play the game as children. The Americans go to the stadiums to watch the game or just stay at home watching the game broadcast live on TV. Huge crowds gather in the stadiums and before television sets. Thus baseball serves as a kind of national religion that brings the communities together. Baseball is a democratic game. Unlike football and basketball, baseball can be played well by people of average height and weight. Baseball has long been associated with a fundamental American mythology of "rags-to-riches individualism" (Osteen, *American Magic and Dread* 218). It provides the players of all races with opportunities to succeed and become rich. The prologue of *Underworld* depicts a legendary baseball game between the Giants and Dodgers in 1951. DeLillo uses this game as access to the history of postwar America, the country which was under the nuclear threat. The game was described by American media as "the Shot Heard Round the World."

1. "The Shot Heard Round the World"

As a fictional historian whose interest is the media-saturated America, DeLillo often depends on newspapers, TV footage, and other media texts—in Montrose's words, "the textual traces of the society in question" (20)—for access to the past he explores. The media texts constitute a great part of the documents upon which DeLillo, the historian, grounds his texts. Thus they are intertexts of DeLillo's texts.

Newspapers are important intertexts of *Underworld*. In an interview DeLillo told Gerald Howard how he was inspired by a newspaper story and started to explore the history of Bobby Thomson's 1951 home run:

> I was reading a newspaper one morning in October 1991, and there was a story about the fortieth anniversary of a legendary ball game between the Giants and Dodgers, the third game of the play-offs, which the Giants won dramatically on a ninth inning home run by Bobby Thomson. I read it and forgot all about it, but several weeks later began to think about it again in a different context—historical. (121)

The game was played at the Polo Grounds, New York, on October 3, 1951. The next day in the *Daily News*, this home run became known as "the Shot Heard Round the World." But the shot does not only refer to Thomson's historical shot. It also refers to the 1951 Russian atomic blast.

In *Underworld* DeLillo juxtaposes the two historical events which serve as the author's starting points to explore the Cold War history in both fiction and reality. DeLillo writes in the essay "The Power of History" that as a New Yorker living in the Bronx, he did not witness Thomson's heroic shot at the Polo Grounds. He was in the dentist's at that time. Like Bronzini, a character in *Underworld*, many Americans barely knew that the ball game was taking place and "almost missed it completely" (670). But the fall of the Soviet Union on December 25,1991 caused DeLillo to reflect on that baseball game and to put it in the historical context of the Cold War. DeLillo, for the first time, was aware of the implications of the baseball game between the New York Giants and the Brooklyn Dodgers. He went to the library to explore this event. He found a reel of microfilm for the *New York Times* of the following day, October 4, 1951. On the front page there were two headlines, "symmetrically matched" (ibid.). DeLillo makes a reference to his reading of this newspaper in *Underworld*:

> The front page astonished him, a pair of three-column headlines dominating. To his left the Giants capture the pennant, beating the Dodgers on a dramatic home run in the ninth inning. And to the right, symmetrically mated, same typeface, same-size type, same number of lines, the USSR explodes an atomic bombs—*kaboom*—details kept secret. He didn't understand why the *Times* would take a ball game off the sports and juxtapose it with the news of such

> ominous consequence. He began to read the account of the Soviet test. He could not keep the image from entering his mind, the cloud that was not a cloud, the mushroom that was not a mushroom—the sense of reaching feebly for a language that might correspond to the visible mass in the air. (668)

The two headlines gave DeLillo a strong sense of the power of history. This incident caused him to start thinking and writing about the Cold War.

The phrase "the shot heard round the world" has threefold references in *Underworld*. Originally from the opening stanza of Ralph Waldo Emerson's "Concord Hymn" (1837), it referrs to the first clash of the American Revolutionary War in Lexington and Concord, and since then it is applied to other dramatic moments, military and otherwise. This armed conflict started a chain of events which subsequently led to the signing of the Declaration of Independence and the Thirteen Colonies achieving independence from Britain. In *Underworld* "the shot heard round the world" refers to the home run hit by Bobby Thomson and the Russian atomic blast on October 3, 1951. On the next day American newspaper *Daily News* used this phrase to report the home run. In *Underworld*, Bronzini challenges the appropriateness of the media's labelling: "The Shot Heard Round the World? Is the rest of the world all that interested? This is baseball" (669). Father Andrew Paulus, also a character in *Underworld*, defends the media: "We take it that the term applies to the suddenness of the struck blow and the corresponding speed at which news is transmitted these days. Our servicemen in Greenland and Japan surely heard the home-run call as it was made on Armed Forces Radio" (670). Bronzini argues that "the shot heard around the world" was applied to the blast of the Russian atomic bomb which should be a world concern because of its potential threat to global safety. In retrospect, DeLillo thinks that Thomson's epochal home run and the explosion of a Russian nuclear device were both "the shot heard round the World," which were both a dramatic moment in the Cold War. In *Underworld*, DeLillo cleverly combines the two events and digs into the documents so as to unearth American underhistory of the Cold War.

Digging into the historical documents, DeLillo found a historical figure closely related to the American underhistory of the Cold War. This man was J. Edgar Hoover, chief director of the FBI, who makes several appearances in *Underworld*. It is Hoover that enables DeLillo "to blend the two events naturally and seamlessly" (qtd. in Howard 122). In the novel Hoover first appears in the prologue "The Triumph of Death" which was originally published in 1992 as a novella titled "Pafko at the Wall," which chronicles "one of the great events in baseball history" (Fitzpatrick

145). Hoover is at the Polo Grounds, watching the game with Frank Sinatra, Jackie Gleason and Toots Shor, which is a historical fact according to DeLillo. The baseball game is broadcast live on radio. The announcer is Russ Hodges, who broadcasts the game for WMCA. The pennant race has brought New York City to a strangulated rapture. The historical time is 3: 58 pm when Thomson hits the homer. The audience is overwhelmed by the joy. Russ, a Giants' fan, shouts: "The Giants win the pennant." (42) He is so excited that he repeats it many times. Russ's hoarse screams "I don't believe it. I don't believe it. I do not believe it." are recorded in the newsreel and become historical shouts. The Polo Grounds witnesses people's craziness and jubilation: the announcer's hoarse screams, the maddening roar of the crowd, and the shower of paper raining down over the left-field wall. Beyond the Polo Grounds many people are listening to the radio which is the dominant form of mass media, and hear the historical shot which was described by the American media as "the shot heard around the world." This is a shared American moment like the Kennedy Assassination, a turning point in history—"the equivalent (in its sphere) of the defeat of the Armada, the battle of Stalingrad, the Normandy landings" (Fitzpatrick 145). In Russ's view, "this is another kind of history" and people at the Polo Grounds "will carry something out of here that joins them all in a rare way that binds them to a memory with protective power" (*Underworld* 59).

There is a famous line from Jacques Barzun's book *God's Country and Mine: A Declaration of Love Spiced with a Few Harsh Words*: "Whoever wants to know the heart and mind of America had better learn baseball" (qtd. in Early). Obviously in *Underworld* DeLillo echoes support for Barzun's statement. According to Mark Osteen, the early 1950s was the Golden Age of baseball, especially in New York (*American Magic and Dread* 218). Some scholars suggest that baseball may be regarded as a sort of mirror in which values, power, politics, fashion, class, economics and race may be viewed in microcosm, thus can provide an insight into the larger political, social, economic and cultural context in which these values are displayed. In an interview DeLillo was quoted as saying: "In *Underworld*, I felt I was providing a fictional history of the Cold War. This is the unwritten history of the period, as it were" (Fry). He said that *Underworld* was "an attempt to trace history through the objects of our culture: condoms, waste, the (Thomson) baseball itself, all of which is part of the underground stream of our history" (ibid.). The Giants-Dodgers baseball game became DeLillo's entry point to explore the underworld of America and document the history of the Cold War.

Baseball has been perceived as a symbol of American democracy. For example,

Walt Whitman saw the baseball game as a metaphor for America itself and believed that baseball was "an example of democracy at its healthiest" (Rielly 317). DeLillo begins *Underworld* with this sentence: "He speaks in your voice, American, and there's a shine in his eyes that's halfway hopeful" (11). "He" is Cotter Martin, a 14-year-old black "scrawny" boy from Harlem. On October 3, 1951, a school day, Cotter plays truant and jumps the turnstile at the Polo Grounds to watch the baseball game for free. He believes in baseball and to believe in baseball is to believe in America which welcomes everybody and provides opportunities to fulfill their dreams here. Baseball game has truly become the national game with the integration of the black players in 1947. As Whitman believed, baseball is a unifying force. A crowd assembles at the Polo Grounds to participate in the making of history. Cotter, carrying his dream, is eager to join the

> anonymous thousands off the buses and trains, people in narrow columns tramping over the swing bridge above the river, and even if they are not a migration or revolution, some vast shaking of the soul, they bring with them the body heat of a great city and their own small reveries and desperations, the unseen something that haunts the day—men in fedoras and sailors on shore leave, the stray tumble of their thoughts, going to a game. (11)

In my opinion, the Polo Grounds is like the America in the eyes of the immigrants. The audience from different places and of different social backgrounds come to watch the game, unified by the American Dream. Inside the Polo Grounds, Cotter seems to be able to enjoy the equality that is denied him in American society. There is no section marked "Colored" at the Polo Grounds. He sits wherever he chooses to. In the Polo Grounds, Cotter is a representative of the black audience. Among those present at this famous game are four historical icons of America: J. Edgar Hoover, director of the FBI; Frank Sinatra, American singer and film actor; Jackie Gleason, American comedian, actor and musician; and Toots Shor, proprietor of Toots Shor's Restaurant, in Manhattan. They are celebrities in American society. It is amazing that during a time when many places in the United States still practice racial segratation, Cotter, a black and penniless boy, is allowed to sit with them in the same Polo Grounds, watching the same game. Except for Hoover, whose ancestors were European immigrants, the other three were sons of immigrants. Sinatra's parents were Italian, Gleason's parents were Irish, Shor's parents were Jewish, all having working-class backgrounds. The Polo Grounds symbolizes the United States where people of any background and any race from all corners of the world can have their American dreams fulfilled if they are lucky enough, smart enough and hard working enough. This is the deomocracy that the United States boasts.

Cotter has faith in America and is fascinated by the baseball which symbolizes American democracy. Baseball gives Cotter hope and "a local yearning" (11). In 1947, despite the widespread racial segregation, black Americans were allowed to play in the major leagues. As a black baseball fan from New York, Cotter surely knows that in that year Jackie Robinson, a black baseball player, joined the Brooklyn Dodgers and had a breakthrough season. Maybe Cotter dreams of becoming another Jackie Robinson one day. On October 3, 1951, Cotter and other 14 kids, white and black, are waiting at the curbstone outside the Polo Grounds, trying to get in without tickets. With luck and running speed, Cotter makes it without being caught by the cops. He arrives just in time to hear "the crescendoing last chords of the national anthem" and see "the great open horseshoe of the grandstand" (ibid.), which makes him feel proud and excited. As he watches the baseball come in his direction, "he feels his body turn into smoke" (42). He wants to have the baseball that symbolizes democracy and creates history. Thomson's home run ball flies under a seat. After fighting with Bill Waterson under the seat, Cotter gets the ball and takes it home. Thomson's home run ball is the best thing which Cotter has ever possessed. It is Cotter's only treasure. It can remind him of the history it has created and gives him encouragement that he, too, can have his dream fulfilled because anything is possible in the American society: "The game was lost and then they won. The game could not be won but then they won it and it's won forever. This is the thing they can never take away" (148). It is a miracle that Cotter gets the baseball.

But on the very evening Cotter takes the baseball home, Manx Martin, Cotter's father, steals it while he sleeps. Manx sells the baseball at the cheap price of $32.45. The ball, which stands for "people's history," belongs to a black teenager only for a magical moment. After Cotter, its owners are all white people: Charlie Wainwright, an advertising agent, and his son Chuckie, a navigator on a B-52 making bombing runs over Vietnam; Marvin Lundy, an aging Jewish-American memorabilia dealer; and Nick Shay, an executive in waste management, who bought Thomson's home-run baseball from Marvin at $34,500 as an expiation for various losses in his life. Through the depiction of the baseball's journey from the Polo Grounds in 1951 to Nick's study in the early 1990s, DeLillo chronicles American life in the second half of the 20th century.

The baseball bears witness to the racial conflicts in the 1950s' American society. In the Polo Grounds the black boy, Cotter Martin, wrestles with Bill Waterson, a white man, under the seat for the ball and gets it finally. The struggle between "good neighbor Bill flashing a cutthroat smile" (49) and his "buddy Cotter" (53) is a miniature of the era's interracial conflicts in the United States. The crowds gathered in the Polo Grounds were mainly white while the American media bragged about the baseball game's unifying of the white and the black. DeLillo describes the game as a communal event: "All over the city people are coming out of their home. This is the nature of Thomson's homer. It makes people want to be in the streets, joined with others…" (47). But these people were mostly whites. To the minds of many blacks in 1951, the baseball game was still a game of the white in spite of the fact that black players have been allowed to join the baseball leagues since 1947. *Underworld* reveals that racism still remained a major problem in the American society in 1951. Sims, a character in *Underworld*, is insightful enough to notice the inequality and racial discrimination in the baseball game, which exemplifies the severity of racism in America. He takes Ralph Branca, Thomson's rival in the Dodgers, for example: "Branca's a hero. I mean Branca was given every chance to survive this game and we all know why. Because he's white. Because the whole thing is white. Because you can survive and endure and prosper if they let you. But you have to be white before they let you" (98).

  Racial inequality is also displayed by the portrayal of the family lives and the contrasting fates of two boys, the black Cotter and the White Nick, connected by the baseball. Cotter Martin is born into a poor working family in Harlem. His father Manx Martin is depicted as an irresponsible man, a thief and a drunkard. When Manx learns that his son has got the baseball that has helped win the pennant, he quickly has an idea: to sell it. For Manx, if the baseball is kept in his son's room, it will "do nothing and earn nothing." If they sell it, Manx says to Cotter, they will have money to buy things for practical use. By selling the baseball, Manx betrays his son. He sells the ball to Charles Wainwright who pays only $32.45, because Manx cannot show him the ticket stub to prove that this is the ball that hit the home run. There is an illustrative contrast in this selling of the baseball. Manx and Charles are both fathers; Cotter and Chuckie are both sons. Because of poverty and social isolation, the black father betrays his son who sees his dream embodied in the home run ball. DeLillo seems to suggest that the urge to consume ruins the relationship between Manx and Cotter. "Consume or die. That's the mandate of the culture" (287). Cotter and his father, poor people at the bottom of the society, have no money to consume, thus they perish as characters after October 4, 1951. To consume in America is to dream. Cotter's dream is stolen, so his existence is cancelled. The home run ball finally falls into the hands of Nick Shay, who purchases it at $34,500. Nick imagines Thomson's homer will take him back to "the days of disarray, when I didn't give a damn or fuck or a farthing"

(806). He has suffused his entire adolescence into the ball's five ounce. "Yet his ownership of it and the history that congealed around it, DeLillo implies, has been made possible by the initial loss suffered by Cotter" (Heise 234). Cotter and Nick are both betrayed by their fathers. Nick's father abandons the family when he is 11 years old, which is a loss for Nick forever. In contrast to Cotter who disappears after the prologue, Nick remains a main character and major narrator throughout the novel. We see his upward movement in society despite the fact that he killed his neighbor George Manza when he was still a teenager. The shot he fired shocked the local people in the Bronx, a place mainly inhabited by Italian immigrants. "When they took him out to the cop car there were people ... thinking this was a kind of history taking place, here in their own remote and common streets" (781). This is part of Nick's underhistory. He grows up to be an expert in waste management, successful and accomplished, making big bucks so that he can pay that huge sum of money for the home run ball. As a son of an Italian immigrant, he has his American dream of rags to riches come true. In the American society, it is not "I think, I exist," but "I consume, I exist." Consumerism helps the troubled white boy fullfil his dream.

With "the shot heard round the world", started another conflict, this time, not between two baseball teams of America, but between two superpowers of the world. The age of innocence for the American people ended. When the Americans enjoyed watching the baseball game and were proud of "the shot heard round the world," the Russians were busy developing nuclear weapons. After the end of World War II, the American people lived in peace, prosperity and security. They did not realize that another war was already started, which is represented in the discussion of "the shot heard round the world" between Father Paulus and Bronzini in *Underworld*:

> Did you see the paper, Father?
>
> [...] Yes, I stole a long look at someone's *Daily News*. They're calling it the Shot Heard Round the World.
>
> How did we detect evidence of the blast, I wonder. We must have aircraft flying near their borders with instruments that measure radiation. Or well-placed agents perhaps.
>
> No no no. We're speaking about the home run. Bobby Thomson's heroic shot. The tabloids have dubbed it for posterity. (669)

It turns out that it is the atomic explosion, with which Albert Bronzini confuses Thomson's home run when he talks about the front page of *New York Times* with Andrew Paulus on October 4, 1951. Father Paulus is the kind of arrogant Americans who are proud of American power and influence and believe that American democracy is spreading far and near. He knows that American servicemen are stationed in Greenland, Japan, Korea, some other parts of the world, and that the baseball players Branca and Thomson are sons of immigrants, one half Hungarian, the other Scottish. "You see why our wins and losses tend to have impact well beyond our borders," Paulus says to Albert.

The "Shot Heard Round the World" heralds the age of nuclear anxiety in America. On the same day of the Dodgers-Giants baseball game, the Soviet Union conducts "an atomic test at a secret location somewhere inside its own borders" (23). The news is secretly revealed to Hoover who is watching the baseball games in the Polo Grounds. In history the American government attempts to suppress the news of the atomic blast. The Soviet's bomb was "born secret" and "was often depicted in popular journalism as the era's biggest secret" (Osteen, *American Magic and Dread* 217). Yet despite the government's suppression, *New York Times* quickly learned the news and published it in the newspaper. The news of the Soviet's atomic test which is referred to as a "blast" (23, 51) in *Underworld* was quickly spread all over the world. This blast caused anxiety among Americans, who realized, as Edgar Hoover does in the novel, the Russian bomb was "an instrument of conflict … It is not some peaceful use of atomic energy with home-heating application. It is a red bomb that spouts a great white cloud" (23) like the atomic bombings of Hiroshima and Nagasaki in Japan in 1945 which killed at least 150, 000 people. This blast ignited the nuclear arms race between the United States and the Soviet Union. "The revelation of the Soviet test occurred just as the U. S. military was announcing a new series of atomic tests in Nevada …" (Osteen, *American Magic and Dread* 217) With McCarthyism on the rampage and weapon testing accelerating, John Duvall suggests, October 4, 1951, "when the United States had to acknowledge that the Soviets were regularly testing atomic weapons, was the first day of the Cold War" (ibid. 218).

In *Underworld*, the baseball game and the nuclear bomb test partake of each other. The prologue, the three "Manx Martin" chapters, and Part Six portray the kinship between the two games and give us a snapshot of America in the middle of the 20th century. The existence of the baseball is a historical fact, but Cotter and the white owners are fictional characters. In an interview DeLillo expresses his view on the purpose of his creation of fictional characters who share the fictional world with the historical figures: "The fictional characters fill the gaps, so to speak. They provide the lost knowledge" (qtd. in Fry). The baseball is first owned by a poor black kid, and then falls into the hands of four white men. The fictional movement of the baseball from one owner to another in *Underworld* connects the life stories of the owners and uncovers the underworld history of America in the Cold War years in which the American people were plagued by nuclear anxiety and paranoia.

2. "We're All Gonna Die"

Underworld depicts America during the years of nuclear armament. English writer Martin Amis calls it a "wake for the Cold War" (qtd. in Echlin, "Baseball and the Cold War" 145). It explores how anxiety in the Cold War "displaces religious faith" with "radioactivity, the power of alpha particles and the all-knowing systems that shape them, the endless fitted links" (*Underworld* 241), a chain reaction of fear that extends across the nation, "becoming in effect the glue that cements the nation together" (Knight, "Everything Is Connected: *Underworld*'s Secret History of Paranoia" 287). It documents the apocalyptic anxieties and paranoia of Americans who were living under the shadow of the nuclear war.

2.1 Soviet's Second Atomic Test and *The Triumph of Death*

On October 3, 1951, the day when Thomson hit his home run, the Soviet Union had its second atomic test on the Kazakh Test Site. Before the news reached the public, the FBI director John Edgar Hoover was informed by a secret agent. The prologue of *Underworld* describes Hoover's reaction to the news which exemplifies America's concern over the Soviet's nuclear test.

The news of the atomic test reaches Hoover when he is in the Polo Grounds watching the baseball game with his friends. It makes him think of "the prospect of warheads being sent to communist forces in Korea," the "Pearl Harbor" (23-24) and the nuclear threat to the patriots. When he looks at the audience whose faces are "open and hopeful," what comes to his mind is not the American democracy or American values that unite the people from all walks of life and backgrounds, but the potential nuclear threat that connects them. "These people … have never had anything in common so much as this, that they are sharing in the furrow of destruction" (ibid.).

The Triumph of Death best manifests the Americans' nuclear anxiety. The crowd of fans in the Polo Grounds is juxtaposed with the crowd of the dead in a 16-century picture painted by "a Flemish master, Pieter Bruegel, and it is called *The Triumph of Death*" (50). This oil painting that gives the prologue its title, "The Triumph of Death," was reproduced in the October 1, 1951 issue of *Life* magazine. In the novel Hoover happens to see the painting while at the baseball game when someone in the stands above tears up a copy of the magazine and tosses the pieces and a magazine page with the reproduction of the Bruegel painting falls on his shoulder. In the painting the agents of death spare no one. When he first sees the painting, he wonders "why a magazine called *Life* would want to reproduce a painting of such lurid and dreadful dimensions" (41). Hoover is intrigued by death's final conquest of humanity. He sees death in the "great white cloud" spouted by the "red bomb" (23) which can create the scary spectacle represented in the painting: "Terror universal" (50) and the "scorched, barren earth, devoid of any life as far as the eye can see" (Snyder 486).

The news of the Soviet's second atomic blast sharpened the tension between Us and Them and increased American fear of communist subversion and conquest. It "will give Hoover the 'ammunition' to pursue even more fully his anticommunist agenda" (Duvall, "Excavating the Underworld of Race and Waste in Cold War History" 265). Hoover was Senator Joseph McCarthy's friend. In 1950 McCarthy charged about 205 communists working in the State Department. During the height of McCarthyism, from 1950—1953, "McCarthy became a media star, but Hoover made it happen by supplying the senator with embarrassing information about individuals, often illegally obtained and consisting largely of gossip and rumor …" (ibid. 266) Hoover loved celebrities. "He likes to be around movie idols and celebrity athletes" (17) and spied on them. "He wants to be their dearly devoted friend provided their hidden lives are in his private files, all the rumors collected and indexed, the shadow facts made real" (ibid.). He dug into the personal files and tried to detect any possible connection between "us and them." As a fervent anticommunist, he was in part responsible for the Red Scare or McCarthyism.

Underworld portrays the fear incited by the media news of the second Russian atomic blast. On the day of the atomic explosion, a preacher on Amsterdam Avenue in New York City is persuading people to believe in God by using the terrifying news of the blast:

> This is what they say and I believe them because they study the matter. All the creatures God put on earth, only insects survive the radiation. […] And I believe them when they say the insects will still be here after the atom bombs will fell the buildings and destroy the people and kill the birds and the animals and emasculate the dogs and cats so they can't begat their young. (352)

The preacher is describing the horrible scene, the left-over of nuclear mass destruction. But to my mind, he is also describing the Bruegel's painting *The Triumph of Death*. Actually he is only repeating what the radio keeps saying after the Soviet atomic explosion: "Russians explode an atom bomb on the other side of the world. You got your radio tuned to the news? I'm telling you the news. Clear across the world." (352-53) The man preaches that no one and nothing except God can save them from being wiped out. But the majority of Americans did not realize the significance of the nuclear weapon test at the time. In Hoover's opinion, "they are sitting in the furrow of destruction" (28), unknowingly. Even if they knew the news, they did not care. Some people thought it was the "business of the generals and the diplomats" (353). Ordinary Americans just wanted to carry on their lives as usual. But the American government and mass media would not leave it alone. The government employed the Soviet's second nuclear test to persuade the Congress to increase its military budget, for the anticommunist agenda needed financial support and the nuclear arms race was costly. The mass media used the Russian atomic explosion to attract more consumers of their news products. In *Underworld*, the preacher, the government and the media all take advantage of the atomic blast and the subsequent public fear for their respective purposes, which can only result in the aggravated anxiety of the American public. Fear leads to more military expenditure, hence escalating the arms race between the United States and the Soviet Union.

  Due to the propaganda of the Cold War ideology by the media, throughout the 1950s Americans lived in the shadow of the nuclear war. How the American people reacted to the threat of an allegedly upcoming nuclear war is represented in *Underworld*. On October 3, 1951, in the Polo Grounds, there were 20000 empty seats. According to Marvin, a baseball collector and Cold War paranoia in *Underworld*, the reason why there were so many empty seats for the most important game of many years was that people "sensed some catastrophe in the air" (171). They stayed indoors to avoid being exposed to the nuclear fallout. To protect against the nuclear fallout, the American government built "bomb shelters that hold twenty-five thousand people under the streets of this city" (353). Sister Edgar, a minor character in *Underworld*, was "a cold war nun who'd once lined the walls of her room with Reynolds Wrap as a safeguard against nuclear fallout" (245). The children she taught had to wear dog tags which "were designed to help rescue workers identify children who were lost, missing, injured, maimed, mutilated, unconscious or dead in the hours following the onset of atomic war" (717). American children were being taught to "duck and cover" in case of nuclear attacks and were being herded into school basements for terrifying bomb drills. As the Cold War between the United States and the Soviet Union stepped up, fear of the atomic bombs and anxiety over the possibility of a nuclear war drove many Americans to build bomb shelters in their backyards in an effort to survive what seemed at the time the inevitable nuclear attack from their enemies. Radio bragged about the dangers and the imminence of a nuclear war. Newspapers carried radiation readings beside daily weather reports. Hollywood began producing nuclear war doomsday films, including "On the Beach," "The Last Man On Earth," "The Day the World Ended," "Atomic Kid," and "Dr. Strangelove." Television produced its own prime time doomsday. *Life* magazine published a reproduction of Bruegel's painting "The Triumph of Death" on October 1, 1951, which has been interpreted as an allegorical representation of the horrors of nuclear war in which death takes anyone and spares no one—a projection of the social mood in America. With media's indoctrination of an impending nuclear war and the havoc it may cause, the 1950s was a time of unprecedented anxiety in spite of the unprecedented prosperity evidenced by the popularity of the baseball games in America. Fear became a part of American everyday life.

American mass media played an important role in its struggle for global dominance with the Soviet Union. The media extended the propaganda to every aspect of American life, from radio, film, television and print to even schools. Media manipulation intensified the mood of anti-communism in American society, reinforced the American dominant ideology of capitalism and helped to redefine national identity as a virtuous and patriotic America, against a dangerous and destructive Soviet Union. Through the media's indoctrination in the 1950s, the United States was plunged into an intense hysteria over communism and nuclear fear.

2.2 "We're All Gonna Die"

Things did not improve in the 1960s. The conflict between the US and the USSR escalated after the young President Kennedy took office. Kennedy recommended a course of action to his fellow Americans. "A fallout shelter for everybody," he said, "as rapidly as possible." (qtd. in Zacharias, "When Bomb Shelters Were All the Rage") On October 14, 1962, the Cuban Missile Crisis occurred. It was one of the major confrontations of the Cold War, shoving the world to the brink for 13 agonizing days. The performances of Lenny Bruce depicted in *Underworld* reproduce the nation's panic and anxiety over the Cuban Missile Crisis.

Lenny Bruce (1925—1966) was an American stand-up comedian, social critic and satirist. In an interview, DeLillo told Gerald Howard: "Lenny Bruce was a very strong influence on the culture and deserves recognition at the level of Ginsberg and Burroughs and Kerouac" (qtd. in Howard 129). Bruce appears in Part 5 of *Underworld* as "the infamous sick comic" (504), giving his performances in October, 1962, and is found dead at his home in Los Angeles in 1966. He is "one of *Underworld*'s primary spokesmen" (Osteen, *American Magic and Dread* 247) for the "secret history that never appears in the written accounts of the time or in the public statements of men in power" (*Underworld* 594). In his performances during the crisis, he screams to his audience: "We're all gonna die!" (506, 507, 508, 584), frankly articulating his audience's panic. "In his giddy shriek the audience can hear the obliteration of the idea of uniqueness and free choice. They can hear the replacement of human isolation by massive and unvaried ruin" (507).

In *Underworld* Bruce's criticism mainly focuses on President Kennedy and his administration during the Cuban Missile Crisis. He starts his performances by vividly imitating President Kennedy's opening line of his speeches: "Good evening, my fellow citizens," which causes the audience to laugh. He makes satirical comments on the Kennedy Administration's approach to foreign policy guided by an elaborate theorizing rooted in school-playground view of world politics. He points out that it is these white elites, the "twenty-six guys from Harvard," who control the country and decide the fate of the American people. He criticizes the Kennedy Administration for its incompetency, selfishness and irresponsibility in times of crisis: "These guys wear boxer shorts with geometric design that contain the escape routes they've been assigned when the missiles start flying" (505). When the nuclear war between the US and the USSR starts, all the American people will be killed except the elite top leaders, for they have constructed bomb shelters for themselves. Bruce also criticizes the elite American government for their luxury and squandering of taxpayers' money:

> Twenty-six guys in Clark Kent suits getting ready to enter a luxury bunker that's located about half a mile under the White House and the faggot decorator's doing a last minute checklist. Let's see, peach walls, stunning. Found the chandelier in a little abbey outside Paris. None of that Statler Hilton dreck in my bomb shelter. [...] Rugs, fabulous, the purest Persian slave labor. Arched windows [...] dining table, plantation mahogany, eleven bottles of Lemon Pledge. Centerpiece, designed it himself, the highlight of his career. A huge mound of crabmeat carved in the shape—they're gonna love this, it's so forceful and moving—yes, Kennedy and Khrushchev wrestling in the nude. Lifesize. (506)

Bruce's political satire seems comic at first, causing laughter among the audience. The narrator wonders: "How real can the crisis be if we're sitting in a club on Santa Monica Boulevard going ha ha ha." (507) Bruce's comic stand-up routine about the Cuban Missile Crisis is the gallows humor.

The Cuban Missile Crisis started in 1962, after Bay of Pigs and Operation Mongoose, two unsuccessful operations by the United States to overthrow Castro's Cuban government. In the late summer the Cuban and Soviet governments began to build bases in Cuba for missiles with the ability to strike most of the United States These preparations were noticed and on October 14, a US U-2 aircraft took several pictures clearly showing sites for medium-range and intermediate-range ballistic nuclear missiles (MRBMs and IRBMs) under construction. These images were processed and presented on October 15, which marks the beginning of the 13-day crisis from the United States perspective. The United States considered attacking Cuba via air and sea, but decided on a military blockade instead. The Kennedy Administration held only a slim hope that the Kremlin would agree to their demands, and expected a military confrontation.

Lenny Bruce, in *Underworld*, criticizes the President's incompetent handling of the crisis and the complicity of TV in intimidating the public. He thinks that the Americans are reduced to being powerless, which is their "basic state" although the United States "is putting up a naval blockade ... Any offensive military equipment being shipped to Cuba get stopped dead in the water by the U. S. fleet" (507). On TV there is nothing else except the President's speech played again and again. In the speech President Kennedy has addressed his nation on the Cuban Missile Crisis. Bruce says, a woman worker "comes home exhausted and turns on the TV and it's the President of the United States and he's saying, Abyss of destruction" (ibid.). Kennedy's grim speech goes on and on. The woman does not know "Abyss of destruction" refers to the Cuban Missile Crisis. She thinks it is a movie title. So she calls her friend, asking: "Who was in that movie the President's talking about on TV?" Her friend says, "You're asking me about movies? At a time like this?" (508) At the time of "the highest national urgency" (504), with the bombardment of Kennedy's speech, the Americans are united by the fear of the impending mass annihilation.

But the bomb never dropped. In his show at Carnegie Hall, New York City, on October 29, 1962, Lenny Bruce announces: "What a crazy nerve-wracked morbid week. We're all drained. We were minutes from being fireballed. But now, but now, but now. We're not gonna die!" (624). In secret back-channel communications, Kennedy and Khrushchev initiated a proposal to resolve the crisis. After much deliberation Kennedy secretly agreed to remove all missiles set in Europe in exchange for Khrushchev removing all missiles in Cuba. "Russians agree to remove missiles and end construction of missile bases in Cuba" (625). The confrontation ended on October 28, 1962. The whole world was relieved. Even Khrushchev is "taking hot baths to relax, like a plastic pouch of corn coming to a boil" (ibid.).

In *Underworld*, through Bruce's performance, DeLillo represents the nuclear anxiety suffered by the Americans during the Cuban Missile Crisis. At the same time he digs into the secret history of those critical moments. Firstly, Kennedy asserted in his October 22 televised address that the missiles were "an explicit threat to the peace and security of all the Americas" (qtd. in Schwarz, "The Real Cuban Missile Crisis"). But it is found out that the threat was exaggerated by the media and Kennedy for a political reason: America's "Red Scare." Kennedy himself held conspicuous and fervent hostility toward the communist Castro regime. Secondly, Kennedy should not have taken all the credit for all the efforts to end the crisis. In his performance Bruce reveals, "Khrushchev wrote a letter to Kennedy. He wants a summit" (586). It was Moscow that took the initiative and dismantled the missiles, and a cataclysm was averted. But in American official history and media coverage it is "the Kennedy Administration's placid resolve and prudent crisis management—thanks to […] the president's combination of toughness and restraint, of will, nerve, and wisdom, so brilliantly controlled, so matchlessly calibrated, that dazzled the world" (ibid.). With Bruce's satire, DeLillo excavates the secret history of the Cuban Missile Crisis.

The end of the Cuban Missile Crisis did not stop the nuclear rivalry between the United States and the Soviet Union. The conflicts between the two superpowers continued. In 1991 the nuclear arms races dragged down the Soviet's economy, which partly resulted in the falling apart of the Soviet Union, hence the Cold War ended, leaving behind a large quantity of nuclear waste and human waste.

3. "Waste Is the Secret History"

With the end of the Cold War, "[t]he missiles remained in the underwing carriages, unfired" (76). They become garbage and waste material. "Plutonium waste is getting to a point that's very crazy. Worldwide, who is counting? Maybe twelve hundred metric tons" (795). How to deal with them becomes an international issue. In the epilogue to *Underworld*, which takes place after the collapse of the Soviet Union, Nick Shay visits Kazakhstan "to witness an underground nuclear explosion" (788) and to meet Victor Maltsev, a Russian trading company executive. In the post-Cold War era, nuclear explosion becomes a commodity that Victor's company trades in. The Russian businessmen "sell nuclear explosions for ready cash. They want us to supply the most dangerous waste we can find and they will destroy it for us. … They will put up waste anywhere in the world, ship it to Kazakhstan, put it in the ground and vaporize it. We will get a broker's fee" (ibid.).

3.1 Globalization in the Post-Cold War Era

Globalization is the process of international integration arising from the interchange of world views, products, ideas and other aspects of culture (Albrow and King 8). It is a process driven by international trade and investment and aided by information technology. Globalization is not new. It has existed for centuries. In the 1980s globalization quickened and produced tremendous effects on the Soviet Union and the Third World countries.

In *Underworld* DeLillo argues that how the Americans won the Cold War was "at least as much the work of American media and consumer culture as it was US nuclear tonnage" (Duvall, "The Power of History and the Persistence of Mystery" 3). As many scholars claim, globalization was predominantly driven by the outward flow of culture and economic activity from the United States and was better understood as Americanization or Westernization. New technology and multinational corporations created the appropriate environment to present aspects of American and "democratic culture" to Russians, which, in combination of other reasons, led to the collapse of the Soviet Union.

The epilogue is titled "Das Kapital" which is named after Karl Marx's famous book, *Das Kapital, Kritik der Politischen Ökonomie*, whose English translation, *Capital: Critique of Political Economy*, is familiar to us. The epilogue presents a postmodern Russia virtually identical to the postmodern United States which DeLillo depicts in *Cosmopolis* and "In the Ruins of the Future":

> Capital burns off the nuance in a culture. Foreign investment, global markets, corporate acquisitions, the flow of information through transnational media, the attenuating influence of money that's electronic and sex that's cyberspaced, untouched money and computer-safe sex, the convergence of consumer desire—not that people want the same things, necessarily, but that they want the same range of choices. (785)

The post-communist Russia is westernized; the "them-us" binary opposition of the United States and Russia disappears. Capital prevails, connecting the two countries which used to be ideological enemies combating against each other for nearly 50 years. "The bilateral animus and the geographic spheres of influence of the NATO and Soviet blocs have dissipated" (Conte 183), ushering a new global order of transnational politics. Globalization is transforming Russia from planned economy to market economy: "A method of production that will custom-cater to cultural and personal needs, not to cold war ideologies of massive uniformity" (785-86).

In the epilogue, "DeLillo shows the way Russian culture is attempting to ape the worst of Western consumerism" (Duvall, "Excavating the Underworld of Race and Waste in Cold War History" 278). Nick Shay and his "old buddy Brian" (785) witness a changed Russia when they stay in Moscow on business after the fall of the Soviet Union. They sit in "a pub called the Football Hooligan" (ibid.), listening to music and observing Russians eat, drink and dance. They serve ethnic fast food and five-star cognac. The music is called cult rock, loud, "but mostly piercing and repetitive, on an icy kind of wavelength" (ibid.), played by a live band "with fuzz heads and fatigue pants and bombs packed strapped to their bare chests—college boys probably who've appropriated a surface of suicide terror" (786). Brian finds this place frightening because of "the sense of displacement and redefinition" (786). The club is located

> on the forty-second floor of a new office tower filled with brokerage houses, software firms, import companies and foreign banks, where private guards hired by various firms to patrol the corridors sometimes shoot at each other and where the man at the next table, with a bald dome, slit eyes and a jut beard, turning this way at last, is clearly a professional Lenin look-alike. (786)

Later Victor tells Nick that he would see the paid doubles of Marx and Trotsky in the club if he stayed long enough. Obviously the club is an exemplary staging of postmodern pastiche which Jameson characterizes as "a neutral practice of such mimicry, without any of parody's ulterior motives, amputated of the satiric impulse, devoid of laughter … Pastiche is thus blank parody, a statue with blind eyeballs" (*Postmodernism* 17). The new office tower represents the capitalist Russia which is more and more like its counterpart, its former Cold War foe. Nick and Brian take an ambulance-turned taxi to the airport where they are flying to "The Kazakh Test Site" (789) to see bomb explosions. On the way they see "a huge billboard advertising a strip club" (787). In the strip club called Interactive Sonya, people can watch "nude dancing on the information highway." When they arrive at the airport, instead of asking for the Russian rubles for the fare, the driver wants US dollars which are highly valued in Russia now. Globalization has transformed Russia. US technology, companies and money flow to Russia. The contesting relationship between the United States and Russia in the Cold War is now replaced by the business partnership. The Russians not only change the ambulances into taxies, passenger planes and military planes, which were "originally designed for mixed loads of cargo and troops" (787), but they also change the atomic bombs, now dangerous waste, into commodities.

Underworld is a history of waste. As is showed in the epilogue, waste connects everything: the East and the West, the former communist country and the most advanced capitalist country, the black and the white, the nuclear bomb and baseball, the fictional characters and the historical figures. Victor, a Russian waste dealer, and Nick, an American waste manager, arrive at a nuclear test site known as Polygon in Kazakhstan, the exact spot of the 1951 atomic blast mentioned in the prologue. At the gate to the site, Brian says the gate "resembles the entrance to a national park" (792). Forty years ago a black teenager fan Cotter stood at the gate to the Polo Grounds, trying to enter the ballpark to watch the baseball game. During the game the FBI director Hoover was informed of the Soviet nuclear test in Kazakhstan. Now in the epilogue Nick is invited to witness a test for the potential commercial use of underground nuclear explosion. At this point the novel brings the reader full circle, thus ending its excavation of American underhistory of the Cold War.

3.2 The Waste Land

Waste is everywhere in *Underworld* and "it is one of the novel's 'secrets,' one of the simultaneously hidden and transparently manifest underworlds to which the novel's title refers" (O' Donnell, "*Underworld* " 110). Waste in the novel refers to nuclear waste, disused arms, architectural ruins, urban slums and household garbage. *Underworld* is DeLillo's Waste Land of the Cold War.

The Cold War ended in 1991, leaving behind more than "twelve hundred metric tons" (795) of Plutonium waste and a large number of weapons to dispose of. By making the "curious connection between weapons and waste" (791), DeLillo finds the clue to rewriting the Cold War history. Waste is "the devil twin" (ibid.) of weapons. Waste always goes to the landfills, buried underground. Waste is "the secret history, the underhistory" (ibid.). DeLillo, like the "archaeologists who dig out the history of early cultures", finds "every sort of bone heap and broken tools" (ibid.), figuratively from under the ground, and detects connections between them, excavating the secret history of the Cold War in the United States.

3.2.1 The Kazakh Test Site

The nuclear arms race between the United States and the Soviet Union led to large spending on armaments and the stockpiling of vast nuclear arsenals. This competition in developing nuclear weapons placed great strains on the Soviet economy. The armament and Mikhail Gorbachev's reform accelerated the end of the Cold War and the collapse of the Soviet Union. The United States survives as the only superpower. The Soviet Union lost the contest and dissolved as a communist country. The political consequences of the arms race are obvious, but its side effects on the environment and humans need to be explored.

The nuclear tests victimized the residents and their progeny near the test sites. In the epilogue to *Underworld*, before flying back to Moscow, Victor takes Nick and Brian to two places close to the nuclear test site: the Museum of the Misshapens and a radiation clinic. In the museum they see some disfigured fetuses on display. Some of the fetuses are horrifying: "the two headed specimen," "the single head that is twice the size of the body," "the normal head that is located in the wrong place, perched on the right shoulder," "the cyclops," with the eye "centered, the ears below the chin, the mouth completely missing" (799). These fetuses are victims of nuclear radiation. On the outskirt of the city of Semipalatinsk, Nick sees more victims of nuclear radiation. These victims live in the village "downwind of the testing in the years of frequent detonations" (800). The villagers, their children, and their grandchildren are patients of the clinic which has "disfigurations, leukemias, thyroid cancers, immune systems that do not function. The doctor says … there are unknown diseases here. Sickness everywhere around" (800-01) in the contaminated land. It seems Pieter Bruegel's painting "The Triumph of Death" comes into reality.

The tragedy brought about by the nuclear arms race will possibly continue for future generations in spite of the end of the Cold War. The environment near the nuclear tests was contaminated without warning. The villagers living near the Kazakh Test Site were kept in darkness about the testing and the radiation. "Five hundred nuclear explosions at the test site" (799) contaminated the atmosphere and the land. The villagers were not aware of the dangers because they did not know they were living close to a nuclear test site, a highly secret place which was not marked on the map. The Kazakhs were exposed to nuclear radiation but the Russians kept it as a secret. "For many years the word radiation was banned" around the test site (801). "The Kazakh Test Site" will see more atomic blasts which are to be shot underground, for the Russian businessman Victor "is trying to merchandise nuclear explosion" (800) for ready cash. Unused nuclear bombs will be carried here and destroyed "in granite about one kilometer down" (794). At the site gather waste traders, venture capitalists, arms dealers, "looking to make bids … on the idle inventory of weapons-grade plutonium floating at the fringes of the industry" (ibid.).

In the Polo Grounds on October 3, 1951, after having been informed of the

Soviet's second nuclear test at a secret location in Kazakhstan, Hoover wonders:

> What secret history are they writing? There is the secret of the bomb and there are the secrets that the bomb inspires, things even the Director cannot guess [...] This is what he knows, that the genius of the bomb is printed not only in its physics of particles and rays but in the occasion it creates for new secrets. For every atmospheric blast, every glimpse we get of the bared force of nature, that weird peeled eyeball exploding over the desert—for every one of these he reckons a hundred plots go underground, to spawn and skein. And what is the connection between Us and Them, how many bundled links do we find in the neutral labyrinth? (50-51)

In my view, the connection between the United States and the Soviet Union is a mindset focused on secrecy. In this self-reflexive passage, DeLillo ponders over the nuclear bomb, its effects and various links. He steers clear of the obvious links, digs into the underground, finds out secret links, and writes a secret history of the Cold War.

Among the links is the Kazakh Test Site which held many secrets of the Soviet Union, which leads to the popularity of false beliefs and conspiracy theories after the fall of the Soviet Union. There is a belief popular with the Kazakhs that Russians "tried to murder the whole population" because "Red Army did not always evacuate villages before a test" and in every test "hundreds of towns and villages exposed to radiation" (801). Communism, which used to be a binding force for the Soviet Union, has become a thing of the past. The Kazakhs blame the communist Russian government for holding back the truth and its disregard for public safety. As I see it, the consequences of nuclear explosions at the Kazakh Test Site are similar to those of Chernobyl. Lack of safety culture was one of the reasons for the 1986 Chernobyl disaster in Ukraine. Overlooking nuclear safety is disregard for human life. After the disaster took place, the Soviet government offered no warning or advice of any kind about the dangers from the radiation exposure, leading to widespread illness as all involved were struck with severe symptoms of radiation poisoning. The accident contaminated large areas of the Soviet Union and its neighboring countries, but the government tried to cover the whole thing up, making only a vague announcement about the explosion after two days had passed; the world only became aware of the true horror of the accident after a radioactive cloud that had drifted into Sweden was sourced back to Chernobyl. Distrust can be contagious, as is revealed in *Underworld*. As horror stories about Chernobyl and the nuclear radiation poisoning that followed began to spread, the citizens of the Soviet Union began to lose faith in their nation's ability to inform and protect them; the government quickly began to lose control over its public. In the past, the people believed in the Soviet system, and trusted that it had led them to be the leading power in the world. After Chernobyl, they realized that the Soviet Union lagged politically, economically and technologically behind many Western countries, and that the system was flawed and potentially dangerous. On Christmas day in 1991, just six years after Chernobyl, the Soviet Union ceased to exist, as dissent amongst citizens, once completely satisfied with, and trusting, their government, grew over issues such as public safety and political transparency. Gorbachev stated that Chernobyl was "perhaps the real cause of the collapse of the Soviet Union" (qtd. in Kennedy, "Chernobyl's Role in the Fall of the Soviet Union).

The arms race, especially Reagan's "Star Wars" programs in the 1980s, by outspending the Soviet Union, weakened its stagnating and inefficient state-run economy. Globalization, which accelerated in the late 1980s as is depicted in *Mao* II, benefited American economy but bankrupted the Soviet's economy. Consumerism accompanying globalization eroded the Soviet people's faith in communism, and resulted in the dominance of popular culture in Moscow, as is depicted in the beginning of the epilogue to *Underworld*. DeLillo is insightful in arguing that "perhaps as much as proliferation of nuclear weapons, the proliferation of consumerism and disposable goods was a key weapon in America's Cold War arsenal" (Duvall, "Excavating the Underworld of Race and Waste in Cold War History" 260).

In *Underworld* the post-Cold War Russia has become a capitalist country like America: Postmodern culture, free market and entrepreneurialism. Like in *Mao* II, DeLillo is keenly aware that the old binary between communism and capitalism is replaced by the new binary between the West and Islam. He knows that terrorism in Central Asia is getting stronger. In Kazakhstan, Nick notices a dwarf girl in the clinic wearing "a T-shirt advertising a Gay and Lesbian Festival in Hamburg, Germany" (800). Victor tells Nick a local businessman bought 10000 T-shirts without knowing they were "leftovers from a gay celebration in Europe" (ibid.). "T-shirt," "advertising," and "Gay and Lesbian" are images of the corrupted West. Islam treats homosexuality as a sin and crime and should forbid it. Thus, it was a very "crazy thing … bringing these shirts into a place where Islam is stronger every day" (ibid.). The Islam fundamentalists would interpret this garbage as offensive and profane—as a threat to their faith or traditions, an invasion from the West, the leader of which is the United States of America. I admire DeLillo's insight and prophecy in *Underworld*. He is not only a historian, but also a prophet. In *Underworld* he predicts the upcoming Age of Terror. The planes that flew into the Twin Towers in New York City are alluded to on the cover of the novel. Four years after the publication of *Underworld*, the Islamic terrorists would attack the Twin Towers and the Pentagon. Driven by "the old slow furies of cut-throat religion" (DeLillo, "In the Ruins of the Future), the terrorists were training in Afghanistan and plotting in the mosque of Hamburg, Germany, preparing themselves for launching a terrorist attack against America, in an attempt to resist the invasion of Western culture and globalization.

3.2.2 The Nevada Test Site

In *Underworld* DeLillo also makes references to American nuclear test sites. The United States conducted around 1,054 nuclear tests (by official count) between 1945 and 1992, 300 more than the Soviet Union did. The test sites were located across the country, but mostly in Nevada and New Mexico. The US first atomic test Trinity was conducted on July 16, 1945 in the Jornada del Muerto desert of New Mexico. On August, 6 and 9, 1945, the US conducted the atomic bombings of Hiroshima and Nagasaki, two cities of Japan, causing massive casualties and the surrender of Japan. The bombings in Japan were the only use of nuclear weapons in war to date. At the news of America possessing atomic bombs with such unusual destructive force, Stalin gave orders for the Soviet scientists to develop their own nuclear weapons. Thus was started the nuclear arms race between the Soviet Union and the United States. They competed for advanced technology which could be used to produce more destructive yet safer nuclear weapons. DeLillo writes in *Underworld*: "All technology refers to the bomb" (467).

Nick's brother, Matty, worked in the development of nuclear weapons in the hills of southern New Mexico. One day Eric, one of "the bombheads," told Matty of the latest secret concerning the Nevada Test Site which was located in the Nevada desert. Workers at this site "in the days of the aboveground shots" were exposed to radiation and were reported to suffer from some diseases like multiple myelomas, kidney failures, and so on. These people were called "downwinders" (405). In the "[l]ittle farm communities downwind of the tests," which were mainly in southern Utah, "[n]early all the kids wear wigs" (406). Some kids were "born with a missing limb or whatnot" (ibid.). Some downwinders had teeth fall out or hair fall off, hence toothless and bald. Eric told Matty, the US Army used soldiers for experiments which exposed them to radiation without their knowledge or consent: "They marched troops to zero point after the detonations. They sent manned aircraft through radiation clouds" (417-18). DeLillo says in an interview that it is history that "the U.S. Army has truly conducted radiation experiments with soldiers. ... Every government is hiding secrets from its citizens" (qtd. in Burger, "Mr. Paranoia"). "History is the sum total of all things they don't tell us" (321), as DeLillo wrote in *Libra*.

The nuclear arms race took its toll. For 40 years the Americans competed against the Soviets to make more and better atomic bombs. "But the bombs were not released… The missiles remained in the rotary launchers." (122) The nuclear weapons along with the plutonium waste became hazardous garbage. The dissolution of the Soviet Union turned the nuclear test sites into waste land. When testing at the Nevada Nuclear Site ended in 1992, the US Department of Energy estimated that more than 300 million curies of radiation remained in the environment at that time, making the Nevada Nuclear Test Site one of the most radioactively contaminated locations in the United States. In the worst-affected zones, the concentration of radioactivity in affected groundwater reaches millions of picocuries per liter while the federal standard for drinking water is 20 picocuries per liter. Although radiation levels in the water continue to decline with the passage of time, the longer-lived isotopes could pose risks to workers or future settlers on the NNSS for tens of thousands of years (Vartabedian). Like the Russian businessman Victor, Jesse Detwiler, the American waste theorist in *Underworld*, predicts that the nuclear test site will become "Plutonium National Park" to be visited by tourists "wearing respirator masks and protective suits" (289).

DeLillo's descriptions of the deserted Kazakh Test Site and the Nevada desert and the repeated allusions to the wind recall "the landscape of *The Waste Land*, which Eliot's speaker characterizes as sterile, void of human habitation, and home only to the wind" (Gleason 133). But the waste land not only refers to the land contaminated by nuclear waste, but also the land occupied by social outcasts and consumerist waste.

3.2.3 The Bronx

In order to contain the Soviet Union, the United States produced more and more nuclear weapons that it could never use, leaving behind mountains of waste. For DeLillo, two forms of waste define American culture in the second half of the 20th century: "nuclear waste and waste produced by mass-media capitalism" (Gleason 133).

3.2.3.1 The Mafia

Many sections of *Underworld* unearth secrets which New York harbored during the Cold War years: the underworld of organized crimes; the underworld of drugs; the underworld of the underclass; and the underworld of subway graffiti artists. *Underworld* has autobiographical elements, as Dewey says, the novel is "DeLillo's touching gesture at autobiography, his most intimate record of his own childhood in the Bronx" ("A Gathering under Words: An Introduction" 10). DeLillo himself admits in an interview that "the Bronx episodes in Part Six particularly were written out of a sense of intimate knowledge" (qtd. in Howard 126). As a New York native, DeLillo witnessed recent decades' changes of New York City. On November 20, 1936, DeLillo was born into the family of an Italian immigrant couple in the Bronx. He grew up in an Italian-American neighborhood, attending Cardinal Hayes High School and later enrolling at Fordham University. In 1958 he graduated from the university. Except for three years (1979—1982) abroad, he lived in New York City most of the time. Now DeLillo lives "just north of New York City—not terribly far from the Bronx neighborhood and the now-vanished Manhattan stadium where key sections of *Underworld* take place" (Howard 121). DeLillo chronicles the underhistory of contemporary New York City in *Underworld*.

In *Underworld* there are many characters from the Bronx: Nick Shay, Matthew Shay, Klara Sax, Sister Edgar, and so on. They are fictional characters, but based on DeLillo's intimate knowledge of real people he knew in his childhood in the Bronx. Nick, a central character, was born in the Italian Bronx. He grows up in an apartment building near DeLillo's old house. When Nick was "eleven years old," his father, James Costanza, "went out for cigarettes," and disappeared since then (118). Nick thinks his father may have been killed by the mob for not paying off a debt. "They took him out to the marshes and wasted him." (106) In his childhood DeLillo witnessed that Arthur Avenue, the heart of the Italian Bronx, was thick with mobsters. In an interview DeLillo told David Remnick:

> There was a Mob hit here when I was a kid—a mobster killed while he was buying fruit. I think it must have been a model for that scene in *The Godfather* when Mario Puzo has Don Corleone getting shot while he's buying fruit in the street. He was a mobster from City Island who came here to shop. There were actually three events like that when I was growing up. One was the uncle of a kid I knew. And the other was in a liquor store. (137)

The Godfather, a novel written by Italian American author Mario Puzo in 1969, tells the story of a fictitious New York Mafia family involved in a range of underworld activities like loan-sharking, drug trafficking and prostitution during the years from 1945 to 1955. *The Godfather* is an intertext of *Underworld*. Perhaps because Nick sees mobs kill and get killed in the street, he imagines his father borrows money from the Mafia, but unluckily cannot repay them. The mobs cannot get their money back and so kill Costanza in order to warn others against following his example. The drug trafficking of the Mafia leads to easy access to drugs in the Bronx. George the waiter has trouble in sleeping and feels lonely and empty like the old waiter in Hemingway's famous short story "A Clean, Well-Lighted Place." He takes drugs to anesthetize himself, which makes things worse. One day in a basement George puts a shotgun in Nick's hand and tells Nick it is not loaded. Nick pulls the trigger and kills doped George, which can be interpreted as a revenge on the community plagued by the Mafia.

The title "Underworld" not only refers to the underworld of waste: human waste and nuclear waste; the underworld of baseball memorabilia, but also points to the Mafia, the underworld of organized crime, the dark side of the Bronx which witnessed lives wasted, moral decay, and spiritual death.

3.2.3.2 The Wall

"Underworld" also refers to the underworld of the underclass in the South Bronx in the late 1980s and the early 1990s. "In the book there's a wasted section of the South Bronx called the Wall. It's an area outside the reach of basic services such as water and electricity" (qtd. in Howard 127). DeLillo depicts many types of waste, and "the Wall is a particular part of the waste—the part that includes human lives" (ibid.).

The decay of the South Bronx started in the 1960s, but in *Underworld* the South Bronx passages "are set around the time of the fall of the Berlin Wall" (qtd. in Howard 127), in Part 2 "Elegy for Left Hand Alone: Mid-1980s—Early 1990s." This is a landscape in the South Bronx

> of vacant lots filled with years of stratified deposits—the age of house garbage, the age of construction debris and vandalized car bodies, the age of moldering mobster parts. Weeds and trees grew amid the dumped objects. [...] At the far end was a standing structure, a derelict tenement with an exposed wall where another building had once abutted. [...] This area was called the Wall, partly for the graffiti façade and partly the general sense of exclusion—it was a tuck of land adrift from the social order. (238)

An underworld artist Ismael Muñoz and his crew of graffiti writers spray-paint a memorial angel on the wall every time a child died in the neighborhood. The causes of the children's terrible death are "TB, AIDS, beatings, drive-by shooting, measles, asthma, abandonment at birth" (239). In the streets of the South Bronx there are teenager boys in clusters, armed drug dealers and monks who run a shelter for the homeless and collect food for the hungry. At night shootings can be heard all the time, "death interchangeable on the street and TV" (249). In the derelict tenement a number of floors are occupied by squatters, "a society of indigents subsisting without heat, lights or water" (242). Ismael's crew consists of kids who are illiterate and speak broken English. They help with Ismael's spray-painting and Nun Edgar's distributing free food, condoms and needles to the poor people in the area, who "paid rent for plywood cubicles worse than prison holes" (246). These people are social outcasts: either handicapped, or heroin addicts, or suffering cancers, or unemployed prostitutes, or small children abandoned by parents. Living in the ghetto is a 12-year-old girl named Esmeralda, who forages in empty lots for discarded clothes, and plucks spoiled fruit from garbage bags behind bodegas. Abandoned by her mother, she is sometimes seen running in the thickest part of the lots with dumped hospital waste and laboratory waste, which is frequented by bats and rats. One day somebody rapes her, throws her off a roof and kills her. Onto the painted wall another angel is sprayed. "A winged figure in a pink sweatshirt and pink and aqua pants and a pair of white Nike Air Jordans with the logo prominent—she was a running girl so they gave her running shoes." (815)

In *Underworld* DeLillo depicts the nuclear wasteland and the urban wasteland in America. During the period of US-Soviet rivalry, Americans were living in the shadow of the threat of nuclear warfare, which caused great damage to the psyche of Americans. The United States won the Cold War, but at what cost? DeLillo urges Americans to acknowledge the cost of their victory that is not included in the official history of the Cold War. The nuclear arms race produced the underworld of weapons and waste, leaving behind a waste land. There were "pyramids of waste above and below the earth" (106), downwinders—victims of nuclear testing, and the underclass in the South Bronx. In an interview, Howard asked DeLillo: "Was the near death of the Bronx ... as clear a cost of the Cold War as, say, the devastating pollution of certain Soviet Union?" DeLillo answered:

> There is certainly no explicit connection. There is a kind of shadow, a whisper. And there are themes of weapons and waste. The beautiful, expensive, nobly named weapons systems. And then the waste, many types of waste, and the Wall is a particular part of the waste—the part that includes human lives. (qtd. in Howard 127)

Like the nuclear waste, the Wall in the South Bronx was a by-product of American arms races with the Soviet Union, a price America paid for its victory in the Cold War. The containment, the military build-up, the covert actions, the economic sanctions and the Strategic Defense Initiative called for high spending, which did not bankrupt America, but did have economic and social costs which were exemplified by the South Bronx. In *Underworld* the passages about the Wall in the South Bronx "are set around the time of the fall of the Berlin Wall" (ibid.). The Berlin Wall was built in 1961 by East Germany and was called "the Wall of Shame" by West Germany. The physical Wall itself was primarily destroyed in 1990. "The Iron Curtain" was destroyed and then at the end of 1991 the Soviet Union dissolved. Thus ended the Cold War. But at the time of the fall of the Berlin Wall, DeLillo "builds" a wall in the South Bronx, which exposes the underbelly of American society. Which one was more pathetic, the downwinders in the victimized Kazakh villages, or the underclass in the South Bronx? The Wall in the South Bronx is "the Wall of Shame" in the United States.

3.3 Redemption of the Waste Land

Is there any possibility of redeeming the waste land? Art has a synthesizing and redemptive force. DeLillo's portrayal of artist characters in *Underworld* seems to suggest a positive answer: the hope of redemption is situated in art.

In *Underworld* DeLillo depicts a group of artists: satirist Lenny Bruce, sculptor Klara Sax, graffiti writer Ismael Muñoz, film-maker Sergei Eisenstein and visionary sculptor Simon Rodia. Lenny, Sergei and Simon are historical characters while Klara and Ismael are fictional. Sergei and Simon do not appear personally. Their names are mentioned because of their works. Sergei was a Soviet movie director. In the novel DeLillo invents a Sergei movie *Unterwelt* which has been suppressed and thus remains in the underground until it is "recently found in East Germany, meticulously restored and brought to New York under the aegis of the film society" (424). Simon was an Italian-American who created the Watts Towers, a Los Angeles landmark, out of garbage. Although the novel is full of artists, my discussion in this section focuses on Klara, Sabato and Ismael.

Klara is a conceptual artist. She is called "the Bag Lady" (70) because she has been using garbage as material to construct art. Klara retreats to the desert of Arizona from Manhattan where she has been working with "castoffs" for years. In her desert atelier, she repaints B-52 long-range bombers which were used during the Vietnam War. This project draws many volunteers, who come to the desert to paint the deactivated aircraft which were weapons but are now waste after having been "stripped of most components that might still be useful or salable to civilian contractors" (69). Klara is not "going to let these machines expire in a field or get sold as scrap" (70). As she affirms in 1974, "We took junk and saved it for art" (393), she is employing the decommissioned B-52 bombers to create works of art, not just for the sake of art, but also for peace, because there are redemptive qualities in "the things we use and discard" (809).

From recycling the cast-off materials in daily life to the Cold War weaponry, Klara gets inspiration from rubbish. Her recycling of discarded objects links her with Simon Rodia, who built Watts Towers from "steel rods and broken crockery and pebbles and seashells and soda bottles and wire mesh, all hand-mortared, three thousand sacks of sand and cement" (276). Sabato Rodia, an illiterate Italian immigrant, spent more than 30 years in the south Los Angeles neighborhood "with glass specks crusting his hands and arms and glass dust in his eyes as he hangs from a window-washer's belt high on the towers, in torn overall and a dusty fedora, face burnt brown, with lights strung on the radial spokes so he could work at night, maybe ninety feet up, and Caruso on the gramophone below" (ibid.). He worked single-handedly without benefit of machine equipment, scaffolding, bolts, rivets, welds, drawing board designs or even nails. "When he finished the towers, Sabato Rodia gave away the land and all the art that was on it" (277). For decades Rodia was engaged in turning rubbish into artistic work. In my view, he was a great artist in spite of his illiteracy. Although the Towers fall into no strict art category, international authorities and the general public alike have honored them as a unique monument to the human spirit and the persistence of a singular vision. His Watts Towers has become a landmark of Los Angeles and attracted visitors from all over the world.

Ismael Muñoz is a Puerto Rican graffiti artist living in the decayed part of the Bronx. In the eyes of Sister Edgar, Ismael is waste because he is homosexual. His work is not regarded as art, but waste or an act of vandalism, by the authorities. The merits of graffiti lie in its subversion or resistance as Mark Osteen remarks: "Ismael's work is multiply subversive: in writing his name with stolen materials, he ironically appropriates the consumer society's fixation on brand names and transforms it into an attack on private property" (ibid.). Ismael's work is truly a counter-discourse from the underworld which "rushes" through the 1970s' American society.

In the late 1980s Ismael stops tagging the trains. He is doing community work in the Wall of a derelict tenement in New York's urban waste land. Ismael and his crew of graffiti writers spray-paint a memorial angel on the Wall every time a child died in the neighborhood, thus transforms the waste land into a piece of art work which draws public attention to the urban ghetto communities that mainstream America does not want to acknowledge. Tourists from Europe are drawn to the Wall and name it *South Bronx Surreal*. Ismael not only uses art to tell the backstreet stories to the public, but also helps to take care of the inhabitants of the Wall by his salvage business which is recycling junk cars. He earns money from recycling the junk, "using it more or less altruistically, teaching his crew of stray kids … giving them a sense of responsibility and self-worth" (813) and helping the nuns feed the hungry. With his recycled art, Ismael joins in the efforts of the nuns and priests to bring changes to the Wall and redeem the postmodern waste land.

Simon Rodia, Ismael Muñoz and Klara Sax work both on and with elements provided by consumer culture. Sabato Rodia constructed his towers out of the detritus of the consumer society. Ismael uses spray paints stolen from hardware stores. Though many of Klara Sax's materials are donated, she admits that "[W]e still have to scratch and steal to get many of the things we need" (69) and thus earns the nickname "the Bag Lady" of garbage. Then after the end of the Cold War, Klara takes another kind of waste—the decommissioned B-52s that had been used to carry the nuclear payload that could have removed humanity from the earth—and recycles it into "works of singular beauty" (Osteen, *American Magic and Dread* 256). For DeLillo, Rodia's Watts Towers, Ismael's graffiti and Klara's "Long Tall Sally" project in Arizona's desert exemplify "how art can become an agent of redemption, reconstructing hope and beauty out of the wreckage of history, as such it offers a model for all post-Cold War artists" (ibid. 255).

DeLillo himself is such an artist. Like Simon Rodia, Ismael Muñoz and Klara Sax, his method of waste disposal is recycling. He "has taken the effluvia of modern life, all the detritus of our daily and political lives, and turned it into a dazzling, phosphorescent work of art" (qtd. in Cowart, *The Physics of Language* 197). DeLillo, along with the artist figures in his fiction, shows us how art can become an agent of redemption by transforming waste into art. DeLillo, like Nick Shay, the waste manager of *Underworld*, recycles the wasteful culture, sifting and sorting through the physical, metaphysical and spiritual excesses, contaminants, and wastes of postmodernity, and writes a counter-history of contemporary America.

4 "Everything Is Connected in the End"

Underworld ends in cyberspace where "[t]here are only connections" (825). Cyberspace, the virtual world, is where Sister Edgar goes to after she died. As a Cold War nun, she witnesses the end of the conflict between the socialist East and the capitalist West and the beginning of a new era in which people, countries and cultures interact more closely. Like Úrsula Iguarán in Gabriel García Márquez's *One*

Hundred Years of Solitude, Sister Edgar has lived long enough to experience the paranoia of the Cold War and the paranoia of the web in the era of globalization: "from the apocalyptic anxiety of the early Cold War through the tense brinkmanship of the Cuban Missile Crisis and the doomed containment crusade of Vietnam and ultimately, to the giddy flush that followed the speechlessly swift collapse of the Soviet empire and the late-century emergence of capitalist commodity-culture as the defining world market" (Dewey 114). With her death comes the end of an age which was dominated by conflicts, containment and the decline of spirituality.

Does her death signal the dawn of a new faith? Probably yes, for Sister Edgar finds a new God in the cyberspace. After her death, she does not go to heaven but to cyberspace where she "joins the other Edgar" (826), the late FBI director J. Edgar Hoover, who died in 1972. One logs onto the H-bomb home page and finds Sister Edgar is right in it. She sees the flashes of the atomic bomb tests and merges with the God of atoms, its "dripping christblood colors, solar golds and reds" (825). When the atomic nuclear bombs detonate across the screen, again and again, "there is another fusion taking place" (826), which not only brings together Sister Edgar and Edgar Hoover—the fictional and the historical—but also connects the religious and the political; the Church and the State; and the magic and the dread of the Cold War. This new faith seems to have a unifying force that connects everything. Thus DeLillo ends his novel with the world "Peace," which expresses the author's tentative hope.

This ending catches the general mood in the post-Cold War American society. The collapse of the Soviet Union boosted the Americans' confidence in capitalism and Western democracy which they believe may dominate the earth in the future. An American scholar, Francis Fukuyama, elaborates his optimistic belief in the final peace of the world in his book *The End of History and the Last Man* (1992). In the book, Fukuyama writes: "What we may be witnessing is not just the end of the Cold War, or the passing of a particular period of post-war history, but the end of history as such: that is, the end point of mankind's ideological evolution and the universalization of Western liberal democracy as the final form of human government." As soon as the book was published, Fukuyama was criticized. I think DeLillo is among his critics. Throughout his career, DeLillo is a satirist of American capitalist society which highlights democracy but is still plagued by social problems like poverty, racial tension and violence. He also detects authoritarian elements in American consumer culture which is dominated by mass culture. At the same time, DeLillo sharply observes the rise of terrorism and the threat of Islamic fundamentalism to the spread of liberal democracy. Even if capitalism triumphs as is depicted in the epilogue of

Underworld, there remains the clash of civilizations.

The invention of the Internet and the development of globalization have strengthened the interconnectedness of different nations and people, but they will not lead to Fukuyama's "end of history." The September 11 terrorist attacks proved that Fukuyama was wrong in thinking that the end of the Cold War also represented the end of major global conflicts and that the optimism of the Western world during the 1990s was too naive in various senses.

Chapter Three

Narrative Strategies in DeLillo's Fictional Texts

DeLillo is a serious author who writes with a great moral sense. His work is a critique of American society in which individuals are subject to the controlling influence of mass media, corporations and other social organizations. Throughout DeLillo's work runs his resistance to the established order and the social forces which are the enemy of democracy and individualism. But DeLillo's subversion of the socio-economic and political structures is contained by the dominant power structures. His criticism of American society becomes more subtle and less provocative than when he wrote *Libra* and *White Noise*. After *Underworld*, DeLillo's career turned towards the miniature: *The Body Artist*, *Cosmopolis*, *The Falling Man* and *Point Omega* are much slighter books. As he is getting old with years and gets well-established as a canonical writer, he becomes less of a postmodernist than early DeLillo reception indicated, and becomes increasingly a modernist, as some critics have observed (Nel, "DeLillo's Return to Form" 736-38).

There has been a lot of debate as to whether DeLillo is a modernist or a postmodernist. It is no doubt that DeLillo's work examines the effects of social, political, or cultural changes in American society and that DeLillo's fiction after *White Noise* continues to address his concerns of postmodernity, but their forms move toward modernism. After a close examination of DeLillo's fiction of the later period, it can be found that the major narrative forms DeLillo exploits were also used by canonical modernist masters like James Joyce, William Faulkner and Virginia Woolf. Multiple points of view, discontinuity in narration, black humor and intertextuality are associated with the avant-garde in modernism. DeLillo's employment of those strategies helps represent the chaos, fragmentation, randomness, absurdity and indeterminacy in postmodern American society. It manifests clearly that he "has a greater formal and spiritual affinity with the early twentieth-century avant-garde in particular and modernism in general than with other contemporary postmodernist writers" (Knight 27).

DeLillo's use of multiple points of view matches the postmodern spirit manifested by Lyotard's "petit narrative." Discontinuity in narration is used to render contemporary disorder and lost coherence. Black humor and intertextuality have existed for a long time. Jonathan Swift was identified as the originator of black humor. Since the 1960s black humor has been associated with postmodernism. DeLillo employs black humor to criticize American society. His black humor contains both realism and postmodernism. The term "intertextuality" was coined by poststructuralist Julia Kristeva in 1966. But it is not new as a device. The New Testament passages quote from the Old Testament, and in the Old Testament the events described in some books are referred to in some other books. Now intertextuality has become the very trademark of postmodernism. Many of DeLillo's novels blend different literary genres and various narratives so much so that it is difficult to classify them according to traditional literary rubrics, hence the on-going debate among the critics. In my view, the blending of the genres and narrative forms that used to be associated with realism and modernism is an important feature of postmodern American culture and is suitable for the representation of the paradoxes and contradictions of postmodern culture.

I. Multiple Points of View

Point of view is the position from which the events of a story seem to be observed and presented to readers. It is one of the most important basics for any piece of fiction. There are two types of point of view that tend to dominate most current writing: first person, or stories that are narrated by "I"; and third person, where the point of view, using "he" or "she", is limited to one or more characters; and the third person omniscient, where the writing moves in and out of various characters' points of view fluidly. Many novels use multiple points of view, in which the events are presented from the positions of two or more different characters, alternating between first and third person point of view. DeLillo employs multiple narrative points of view in his fiction. The narration sometimes shifts from the first person point of view to the third, and sometimes the dominant third person narration is embedded by the first person point of view. Let's take *Libra* for example.

There are 24 chapters in *Libra*. The odd chapters are Oswald's biographical chapters and the even chapters are conspiracy chapters. The two narratives converge at the end of Chapter 17 "In New Orleans" in which Oswald begins to interact with the conspirators. At this point the novel "becomes one headlong scream toward November 22" (qtd. in Connolly 34). Throughout the novel, the dominant narrative technique is the third person accounts conducted in interior monologue. In Oswald's chapters the story is told mainly from the third person point of view, and occasionally from the first person point of view. The novel starts with the following paragraph:

> This was the year he rode the subway to the ends of the city, two hundred miles of track. He liked to stand at the front of the first car, hands flat against the glass. The train smashed through the dark. People stood on local platform staring nowhere, a look they'd been practicing for years. He kind of wondered, speeding past, who they really were. His body fluttered in the fastest stretches. They went so fast sometimes he thought they were on the edge of no-control. The noise was pitched to a level of pain he absorbed as a personal test. Another crazy-ass curve. (3)

This chapter in which this paragraph appears is entitled "In the Bronx." It recounts Oswald's early life in the Bronx, New York. The story of Oswald's roaming the city is apparently told in the third person limited point of view. But the inner voice is Oswald's. Interior monologue provides a chance to see inside the heads of characters. We see New York City through Oswald's eyes and in the meantime are offered Oswald's inner thoughts and impressions. This unique narrative strategy is employed throughout the novel, offering characterization and motivation and giving a mimetic reproduction of soical reality in the United States in the 1950s and the early 1960s.

In the modernist works runs the "blood" of realism. Virginia Woolf advocated a new realism based on consciousness:

> Examine for a moment an ordinary mind on an ordinary day. The mind receives a myriad of impressions—trivial, fantastic, evanescent, or engraved with the sharpness of steel. From all sides they come, an incessant shower of innumerable atoms . . . Let us record the atoms as they fall upon the mind in the order in which they fall, let us trace the pattern, however disconnected and incoherent in appearance, which each sight or incidence scores upon the consciousness. (qtd. in Jahn 95)

DeLillo follows this doctrine in his fiction writing as he admits in an interview: "I tend to write through character consciousness, and different people in my books have different feelings about this matter" (Binelli). In *Libra*, DeLillo enters the consciousness of Oswald and other characters' consciousness as well. Thus the story is told by multiple narrators, resulting in multiple perspectives. This contributes to the construction of the fictional world which is full of uncertainties, ambiguities and chaos, and accurately represents the fabric of American postmodern reality.

In the chapters about Oswald, the narrator voices shift among Oswald, Marina and Marguerite, alternating between the third-person point of view and first-person point of view. When Oswald is accused of truanting, and Marguerite is accused of neglecting her duty as a mother and being "the looming mother of a boy's bad dream" (49), Marguerite tries to defend her son and herself by narrating her difficult life story as a single mother and put the blame on the unfair society. In these parts of the novel DeLillo chooses to use Marguerite's viewpoint and carefully mimic her speech patterns. Here are examples:

> Does he have religious affiliation and whatnot? Is he disruptive in class? He doesn't know the slang, your honor. The place is full of New York-type boys. They see my son in Levis, with an accent. Well many boys wear Levis. What is strange about Levis? […] He is advanced, your honor. I have said from early childhood he liked histories and maps. He knows uncanny things without the normal schooling. The boy slept in my bed out of lack of space until he was nearly eleven and we have lived the two of us in the meanest of small rooms when his brothers were in the orphans' home or the military academy or the Marines and the Coast Guard. Most boys think their daddy hung the moon. But the poor man just crashed to the lawn and that was the end of the only happy part of my adult life. It is Marguerite and Lee ever since. We are mother and son. It has never been a question of neglect. (11)
>
> […] As far as his mother's place in his heart, he has worked as a messenger and office boy and bought me a thirty-five-dollar coat with his first pay and who gives over money to his mother for room and board and bought me a parakeet in a cage that came with a stand and with a planter. […] I cannot say enough how hard it is to raise boys without a father. […] I am mother of three who sold needles and thread and yarn in her own shop in the front room of the house […] I was a popular child, your honor. I was raised by a father with five other children to be happy and patriotic. I have made my best effort to raise my boy in this manner, regardless. (48-49)

Marguerite is talking to a person she addresses as "your honor", probably a lawyer, to defend her son and herself. She denies all those accusations against her. Her viewpoint, or perspective, of a mother adds to the reliability of her story, for what she recounts is all about herself and Oswald and no one can have more knowledge of their life. Marguerite's accounts portray the poor people's life in the American Southern states in the early 1950s. The United States in the 1950s experienced marked economic growth—with an increase in manufacturing and home construction in a post-World

War II economic boom. But Marguerite's story shows that not every American benefits from the economic boom. She is a working single mother with three children to take care of. No one offers help to them. Instead, they suffer unfair treatment and discrimination because of poverty, bad education and accent. She is speaking not only in defense of her son and herself, but also as a kind of counteraccusation of the social neglect of the poor.

Marguerite's viewpoint is consistent with Oswald's. They are critical of American society. When they move back to the southern city of New Orleans, their life is still miserable. This is what Oswald sees and how he feels about their living condition:

> Ever since he could remember, they'd shared cramped spaces. It was basic Oswald memory. He could smell the air she moved through, could smell her clothes hanging behind a door, a tropical mist of corsets and toilet water. He entered bathrooms in the full aura of her stink. He heard her mutter in her sleep, grinding the death's-head teeth. He knew what she would say, saw the gestures before she made them. (35)

The family's poverty partly drives Oswald to reading communist works which becomes a hobby in his spare time, an escape from the depressing reality, something to show his uniqueness and individuality because he has nothing to show off in front of his classmates and colleagues. As Oswald grows up, he sees himself as a Marxist. When he is stationed in Japan, he meets Dr. Braunfels, a Russian spy. He tells her that he wants to defect to Russia:

> I studied Marxist ideology. I could lift my head from a book and see the impoverishment of the masses right there in front of me, including my own mother in her struggle to raise three children against the odds. These socialist writings showed me the key to my environment. [...] There is hysteria in the air, like hating Negroes and communists. [...] I'm ready to go through pain and hardship to leave my country forever. (110)

No matter whether DeLillo uses the third person point of view or the first person, the fictional world in *Libra* is seen through the eyes of the characters, not dominated by one controlling voice and the omniscient perspective, representing a world shaped by individual perceptions.

The narrative form that is often used in *Libra* is called "figural narrative" by Franz K. Stanzel, that is, "a third-person narrative in which the story world is seen through the eyes of a character" (Jahn 95). In his theoretical writings, Henry James called such central perceiving characters "centers," "mirrors" or "reflectors". The French narrative theorist Gerard Genette called these characters "focal characters." Genette coined a term "focalization" which refers to the perspective through which a narrative is presented, and the way the events, characters and objects of the story are perceived. In the Oswald chapters of *Libra*, Oswald is the major internal focalizer. His life story is the focalized object, moving from the Bronx, New York; New Orleans; Atsugi, Japan, as a US Marine; back to Fort Worth, Texas; then to Moscow and Minsk, as a defector; two years later back to Fort Worth; to New Orleans and Dallas, looking for jobs; to New Mexico for a visa to Cuba; finally to Dallas where he shot at the President and was killed. What happens to him is seen through his eyes and filtered through his perceptions. We follow his eyes from event to event, from place to place, and gain an insight into American society in the 1950s and the early 1960s. Not only is the external world presented, but also Oswald's internal world. DeLillo lets us look into the mind of Oswald, striving to create a truer Oswald with depth and character, not the stereotypical assassin in a government file. Oswald, on the surface, is a man with communist views who struggles to function in an unequal American society. However, DeLillo does what many others would not think of when addressing the presidential assassin, he attempts to understand Oswald as a person and describes Oswald in this sense as a human being with multiple parts as opposed to a singular entity with no background. The result of DeLillo's assessment is the title and theme of the novel, as Libra is Oswald's zodiac symbol and also a representation of balance in his actions.

The conspiracy chapters cover the plot against Kennedy and are named after the dates that mark its development between 17 April and 22 November 1963. DeLillo employs multiple internal focalization and represents the history of the Kennedy Assassination from multiple perspectives. Through the eyes of Oswald, Marguerite, the conspirators Everett, Parmenter, Banister, Ferrie and Mackey, and the present day view of Nicholas Branch, DeLillo formulates a conspiracy that embodies what American culture desires out of the Kennedy Assassination: a reason or an answer to why and how the President was killed. From Oswald's point of view, he is a socially battered man. His life consists of truancy, defection, the undesirable discharge and lost jobs. He is an unwelcome Marxist, but he is not a political fanatic as the media paint him to be. He sees himself a patsy. In Marguerite's viewpoint, Oswald is set up for the role of the assassin. She thinks Oswald is used by the American government but does not get a decent burial. She sees Oswald's body buried "in the utmost sheepish hurry" (449) without being allowed to stay in the chapel for a brief service. She thinks her son works for CIA. "There are stories inside stories, judge. Lee collected stamps in a book and practiced chess alone at the kitchen table and they sent him to Russia to infiltrate" (450). She wonders: "Who arranged the life of Lee Harvey Oswald?" (455).

The conspirators' perspectives display why they hold grudges against the President, how they plot against the President and how they try to manipulate and use Oswald. They are all anti-communists, furious about the President's half-heartedness about the Bay of Pigs Invasion and anxious about the spread of communism in Cuba. But each conspirator has his own story and intention. Everette plans to stage a mock assassination, but Mackey wants to kill the President for those anti-Castro Cuban exiles. Is Oswald the lone gunman? At the Dealey Plaza there are three gunmen: Raymo and Frank Vásquez, two Cuban shooters arranged by Mackey, and Oswald. The shootings at the President are perceived by Raymo and Oswald:

> Leon fired too soon, with the car passing under the tree. The report sounded like a short charge, a little weak, a defect, not enough powder.
> Kennedy reacted late, without surprise at first, his arms coming up slowly like a man on a rowing machine. (397)

Oswald fires the first two wounding and distracting shots, but Raymo fires the fatal shot from the fenced parking area. Oswald is not the lone gunman. He does not intend to kill the President, instead he feels shocked, even somewhat upset, when he perceives the murdering and death of Kennedy. *Libra* thus becomes one of many rebuttals of the Warren Report. It challenges "the lone gunman" verdict of the Warren committee. By employing the multiple perspectives and probing into the consciousness of the characters, DeLillo patches up the complex reality of the United States in the 1950s and the early 1960s, and explores the possible motive for the JFK Assassination. In the meantime, he depicts a more convincing Oswald who can arouse our sympathy and pins blame for the JFK Assassination on the CIA agents who were extremely unsatisfied with the President's handling of the Cuban Missile Crisis.

By using the multiple points of view, DeLillo makes the novel a medium of democracy. This narrative strategy allows us to enter the consciousness of the characters and hear their different voices and treat each character as an equal human being with dreams, emotions, frustrations, fears and anxiety. DeLillo is justified in using this strategy which contributes to the representation of the reality, both social and personal, psychological.

II. Discontinuity in Narration

Apart from the multiple points of view, discontinuity is a technique employed by DeLillo to portray the fragmentation, confusion and chaos which are the postmodern reality. This nonlinear narrative technique, like the multiple points of view or stream of consciousness, was used by modernist writers such as Joseph Conrad, Marcel Proust and William Faulkner who upset the accepted continuity of chronological development valued by the 19th century traditions. The multiple points of view are, in fact, a kind of discontinuous narrative, with the disjuncture arising out of the medley of voices and perceptions.

Discontinuous narrative is a narrative style in which the narrative moves back and forth through time. It is used in many of DeLillo's works. DeLillo is thus regarded as "the master of discontinuity, and the moment you start to settle into the narrative flow is just when you can count on a change in scenery" (Gioia, "*Underworld* by Don DeLillo").

Libra is apparently organized in a fragmented way, as it stresses the confusion and uncertainty that floats around the events that took place in Dallas. DeLillo employs three types of discontinuity in narration to depict the chaos and randomness arising from the JFK Assassination. First is the discontinuity of narrative perspective. There are three parallel stories in *Libra*: a biography of Lee Harvey Oswald, a CIA plot against Kennedy, and the efforts made by a retired CIA agent to write a secret history of the assassination for the CIA. There are 24 chapters in the novel. The odd-numbered chapters are Oswald chapters and entitled after the places where he lived. The even-numbered chapters are conspiracy chapters which cover the plot against Kennedy and are named after the dates that mark its development between April and November 1963. Oswald's biography and the conspiracy narrative converge at the end of the long New Orleans chapter when Ferrie talks to Oswald. Ferrie said:

> Think of two parallel lines [...] One is the life of Lee H. Oswald. One is the conspiracy to kill the President. What bridges the space between them? What makes a connection inevitable? There is a third line. It comes out of dreams, visions, intuitions, prayers, out of the deepest levels of the self. It's not generated by cause and effect like the other two lines. It's a line that cuts across causality, cuts across time. It has no history that we can recognize or understand. But it forces a connection. It puts a man on the path of his destiny. (339)

Here Ferrie acts the role of the author explaining the plot and structure of the book when he was trying to explain to Oswald that "what they in fact want from him is for him to assassinate the president. He is actually laying out the plot for the novel *Libra*" (Connolly 34). The two narratives develop chronologically, respectively. The narration of the novel alternates between Oswald's biography and the conspiracy of the conspirators, shifting from place to place, which results in the second type of discontinuity in narration: spatial discontinuity. The first chapter describes Oswald's life in the Bronx, New York City in 1952. Chapter 2 is titled "17 April, 1963," the second anniversary of the Bay of Pigs Invasion. On this day the main conspirators and veterans of the Bay of Pigs meet in Dallas to discuss their plan to get back Cuba by plotting against the President's life. Oswald as the gunman was alluded to, too. "On the radio a new announcer said that police were still keeping watch over Major General Edwin A. Walker's home and grounds following a gunman's attempt to kill the controversial rightwing figure one week earlier." (30) This chapter points to Chapter 22, "22 November," on which day the conspirators' plan was carried out in Dallas, hence forming a loop. On the surface the narration follows roughly the chronological development of the novel, from Oswald's teenage to his death. But as I have mentioned, the Oswald narrative and the conspiracy narrative alternate chapter by chapter and are interwoven by Nicholas Branch's investigation, speculation and reflection, which gives the feeling that "we enter the world of randomness and ambiguity" (qtd. in Connolly 28).

The third type of discontinuity in narration employed in *Libra* is temporal discontinuity. In Chapter 2 there are four narrative points of view. Branch's story is told in the present tense while the rest of the novel is written in the past tense. At the beginning of Chapter 2 we read

> Nicholas Branch sits in the book-filled room, the room of documents, the room of theories and dreams. He is in the fifteenth year of his labor and sometimes wonders if he is becoming bodiless. [...] This is the room of growing old, the fireproof room, paper everywhere. (14)

Branch's room is filled with books, reports, papers, all kinds of materials about the assassination and it is from the closeness of his room that the reader is pushed towards a confused world peopled with a myriad of different characters. Thus the novel becomes a collective representation of contemporary American society. It is through the documents collected in Branch's study that we come across some of the public

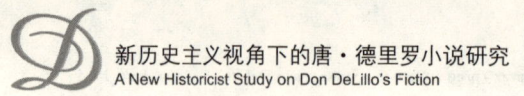

figures that have filled the chronicles of contemporary history in the last five decades:

> He enters a date on the home computer the Agency has provided for the sake of convenient tracking. April 17, 1963. The names appear at once, with backgrounds, connections, locations. The bright hot skies. The shady street of handsome old homes framed in native oak. (15-16)

The present tense and the home computer that appear in the quoted passage pinpoint Branch as DeLillo's contemporary. Some critics see Branch as DeLillo's double (Lentricchia, "*Libra* as Postmodern Critique" 215). There is no denying that Branch sounds like DeLillo. Both are postmodern historians, paying great attention to the close reading of historical texts and believing that our only access to history is through texts. Throughout the novel, DeLillo's narration jumps back and forth on the time line. Branch "speaks" at the time when his story takes place, at least 15 years after the assassination. It is through his introduction that we enter the conspirators' world. Win Everett and his fellow conspirators are engaged in the conspiratorial activities which take place from 17 April, 1963 to 24 November, 1963. Through the flashbacks of the conspirators we learn about their stories during and after the Bay of Pigs Invasion and understand their fear, anxiety and anger toward Kennedy. In order to answer who Lee Oswald was, why he assassinated the President if he was the assassin, and whether there were other gunmen involved, DeLillo examines the fragmented and enigmatic life story of Oswald. He deconstructs the official history by offering his own theory of the assassination. DeLillo explores the possible motives of the conspirators. Moving back and forth through time, DeLillo's discontinuous narration captures the fragmented nature of the postmodern society and reconstructs the historical environment of the JFK Assassination.

Underworld is DeLillo's longest and most complicated novel. One of the most striking features of *Underworld*'s narrative is its sprawling, nonlinear structure. The novel opens on October 3, 1951, when a boy named Cotter Martin sneaks in to watch the New York Giants play against the Brooklyn Dodgers at the Giants' home field Polo Grounds. After the prologue of the baseball game, the novel cuts to 1992 and begins to work backward through the years of the Cold War until back to 1951 again. The novel ends in the late 1990s when the Soviet Union collapses and capitalism starts to develop in Russia. Its dislocations of temporality are seen in the scrambling of chronology as well as the mixing of present-tense and past-tense narration. At first glance haphazard and fragmentary, the narrative is stitched together with the help of a number of objects (like the baseball and the waste) and characters (like Nick Shay and

Klara Sax) whose transformations the reader witnesses from the 1950s to the closing years of the millennium. DeLillo himself has likened the structure of the book to the countdown to zero that precedes a missile or rocket launch:

> Once I set the structure and once I figured it out, I took it for granted and haven't really thought much about it. But it occurred to me recently that in a curious way it duplicates the countdown voice we associate with a nuclear test—ten, nine, eight, seven [...] (Gerald Howard 122)

This structure, then, is perfectly suitable for DeLillo's representation of American experience in the nuclear age.

The backward movement of the narration also suggests

> a number of self-evident analogues, especially the activity of memory, and to a kind of psychoanalytic and cultural archaeology. As archaeology, the movement backward is also a movement down, under, and within—each suggestive of an underworld to be revealed. (Hendin 71)

Underworld models the activity of memory so as to explore the whole landscapes of experience in the Cold War. Like an archaeologist, DeLillo digs into the past of American society to discover the unwritten history of America during the Cold War.

Another nonlinear narrative technique used in *Underworld* is parallel distinctive plot lines. Embedded in the reverse narration mentioned in the above paragraph is the story of Manx Martin, Cotter Martin's father, which is told in three separate chapters. The chapters of Manx Martin move forward and the rest of the book moves backwards. Manx Martin I, II, and III come after Part I, Part III and Part V respectively and develop chronologically. These three chapters follow the narrative time of the prologue and "recounts a heart-twisting story of a day and a night in the life of Manx Martin" (qtd. in Echlin 149). Manx and his family do not appear in all the chapters about Nick's family and friends. Only after Manx steals the baseball from Cotter and sells it at about 32 dollars do the Manx chapters become part of the larger chronology of the book. Then starts Part VI where the Manx episodes join the rest of the novel. The Manx chapters are marked off with black pages and do not interact with the adjoining chapters. This structure symbolizes the alienation of the blacks from the white-dominated society. This narrative strategy foregrounds the racial issue and social conflicts in American society. Cotter's young spirit and passion for the baseball is evident as he runs on a wild chase to protect the winning ball that he fought so eagerly for. The baseball game at the Polo Grounds "dramatizes class, racial, and ethnic differences approaching the age of the melting pot and celebrates postwar American democracy and diversity" (Hendin 104).

The formidable chronological complexity of the structure has challenged all its readers. "Even distinguished critics of the modern American novel find themselves thwarted by the novel's trickiness" (Robson). And according to DeLillo, playing tricks like this is why writing fascinates him: "This is why I write. To try to do things like this" (qtd. Echlin 149). Of course, this is not the only reason why DeLillo writes. But his passion for language and experimenting with literary convention can explain why he ranks among the finest stylists and best postmodernist novelists in America.

III. Black Humor

Apart from the multiple points of view and discontinuity in narration, black humor is another characteristic of DeLillo's narrative. As Anthony DeCurtis observes, humor plays an important role in DeLillo's novels (66). Frank Lentricchia also points out in the introduction to his book *New Essays on White Noise*:

> What is characteristic about DeLillo's novels, aside from their contemporary subjects, is their irredeemably heterogeneous texture; they are montages of tones, styles, and voices that have the effect of yoking together terror and wild humor as the essential tone of contemporary America. Terrific comedy is DeLillo's mode [...] (1)

This view is shared by Harold Bloom who comments on DeLillo's narrative style: "DeLillo is a comedian of the spirit, haunted by omens of the end of our time" ("Introduction" 1). Although these critics do not use the term, what they say about DeLillo's humor is exactly black humor, an important narrative technique employed by DeLillo in his social criticism.

According to *The Oxford English Dictionary*, black humor is defined as "combining the morbid and grotesque with humor and farce to give a disturbing effect and convey the absurdity and cruelty of life." The term "black humor" was coined by the French theoretician André Breton in 1935. Breton credited Jonathan Swift as the originator of black humor and gallows humor. Black humor is an important feature of postmodern literature. The postmodernist writers Thomas Pynchon, Kurt Vonnegut, John Barth and Joseph Heller are called black humorists. Black humor often relies on topics such as death and is related to the grotesque genre. Topics and events that are usually regarded as taboo are treated in an unusually humorous or satirical manner while retaining their seriousness. Thus black humor is often intended for readers or audience to experience both laughter and discomfort, sometimes simultaneously.

A main feature of DeLillo's black humor is the juxtaposition of impending calamity and humor. *White Noise* is regarded as a black comedy. It is very funny, but at the same time very disturbing. In the novel DeLillo juxtaposes airborne toxic events, the disaster, with humor and farce, thus producing a disturbing effect. In an interview when he talked about his writing of *White Noise*, he revealed: "I never felt that I was writing a comic novel before *White Noise*. Maybe the fact that death permeates the book made me retreat into comedy" (Phillips). In such a book about death, humor is employed to satirize postmodern American society while invoking laughter and discomfort simultaneously.

To achieve his desired purpose, burlesque is employed. In Chapter 21 an "airborne toxic event" takes place and forms the dark billowing cloud which is full of Nyodene D. Everybody in the town has to evacuate. Jack Gladney's family joins in the evacuation which is like a farce. The depiction of the evacuation is modelled on a war movie, with air-raid sirens sounding and jet fighters scouting in the sky. On the other hand, the messages about the effects of exposure to Nyodene D. are confusing and amusing. While they are fleeing from the toxic event, chemical cloud on the snowy roads, Jack turns on the radio and hears a woman "identified as a consumer affairs editor discuss the medical problems that could result from personal contact with the airborne toxic event" (210). The radio quotes a series of symptoms ranging from sweaty palms to déjà vu to coma. Denise and Steffie have developed some of these symptoms. "But they were late with sweaty palms, late with nausea, late again with déjà vu." Jack wonders whether her daughters are developing real symptoms or simply "have a false perception of an illusion" (126). On the way Jack finds himself

> giving and taking an oral examination based on the kind of quibbling fine points that had entertained several centuries' worth of medieval idlers. Could a nine-year-old girl suffer a miscarriage due to the power of suggestion? Would she have to be pregnant first? Could the power of suggestion be strong enough to work backward in this manner, from miscarriage to pregnancy to menstruation to ovulation? Which comes first, menstruation or ovulation? Are we talking about mere symptoms or deeply entrenched condition? (126)

DeLillo is being playful in parodying the medieval theologians. On the one hand, there is the grim situation Jack's family is now in: threatened by the toxic event yet uncertain about the result of the exposure. But on the other hand, the grimness is relieved by the comedy or the farce they are put in. Jack compares himself to the medieval scholars, who have a lot of free time quibbling about some scholastic questions like "how many angels can dance on the point of a very fine needle, without jostling one another?"

Mention the medieval scholars and we can't help remembering Jack comically dressing himself up like a medieval scholar in Chapter 3:

> Department heads wear academic robes at the College-on-the-Hill. Not grand sweeping full-length affairs but sleeveless tunics puckered at the shoulders. [...] Idling students [...] as they witness the chairman walking across campus, crook'd arm emerging from his medieval robe [...] The robe is black, of course, and goes with almost anything. (9)

The terror and humor are thus combined and become components of the narrative. The cloud of death is hovering in the air, and the narrator or sometimes the writer uses humor to offset "a particular moment of discomfort or fear, but this reflex is so deeply woven into the original fear that they almost become the same thing" (qtd. in DeCurtis 66). DeLillo's use of black humor helps to represent the absurdity of postmodern society and satirize the depthlessness of postmodern culture and the shallowness and commodification of the academia. In the postmodern society where there is no absolute truth and God is believed to be dead, people are as gullible as people in the medieval age. But their religion is consumerism, not Christianity.

The brilliantly mixed terror and humor are more striking in Chapter 39 of the novel. DeLillo represents the widespread violence; the manipulation of consciousness by mass media; and the loss of faith. When something happens, the characters in the novel will think: "How should I react?" Of course, they model on TV and movies. How should a betrayed husband respond to an adulterer? Jack acts according to a movie plot. Thus his revenge is a melodrama. When Jack finds Mink in the motel and fires at him, he describes the morbid crime scene in the cold-blooded and even aesthetic manner:

> I watched blood squirt from the victim's midsection. A delicate arc. I marveled at the rich color, sensed the color-causing action of nonnucleated cells. The flow diminished to a trickle, spread across the tile floor. (312)

In this episode DeLillo juxtaposes murder and farce. When Jack put the gun into the hand of Mink to fake the crime scene in the way that Mink shot himself, Mink the victim raised his hand, pulled the trigger and wounded Jack in the wrist. When Jack finds the dying Mink gasping for oxygen, he "decided to attempt mouth to mouth." He leans over Mink and tries to reach his mouth in order to breathe powerful gusts of air into his lungs. "My lips were gathered, ready to funnel. His eyes followed me down. Perhaps he thought he was about to be kissed" (314). The irony and jokes make us laugh. DeLillo's narrative strategy renders the humor more palatable, hence more effectively drives home his satire on the media-saturated society.

Black humor is also an important narrative strategy in *Underworld*, a black comedy "about the psychic fallout of nuclear terror: what it felt like to exist year after year with the knowledge that every privilege in your life and every thought in your mind depends on the ability of the two great powers to hang a threat over the planet" (Haven). In Part V of the novel DeLillo depicts Lenny Bruce's performances in the nightclub in late October, 1962, during the Cuban Missile Crisis. Bruce juxtaposes death and humor to reveal Americans' fear and helplessness in the face of nuclear annihilation. He starts his performance by imitating Kennedy's opening line in his dramatic television address to the nation regarding the Cuban Missile Crisis: "Good evening, my fellow citizens." Hearing President Kennedy's voice from funny Bruce, the audience roars with laughter. When the audience thinks that he is going to do a Kennedy imitation, he switches to satirize the American elite leaders and expresses his deep concern for these leaders' management of the country: "Dig it. These are the guys from the eating clubs and the secret societies. They have fraternity handshakes so complicated it takes three full minutes to do all the moves. One missed digit you're fucked for life." (505) Then he jokes about the leaders of the superpowers: "A huge mound of crabmeat carved in the shape—they're gonna love this, it's so forceful and moving—yes, Kennedy and Khrushchev wrestling in the nude. Lifesize" (506). During his performance, he does "the shrillest sort of falsetto": "We're all gonna die!" (506) With it, he can't help laughing. He continues: "Dig it, JFK's got this Russian man-bull staring him down, they're pizzle to pizzle, and this is a guy Jack doesn't know how to deal with. This is a guy who craps with the door open on state occasion. He has sex with his bowling trophies" (506-07). His famous line "We'll all gonna die" resonates in the novel. In Bruce's "giddy shriek the audience can hear the obliteration of the idea of uniqueness and free choice. They can hear the replacement of human isolation by massive and unvaried ruin" (507). In spite of the immediate threat of mass death, the audience laughs with Lenny Bruce. This is so-called gallows humor employed by Bruce to dramatize the powerless situation of Americans when confronted with the nuclear threat. The audience has no choice but to respond to the overwhelming danger with laughter. In 1966 Bruce died, according to the government, "of acute morphine poisoning ... the syringe still stuck in his arm," but some others suspect that "Lenny's been killed by shadowy forces in the government" (574-75). By cleverly using the fictionalized narrative of Lenny Bruce, DeLillo conducts his social criticism and digs out American secret history in the 1960s.

In *Underworld* black humor is also utilized in the characterization of two Edgars, who are both paranoids. In J. Edgar Hoover's case, DeLillo uses exaggeration to ridicule the late FBI director who led the FBI to spy on tens of thousands of American people in despised and secret ways. In the novel DeLillo humorously depicts the conflict between Hoover and the guerrillas. Hoover's garbage is allegedly stolen by garbage guerillas to be exhibited and analyzed after the FBI publicizes its methods regarding organized crime figures: ransack their garbage in the night in order to find their criminal evidence. The urban guerrillas will take revenge and do the same to Hoover. His aide Clyde reports to him:

> Confidential source says they intend to take your garbage on tour. Rent halls in major cities. Get lefty sociologists to analyze the garbage item by item. Get hippies to rub it on their naked bodies. More or less have sex with it. Get poets to write poems about it. And finally, in the last city on the tour, they plan to eat it. And expel it publicly. Confidential source says they will make a documentary film of the tour, for general release. (558)

This is disgustingly humorous. Hoover penetrates secretly into the private life and sets up dossiers for thousands of American citizens. Now ironically, his private life is going to be pried into and even publicly exhibited. As the FBI director during the Cold War, Hoover must have made many enemies. The way to deal with such people is to compile massive dossiers. "In the endless estuarial mingling of paranoia and control, the dossier was an essential device. ... The file was everything, the life nothing. And this was the essence of Edgar's revenge." (559) In *Underworld* DeLillo subverts the official image of Hoover as the first FBI director in the United States. The fictional Hoover is indulged in amassing secret files by using illegal methods to harass and persecute political dissenters and activists, even to intimidate and control top political leaders and powerful figures like the sitting American President out of his fear of communism and other subversives, and also out of his desire for power. By characterizing the FBI director as such, DeLillo satirizes American democracy and criticizes the darkness of American politics in the Cold War, especially from the 1950s to the 1960s.

The characterization of Sister Edgar involves black humor, too. For example, at the end of the novel, the nun, "bride of Christ, passing peacefully in her sleep" (824), does not ascend into the heaven as she hopes, but ironically she is trapped in cyberspace:

> In her veil and habit she was basically a face, or a face and scrubbed hands. Here in cyberspace she has shed all that steam-ironed fabric. She is not naked exactly but she is open—exposed to every connection you can make on the world wide web. (824)

She does not reside in the paradise with the Lord. In the cyberspace she is merging with the god of atoms, its "dripping christblood colors, solar golds and reds" (825), feeling the power of information technology, a new faith in the 21st century.

Sister Edgar, "the Cold War nun," and J. Edgar Hoover, the director of FBI, merge in the cyberspace as "Sister and Brother." In the Internet age, cyberspace is heaven. As long as there is a password, just with a click, everyone can have instant access to it. In this heaven, "all human knowledge gathered and linked, hyperlinked, this site leading to that, this fact referenced to that, a keystroke, a mouse-click, a password—world without end, amen" (825). When the bomb explodes, she thinks she sees God. But DeLillo humorously writes: "No, wait, sorry. It is a Soviet bomb she sees, the largest yield in history, a device exploded above the Arctic Ocean in 1961, preserved in the computer that helped to build it ..." (826). Here by his innovative employment of black humor, DeLillo satirizes American society in which paranoia displaces religious faith with "radioactivity, the power of alpha particles and the all-knowing systems that shape them, the endless fitted links" (241, 251).

IV. Intertextuality

Intertextuality is a major feature of postmodern literature. As a postmodernist writer, DeLillo, whose fiction has a hybrid character, inevitably uses this technique. Examples of intertextuality proliferate in DeLillo's novels.

What does intertextuality mean? According to *Oxford Concise Dictionary of Literary Terms*, intertextuality is

> a term coined by Julia Kristeva to designate the various relationships that a given text may have with other texts. These intertextual relationships include anagram, allusion, adaptation, translation, parody, pastiche, imitation, and other kinds of transformation. (112)

Although predominantly attributed to Kristeva, the notion of intertextuality finds articulation in the works of Barthes, Jakobson, and especially Bakhtin. Barthes regards intertextuality as a "prerequisite for any text":

> Every text is an intertext; [...] every text is a new fabric woven out of bygone quotations. [...] A prerequisite for any text, intertextuality cannot be reduced to a problem of sources and influences; it is a general field of anonymous formulas whose origin is seldom indentifiable, of unconscious or automatic quotations given without quotation marks. (qtd. in Gresset 4)

In the introduction of her *A Poetics of Postmodernism: History, Theory, and Fiction*, Hutcheon says: "No text is without its intertexts, we have been taught" (vii). What she said is true. Jacques Derrida has already said that "there is nothing outside the text" (Derrida 1976, 158). "Writing is a means of taming both texts and contexts…. Texts talk to one another; they echo one another; they push one another; they war with one another. They are voices in chorus, in conflict, and in competition" (Fewell 1992, 11-2). T. S. Eliot is quoted as saying: "Minor poets borrow, major poets steal" (Plottel 1978, xvi). What Hutcheon, Derrida, Fewell and Eliot talk about is intertextuality. For many years intertextuality has already become an important literary conception. "Offering new insights into textual relations, intertextuality is changing the way we think about textual production and interpretation" (Fewell 1992, 10).

The term "intertextuality" was coined in the late 1960s by Julia Kristeva, who combined ideas from Bakhtin on the social context of language with Saussure's positing the systematic features of language. According to Kristeva, intertextuality is "a mosaic of quotations; any text is the absorption and transformation of another. The notion of intertextuality replaces that of intersubjectivity, and poetic language is read as at least double" (Kristeva 1986, 37). It indicates that it is a "way in which a text reads history and places itself in it" (Caselli 2005, 8). It is a term for all the relations between texts whether explicit or implicit. It can refer to the relation between a text and historical or cultural contexts. It can be the reference to another separate and distinct text within a text. "Texts, whether they be literary or non-literary, are viewed by modern theorists as lacking in any kind of independent meaning. They are what theorists now call intertextual. …The text becomes the intertext" (Allen 2000, 1). The idea of the text, and thus of intertextuality, depends, as Barthes argues, on the figure of the web, the weave, the garment (text) woven from the threads of the "already written" and the "already read." Every text has its meaning, therefore, in relation to other texts. Intertextuality seems such a useful term because it foregrounds notions of relationality, interconnectedness and interdependence in modern cultural life. (Allen 2000, 5) Intertextuality is not exclusively related to works of literature or other written texts, including virtual texts. And it has a critical function: intertextuality, like influence or imitation, is not neutral, and thus hints at its underlying socio-political importance. (Martin 149)

Intertextuality is an important narrative technique that DeLillo employs to represent American contemporary history and postmodern culture. History, like literature, is a text, a narrative, a linguistic construct that can be told and retold, and is subjective and fictive. As a reaction to old historicism, New Historicism calls this postmodern situation of history "textuality". Historical facts can exist only as textual traces, and we can only know history in textual forms and by way of prior textualization. "Once society, history, and culture are seen as 'texts', intertextuality becomes central to New Historicism" (Herman et al. 258). Intertextuality abounds in DeLillo's novels. DeLillo employs a large number of pre-existent texts, which include official records, newspaper articles, films, TV footages, the Bible, paintings, novels, essays, magazines and photos. Intertextuality in DeLillo's novels is shown in allusion, adaptation, pastiche and historiographic metafiction.

1. Allusion

An allusion is "a passing reference, without explicit identification, to a literary or historical person, place, or event, or to another literary work or passage" (Abrams 9). DeLillo's novels are highly allusive.

In *Mao II* there are abundant allusions to historical events. The prologue titled "At the Yankee Stadium" depicts a mass wedding at Yankee Stadium, performed by the priest Mr. Moon, of 13,000 men and women. It alludes to the wedding of 13, 000 people, conducted by Reverend Moon of the Unification Church in Seoul. DeLillo saw the photograph of the Korean wedding and was struck by it. DeLillo said in an interview he was inspired by a photo of this Korean mass wedding (Passaro 80). This photo has found its way into the novel. It perfectly matches the content of the prologue and the theme of authoritarianism. "Here they come, marching into American sunlight." The brides and bridegrooms are "one body now, an undifferentiated mass"

(DeLillo, *Mao* II 3). And Master Moon becomes "their true father," the Messiah, who "lives in them like chains of matter that determine who they are" (6) and who comes to the United States "to lead them to the end of human history" (6). The Korean wedding is a real event and Reverend Moon is a real priest who organized the Unification Church in Korea in 1954 and moved to the United States in 1972. The Unification Church flourished in the 1970s and 1980s. DeLillo's fictional portrayal of the mass wedding and Master Moon reveals his concern about the threat to freedom and individuality that are the core values of Americans.

Besides the mass wedding, *Mao* II alludes to the following real events in history: the mass trampling at Hillsborough Soccer Stadium; the funeral of Ayatollah Khomeini; and Warring Beirut. The historical events constitute historical intertexts of *Mao* II and provide access to DeLillo's fictional world which according to DeLillo has the tendency to move toward authoritarianism.

Mao II employs Andy Warhol's paintings of Chairman Mao as the book cover. The cover picture exhibits the power of the image in the society of spectacle. It also refers to Chairman Mao's portrait hung in the Tian'anmen Square and the Andy Warhol Exhibition held in the Museum of Modern Art, New York City, in 1989. In the novel there is a room "filled with images of Chairman Mao. Photocopy Mao, silk-screen Mao, wallpaper Mao, synthetic-polymer Mao" (21). Andy's paintings of Chairman Mao tapped into the historic easing of relations between the United States and China in 1972 when President Nixon paid his "ice-breaking" visit to China. Chairman Mao's image was everywhere and Warhol captured that phenomenon and transformed Mao, a communist leader, into a new icon, and a commodity to be consumed in the capitalist America. Andy's paintings of Chairman Mao achieved both critical and commercial success. DeLillo, the novelist historian, captured the postmodern phenomenon and chronicled it in his novel.

Mao II also alludes to Barthes' 1968 landmark essay "Death of the Author," in which Barthes argues that the author is nothing more than a social and historically constituted subject. It is hard for the author to stand outside of the society and take an oppositional stance to the dominant power. Even when Bill Gray lives in complete reclusiveness, he cannot escape the influence of consumerism and the hegemony of the images. Bill's physical death

> completes a process of diminution at once personal and cultural. [...] Bill perishes first in the simple exhaustion of his talent. But, more insidiously, he suffers death as the victim of societal indifference or cultural forces that turn him and the books he writes into commodities.

(Cowart 114-15)

2. Adaptation

Adaptation means changing a written work so that it can be presented in another form. It is an important narrative strategy employed in *Libra*.

Libra relies heavily on *The Warren Commission Report*. The fictionalized biography of Lee Oswald is based on this report. In an interview DeLillo admitted to his reading of *The Warren Report* before writing *Libra*: "I did do extensive research, and the heart of it was *The Warren Commission Report* and its twenty-six volumes of testimony and exhibits." (Connolly 2005, 25) *The Warren Commission Report* provides Lee Oswald's biography and an analysis of why Oswald became the man he was. "A full third of the Report's 816-page text is devoted exclusively to Oswald, more than 150 pages are explicitly biographical." (Keener 2001, 71) *The Warren Commission Report* contains two complete, self-contained biographies. Appendix 13 to the Report is entitled "Biography of Lee Harvey Oswald" which is a linear and detailed life history of Oswald: early years; Marines; Soviet Union; Fort Worth, Dallas, New Orleans; Mexico City; and Dallas. The other biography is Chapter 7, entitled "Lee Harvey Oswald: Background and Possible Motives," which includes a life history of Oswald but with the added dimension of overt, clinic analysis, a blend of sociology and physiology. This is a form of biography that seeks to "define the growth of a person in a cultural milieu" (Keener 2001, 71).

After examining Oswald's past and the environment in which his character was shaped, the Warren commission draws a conclusion:

> Many factors were undoubtedly involved in Oswald's motivation for the assassination, and the Commission does not believe that it can ascribe to him any one motive or group of motives. It is apparent, however, that Oswald was moved by an overriding hostility to his environment. He does not appear to have been able to establish meaningful relationships with other people. He was perpetually discontented with the world around him. Long before the assassination he expressed his hatred for American society and acted in protest against it. Oswald's search for what he conceived to be the perfect society was doomed from the start. He sought for himself a place in history—a role as the "great man" who would be recognized as having been in advance of his times. His commitment to Marxism and communism appears to have been another important factor in his motivation. He also had demonstrated a capacity to act decisively and

> without regard to the consequences when such action would further his aims of the moment. Out of these and the many other factors which may have molded the character of Lee Harvey Oswald there emerged a man capable of assassinating President Kennedy. (*National Archives*)

This conclusion can also be reached after reading DeLillo's *Libra*. It can be found that DeLillo is faithful to the archive as far as Oswald's biography is concerned. In an interview with Donn Fry, DeLillo remarked that the Oswald of *Libra* was as close to the known record as he could possibly make him and such historical accuracy was his "duty." Of course, he created some characters, dialogues and psychological activities of the characters. And more importantly, he subverted the conclusion of The *Warren Commission Report* by adding the conspiratorial plot.

DeLillo's adaptation of *The Warren Commission Report* is unique and successful. He is faithful to the hard historical facts. Besides, his creation of dialogues and mental activities of the characters can only increase the authenticity of the history narrated in the novel while "[t]he fictional characters fill the gaps […]. They provide the lost knowledge" (Fry). The conspiracy plot is not purely a product of the author's imagination. It is based on his research, too. The addition of the conspiracy plot embodies DeLillo's attitude toward the American government which was involved in the Watergate Scandal and the Iran-Contra Scandal. In my view, DeLillo's representation of the JFK Assassination is surely shaped by what he was most concerned about at the time of his writing the book, as Stephen Greenblatt writes in *Renaissance Self-Fashioning: From More to Shakespear*: "It is everywhere evident in this book that the questions I ask of my material and indeed the very nature of this material are shaped by the questions I ask of my self" (5).

3. Pastiche

Pastiche is another important narrative technique DeLillo employs in his novels. It means to combine, or "paste" together, multiple elements. It can be seen as a representation of the chaotic, pluralistic, or information-drenched aspects of postmodern society. It can be a combination of multiple genres to create a unique narrative or to comment on situations in postmodernity. DeLillo's novels are very often a combination of multiple genres, blurring the distinction between high culture and low culture, accurately representing the chaotic postmodern American reality.

Fredric Jameson argues that pastiche is one of the most significant features or practices in postmodernism. He defines "pastiche" as "like parody, the imitation of a peculiar or unique style, the wearing of a stylistic mask, speech in a dead language." He declares: "Pastiche is blank parody, parody that has lost its sense of humor" (163-67). He contends that postmodern pastiche is symptomatic of a general loss of historicity and the incapability to achieve aesthetic "representations of our own current experience" (qtd. in Homer 182). But Linda Hutcheon does not agree with Jameson's definition of pastiche. According to her, postmodern parody is not ahistorical or dehistoricizing. She states:

> Parody in postmodern art is more than just a sign of the attention artists pay to each other's work [...] and to the art of the past. It may indeed be complicitous with the values it inscribes as well as subverts, but the subversion is still there: the politics of postmodern parodic representation is not the same as that of most rock videos' use of allusions to standard film genres or texts [...] This is what should be called pastiche, according to Jameson's definition. ("The Politics of Postmodern Parody" 234)

As Hutcheon puts it: "Postmodernism is both academic and popular, élitist and accessible" (*Poetics of Postmodernism* 44). It is thanks to such contradictions that postmodernism can mount a successful critique. Hutcheon believes that postmodern parody is more willing to break down distinctions between "reality" and "fiction," as in such works as E. L. Doctorow's *Ragtime*, a postmodern generic trait that Hutcheon terms "historiographic metafiction." (Felluga, "Modules on Linda Hutcheon")

White Noise combines popular and literary genres. It mixes the genres of the campus novel, the existential drama, the disaster novel, the domestic melodrama and the detective novel. Besides, *White Noise* includes elements of porn novels, films and commercials. *Libra* incorporates the genres of biography, conspiracy thriller, the spy novel and the historical novel.

Underworld is regarded as one of the "contemporary American epics" (Morley 6), like all epics, whose action takes place on a grand scale. But it is not an epic like the English epic *Beowulf* or John Milton's *Paradise Lost* which contains "military heroics or fantastic encounters with a collection of gods and demi-gods" (ibid. 125). Catherine Morley compares *Underworld* to James Joyce's well-known epic *Ulysses* (125). Indeed, DeLillo shares Joyce's commitment to the mundane and the ordinary:

> Joyce provided a model of how a narrative of epic scope and tenor could also become a homage to the quotidian, the bland 'everyday life' [...] DeLillo takes up this preoccupation with the ordinary: *Underworld* is a vast exploration of the small, unofficial pockets of individual American

histories throughout the past half-century. (Morley 126).

Underworld also includes the elements of comedy. There are two comedians in the novel: Jackie Gleason and Lenny Bruce, who form the two poles of comedy in the novel, "the comedy of reassurance, domesticity, and the canned laughter of the situation comedy vs. the decentering, threatening, off-color humor of the satirist" (Nadel 178). And in daily life, humor abounds. The humor of the street with Nick and his youthful friends dominates the sense of the comic in the novel. Even the paranoids Hoover and Sister Edgar are sometimes comic. Besides, *Underworld* is also a work of hysteria realism, a term coined by the literary critic James Wood to label the enormous and encyclopedic novels like David Foster Wallace's *Infinite Jest* and Thomas Pynchon's *Mason and Dixon*. Novels of hysteria realism are often "anxiety-riddled, emotionally confused and intellectually scattershot—in a word, hysterical" (Zalewski). Although Wood is critical of the so-called hysteria realist novels, he is correct in pointing out that in *Underworld* DeLillo adopts the conventions of realism to depict the postmodern American reality. The novel is viewed as a work of realism for its focus on showing accurately the everyday, quotidian activities and life and its emphasis on the ugly or sordid in American society. Thus far, I can conclude that *Underworld*, a combination of multiple genres, is a good example of pastiche.

4. Historiographic Metafiction

Linda Hutcheon defines historiographic metafiction as

> those well-known and popular novels which are both intensely self-reflexive and yet paradoxically also lay claim to historical events and personages: *The French Lieutenant's Woman*, *Midnight's Children*, *Ragtime*, *Legs*, *G.*, *Famous Last Words*. [...] Historiographic metafiction incorporates all three of these domains: that is, its theoretical self-awareness of history and fiction as human constructs (historiographic metafiction) is made the grounds for its rethinking and reworking of the forms and contents of the past. (*A Poetics of Postmodernism* 5).

Beyond reconnecting history and fiction, Linda Hutcheon remarks that "postmodern fiction suggests that to re-write or to re-present the past in fiction and in history is, in both cases, to open it up to the present, to prevent it from being conclusive and teleological" (*A Poetics of Postmodernism* 110). To accomplish this re-presentation of the past, historiographic metafiction "plays upon the truth and lies of the historical record. ... certain known historical details are deliberately falsified in order to foreground the possible mnemonic failures of recorded history and the constant potential for both deliberate and inadvertent error" (*A Poetics of Postmodernism* 114).

DeLillo's major works such as *Libra*, *Mao II*, *Underworld* and *Falling Man* are dubbed "historiographic metafiction" because they blend the reflexivity of metafiction "with an explicit questioning of official history" (Duvall, "Introduction" 3). By using intertexuality, DeLillo alludes to historical events and figures, juxtaposes fictional characters and historical figures, literally incorporating the textualized past into his own texts.

Libra is such a self-reflexive historical fiction, combining historical narration with metahistoriographic and metafictional commentary. There are three parallel stories in *Libra*: a biography of Lee Harvey Oswald, a CIA plot against Kennedy, and the efforts made by Nicholas Branch, a retired CIA agent, to write a secret history of the assassination for the CIA. It is through Nicholas that DeLillo introduces an element of self-reflexivity in historiographic metafiction. Branch's stories are set outside the doubled time scheme of the novel, probably in the 1980s, when DeLillo planned to write *Libra*. Some critics regard Branch as DeLillo's double, who keeps echoing DeLillo's meditative voice of commenting on the mysteries surrounding the assassination and the difficulties in writing a coherent history. Branch's long and difficult process of collecting and studying the data is a representation of DeLillo's long interest in and investigation into the tragic assassination. Both DeLillo and Branch were amazed by the amount of data generated by the assassination. In an interview with Adam Begley, DeLillo talked about his research for writing *Libra*. The documents seemed endless to him. Working into them was like walking into a maze or labyrinth. "Then there was the *Warren Report*, which is the *Oxford English Dictionary* of the assassination and also the Joycean novel. ... the *Warren Report*, which totals twenty-six volumes" (qtd. in Begley 98). In *Libra* DeLillo writes: "There is also the *Warren Report*, of course, with its twenty-six accompanying volumes of testimony and exhibits, its millions of words. Branch thinks this is the megaton novel James Joyce would have written if he'd moved to Iowa City and lived to be a hundred." (181) "Anyone who enters this maze" has to become "part scientist, novelist, biographer, historian, and existential detective. The landscape was crawling with secrets" (qtd. in Begley 98). At the end of the novel, Branch is still working hard, after 15 years' research, trying to work out a clue to the mysteries hovering over the assassination. As the author's alter ego, Branch discusses the fictional nature of historiography and textuality of history. By utilizing self-reflexive narrative techniques, DeLillo exposes the fictionality of recorded official history and the futility of separating the real past from the constructed.

According to Hutcheon, postmodern novels are not only self-reflexive, but also historically and ideologically grounded (*Politics of Postmodernism* 2). *Libra* incorporates social and political history. The historical narrative represents the complex political and social reality of post-war America: from the US invasion of Guatemala in 1954, to the U-2 spy plane event, to the Bay of Pigs invasion in 1961, to the Cuban missile crisis, and to the national crackdown on the organized crimes, "against the backdrop of hostilities in Vietnam, the Cold War, and the threat of nuclear apocalypse," *Libra* produces "a sense of an unstoppable wheeling towards the assassination as the event which mediates the struggle between communist east and capitalist west in the wake of 1945" (Boxall 142). As has been revealed in the previous discussion in this book, *Libra* draws heavily on historical documents. There are two types of historical documents. One major historical intertext in the novel is the *Warren Report*. Oswald's biographical material comes from this archive. The other type is the image intertexts: The famous Zapruder film, and the news footage on TV recording Jack Ruby's murder of Oswald. In addition to these historical documents, the novel refers to the Marxist publications such as the *Militant* and the *Worker*, works by Marx, Trotsky, Castro, Orwell, Wells, Dostoevsky, and Whitman which Oswald reads and the two movies about assassinations which Oswald watches before he assassinates the President. Besides, *Libra* alludes to DeLillo's essay "American Blood: A Journey through the Labyrinth of Dallas and JFK" which was published in 1983. Originally DeLillo intended to title his novel "American Blood." With these intertexts, *Libra* is truly a densely intertextual novel.

Historiographic metafiction blurs the borderline between fact and fiction, between the documented and invented. In the self-reflexive historical fiction like *Libra* the historical facts and fictional events are interwind; the historical figures and the invented characters interact. The majority of the characters involved in Oswald's biography section are historical figures while the characters participating in the conspiracy are mostly invented by DeLillo. But no matter whether they be imagined or real, we can only know them through the texts which are human constructs. Like Hayden White, Hutcheon asserts: "We know the past (which really did exist) only through its textualized remains. And every representation of the past has specifiable ideological implications" because the writer manipulates those events as historical facts "by selection and narrative positioning" (*Poetics of Postmodernism* 119-20). Hutcheon continues: "Narrativized history, like fiction, reshapes any material (in this case, the past) in the light of present issues" (*A Poetics of Postmodernism* 137). This is the "historicity of texts" of New Historicism. *Libra* was written against the backdrop of Watergate, Iran-Contra and rampant consumerism in the United States. By employing the "parodic intertextuality", DeLillo incorporates his conspiracy theory in the fictionalized history in an attempt to give order and meaning to the chaotic and absurd political world and presents a critique of the postmodern American society "where acts of consumerism and violence overlap" (Green 97).

Multiple points of view, discontinuity in narration, black humor and intertextuality have existed long in literature, but since the 1960s they have become dominant techniques of postmodernist literature, to which DeLillo has made great contributions by means of recycling: he recycles Joyce, Eliot, Faulkner, Mailer, Godard and Lenny Bruce. Like the artists in *Underworld*, DeLillo picks through the landfills of history in search for a vision with which to create and to look for his own ways to represent fragmentation, multiplicity and absurdity in postmodern American society.

Conclusion

According to New Historicism, literary texts are necessarily embedded in their social, historical and institutional provenance. There is no text apart from its historical context. DeLillo's writing career parallels the progress of postmodernity in America. The postmodern condition constitutes the context of his texts which were produced from 1960 to the early 21st century. Postmodern theorists like Daniel, Jameson, Lyotard and Baudrillard all agreed that the 1960s' American society had entered the postmodern era, in which there is no distinction between simulation and reality, between fiction and history, and between high culture and popular culture. As an acute observer, DeLillo surely noticed these changes. He has publicly remarked that he does not read much of "the theoretical work being done in philosophy and literary criticism these days. [...] Yet to read DeLillo is to encounter in his fiction many of the observations articulated by contemporary theorists of the postmodern. His work lends itself to definition by way of example rather than formulation" (Morley 124).

DeLillo viewed the assassination of President Kennedy originated American postmodern condition. The deaths of Kennedy and Oswald ushered in the society of spectacle in the United States. The assassination has changed the ways Americans view knowledge, reality and government. In the view of a New Historicist, man is a social construct. A writer can never escape his or her time and history. The JFK Assassination has undoubtedly shaped DeLillo. As he once said in an interview: "I don't think my books could have been written in the world that existed before the Kennedy Assassination. [...] It's conceivable that this made me the writer I am" (Passaro 77-78). It was the assassination that invented him as a writer. In a 2005 interview he again talked about the influence of the JFK Assassination on his writing:

> November 22nd 1963 marked the real beginning of the 1960s. It was the beginning of a series of catastrophes: political assassinations, the war in Vietnam, the denial of Civil Rights and the revolts that occasioned, youth revolt in American cities, right up to Watergate. When I was starting out as a writer it seemed to me that a large part of the material you could find in my novels—this sense of fatality, of widespread suspicion, of mistrust—came from the assassination of JFK. (Bou and Thoret)

The assassination is alluded to at the end of *Americana* when David ends his journey to the American West at Dallas. The ending signals the beginning of a new journey which DeLillo was going to embrace. This was a journey to explore the culture saturated by violence, simulations and paranoia which DeLillo remarked originated from the assassination of JFK.

Libra exemplifies Montrose's "historicity of texts" which means that "the past has shaped the present and the present reshapes the past" (Montrose 24). As a writer with a bachelor's degree in Communication Arts and five years' media working experience, DeLillo saw the JFK Assassination from a perspective different from the Warren Commission and Norman Mailer. DeLillo's focus is on the media-saturated phenomenon in American society. He was concerned with the media's negative effects on the individuality and identity. In the early 1980s, cable TV began to enter most of American families. This cultural phenomenon of rampant consumerism and media-saturation shocked DeLillo who just returned to America after having lived abroad for three years, and motivated him to write "American Blood," *White Noise* and *Libra*, three works which were published in the 1980s and thematically related. Another thing that influenced DeLillo's perception of the JFK Assassination was the media coverage of political scandals. The Iran-Contra affair was a huge political scandal of the 1980s. The scandal hearings were covered on TV every day and consumed as media commodities. Along with other political scandals in the 1960s and the 1970s, the Iran-Contra affair eroded the public's confidence or trust in the American government. DeLillo perceived the history of the JFK Assassination through the lens of post-Watergate-Iran-Contra America. Reading his *Libra*, one gets the impression that Watergate and Iran-Contra seemed to precede November 22, 1963, "as if the novel's narration of the events of twenty-five years past made that day in November contemporaneous with its retelling" (Lentricchia, *Introducing Don DeLillo* 200). As historians as interpreters of history are embedded in the culture and society they are located in, they conduct dialogues not only with the dead, but also with their own cultures. As Stephen Greenblatt puts it in *Renaissance Self-Fashioning: From More to Shakespeare*, "the questions I ask of my material and indeed the very nature of this material are shaped by the questions I ask of myself" (5), the critique of American postmodernity dictates DeLillo's writing of *Libra*.

Another novel to exemplify the "historicity of texts" is *Falling Man*. 9·11 can be understood both as a psychic/personal trauma and a cultural/collective one. Despite DeLillo's previous interest in cultural issues, he chose to write a post-9·11 novel of psychic rather than cultural trauma. The novel was criticized for its lack of the visionary scope and depth of *Underworld*, which so brilliantly captured the American experience of the Cold War era. I think this kind of criticism is unfair. In my view, DeLillo displays his vision and bravery in confronting such a traumatic event which many Americans equate with the Pearl Harbor. He not only provides the counter-narrative to terrorism he promised in his essay "In the Ruins of the Future," but also a counter-narrative to the prevailing nationalistic rhetoric which dominated American media after 9·11 and "sought to transform vulnerability into triumphant profiles in courage" (Versluys 23). By depicting the emotional effects of the terrorist attacks on the victims and their families in documentary accuracy, DeLillo denounces the brutality of the terrorists in his unique way. At the same time he seems to write the novel as a critique of American mass media, which treated the disaster as a commodity, and as a warning of the after-disaster amnesia. DeLillo, like the Falling Man, the performance artist, makes art out of horror and reenacts the suppressed history of the 9·11 terrorist attacks. DeLillo is a "Brave New Chronicler of the Age of Terror" (*Falling Man* 220).

From *Americana* (1971) to *Point Omega* (2010), DeLillo presents the picture of contemporary American society. As an American who was born in 1936 and has lived in New York most of his life, DeLillo witnessed and experienced all the important historical events: the JFK Assassination, the Cold War and the 9·11 terrorist attacks. He and Oswald had once lived in the same neighborhood in the Bronx although they did not know each other. He had shared the anxiety of living in the shadow of nuclear threat. When the terrorist attacks brought down the World Trade Center, DeLillo was in New York. He was saddened by the great number of casualties and the howling space at the Ground Zero. He observed carefully and acutely and painted a portrait of postmodern America. In an interview DeLillo said: "When I work," he goes on, "I'm just translating the world around me in what seems to be straightforward terms. For my readers, this is sometimes a vision that's not familiar. But I'm not trying to manipulate reality. This is just what I see and hear" (McCrum). DeLillo has been "reading" American reality and interpreting it, the result of which is DeLillo's version of American history.

DeLillo's fiction is a chronicle of America from the 1950s to the early 21st century, through which we can have some knowledge of the history of contemporary America. Postmodern theorists have told us that historical knowledge can only be attained through texts. Fredric Jameson claims in *The Political Unconscious* that although history or the past does exist, "history is inaccessible to us except in textual form, or in other words, that it can be approached only by prior (re)textualization" (82). Linda Hutcheon argues in her famous book *Politics of Postmodernism*: "The past really did exist, but we can only know it today through its textual traces, its often complex and indirect representations in the present: documents, archives, but also photographs, paintings, architecture, films, and literature" (75). Hutcheon echoed Hayden White's influential theory of historical narratives. According to White, the writing of history is a poetic process, "history" is a verbal construct, and a historical text is a literary artifact. Both history and fiction are discourses, and both constitute systems of signification by which we make sense of the past. White's theory of historical narratives was embraced by Montrose, who characterized New Historicism "as a reciprocal concern with the historicity of texts and the textuality of history" (20). DeLillo's texts which represent American postmodernity are embedded in the presuppositions, the attitudes and values of the age in which they were written and conditioned by the author's ideological commitment. DeLillo presents a version of American contemporary history which is often buried underground to question the official version of historical events. Thus he is regarded as "an excavator, a pathfinder—a specialist in the 'secret history' of observable phenomena and recorded facts" (Robson).

By "historicity of texts, and textuality of history," Montrose suggests that literature or any particular text is not only socially produced but also socially productive (Montrose 23). By constructing a unique narrative of American postmodern condition and anatomizing American society, DeLillo, like Norman Mailer, has made a revolution in the consciousness of his time, and at the same time has fashioned himself as a writer in opposition.

DeLillo is an oppositional writer. He claimed in an interview: "Writers must oppose systems. It's important to write against power, corporations, the state, and the whole system of consumption and of debilitating entertainments" (qtd. in Bou and Thoret). This is what DeLillo has been practicing for decades. In *Libra* he shows his sympathy for Lee Harvey Oswald, the so-called assassin of President Kennedy, and challenges the conclusion of the Warren Commission. DeLillo probes the mind and motives of Oswald and creates a figure who has lived a life in small rooms. In DeLillo's view, Oswald's life "in small rooms is the antithesis of the life America seems to promise its citizens: the life of consumer fulfillment" (qtd. in DeCurtis 60). DeLillo seems to suggest that American society was in part to blame for Oswald's failed life. For his conspiracy theory, sympathy for Oswald, and critique of American society, DeLillo was criticized by George Will who wrote that *Libra* "is an act of literary vandalism and bad citizenship" ("Shallow Look at the Mind of an Assassin" 56). DeLillo's response to Will is as follows:

> I don't take it seriously, but being called a 'bad citizen' is a compliment to a novelist, at least to my mind. That's exactly what we ought to do. We ought to be bad citizens. We ought to, in the sense that we're writing against what power represents, and often what government represents, and what the corporation dictates, and what consumer consciousness has come to mean. In that sense, if we're bad citizens, we're doing our job. (qtd. in Remnick 142)

DeLillo is not alone as a novelist in criticizing American society. In the history of American literature there is a long list of such novelists: Henry David Thoreau, Mark Twain, Theodore Dreiser, John Steinbeck, Dos Passos, E. L. Doctorow, Robert Coover, Norman Mailer, Ishmael Reed, Kurt Vonnegut, to name just a few. These canonical novelists are adversarial critics of American society and culture. From Thoreau to DeLillo, "[t]he main literary line is political, but not in the trivial didactic sense of offering programs of renovation, or of encouraging us to go out and 'do something'" (Lentricchia, "The American Writer as Bad Citizen" 5). DeLillo has been denounced as a member of the paranoid left after the publication of *Libra* which he admitted in an interview "is saturated with politics, of necessity" (qtd. in DeCurtis 73). In spite of the politics in his books and his explicit statements about the writer's oppositional role, DeLillo says that he does not have a political program for social changes. He would rather be an outsider—"to stand and live in the margins"—in order to be able to observe reality from a "sideline vantage" point and to keep his capacity to denounce and criticize it: "to alter the inner life of the culture" (*Mao* II 41).

The opposition to the capitalist socio-economic system runs through DeLillo's works. According to *Merriam-Webster Dictionary*, "Americana" refers to artifacts, or a collection of artifacts, related to the history, geography, folklore and cultural heritage of the United States. DeLillo chose it as the title of his debut, by which he made known his ambition to write Great American Novels exploring American life and culture. In *Americana* DeLillo represents an America in which commercialism prevails, Christianity declines, and the land is being destroyed. *Americana* explores the malaise of the modern corporate man, interrogates mass media's power to misrepresent reality, and addresses the roots of American pathology. *Americana* initiates DeLillo's criticism of postmodern America.

The resistance to the American status quo is continuous in the rest of DeLillo's works. *Players* is a critique of late capitalism. Lyle and Pammy, two main characters in the novel, joylessly work in the Stock Exchange and the World Trade Center, two symbols of American capitalism, and live their lives like zombies. They "are aimless victims of the contemporary urban anomie—each tries, ironically, to defeat ennui by escaping into forms of play that ultimately prove even less centered or purposeful than their present lives" (Cowart, *The Physics of Language* 45). Pammy, the wife, is involved with a gay couple, which leads to a suicide. Lyle, the husband, playfully involves himself in a terrorist plot to blow up the Stock Exchange which stands for the secret power of capitalism and the hegemony of America. The terrorists want to "disrupt the system, the idea of worldwide money. It is this system that we believe is their secret power. […] It was this secret of theirs that we wanted to destroy, this invisible power. […] They have money. We have destruction" (*Mao II* 105). The terrorists' violent acts seem to be justified by the corrupted bourgeois life in American capitalist society and America's hegemony.

White Noise and *Libra* are published during Ronald Reagan's presidency when consumer culture swept across America like a new wave. In these novels DeLillo, like a Frankfurt School critic, offers his critique of American society which is dominated by rampant consumerism and is saturated by mass media. In this society consumerism has become a new religion and the supermarket is the church because the Old God has left the world. Everyone is shopping either in the supermarket or on TV. Shopping seems to be able to relieve temporarily the fear of death which haunts Jack Gladney and Babette who are exposed to the daily news of disasters and violence. America has entered the society of the spectacle since the JFK Assassination and the murder of Oswald, as is described in *Libra*. According to Debord, social life is not about living, but about having; the spectacle uses the image to convey what people need and must have (Thesis 17). Hence the issues of class alienation, cultural homogenization, manipulation of mass media, and commodity fetishism, which DeLillo explores in his novels.

Throughout DeLillo's works there is an anxiety that American individualism is dying due to the rampant consumerism and manipulating mass media. DeLillo's entire career has been a critique of authoritarian thinking which is related to cult, rampant consumerism and manipulation of the mass media. In *White Noise*, television symbolizes authoritarianism in American society. It imposes images, role models and values that shape individual thoughts and behavior. It is all-pervasive and manipulative. Through the use of mass media, the consumer society succeeds in manipulating the conscious and the unconscious, which is one of the most important mechanisms of control in capitalist societies. The manipulation of mass media has the danger of resulting in authoritarianism. His exploration of authoritarianism in the contemporary world is continued in *Mao* II. The novel represents the cultural environment of America in the late 1980s which was dominated by rampant consumerism. DeLillo was concerned about this culture of images which keeps proliferating and becomes a tyranny. Images are everywhere, pushing their way into the social fabric of people's social lives: "In our world we sleep and eat the image and pray to it and wear it too" (*Mao* II 37). The media image is ubiquitous, like the omnipresent God. It shapes the media consumers' identity and dictates their perception of reality. DeLillo is concerned that this cultural environment may lead to authoritarianism in American society. In this society consumption is a top priority. The American consumerist capitalism has turned everything into a commodity. Disasters are turned into media images and consumed as commodities by the television viewers. Academic research is trivialized. Religions are commercialized. Individuals are engulfed by consumer culture and are turned into Xerox copies, losing their individuality.

As a writer, DeLillo is subversive. He challenges the traditional view of history as a totalizing grand narrative. His novels represent American history since the 1950s. But they are a petite histoire, rather than a grand narrative. According to New Historicism, history is verbal construct, interpretation and narrative. Thus with historians of different political commitments, there are naturally different versions of history. DeLillo's version of history is underhistory or counterhistory: the secret history, the lost history, the unwritten history, those experiences and memories that have not been heard and integrated in official histories. DeLillo, like a muckraker, has devoted his writing to the shadow side of American life. Take *Underworld* for example. In the novel DeLillo explores the "underworld" of America and excavates the underhistory of the Cold War, as he remarked in an interview, "[i]n *Underworld* I felt I was providing a fictional history of the Cold War. This is the unwritten history of the period, as it were. It's an attempt to trace history through the objects of our culture: condoms, waste, the (Thomson) baseball itself, all of which is part of the underground stream of our history" (Fry).

DeLillo's version of the Cold War history is about waste and weapons. It was right after the end of the Cold War that DeLillo began to compose the novel. He was inspired by a newspaper article concerning the 40th anniversary of a famous ballgame played in New York in 1951 and started his journey exploring the underworld of America during the Cold War. Instead of celebrating the triumph of American capitalism, he exposed various kinds of waste in American society which had been excluded in the official history. It is true that "the proliferation of nuclear weapons, the proliferation of consumerism and disposable goods are a key weapon in America's Cold War arsenal" (Duvall, "Excavating the Underworld of Race and Waste in Cold War History" 260), but the arms races and the conspicuous consumption produced a large amount of waste, hence was born the American Waste Land. "If an archaeology of Cold War America is ever to be performed, [...], it must take place in the massive landfills near our urban areas" (ibid.). Waste does not only end in the landfills surrounding the urban areas. In fact, waste is omnipresent, permeating all corners of the American society depicted in *Underworld*. There is household garbage, memorabilia junk, nuclear waste, heroin, retired B-52 aircrafts, unreleased bombs, decayed urban areas and wasted lives, to name but a few. DeLillo depicts Cold War America as "a Splendid Junk Heap" (Kakutani), a postmodern Waste Land, exposing the fin de siècle crisis of American culture as part of a global system and generator of a global overruling discourse, to protest the toll of capitalism and the effects of an exaggerated consumerist discourse.

DeLillo's fiction has been committed to the "underside" of the United States: the side that the state and its discourse tend to mask or forget. DeLillo describes the destruction of American landscape by technology and consumerism; the damaging effects of the image-driven consumer society; authoritarianism in American society arising from the manipulation of mass media and the predominance of consumer culture; the underclass and the homeless in urban areas; the anxiety and paranoia brought on by the Cold War; and the trauma caused by the 9·11 terrorist attacks. Throughout his career, DeLillo has been exploring the damaging effects of American consumerism which has come to dominate the world system with its own discourse, supported by the expansion of technological power. With the end of the Cold War, capitalism has become dominant in the world, as is depicted in the epilogue of *Underworld*. In 1992, a year after the collapse of the Soviet Union, American scholar Francis Fukuyama published *The End of History and the Last Man* which argues that the progression of human history as a struggle between ideologies is largely at an end, with the world settling on liberal democracy after the end of the Cold War and the fall of the Berlin Wall in 1989. He predicted the eventual global triumph of political and economic liberalism, which contradicts the position of Karl Marx who imagined that antagonistic history would end with communism displacing capitalism. Fukuyama's view represented the prevalent optimism of the Western world during the 1990s, when many Americans thought that the end of the Cold War also represented the end of major global conflicts. As a chronicle of the Cold War and the 1990s' America,

Underworld depicts not only the conflicts between nations, races, men and women, the individual and the government during the War, but also the optimistic mood which characterized the 1990s' America. Thus the novel ends with the word "peace," which to some people like Fukuyama refers to the reality, but which in DeLillo's view is "all about longing, [...] certainly not a realistic expectation" (qtd. in Moss 157).

For as early as in the late 1980s when the Berlin Wall collapsed, DeLillo perceived the threat of terrorism with the quickening of globalization and considered it an essential issue in international affairs. In *Mao* II George Haddad, a representative of the terrorists in Beirut, says to Bill Gray: "In societies reduced to blur and glut, terror is the only meaningful act. [...] It's confusing when they kill the innocent. But this is precisely the language of being noticed, the only language the West understands" (157). He continues to say that the terrorists "carry the old wild-eyed vision, total destruction and total order" (158). In 1993, two years after the publication of *Mao* II, the Islamist terrorist group al-Qaeda carried its initial attack on the World Trade Center. But in spite of the terrorist attacks, Americans' triumphalist optimism did not recede. It was sustained by the prolonged economic boom in the United States, which was fed by extraordinary productivity gains from new technology, especially the application of IT. As DeLillo depicts in the epilogue of *Underworld* and *Cosmopolis* which sets its story on a single day in April 2000, the 1990s was a decade of technology boom and globalization, "marked by the technological acceleration and financial excesses of the information economy" (Conte 179). Internet and digital technology boosted the virtual economic development of America and created a surging stock market. With the widespread use of the Internet "[e]verything is connected" (*Underworld* 825). Business could be done worldwide online. Even originally subversive artist Ismael is "planning to go on-line real soon with his junk car business" (ibid. 812). Thus America entered the second era of globalization, which led to American cultural dominance, the widening gap between the rich and the poor, and inequality between nations. Islamic fundamentalists tried to resist the influences of the West, and America in particular which Bin Ladin called "the head of the snake" (*The 9·11 Commission Report* 54) should perish from the earth. The Islamic extremists viewed American society and culture as immoral, corrupt and godless. They abhorred the "power of American culture to penetrate every wall, home, life and mind" (DeLillo, "In the Ruins of the Future"). They wanted to destroy America, stamp out its influence, and bring back "what they used to have before the waves of western influence" (ibid.). With the end of the Cold War, DeLillo saw that there was "a global theocratic state, unboundaried and floating and so obsolete it must depend on suicidal fervour to gain its aims" (ibid.). The terrorists planned for a long time before they targeted the World Trade Center and brought "this symbol of the United States' preeminent place in multinational capitalism to ruins" (Conte 179). The Americans were totally unprepared for the 9·11 terrorist attacks because they had believed that they were in the age of peace. In the weeks after the attacks, Fareed Zakaria called the events "the end of the end of history" (*Newsweek*), while George Will, who charged DeLillo with literary vandalism and bad citizenship for his *Libra*, wrote that history had returned from vacation in *Jewish World Review* ("The End of Our Holiday from History"). As a native New Yorker, DeLillo was especially saddened by the terrorist attacks. In December he published the essay "In the Ruins of the Future: Reflections on Terror and Loss in the Shadow of September" which "reveals that he has more presciently understood the character of this major phase-change in American culture than most of the 'first responders' in newspapers, journals, and broadcast media" (Conte 180). The 9·11 terrorist attacks had already been foreshadowed in some of his novels.

In several of his novels, DeLillo depicts terrorists who are anti-capitalists. In *Players* a group of terrorists attempt to blow up the New York Stock Exchange which is regarded as the symbol of American capitalism. The terrorists choose to hit the Exchange for they believe: "It's all in that system, bip-bip-bip-bip, the flow of electric current that unites moneys, plural, from all over the world. Their greatest strength, no doubt of that. They have money. We have destruction" (*Players* 109). In *Cosmopolis*, which DeLillo had just finished writing when the 9·11 terrorist attacks took place, there is a violent anti-globalization demonstration at the Nasdaq Exchange in New York, trading floor for technology stocks in the new economy. The protagonist Eric Packer is a 28-year-old extremely rich currency trader, who has a 45-room apartment on the East Side of Manhattan. He controls the global flow of cyber-capital from his highly technologically equipped limousine stuck in the traffic jam in the midtown of Manhattan. "It's cyber-capital that creates the future" (*Cosmopolis* 79). As "the very avatar of cyber-capital" (Conte 182), Packer embodies the global capitalism which was characteristic of the 1990s. The anti-capitalism protesters attack Packer's car, set off a bomb outside an investment bank and change the electronic stock ticker to declare: "A specter is haunting the world—the specter of capitalism" (89). This slogan is a variation on the famous first sentence of Karl Marx and Friedrich Engels' *The Communist Manifesto*: "Europe is haunted by the specter of communism" (96). A protester self-immolates on the street to resist being incorporated by capitalism. At the end of the novel Packer loses incredible amounts of money for his clients by betting against the rise of the yen through the course of the day. He loses everything, including his own life. Packer, the rogue capitalist, is killed by his former employee Benno Levin, a grave digger of capitalism in Karl Marx's term. Levin is the product of the system that Packer represents. It is the capitalist system that created the conditions for its own destruction. *Cosmopolis* offers a critique of Jameson's late capitalism and gives an insight into the 9·11 terrorist attacks.

DeLillo is often "seen as a novelist who describes the present moment but at the point of a future warning" (Bou and Thoret). Take *Cosmopolis* for example again. It not only foreshadowed the imminence of 9·11, but also prophesied the 2008 financial crisis. He is therefore regarded as a prophet. But DeLillo himself denied being called a prophet. In an interview he said:

> September 11 aroused all sorts of anxieties ('hantises') present in my books, where you find various elements that set in motion aircraft hijackings, buildings being blown up, terrorists. [...] Perhaps the novelist is able to see in a clearer, sharper manner what's already there. But that doesn't make the writer a prophet (ibid.).

As a writer who stands and lives at the far margin of the society, DeLillo is always more capable of detecting the social undercurrents and seeing a reality that the average Americans cannot make out. The result is that his works appear both prophetic and realistic.

DeLillo has been committed to writing about postmodern America. His books can almost be taken as a systematic look at various aspects of contemporary American life. DeLillo is an acute novelist historian and a great chronicler of his age, for

> no other contemporary novelist could be said to outstrip DeLillo in his ability to depict that larger social environment we blandly call everyday life. Brand names, current events, fads, the society of the spectacle, and the rampant consumerism that has become our most noticeable, if not our important, contribution to history, are all plentiful and accurately recorded throughout DeLillo's work. (Molesworth 143)

It is beyond doubt that DeLillo's works depict the postmodern reality of America and probe its postmodernity. In the meantime he is the American Jonathan Swift, satirizing the American society which is engulfed by consumerism and plagued by terrorism. He is the American Charles Dickens, using noxious elements of postmodern life "to embody the moral defects of the society that produces them" (Ryan 794). DeLillo is an adversarial critic of American society which is in his view "the worst enemy that the cause of human individuality and self-realization has ever had" (Lentricchia, *Introducing Don DeLillo* 5). His works are thronged by artists who resist the systems in which they are enmeshed. DeLillo sees himself as one of the artists in opposition to the "endless cycle of consumption and instantaneous waste" (qtd. in Moss 94), in opposition "to power, corporations, the state, and the whole system of consumption and of debilitating entertainments" (qtd. in Bou and Thoret). His works reveal the moral force which is rare in the postmodern age. Despite the "blur and glut" (*Mao II* 157) and the marginalization of literature, DeLillo remains "the world's faithful mirror and conscience" (Cowart, *The Physics of Language* 119). Thus some critics argue that DeLillo is neither a modernist nor a postmodernist, but a realist (Giaimo 17) since he follows the line of Dickens, Mark Twain and Dreiser. In my view, the work of DeLillo is distinctly postmodernistic, because it not only depicts American life in a postmodern, post-industrial and media-saturated society, but also embodies its author's postmodern views of history and culture and exemplifies some innovative narrative strategies of postmodernist fiction. The realistic elements in DeLillo's work suggest that DeLillo is a novelist with social responsibility, high morality and a strong sense of historical consciousness.

Linda Hutcheon argues: "[A]s a cultural activity […], what I want to call postmodernism is fundamentally contradictory, resolutely historical, and inescapably political" (*A Poetics of Postmodernism* 4). This statement applies to DeLillo's writing. Politics plays a part in his books as it always does in postmodern American literature. DeLillo, like Norman Mailer and Robert Coover, is a political writer. DeLillo's political commitment is to subvert the power in the late capitalist society which is the enemy of American traditional values of human rights, democracy and individualism. He claims: "Writers must oppose systems. It's important to write against power, corporations, the state, and the whole system of consumption and of debilitating entertainments" (Bou and Thoret). For five decades, with his writing, DeLillo has been resisting this system of consumer capitalism.

Linda Hutcheon claims that postmodern writing can engage in a kind of "complicitous critique" by narrative strategies such as historiographic metafiction and intertextuality (Felluga, "Modules on Hutcheon"). DeLillo's postmodernist novels are doing a complicitous critique of the postmodern condition in America. He criticizes the contemporary American society which is pervaded by mass media and commodifies everything. Yet his novels "ring with the clamour of the marketplace" (Boxall, "DeLillo and Media Culture" 43). He has incorporated mass-market forms in its critique. He recycles both high literature and popular fiction, blurs the distinction between high culture and pop culture, and defamiliarizes specialized languages. His novels have incorporated the influences of canonical writers such as James Joyce, Virginia Woolf, Mark Twain, Ernest Hemingway and John Dos Passos; and pop stars like Bob Dylan, Lenny Bruce and Andy Warhol. "Hollywood film blends with the auteurist films of Ingmar Bergman, Jean-Luc Godard, and Michelangelo Antonioni" (ibid.), the European movies in the 1960s, which figured in almost all of DeLillo's novels. In *Americana* David calls himself "child of Godard and Coca-Cola." This label also applies to DeLillo himself who was shaped by the movies of Jean-Luc Godard and the American popular culture symbolized by Coca-Cola. Godard's movies are a critique of capitalist consumerism from the approach of Marxism, which has apparently influenced DeLillo's stance on capitalism in America. At the same time DeLillo lives in the capitalist society and has been fashioned by capitalist culture which is ubiquitous and pervasive, which accounts for his susceptibility to cooptation and his fascination with the very cultural forces he deplores. Thus his opposition to the American postmodern society is not monolithic.

DeLillo advocates that the writer's role should be subversive. But he admits that it is difficult to keep the resistance. The containment comes from the system and culture he resists. The writer as a social critic is under threat from ever more advanced modes of surveillance and control and suffers from being incorporated by the power he/she is trying to subvert. In his "Invisible Bullets" Greenblatt argues that "subversiveness is the very product of that power and further its end" (48). With more books published, more awards received and more interviews given, DeLillo is not so "dangerous" any more. His latest novel *Point Omega*, an abstract minimalist work on time and death, becomes more mysterious, philosophical and inaccessible. His criticism of American society becomes more subtle and less provocative.

As DeLillo understands that capitalism has the capacity to consume its own opposition, he has been trying to live in the margins of the society in order to distance himself from its influence and to keep from being incorporated by the almost all-encompassing systems of capitalist control. He takes this outsider position so as to observe more insightfully and subvert more powerfully. In the era when fiction has been marginalized by consumerism, terrorism and their media confederates, DeLillo remains true to his calling—as a functional artist and public intellectual, to be America's faithful mirror and conscience.

Works Cited

Abrams, M. H. *A Glossary of Literary Terms*. Beijing: Foreign Language Teaching and Research Press, 2004.

Adams, Tim. "The Chronicle of America." *The Observer*. May 8, 2011. <http://www.guardian.co.uk/books/2007/apr/22/dondelillo>

Albrow, Martin, and Elizabeth King, eds. *Globalization, Knowledge and Society*. London: Sage, 1990.

Allen, Graham. *Intertextuality*. New York: Routledge, 2000.

Amis, Martin. "Laureate of Terror." *The New Yorker*. April 29, 2012. <http://www.martinamisweb.com/commentary_files/MA_Delillo_2011.pdf>

Arensberg, Ann. "Seven Seconds." *Conversations with Don DeLillo*. Ed. Thomas DePietro. Jackson: Mississippi University Press, 2005.

Baldick, Chris. *Oxford Concise Dictionary of Literary Terms*. Shanghai: Shanghai Foreign Language Education Press, 2000.

Barrett, Laura. "*Mao II* and Mixed Media." *Don DeLillo: Mao II, Underworld, Falling Man*. Ed. Stacey Olster. New York: Continuum, 2011.

Barron, John. "DeLillo Bashful? Not This Time." *Chicago Sun-Times*, March 23, 2003.

Barthes, Roland. *Image, Music, and Text*. Trans. Stephen Heath. New York: Hill and Wang, 1977.

—. "Theory of the Text." *Untying the Text: A Post-structuralist Reader*. Ed. Robert Young. Boston, London, and Henley: Routledge Kegan & Paul, 1982.

Baudrillard, Jean. "*Simulacra und Simulation*." *Modernism/Postmodernism*. Ed. Peter Brooker. London and New York: Longman, 1992.

—. "The Spirit of Terrorism." Trans. Donovan Hohn. *Harper's*. February 2002.

Begley, Adam. "The Art of Fiction CXXXV: Don DeLillo." *Conversations with Don DeLillo*. Ed. Thomas DePietro. Jackson: Mississippi University Press, 2005.

Bell, Daniel. *The Coming of Post-Industrial Society*. New York: Basic Books, 1973.

Benson, Michael. *Encyclopedia of the JFK Assassination*. New York: Facts on File, Inc., 2002.

Berthoff, Warner. "Fiction, History, Myth: Notes toward the Discrimination of Narrative Forms." *The Interpretation of Narrative: Theory and Practice*. Ed.

Morton W. Bloomfield. Cambridge: Harvard University Press, 1970.

Binelli, Mark. "Intensity of a Plot. An Interview with Don DeLillo." *Guernica*. March 2, 2011. <http://www.guernicamag.com/interviews/373/intensity_of_a_plot/>.

Bing, Jonathan. "The Ascendance of Don DeLillo." *Publisher's Weekly*, August 11, 1997. http://www.publishersweekly.com/pw/print/19970811/22663-the-ascendance-of-don-delillo.html

Bloom, Greg. "The Terrifying World of *Mao II*." *The Chronicle*. January 5, 2013. <http://www.dukechronicle.com/articles/2002/04/11/terrifying-world-mao-ii>.

Bloom, Harold. *Don DeLillo (Bloom's Major Novelists)*. Philadelphia: Chelsea House Publisher, 2003.

—. Introduction. *Don DeLillo's White Noise*. Ed. Harold Bloom. Philadelphia: Chelsea House Publisher, 2003.

Bou, Stéphane, and Jean-Baptiste Thoret. "*Panic* Interview with DeLillo—2005." *Panic*. March 20, 2013. <http://perival.com/delillo/interview_panic_2005.html>.

Boxall, Peter. *Don DeLillo: The Possibility of Fiction*. London and New York: Routledge, 2006.

Brannigan, John. *New Historicism and Cultural Materialism*. New York: St. Martin's Press, 1988.

Bryson, J. R., and Peter W. Daniel. *The Handbook of Service Industries*. Northampton, Massachusetts: Edward Elgar Publishing, 2007.

Buhle, Paul. "Daniel Bell Obituary: Influential American Sociologist Best Known as the Author of *The End of Ideology*." *The Guardian*. June 2, 2012. <http://www.guardian.co.uk/education/2011/jan/26/daniel-bell-obituary>.

Burger, Jörg. "Mr. Paranoia." *Perival*. January. 21, 2013. <http://www.perival.com/delillo/interview_burger_1998.html>.

Bush, George. W. Jr. "Text of Bush's Address." *CNN US*. Dec. 2, 2012. <http://articles.cnn.com/2001-09-11/us/bush.speech.text_1_attacks-deadly-terrorist-acts-despicable-acts?_s=PM:US>.

Cantor, Paul A. "Adolf, We Hardly Knew You." *New Essays on White Noise*. Ed. Frank Lentricchia. Cambridge: Cambridge University Press, 1991.

Caselli, Daniela. *Backett's Dantes: Intertextuality in the Fiction and Criticism*. Manchester: Manchester University Press, 2005.

Champlin, Charles. "The Heart Is a Lonely Craftsman." *Los Angeles Times Calendar*, July 29, 1984.

Charles, Ron. "Novelist Don DeLillo Named First Recipient of Library of Congress Prize for American Fiction." *The Washington Post*. June 24, 2013. <http://www.

washingtonpost.com/lifestyle/style/don-delillo-is-first-recipient-of-library-of-congress-prize-for-american-fiction/2013/04/24/ae1ff5f8-acd5-11e2-b6fd-ba6f5f26d70e_story.html>.

Cohen, Morris Raphael. "Baseball as a National Religion." *The Faith of a Liberal*. Ed. Morris Raphael Cohen. New Brunswick, NJ: Transaction Publishers, 1993.

Conte, Joseph M. "Conclusion: Writing amid the Ruins: 9/11 and *Cosmopolis*." *The Cambridge Companion to Don DeLillo*. Ed. John N. Duvall. Cambridge and New York: Cambridge University Press, 2008.

Coonan, Clifford. "'Messiah' Moon Leaves a Vast Business—and a Tainted Image." *Unification Church and the Rev. Sun Myung Moon*. The Rick A. Ross Institute. January. 2, 2012. <http://www.rickross.com/reference/unif/unif411.html>.

Cowart, David. *Don DeLillo: The Physics of Language*. Athens: University of Georgia Press, 2002.

Debord, Guy. *The Society of the Spectacle*. Trans. Donald Nicholson-Smith. New York: Zone, 1995.

DeCurtis, Anthony. "'An Outsider in This Society': An Interview with Don DeLillo." *Conversations with Don DeLillo*. Ed. Thomas DePietro. Jackson: Mississippi University Press, 2005.

DeLillo, Don. "American Blood: A Journey through the Labyrinth of Dallas and JFK." *Rolling Stone*. December 8, 1983.

—. *White Noise*. New York: Viking, 1985.

—. *Mao II*. New York: Viking, 1991.

—. *Underworld*. New York: Scribner, 1997.

—. *Falling Man*. New York: Scribner, 2007.

—. *Point Omega*. New York: Scribner, 2010.

—. *Libra*. New York: Viking, 1988. New York: Quality Paperback Book Club, 2001.

—. *Running Dog*. New York: Knopf, 1978.

—. *Americana*. Boston: Houghton Mifflin, 1971. New York: the Penguin Group, 1989.

—. "The Power of History." *New York Times Magazine*. September 7, 1997.

—, and Paul Auster. *Salman Rushdie Defense Pamphlet*. The Rushdie Defense Committee USA, February 14, 1994. http://www.perival.com/delillo/rushdie_defense.html, accessed March 2, 2011

DePietro, Thomas. "Introduction." *Conversations with Don DeLillo*. Jackson: Mississippi University Press, 2005.

Derrida, Jacques. *Of Grammatology*. Trans. Gayatri Chakravorty Spivak. Baltimore and London: Johns Hopkins University Press, 1976.

—. *Limited Inc*. Trans. Samuel Weber and Jeffrey Mehlman. Evanston, Illinois: Northwestern University Press, 1988.

Dewey, Joseph. *Beyond Grief and Nothing: A Reading of Don DeLillo*. Columbia: University of South Carolina Press, 2006.

—. "A Gathering Under Words: An Introduction." *UnderWords: Perspectives on Don DeLillo's Underworld*. Eds. Joseph Dewey et al. Newark: University of Delaware Press, 2002.

Douglas, Christopher. "Don DeLillo." *Postmodernism: The Key Figures*. Eds. Hans Bertens and Joseph Natoli. Malden, Massachusetts: Blackwell Publisher, 2002.

Duvall, John N. "The (Super) Marketplace of Images: Television as Unmediated Mediation in DeLillo's *White Noise*." *White Noise: Text and Criticism*. Ed. Mark Osteen. New York: Penguin, 1998.

—. "Introduction: the Power of History and the Persistence of Mystery." *The Cambridge Companion to Don DeLillo*. Ed. John N. Duvall. Cambridge and New York: Cambridge University Press, 2008.

Early Gerald. "Birdland: Two Observations on the Cultural Significance of Baseball." *The Literature & Culture of the American 1950s*. February. 20, 2012. <http://www.writing.upenn.edu/~afilreis/50s/baseball.html>.

Echlin, Kim. "Baseball and the Cold War." *Conversations with Don DeLillo*. Ed. Thomas DePietro. Jackson: Mississippi University Press, 2005.

Engles, Tim. "DeLillo and the Political Thriller." *The Cambridge Companion to Don DeLillo*. Ed. John N. Duvall. Cambridge: Cambridge University Press, 2008.

Faigley, Lester. "From Fragments to Rationality." *Fragments of Rationality: Postmodernity and the Subject of Composition*. Pittsburgh: University of Pittsburgh Press, 1992.

Fan, Xiaomei. "Consumerism and Its Effects on Contemporary American Society: A Thematic Study on Don DeLillo's *White Noise*." M.A. Diss. Xiamen University, 2001.

—. "DeLillo: a Postmodernist Writer Who 'Xeroxed' Contemporary American Life." *Foreign Literature* 2003 (4).

［范小玫：《德里罗：'复印'美国当代生活的后现代派作家》，载《外国文学》2003（4）。］

Felluga, Dino. "Modules on Fredric Jameson: On Late Capitalism." *Introductory Guide to Critical Theory*. April 27, 2012. http://www.cla.purdue.edu/english/theory/marxism/modules/jamesonlatecapitalism.html

—. "Modules on Linda Hutcheon: On Parody." *Introductory Guide to Critical Theory*.

March. 20, 2012. www.purdue.edu/guidetotheory/introduction/

—. "Modules on Jean Baudrillard II: On Simulation." *Introductory Guide to Critical Theory*. March. 20, 2012. <www.purdue.edu/guidetotheory/introduction/>.

Finney, Daniel P. "Watergate Scandal Changed the Political Landscape Forever." *USA Today*. August. 30, 2012. <http://www.usatoday.com/news/nation/story/2012-06-16/watergate-scandal-changed-political-landscape/55639974/1>.

Fitzpatrick, Kathleen. "The Unmaking of History: Baseball, Cold War, and Underworld." *Underwords: Perspectives on Don DeLillo's Underworld*. Eds. Joseph Dewey, et al. Newark: University of Delaware Press, 2002.

Foucault, Michel. *The History of Sexuality, Volume 1: An Introduction*. Trans. Robert Hurley. London: Penguin, 1981.

Fry, Donn. "Delillo's View: Where Fiction and History Intersect." *The Seattle Times*. September 2, 2011. <http://community.seattletimes.nwsource.com/archive/?date= 19971021&slug=2567332>.

Gardela, Karen, and Bruce Hoffman. "The RAND Chronology of International Terrorism for 1988." *RANA*. December. 10, 2012. <http://www.rand.org/content/dam/rand/pubs/reports/2007/R4180.pdf>.

Gardner, James. "Review of *Underworld*." *National Review* 49.22 November 24, 1997

Giaimo, Paul. *Appreciating Don DeLillo: The Moral Force of a Writer's Work*. Prager: Santa Barbara, 2011.

Gioia, Ted. "*Point Omega* by Don DeLillo." *Great Books Guide*. April 6, 2012. <http://www.greatbooksguide.com/point_omega.html>.

—. "*Underworld* by Don DeLillo." *The New Canon*. May 30, 2012. <http://www.thenewcanon.com/underworld.html>.

Gleason, Paul. "Don DeLillo, T. S. Eliot, and the Redemption of America's Atomic Waste Land." Eds. Joseph Dewey et al. *Underwords: Perspectives on Don DeLillo's Underworld*. Newark: University of Delaware Press, 2002.

Green, Jeremy. "*Libra*." *The Cambridge Companion to Don DeLillo*. Ed. John N. Duvall. Cambridge: Cambridge University Press, 2008.

Greenblatt, Stephen. *Renaissance Self-Fashioning: From More to Shakespeare*. Chicago and London: Chicago University Press, 1980.

—. *Shakespeare Negotiations: The Circulation of Social Energy in Renaissance England*. Berkeley: University of California Press, 1988.

—. "Toward a Poetics of Culture." *The New Historicism*. Ed. H. Aram Veeser. New York and London: Routledge, 1989.

Gresset, Michel. "Introduction: Faulkner between the Texts." *Intertextuality in

Faulkner. Eds. Michel Gresset and Noel Polk. Jackson: Mississippi University Press, 1985.

Gu, Hongli. *A New Historicist and Cultural Materialist Study of Norman Mailer's Work*. Xiamen: Xiamen University Press, 2004.

Heise, Thomas. *Urban Underworlds: A Geography of Twentieth Century American Literature and Culture*. Piscataway, NJ: Rutgars University Press, 2011.

Helyer, Ruth. "Foreword." *Don DeLillo, Jean Baudrillard, and the Consumer Conundrum*. Ed. Marc Schuster. Youngstown, New York: Cambria Press, 2008.

Hendin, Josephine Gattuso. "*Underworld*, Ethnicity, and Found Object Art: Reason and Revelation." *Don DeLillo: Mao II, Underworld, Falling Man*. Ed. Stacey Olster. London and New York: Continuum, 2011.

Herman, David, Manfred Jahn, and Marie-Laure Ryan. *Routledge Encyclopedia of Narrative Theory*. New York: Routledge, 2005.

Hiscock, Andrew, and Stephen Longstaffe. *The Shakespeare Handbook*. New York and London: Continuum, 2009.

Homer, Sean. "Fredric Jameson." *Postmodernism: The Key Figures*. Eds. Hans Bertens and Joseph Natoli. Oxford: Blackwell Publishers, 2002.

Hoover, Dwight W. "The New Historicism." *The History Teacher*. May, 1992, Vol. 25, No. 3. *JSTOR*. Society for History Education. January. 25, 2012. <http://www.jstor.org/stable/494247>.

House Select Committee on Assassinations. *Report of the Select Committee on Assassinations of the U.S. House of Representatives*. Web version based on *the Report of the Select Committee on Assassinations of the U.S. House of Representatives*, Washington, DC: United States Government Printing Office, 1979. 1 volume, 686 pages. <http://www.archives.gov/research/jfk/select-committee-report/ Accessed July 10, 2011.>.

Howard, Gerald. "The American Strangeness: An Interview with Don DeLillo." *Conversations with Don DeLillo*. Ed. Thomas DePietro. Jackson: Mississippi University Press, 2005.

Howard, Jean E. "The New Historicism in Renaissance Studies." *English Literary Renaissance*, 16: 13-43, 1986.

Hutcheon, Linda. *A Poetics of Postmodernism: History, Theory, and Fiction*. London: Routledge, 1988.

—. *The Politics of Postmodernism*. New York: Routledge, 1989.

—. "The Politics of Postmodern Parody." *Intertextuality*. Ed. Heinrich F. Plett. Berlin and New York: Water de Gruyter, 1991.

—. "Historiographic Metafiction: Parody and Intertextuality of History." *Intertextuality and Contemporary American Fiction*. Eds. Patrick O'Donnell and Robert Con Davis. Baltimore and London: Johns Hopkins University Press, 1989.

Ickstadt, Heinz. "Heinz Ickstadt on the Theatricalization of Experience." *Don DeLillo (Bloom's Major Novelists)*. Ed. Harold Bloom. Philadelphia: Chelsea House Publisher, 2003.

Jahn, Manfred. "Focalization." *The Cambridge Companion to Narrative*. Ed. David Herman. Cambridge: Cambridge University Press, 2007.

Jameson, Fredric. *The Political Unconscious: Narrative as a Socially Symbolic Act*. Ithaca: Cornell University Press. 1981.

—. "Postmodernism and Consumer Society." *Modernism/Postmodernism*. Ed. Peter Brooker. London and New York: Longman, 1992.

—. "Globalization and Political Strategy." *New Left Review* 4, July-August, 2000.

—. *Postmodernism, or, the Cultural Logic of Late Capitalism*. Durham: Duke UP, 1991.

Josephson, Eric, and Mary Josephson. *Man Alone: Alienation in Modern Society*. New York: Dell Publishing Co., Inc., 1966.

Junod, Tom. "The Falling Man." *Esquire*. Nov. 17, 2010. <http://www.esquire.com/features/ESQ0903-SEP_FALLINGMAN>.

Kakutani, Michiko. "*Underworld*: Of America as a Splendid Junk Heap." *The New York Times*. October. 20, 2013. <http://www.nytimes.com/books/97/09/14/daily/underworld-book-review.html?_r=1&oref=slogin>.

Kaufman, Linda S. "Bodies in Rest and Motion in *Falling Man*." *Don DeLillo: Mao II, Underworld, Falling Man*. Ed. Stacey Olster. London and New York: Continuum, 2011.

—. "The Wake of Terror: Don DeLillo's 'In the Ruins of the Future,' 'Baader-Meinhof,' and *Falling Man*." *Terrorism, Media, and the Ethics of Fiction: Transatlantic Perspectives on Don DeLillo*. Ed. Peter Schneck and Philipp Schweighauser. New York: The Continuum International Publishing Group, 2010.

Kaufman, Michael T. "Daniel Bell, Ardent Appraiser of Politics, Economics and Culture, Dies at 91." *New York Times*. April 26, 2012. <http://www.nytimes.com/2011/01/26/arts/26bell.html?_r=1&pagewanted=all>.

Kavadlo, Jesse. *Don DeLillo: Balance at the Edge of Belief*. New York: Peter Lang Publishing, Inc., 2004.

Keener, John F. *Biography and the Postmodern Historical Novel*. Lampeter, Wales: The Edwin Mellen Press, 2001.

Keesey, Douglas. *Don DeLillo*. New York: Twayne Publishers, 1993.

Kellner, Douglas. "Jean Baudrillard." *Postmodernism: The Key Figures*. Eds. Hans Bertens and Joseph Natoli. Oxford: Blackwell Publishers, 2002.

Kirsch, Adam. "DeLillo Confronts September 11." *The Sun*. November 10, 2012. <http://www.nysun.com/arts/delillo-confronts-september-11/53594/>.

Knight, Peter. *Conspiracy Culture: From the Kennedy Assassination to the X-Files*. London and New York: Routledge, 2000.

—. "Everything Is Connected: *Underworld*'s Secret History of Paranoia." *Critical Essays on Don DeLillo*. Eds. Hugh Ruppersburg and Tim Engles. New York: G. K. Hall & Co., 2000.

—, ed. *Conspiracy Theories in American History: An Encyclopedia*. Santa Barbara, California: ABC-CLIO, Inc., 2003.

—. "DeLillo, Postmodernism, Postmodernity." *The Cambridge Companion to Don DeLillo*. Ed. John N. Duvall. Cambridge: Cambridge University, 2008.

Kristeva, Julia. *Desire in Language: A Semiotic Approach to Literature and Art*. Trans. Thomas Gora, Alice Jardine and Leon S. Roudiez. Ed. Leon S. Roudiez. New York: Columbia University Press, 1980.

—. "Word, Dialogue and Novel." *The Kristeva Reader*. Ed. Toril Moi. New York: Columbia University Press, 1986.

LaCapra, Dominick. *History and Criticism*. Ithaca, NY: Cornell University Press, 1985.

LeClair, Tom. *In the Loop: Don DeLillo and the Systems Novel*. Urbana and Chicago: University of Illinois Press, 1987.

Lentricchia, Frank. "Introduction." *New Essays on White Noise*. Ed. Frank Lentricchia. Cambridge: Cambridge University Press, 1991.

—. "The American Writer as Bad Citizen." *Introducing Don DeLillo*. Ed. Frank Lentricchia. Durham, NC and London: Duke University Press, 1991.

—. "*Libra* as Postmodern Critique." *Introducing Don DeLillo*. Ed. Frank Lentricchia. Durham, NC and London: Duke University Press, 1991.

Liu, Wensong. *Saul Bellow's Fiction: Power Relations and Female Representation*. Xiamen: Xiamen University Press, 2004.

Loon, Joost van. *Media Technology: Critical Perspectives*. Berkshire: Open University Press, 2008.

Lyotard, Jean-François. *The Postmodern Condition: A Report on Knowledge*. Trans. Geoff Bennington and Brian Massumi. Manchester: Manchester University Press, 1979.

Martin, Elaine. "Intertextuality: An Introduction." *The Comparatist* 2011 (35).

Martucci, Elise A. *The Environmental Unconscious in the Fiction of Don DeLillo*. New

York and London: Routledge, 2007.

McAuliffe, Jody. "Interview with Don DeLillo." *Conversations with Don DeLillo*. Ed. Thomas DePietro. Jackson: Mississippi University Press, 2005.

McCrum, Robert. "Don DeLillo: 'I'm not trying to manipulate reality—this is what I see and hear." *The Observer*. August 2, 2011. <http://www.guardian.co.uk/books/2010/aug/08/don-delillo-mccrum-interview>.

McHale, Brian. *Postmodernist Fiction*. New York: Methuen, 1987.

Melley, Timothy. *Empire of Conspiracy: The Culture of Paranoia in Postwar America*. Ithaca and London: Cornell University Press, 2000.

Molesworth, Charles. "Don DeLillo's Perfect Starry Night." *Introducing Don DeLillo*. Ed. Frank Lentricchia. Durham: Duke University Press, 1991.

Montrose, Louis A. "Professing the Renaissance." *The New Historicism*. Ed. H. Haram Veeser. New York and London: Routledge, 1989.

Morgan, Thaïs. "The Space of Intertextuality." *Intertextuality and Contemporary American Fiction*. Ed. Patrick O'Donnell and Robert Con Davis. Baltimore and London: The Johns Hopkins University Press, 1989.

Morley, Catherine. *The Quest for Epic in Contemporary American Fiction*. New York: Routledge, 2009.

Moses, Michael Valdez. "Lust Removed from Nature." *New Essays on White Noise*. Ed. Frank Lentricchia. Cambridge: Cambridge University Press, 1991.

Moss, Maria. "'Writing as a Deep Form of Concentration': An Interview with Don DeLillo." *Conversations with Don DeLillo*. Ed. Thomas DePietro. Jackson: Mississippi University Press, 2005.

Müller, Wolfgang G. "Interfigurality: A Study on the Interdependence of Literary Figures." *Intertextuality*. Ed. Heinrich F. Plett. Berlin and New York: Walter de Gruyter & Co., 1991.

Nadel, Ira. "The Baltimore Catechism; or Comedy in *Underworld*." *Underwords: Perspectives on Don DeLillo's Underworld*. Eds. Joseph Dewey et al. Newark: University of Delaware Press, 2002.

Nance, Kevin. "Living in Dangerous Times." *Chicago Tribute*. December 6, 2012. <http://articles.chicagotribune.com/2012-10-12/features/ct-prj-1014-don-delillo-20121012_1_mao-ii-angel-esmeralda-printers-row/3>.

National Archives. Report of the President's Commission on the Assassination of President Kennedy. July 10, 2011. <http://www.archives.gov/research/jfk/warren-commission-report/>.

Nel, Philip. "DeLillo's Return to Form: The Modernist Poetics of *The Body Artist*."

Contemporary Literature. Winter, 2002, Vol. 43, No. 4. *JSTOR*. University of Wisconsin Press, Madison. May 11, 2012. <http://www.jstor.org/stable/1209040>.

Nicol, Bran. *The Cambridge Introduction to Postmodern Fiction*. Cambridge: Cambridge University Press, 2009.

The 9·11 Commission Report: Final Report of the National Commission on Terrorist Attacks upon the United States. New York and London: W. W. Norton & Company, 2004.

Olster, Stacy. *Don DeLillo: Mao* Ⅱ*, Underworld, Falling Man*. New York: Continuum, 2011.

—. "White Noise." *The Cambridge Companion to Don DeLillo*. Ed. John N. Duvall. Cambridge: Cambridge University Press, 2008.

Orr, Leonard. *Don DeLillo's White Noise: A Reader's Guide*. New York: Continuum International Publishing Group, 2003.

Osteen, Mark. "'The Natural Language of the Culture': Exploring Commodities through *White Noise*." *Approaches to Teaching DeLillo's White Noise*. Eds. Tim Eagles and John N. Duvall. New York: The Modern Language Association of America, 2006.

—. *American Magic and Dread: Don DeLillo's Dialogue with Culture*. Philadelphia: University of Pennsylvania Press, 2000.

The Oxford English Dictionary. 2nd edition. Oxford: Oxford University Press, 1989.

Parrish, Timothy. *From the Civil War to the Apocalypse: Postmodern History and American Fiction*. Amherst: University of Massachusetts Press, 2008.

Passaro, Vince. "Dangerous Don DeLillo." *Conversations with Don DeLillo*. Ed. Thomas DePietro. Jackson: Mississippi University Press, 2005.

Pfister, M. "How Postmodern Is Intertextuality?" *Intertextuality*. Ed. Heinrich F. Plett. Berlin and New York: Walter de Gruyter & Co., 1991.

Phillips, Jayne Anne. "Crowding out Death." *The New York Times on the Web*. March 21, 2010. <http://www.nytimes.com/books/97/03/16/lifetimes/del-r-white-noise.html?_r=2>.

Plottel, Jeanine Parisier. "Introduction". *Intertextuality: New Perspectives in Criticism.* Vol. 2. Ed. Jeanine Parisier Pottel and Hanna Charney. New York: New York Literary Forum, 1978.

Raab, Scott. "Philip Roth Goes Home Again." *Esquire*. December. 12, 2011. <http://www.esquire.com/features/philip-roth-interview-1010>.

Rader, Mario. "Don DeLillo's Falling Man: Flashbulb Memories of 9·11." *Suite 101*. June 11, 2011. <http://suite101.com/article/don-delillos-falling-man-flashbulb-

memories-of-911-a273215>.

Remnick, David. "Exile on Main Street: Don DeLillo's Undisclosed *Underworld*." *Conversations with Don DeLillo*. Ed. Thomas DePietro. Jackson: Mississippi University Press, 2005.

Rettberg, Scott. "American Simulacra: Don DeLillo's Fiction in Light of Postmodernism." *Undercurrent*. June 20, 2011. <http://retts.net/documents/americansimulacra.pdf>.

Reynolds, Amy, and Brooke Barnett. "'American under Attack': CNN Verbal and Visual Framing of September 11." *Media Representations of September* 11. Ed. Steven Chermak and et al. Westport, Connecticut: Praeger, 2003.

Rielly, Edward J. *Baseball: An Encyclopedia of Popular Culture*. Lincoln, NE: University of Nebraska Press, 2005.

Riepe, Jan. *The Future Belongs to the Crowds: Media in Don DeLillo's Libra, Mao II, and White Noise*. Thesis (MA). Munich, Germany: Grin Publishing, 2006.

Roberts, Margaret. "'D' Is For Danger—And For Writer Don Delillo." *Chicago Tribune*. May 14, 2011. <http://articles.chicagotribune.com/1992-05-22/features/9202150924_1_don-delillo-danger-writers>.

Robson, Leo. "Point Omega." *NewStatesman*. January. 12, 2013. <http://www.newstatesman.com/books/2010/03/white-noise-delillo-jack-novel>.

Robson, Margaret. "Rubbish: Don DeLillo's Wastelands." *IJAS (Irish Journal of American Studies) online*. Issue 2 (Summer 2010). May 20, 2012. <http://www.ijasonline.com/Margaret-Robson.html>.

Rothstein, Mervyn. "A Novelist Faces His Themes on New Ground." *Conversations with Don DeLillo*. Ed. Thomas DePietro. Jackson: Mississippi University Press, 2005.

Rowe, John Carlos. "Global Horizons in *Falling Man*." *Mao II, Underworld, Falling Man*. Ed. Stacey Olster. London and New York: Continuum, 2011.

Ruppersburg, Hugh, and Tim Engles. "Introduction." *Critical Essays on Don DeLillo*. Eds. Hugh Ruppersburg and Tim Engles. New York: G. K. Hall & Co., 2000.

Ryan, Bryan. Ed. *Major 20th-Century Writers*. Volume I. Detroit and London: Gale Research Inc., 1991.

Scheiber, Dave. "JFK: Camelot's Spirit Endures." *St. Petersburg Times*. June 10, 2012. <http://www.sptimes.com/News/111199/JFK/Camelot_s_spirit_endu.shtml>.

Schneck, Peter. "'The Great Secular Transcendence': Don DeLillo and the Desire for Numinous Experience." *Terrorism, Media, and the Ethics of Fiction: Transatlantic Perspective on Don DeLillo*. Eds. Peter Schneck and Philipp Schweighauser. New

York: The Continuum International Publishing Group, 2010.

Schuster, Marc. *Don DeLillo, Jean Baudrillard, and the Consumer Conundrum*. Youngstown and New York: Cambria Press, 2008.

Schwarz, Benjamin. "The Real Cuban Crisis." *The Atlantic*. January 25, 2013. <http://www.theatlantic.com/magazine/archive/2013/01/the-real-cuban-missile-crisis/309190/>.

Simmons, Philip E. *Deep Surfaces*. Athens and London: The University of George Press, 1997.

Snyder, James. *Northern Renaissance Art: Painting, Sculpture, the Graphic Arts from 1350 to 1575*. New York: Harry N. Abrams, 1985.

Søndergaard, Leif. "Relations between Real and Fictional Worlds." *Facts, Fiction and Faction*. Eds. Jørgen Dines Johansen and Leif Søndergaard. Denmark: University Press of Southern Denmark, 2011.

Ssenyonga, Allan Brian. "Americanization or Globalization?" *Global Vision*. December. 5, 2011. <http://www.globalenvision.org/library/33/1273>.

Streich, Michael. "The Camelot Presidency of John F. Kennedy." *American History @ Suite 101*. June 28, 2012. <http://suite101.com/article/the-camelot-presidency-of-john-f-kennedy-a132106>.

Storey, John. *Cultural Theory and Popular Culture: An Introduction*. New York: Pearson Education, 2006.

Sturgis, Sue. "Startling Revelations about Three Mile Island Disaster Raise Doubts over Nuke Safety." *AlterNet*. December 20, 2012. <http://www.alternet.org/story/134977/startling_revelations_about_three_mile_island_disaster_raise_doubts_over_nuke_safety>.

Thomas, Glen. "Glen Thomas on the Fragmentary Nature of History." *Don DeLillo (Bloom's Major Novelists)*. Ed. Harold Bloom. Philadelphia: Chelsea House Publisher, 2003.

Vartabedian, Ralph. "Nuclear Scars: Tainted Water Runs beneath Nevada Desert." *Los Angeles Times*. November 13, 2009.

Veenstra, Jan R. "The New Historicism of Stephen Greenblatt: On Poetics of Culture and the Interpretation of Shakespeare." *History and Theory*. 1995, Vol. 34, No. 3.

Veeser, H. Aram. *The New Historicism*. New York and London: Routledge, 1989.

Versluys, Kristiaan. *Out of the Blue: September 11 and the Novel*. New York: Columbia University Press, 2009.

Weinstein, Arnold. *Nobody's Home: Speech, Self and Place in American Fiction from Hawthorne to DeLillo*. Oxford: Oxford University Press, 1993.

White, Hayden. *Metahistory: The Historical Imagination in Nineteenth-century Europe*. Baltimore: Johns Hopkins University Press, 1973.

—. *Tropics of Discourse: Essays in Cultural Criticism*. Baltimore: Johns Hopkins University Press, 1978.

—. "New Historicism: A Comment." *The New Historicism*. Ed. H. Aram Veeser. New York and London: Routledge, 1989.

Wilcox, Leonard. "Baudrillard, DeLillo's *White Noise*, and the End of Heroic Narrative." *Contemporary Literature.* Autumn, 1991, Vol. 32, No. 3. *JSTORE*. The University of Wisconsin Press, Madison. May 11, 2012. <http://www.jstor.org/stable/1208561>.

Yang, Renjing. *The History of 20th-Century American Literature*. Qingdao: Qingdao Press, 2000.

［杨仁敬：《20世纪美国文学史》，青岛出版社，2000。］

—, et al. *On American Postmodern Fiction*. Qingdao: Qingdao Press, 2004.

［杨仁敬等：《美国后现代派小说论》，青岛出版社，2004。］

—, and Yang Lingyan. *A Concise History of American Literature*. Shanghai: Shanghai Foreign Language Education Press, 2008.

［杨仁敬，杨凌雁：《美国文学简史》，上海外语教育出版社，2008。］

Zacharias, Pat. "When Bomb Shelters Were All the Rage." *The Detroit News*. December 5, 2011. <http://undergroundbombshelter.com/news/when-bomb-shelters-were-the-rage.htm>.

Zalewski, Daniel. "Hysteria Realism." *The New York Times*. May 25, 2012. <http://www.nytimes.com/2002/12/15/magazine/15HYST.html>.

Zhao, Yifan, et al. eds. *Key Words of Western Literary Theories.* Beijing: Foreign Language Teaching and Research Press, 2006.

［赵一凡等编：《西方文论关键词》，外语教学与研究出版社，2006。］

Zhu, Gang. *Twentieth-Century Western Critical Theories*. Shanghai: Shanghai Foreign Language Education Press, 2001.

［朱刚：《二十世纪西方文艺批评理论》，上海外语教育出版社，2001。］

Acknowledgments

My completion of this book would not have been possible without many people's support and help.

First and foremost, I would like to thank Professor Yang Renjing, my supervisor, for his painstaking tutorship, insightful guidance and unfailing encouragement. When I was at a loss for a theoretical framework after I gave up my initial focus on the intertextuality of DeLillo's works, it was Professor Yang who suggested that I take New Historicism as a new approach for my project. It is his insightful suggestions and inspiring criticism that have enabled me to present the dissertation in its present form. I am thankful for his tolerance of my procrastination for he knows that DeLillo is such a tough and challenging project for me. He never rushed me. He encouraged me that I still had plenty of time and that good work takes time. My gratitude also goes to Professor Yang's wife, Ms Xu Baorui, who always comforted and encouraged me when I had difficulty in focusing and outlining the study and was thinking about giving up. I am thankful for her motherly care and confidence that I would complete this project finally.

Secondly, I am also indebted to Professor Chen Dongquan who initiated my interest in Don DeLillo when I was a graduate student by recommending DeLillo's novels to me. When I decided to choose to write about *White Noise* in my MA thesis, he recommended to me Professor Yang Renjing's book *The History of the 20th Century American Literature* which contains groundbreaking work on Don DeLillo in China.

Thirdly, I am deeply grateful to Professor Yang Xinzhang, Professor Su Zixing, Professor Zhan Sukui, Professor Zhang Longhai, Professor Li Meihua and other leaders of the College of Foreign Languages & Cultures in Xiamen University for their generous support by sending me to the US for a year as a visiting scholar in 2010, which helped me immensely.

Next, I would like to take this opportunity to thank Professor Patrick O'Neill, my sponsor, and Professor Henry Veggian in the University of North Carolina at Chapel Hill, whose insightful advice and lectures on DeLillo have benefited me enormously. I am also appreciative of the UNC libraries which allowed me free access to their collections of books, electronic or otherwise, and the computers and the scanners. Without much effort I found all the books and essays I needed in completing the present project. My indebtedness also goes to my friends in Chapel Hill who gave me a lot of help during my one year's stay in the US.

I also want to thank Professor Zhao Yifan and Professor Chen Shidan for their inspiring lectures and warm encouragement.

Above all, I owe a debt of gratitude to my parents, my parents-in-law, my brothers, sister, my son and husband for their love, support, encouragement and faith in me, without which I would not be able to persist and finally complete this challenging and exhausting project.

图书在版编目(CIP)数据

新历史主义视角下的唐·德里罗小说研究/范小玫著. —厦门：厦门大学出版社，2014.12
ISBN 978-7-5615-5328-2

Ⅰ.①新… Ⅱ.①范… Ⅲ.①小说研究-美国-现代 Ⅳ.①I712.074

中国版本图书馆 CIP 数据核字(2014)第 289931 号

官方合作网络销售商：

厦门大学出版社出版发行

(地址:厦门市软件园二期望海路39号 邮编:361008)
总编办电话:0592-2182177 传真:0592-2181253
营销中心电话:0592-2184458 传真:0592-2181365
网址:http://www.xmupress.com
邮箱:xmup@xmupress.com

厦门集大印刷厂印刷
2014年12月第1版 2014年12月第1次印刷
开本:720×1000 1/16 印张:15.25 插页:2
字数:300千字
定价:45.00元
本书如有印装质量问题请直接寄承印厂调换